Love Under Glasse

I0636018

KRISTINA MEISTER

TRITON BOOKS

Triton Books
PO Box 1537
Burnsville, NC 28714
www.Tritonya.com
Triton Books is an imprint of Riptide Publishing.
www.RiptidePublishing.com

Love Under Glasse

Cover art: L.C. Chase, lcchase.com
Editor: May Peterson
Layout: L.C. Chase, lcchase.com/design-portfolio.html

ISBN: 978-1-62649-876-1

First edition
August, 2019

Also available in ebook:
ISBN: 978-1-62649-875-4

Love Under Glasse

KRISTINA MEISTER

TRITON
BOOKS

For my little sister Val, who is sensitive, ferocious, and daring. You never cease to delight and amaze.

Table of Contents

Fairest

The girl slid down the tree trunk, her coat tumbling up over her shoulders in a mantle of black and deep greens. Knees peeking from her torn jeans, she reclined against the roots. As if dismissing the world, she inserted earbuds with the flick of a wrist. Seconds later, she was mouthing lyrics, kissing the humid air with a pout.

El's skin tingled and her pulse rattled in her veins. She was never going to run out of reasons to stare at Riley.

Never.

She pressed against the classroom window as the girl performed a recumbent dance move, face dappled in shade. She moved as if every single tiny gesture had a deeper meaning, and all of it could be decoded if set to music.

There was just no other way to think about Riley. Her face was always composed. Her eyes were always glittering with awareness. She didn't hide in the shadows she could make for herself. Her height and shape were perfectly defined in the mind of every person around her, because like her or hate her, Riley Vanator never folded herself up for anyone . . .

"Elyrra!"

Startled, El's forehead cracked against the cold glass and woke her to reality. At once, she felt small again as a heavy arm fell across her shoulders to the tune of a mean-spirited laugh.

"Hey, I'm gonna pick you up today, okay?"

Shrugging uncomfortably, El clutched her notebook to her chest and tried to look as if she'd been doing something more productive than yet again fantasizing over the gorgeous figure beneath the tree.

"Why?"

Jay was fresh from gym and ruddy, but even physical exhaustion couldn't wipe the perpetual smirk off his face. "Because you're my girlfriend, and I want to take you out."

"Where are we going?"

"It's cool! I already cleared it with your mom."

"I don't—"

"Look, you haven't been out with me in a couple of weeks." His arms coiled around her waist. He clung to her like some kind of sweaty sloth and tried to fondle her. "I'm starting to think you don't like me."

It wasn't the first time he'd said it, but it was the first time she wanted to spit her agreement in his face. He didn't want a girlfriend. He wanted an orgasm. El shoved at him, but there was no disentangling, and not a soul in the quickly emptying study hall seemed to care. While he rooted around in her neck like a pig, she leaned against the glass and rolled her face to the view below.

Riley was sitting cross-legged, eating a small snack before she went to work as she always did right after school. Her thin fingers picked it apart delicately. When her tongue slid out and cleaned them each in turn, El sighed, and the boy attached to her body like a leech gave himself a congratulatory snicker.

"You're gonna have fun tonight. I promise."

"What if I don't?" she whispered.

"What's that mean?" He pulled back and stared at her, brows drawn together in a confusion of wrinkles that somehow painted a perfectly predictive image of his face in twenty years, after he'd done a failed stint in the Army, or bought a car dealership, or something.

Why wouldn't El like him? Jay was *the* boy. The one everyone fought over, the one that the other girls would slander her to obtain, if not for the fact that El was demure and had a powerful family. He was the boy that could do no wrong. He was the boy who just had to be left to be, because boys were boys.

"I don't want to go out tonight."

"Uh . . . but we are."

That was that. His smug grin said it all. He'd long ago figured out that if he went to her mother, it meant that he held the power. El could never get in a moment of defense, because Jay kept her safe. And that came with certain sacrifices.

As he sauntered away, she pictured her mother's face, perfectly feminine makeup below her meticulously highlighted hair. All the little smile lines around her mouth would harden. Her eyes would turn to lead. Her lips would pinch over words that were harsher than anyone else could ever manage.

Why wouldn't El want to go out with a boy, especially *that* boy? Didn't she *like* boys?

Her mother could make doubt into a knife, and carve out the truth like she was delicately eviscerating a quail in her neon pink hunting jacket. Life was bad enough already without the distractions of her sister's pageants and admirers, with her mother downing two bottles of wine a night to counter the stress from the election, with school about to be out. El was alone and center stage.

She hated it.

El packed her things, the world around her blurring in and out of focus. Normal sounds were harsh. Skin numb, feet thudding like dead weights, she dragged herself out into the sun. Her chest ached. Her stomach always seemed to quake. Her heart was constantly trying to claw its way out. Every day was an exhausting dance between blending in and biding time, politics and patience. Every night she went to bed like a narcoleptic, and every morning she woke like a soldier in an air raid.

Soon it would get much, much worse, because Riley, the beautiful respite from the rest of her life, would be gone. Riley didn't have time for this place. She was an explorer. She would move on, and El would be left behind. But that was the way it should be.

Riley was untouchable.

A thrill went through El's body, as Riley's beloved motorcycle growled at the world. Its lithe mistress was astride it, about to charge into battle instead of her shift at Sam's ice cream parlor. Her seamless black helmet was more like a crown. As her high boots coaxed the feral machine backward out of its parking space, Jay leaned from his car window and hurled a wadded-up bag at her. It bounced to the ground lamely, the victim looking after it in a stoic gleam.

"Next time it's a rock, dyke!"

His car jolted, cutting off the motorcycle, but Riley was unperturbed. Slowly tipping at the waist, extended to her full length like a dancer, she plucked the litter off the ground. The boys cackled, but Riley didn't move. Beneath her faceplate, El hoped she was rolling her depthless eyes, wearing that crooked grin that turned her mouth into a beckon. While Jay screeched to the head of the line, Riley squeezed a tighter ball in a gloved hand, tipped forward, and torqued her wrist. Before El could blink, the bike was beside the carful of idiots, the wadded-up bag was bouncing off Jay's face, and the girl was shooting past them, protected by a wall of sound like a legion of demons.

The boys sat for a moment in shock, but there was nothing to be done. It was Riley, and nothing she did was at all surprising, because every glance and word from her was a warning. Jay would have to tackle his hurt pride by himself, because divinity had no time for foolish boys.

El's taut smile was reflexive. She wanted to open her notebook and transcribe every second, but her mother was already there, tapping her watch and making faces.

The car was like a walk-in freezer. Patriotism and bigotry were boxed side by side in every seat and the windows were crowded with campaign signs.

"Come on, Elyrra! I have an appointment at headquarters. Your father has a photo shoot with some magazine."

The radio buzzed with angry voices, debating each other's fitness to live. Someone maligned the local favorite and the host called him "liberal scum." While El sketched her day in ciphers, her mother muttered under her breath in unintelligible venom.

"Mom, can we turn the station?"

"I'm listening to the news," was the flat reply.

"All it does is make you angry."

The smile could be disdainful in the wrong light, but there never seemed to be a right one. "Spiritual warfare doesn't break for your feelings and God doesn't listen to excuses."

Excuses. She'd never really made excuses to God. To herself, sure, but to God? No point. If there was anyone who'd watched her whole life twist into this painful thing, it was God. Which was probably why she was beginning to resent the idea of Him.

As she watched the town drift by in the charm of previous centuries, El realized she measured her life in a series of acquiescences. Every moment was an instance of defeat and compromise, and every day, she became more skilled in being faceless. She was sure that no human could be happy if it came to lying to one's self. It seemed impossible that that could really have been the intent of God.

The radio cut off.

"I sent your camp fees in today, sugar!"

Something about the cheer in the voice was wrong, but then again, there was nothing right about the situation. Three months of perfect girls all wearing bathing suits around the waterfall, ignoring her because she was famous. Three months starved for touch, lonely and cast out into the forest, being bullied by those far more comfortable in their identities. Three months of torture while her mother had a peaceful house and could get all her interviews about family values done without the bother of her family.

"You're gonna have a great summer! I think you're gonna like this camp. It's much more for the *artistic* types!"

El's instincts cut in with a warning. She had never declared herself *artistic*. That would be strategic suicide, because it would mean she could think creatively. Her mother's award-winning works on how to raise godly children in the modern era specifically warned parents about how to sculpt the imagination. Fairy tales were fine so long as they glorified God, but fiction was a kind of lying and so the storyteller had to have a firm hand. El would have done better to pick up the Bible from the center console and slap her mother across the face with it rather than to be "artistic."

Swallowing, she tried to sound content. "What's it called?"

A manicured hand swept the question aside. "Fair Meadows or something. I can't remember. But it's just *perfect* for you."

"It is?"

"You need to learn the *skills* of making healthy friendships!" Exasperation dripped from every word. "You need *support*! You need to really examine yourself and measure yourself by God's standard and learn to *channel* everything you feel into a better relationship with Him. You need to rekindle your faith!"

El needed no help with faith, whatsoever. She had plenty, but her holy words were in her lap in a made-up shorthand. Her worship service took place every Friday evening at an ice cream parlor, where she prayed in daydreams. Her hymns were silent, but her congregation thousands strong—the population of a city hanging on every homily she typed. She needed no fellowship but reblogs and comments, no communion but likes and notes. Her blog of her adoration and suffering was the only religion and a secret sin.

God had apparently only made a few people in His image. The rest were fodder for the Devil.

"So! Jay and a date! I think he has something special planned!"

Something in El's soul began to vibrate like a rung bell. She felt it deep in the center of her abdomen. Soon it filled up her esophagus and was in her mouth before she could stop it.

"He wants to have sex with me. You know that, right?"

Her mother blinked into the silence. El watched that face, fighting to catch her breath, fighting with an unspoken hope that for once, this woman would do right by her. The conflict raged in the air, and then was dashed aside with yet another chemically paralyzed smile.

"The Lord never said a man and woman couldn't be a man and woman. He simply said you have to guard your chastity. You have to demonstrate your virtue to Jay too. You have to learn to strike a balance between your lust and your self-control! That can't happen without testing yourself! You can't beat the demon if you don't ask for the Lord's help."

But the demon wasn't a demon. It was a boy who already wrestled at a professional level. It was disgusting whispers in her ear. It was helplessness. It was fear of being mocked by buxom cheerleaders, or worse still, by boys. It was losing herself to guard herself.

"Why doesn't *he* have to be chaste?"

"He does, Elyrra, but men have urges."

"And if he dumps me for it? If he makes up stories about me—"

Incredibly, her mother turned in the seat and glared at her. "Stop it. Jay is a clean-cut boy. He is going to make some woman very happy one day, and it might as well be you."

The car coasted to a halt at the curb. The church sat back from the street like a red brick castle. El latched her eye on it forlornly.

"So what's wrong with Jay?" Mama demanded.

"I don't like him . . . I mean he—"

"You're too picky! You won't meet a prince."

Closing her eyes, she took a breath. "You love Tom. You never say one bad thing about him. So I guess Rose found a prince."

There was a loud hiss. "Yes, but you're not your sister! She's a beauty queen. And there aren't that many men like Tom! The way you carry on . . . the way you dress—"

"*You* buy my clothes." El stared at her notebook, caressing its cover. "What if I don't ever want to get married?"

Her mother's eyes were wide and blank. Her lips were parted, but petrified. It was as if she was having a premonition of a life without the herd of grandchildren she could parade across the internet for the world to use as a metric of her worthiness. Ever since her father had been elected and her mother's website had gone viral, all she cared about was her reputation. Every week was a list of Mama's radio appearances, podcasts, or website statistics. The whole Christian world knew the faces of Rose and Elyrra Glasse—test subjects of their devoted mother and living proof that God still possessed the heart of modern hedonistic America. Without progeny, the whole experiment was a shambles.

"It's a woman's duty to have a family. The Bible says a woman does not have authority over her own body—"

El opened the door and jumped out. "First Corinthians: 'It is good for a man not to have sexual relations with a woman. But since sexual immorality is occurring, each man should have sexual relations only with his wife.' So wouldn't a woman be more godly if she never married at all and kept men from immorality?"

"You are not a nun, missy! You don't have the fortitude—"

She shut the door and walked toward the shade of the church. Normally, the window would have rolled down and a list of consequences for her disobedience would have been screamed at her, but her mother was late, and the car lurched away.

No fortitude? If Mama only knew what it took her just to get through the day . . .

Reverend Williams was already waiting for her. Everything about this place made her nervous, from the perpetual stink of burned black coffee and dust to the tenacious look in his eye. His questions were pointed, his demeanor intrusive, and his knowledge of her extensive, but it was private sessions with the priest, or her mother would pull her out of school.

The notebook stayed in her lap like a talisman. He dropped into the other chair and patted her hands, knotted anxiously atop it. His knees practically touched hers, but she couldn't retreat, because he would interpret that as withholding.

"So . . . tell me about this week."

Thoughts were squeezed by Jay's hungry fingers, nettled by the other girls' constant jibes at her generically girlish clothes, squashed by the teachers who saw nothing special in her because she hid anything unusual, crushed by the way her mother excused insults as honesty. But then she thought of Riley, stretched out on the grass, her pixie hair at odd angles, her strong limbs, her defiant grin. Suddenly, there were no tests. There were only chances that she wasn't taking, opportunities she was forced to let pass by.

She shook her head. "This week was good."

"And your . . . uh . . ."—he tapped the book—"your little *fixation*?"

Little? There was nothing little about it, but it wasn't the first time he'd tried to compact it into a more pleasing shape. It was at best a phase and at worst a mortal sin, and to him, her future would either result in marriage counseling, or a laying on of hands.

"I wrote about her ten times."

"That's less than last week!" This seemed a relief. It couldn't be easy trying to logic away a feeling so intense it invaded her dreams. "Progress!"

"Yes."

"But we still have a lot of work to do." His sigh whistled like munitions out at the Fort. "The Devil doesn't want to let you go. He had to try for one of you. Especially now that everything is going so well for your family."

El's flesh began to ache like a fever. Suddenly, the quiet ticking of his wall clock and the warmth of the room were too much.

She should never have told him, but her emotions had been a tangle of self-loathing and shame. She'd looked to him for guidance, but only got more confusion, more things to hate about herself, and more reasons to question. The only answers that ever made any sense were gleaned from anonymous online well wishes and emailed articles. Her only real advisors were people she had never met who cared for her as no one had ever cared for them. Without her secret life on the internet, she'd be little more than an automaton.

He took hold of the edge of her book. "May I see?"

El loosened her instinctual grip and watched as he flipped slowly through the pages. Her hieroglyphics were illegible, but the fact that she still wrote in them at all seemed to tell him enough.

"Elyrra, who is the Keeper of Secrets?"

She licked her lips. "You know why I do it, Reverend."

"The Devil is giving you these thoughts to drive a wedge between you and your family. He wants you to be alone and sinful. He wants to cut you off from God."

"But…" She caught herself; his insistent look, however, persuaded her to let it out. "Isn't God everywhere? How can he do that if God is everywhere? Why would God let him?"

He leaned back, taking her scriptures with him. He seemed to be debating something, and as he rose to his feet to pace, her heart plummeted through her sandals. There would be a new exercise, a new prayer, a new prescription for her sickness.

"My dear, you cannot keep doing this to yourself. We've been working on this for months now."

"I know," she breathed. "I'm trying. Really, I am."

"I don't think I have the expertise to help you."

El's pulse began to thrum in her temples. Stillness seemed impossible. She wanted to jump up and bolt, but he was already shaking his head.

"I think I know a way."

As long as he didn't tell her mother, El didn't care if he suggested walking over hot coals; she would do it.

"There's a place where you can go, and they can give you the kind of counsel you need. You'd be with people like you. They would know exactly what to say to you, because they've helped so many already to come back from sin."

Suddenly, it felt as if she couldn't breathe, though her chest rose and fell in the usual fashion. There was simply no oxygen in the room.

This was one of those places her online friend Oscar had talked about. It had to be. The articles he'd sent, the testimonials about conversion therapy, the confessions of people who'd been through it were terrifying in so many tiny ways. He'd warned her. He'd shown her her father's affiliations. And now here they were, affecting her directly.

Tears welled in her eyes, but there didn't seem to be an alternative. If she didn't do what Reverend Williams said, he would tell her mother. If her mother found out, she'd never escape. Her senior year would play out in their parlor with a private tutor, or worse yet, her mother playing educator. Her parents would refuse to pay for college. El would end up living in a studio apartment and picking up roadkill. But if she went to one of those places, if she gave in again . . .

There'd be nothing left of her.

"It's a beautiful camp, right on a lake!" He was smiling, which was supposed to make her feel better, but only made her sick for a variety of reasons. "They have a gourmet chef! And it's more like a summer camp!"

El's throat seemed to swell, but she coughed words out at last. "What's it called?"

"Fairest Meadows!"

The ground swung out from beneath her feet as the world floated away. She knew she was standing, that she had snatched the book from his hand, that she had thrown open his office door, but strangely, it was more like time travel, because suddenly she was outside the church and he was calling after her.

"You told me everything I said was safe!" she shrieked. Her face was wet. Her legs refused to stop. "You told me I could trust you!"

"Elyrra, calm down!"

"No!" He reached for her elbow, and without conscious thought, she swiveled and evaded. "You *lied* to me! You *told* her!"

"I did *not*, young lady!" His voice burned her ears with indignation. "Your *mother* told *me*!"

And there it was. El's robotic movements clicked to a halt. She stared at the swirling chartreuse beneath her feet and flinched as he put a hand on her shoulder.

"Your mother wants to help you. You're too young to know what's best for you. You need to listen."

She pulled away, and in a fierce trot, broke for downtown.

No, what she needed was some ice cream.

2

Magic

"You're early," he said, as if it were a curse.

Riley hung her motorcycle jacket on the hook with a forced smile. "Yeah, Russ? Really?"

He looked down a weasel nose at her. "You can't clock in early."

It had to be today. Just a few more hours, and holy shit, was she going to enjoy her revenge. Knowing what was coming, Riley danced up to the ice cream bar and lounged against the cold glass, blocking the line of patrons.

"My shift doesn't start till 4:30! I get bored!"

He wasn't impressed. "You clock in early so you can get paid more. You can't have any more hours."

"Relax, dude. I'm gonna take my half hour and eat ice cream."

"You can't come behind the counter if you're not wearing your uniform."

What a stickler for the rules, she marveled. When they suited him, of course. "That's okay! I'm cool with you serving me, Russ. Gimme the secret flavor!"

It was amazing how tiny his eyes got when he was angry. "I don't like your attitude."

"Feeling is mutual. One scoop, please!"

He worked the utensil as if using it to carve a hole in her face, and then slid the cup across the bar so fast, it almost fell on the ground— which would have been awesome, frankly, because Riley also wasn't allowed to clean things unless wearing a uniform. Winking at him as he seemed to realize how close he'd come to the germ-coated mop in the backroom, she sauntered to the outdoor seating area and spun one of the heavy iron chairs to face the park.

The first spoonful was . . . interesting. Riley was pretty sure it was supposed to taste like caramel popcorn. Really it tasted like popcorn jelly beans and salty caramel combined. She rolled it around her mouth and couldn't say if she liked it or hated it, but like all of Sam's weekly experiments, it was sure adventurous.

In fact, it was pretty much the only adventurous thing about this fucking town.

Riley missed the city—the snippets of foreign languages, the music out of every window, the food Abuela would cook. All that action and sound traded for Hicksville, hidden somewhere on the Devil's Southern Regions. Now she spent weekends doing weird shit to her hair and disassembling engine components, but it was the way it had to be to keep her dad out of The Life. So it was caramel corn ice cream and mermaid dye jobs, grease and a galumphing mechanic who at least allowed her to get whatever she wanted pierced.

The flavor was giving up more secrets; it had a spine like sweet cream butter and an odd smokiness to it that reminded her of whiskey. Sam would get a detailed note from her on his desk tonight.

She wondered if Miss Glasse would like it—if for once, the girl's hooded, sea-blue gaze and porcelain, deadpan face would change expression. Somehow, she doubted it. Elyrra had been coming every Friday for almost a year, always picking the weekly mystery flavor with a voice so soft that Riley had taken to dishing it up as soon as she walked in, just to prevent the awkward conversation, and never in all that time had she looked as if she had emotions.

Kind of a waste of a pretty face, really.

The swish of Russel's broom scraped against her nerves. "Are you going to put that chair back?"

Tilting her chin over her shoulder, Riley stared him down. "Are you sure I don't need to be wearing my uniform to do that?"

"You're a customer, but it's polite to put the chair back."

Riley rolled her eyes at the park. "Yeah, but not mandatory. Aren't you always telling me how impolite I am?"

"Do I need to talk to Sam?"

"Do what you gotta do, Russ, but I'm pretty sure the customer is always right."

He brushed his way around her, and Riley cracked her knuckles.

Plans came together with patience, she told herself, again and again. It was critical that she wait for the two of them to be alone, for silence and his sticky fingers to start itching. If she didn't get up and walk away at this moment, she was going to end up punching him out before it came to that.

Riley left the chair right where it was, sticking out like a sore thumb that Russel could cram right up his ass. A circuit of the park would only take a couple minutes, if she walked slow. What was she going to do with herself after that?

A feeling tugged on her mind, and triggered a comfortable warmth. By the sorcery that governed the senses, Riley found the girl sitting beneath a tree, and as usual, once she was caught staring, Elyrra Glasse dropped her eyes to her book.

When Riley had recognized the Friday pattern, she was angry. Mama Glasse's opinions about people like her were pretty well known, and there was her daughter coming to stare at the freak, caged in her striped uniform. Over two years and four shared classes, however, Riley had begun to realize Elyrra was painfully shy, polite to the point of getting trampled, and probably just hadn't seen a teenage girl with tattoos. Which, fair enough, since it took parental consent to get ink, and not many parents in these parts would be so liberal.

Coming level with Elyrra, Riley spotted the moist face and the damp spots on her skirt. She had been crying, and even though it was in the 90's and humid as balls, she was shivering. Riley kept going for about ten paces, halted cold, and knew she needed to learn to leave things alone.

She couldn't, though. It was just a fact that defined her as a person. Riley Vanator was a busybody.

Tiptoeing around the tree trunk, she looked down over the girl's shoulder. Page after page of Elyrra's notebook was marked up with weird symbols, as if the kid spent hours copying pictographs from temple walls.

"Are you trying to crack our recipes for Baskin Robbins?"

Elyrra startled as if there were gunfire, the book tumbling off her knees. Shoving her hair from her face, she righted her papers and pushed them into her backpack without a reply.

Riley let out a hiss and plopped herself onto the ground; this was going to be a tough nut to crack. "Look, I get that your mom has this checklist of demonic elements you're s'posed to avoid, but queers don't carry spiritual plague."

The girl froze and cut the silence with a sniffle. "I . . . don't think like that."

Surprised, Riley propped her back against the bark and offered the cup of half-eaten ice cream to her. "Good, because I don't have cooties, I think I hate this, and I want to save you the trouble of paying for it. It's the mystery flavor."

The girl hesitated, but only for a moment, and with two careful hands, accepted the gift as if taking communion. Riley shook her head in amusement as Elyrra lifted the spoon and slowly made her own opinion about Sam's latest alchemical disaster.

"Gross, right?"

Elyrra swallowed. "It tastes like jelly beans."

Waving her hands in the air, Riley laughed. The trembling mouse beside her nearly fell backward in shock, but she pretended not to notice. "Exactly! It's like those fucking Harry Potter beans, but ten times sweeter."

"I've never had those. Mama doesn't like—"

"Oh shit, forgot. Right. They're so gross. Here, give it back, I'll throw it away for you. No one should suffer through that."

"No . . ." Elyrra's cheeks were finally getting some color to them, but the rest of her was still so white Riley wondered if she always wore pink so that her skin would reflect it like some kind of cosmetic optical illusion. "It's okay. I'll eat it."

Riley dropped her wrist onto her knee and let the birds take over the conversation. Dad always said that humans couldn't stand open spaces, gaps, holes. They had to fill them, cover them over, explore them. That included silence, and sometimes what a person chose to put into the silence was the best way to read them. She waited and waited, but Elyrra said nothing. Apparently, the girl was more than happy to be a mystery. Finally, enchanted, Riley fell to her own subterfuge.

"So what happened?"

Dad would scold her. She just couldn't be patient.

"Why do you ask?"

"Uh . . . because I'm not an asshole, and I hate when people cry. Especially girls. Especially pretty girls. It's like kryptonite."

Elyrra seemed to be swallowing very hard, but not getting anywhere. It was probably some weird Glasse family rule that they had to choke down whatever food was given to them. Riley regretted handing her the horror.

"Call me observant, but you're not usually sitting in the park casing our parlor before you come in, are you?"

The girl wiped her face and set the cup on top of her bag. "No."

"So you're not trying to steal our secrets?"

"No."

"Your mom usually picks you up from there."

"Yes."

With a shake of her head, Riley gave up. "This is going to be a really boring conversation if you stick to one-word answers. I mean, I know we don't talk at school—"

"I'm sorry." Elyrra was hugging herself, as if to hold all the other words that might come spilling out in check. "It's so rude."

"It's cool. I understand. If your mom found out you were talking to this social pariah, she'd probably have you exorcised or something."

The mouth twitched. "True."

"Well, see?" Riley reached out with her pinky finger, the tiniest part of her body, and tapped the pale forearm. "Then you're safe. You can tell me what's wrong. Who am I gonna tell?"

Absentmindedly, Elyrra rubbed the spot she'd touched, and Riley tried not to be offended, succeeding only by reminding herself that the Glasse family was pretty stiff. There probably wasn't a lot of physicality in their home.

"Not sure who to trust anymore," the girl mumbled.

"Maybe you could talk to that boyfriend of yours—"

"He's *not* my boyfriend."

Eyebrow cocked to the branches above, Riley cleared her throat. "Maybe somebody should tell *him* that, because he really shouldn't be pawing at you if you aren't dating. Hell, he probably shouldn't be doing it if you are, but I dunno, maybe straight girls *are* into that."

She glanced over. Elyrra's face was a perfect glow of passion fruit punch sorbet. "*I'm* not into it."

"Okay then. Time to uh ... set up some boundaries? Just so I can walk down the hall at school without having to scrub my eyeballs with that powdered soap grit? Can we do that? Save my corneas, save your pride as an added bonus?"

In painstaking inches, Elyrra's gaze had climbed Riley's torso to reach the flowers on her collarbone, but now, in one instant, it was back in her own lap. Riley folded up into a ball and wondered if appearing smaller would make this doll next to her any braver.

"So tell me what's wrong. Talking helps get the facts out there. Somebody lied to you?"

To her shock, Elyrra seemed to shake herself from head to knee like a tree in the wind. Then she twisted in place, stretched out her ghostly white legs, and ran her fingers through her long mass of pitch-black hair.

"I had this secret ... something ... something I didn't want my mom to know. And today, I found out she has apparently known about it for a while."

Riley closed her eyes and let the frail voice tremble through her mind. She caught every note and tenderly examined it for importance. She had an exceptionally sensitive ear, something developed while living with an ex-con. It made keeping track of the truth pretty easy, but it made listening to commercials almost a physical impossibility. That blender/ladder/cubic zirconia was the solution to life's woes? Really?

Yeah, no.

"I'm guessing that she has some way of dealing with it that you know is gonna suck."

"Yes."

"Okay, and why is that upsetting?"

Elyrra's thin fingers were wringing, her expensive manicure of chipped paint sparkling. "It's bad ... because ... because my mother is so much worse than you think."

"Naw . . . You don't look like I do without an expansive imagination."

To her relief, the girl managed a tiny smile. "I'm worried."

"Why?"

Shocked into normal etiquette, Elyrra looked her in the eye, was evidently stunned by the contact, and ricocheted back into her solitude. "That's not obvious?"

"No, I mean, I get it. Your mom's a wicked witch, no offense."

"None taken."

"Yeah. Right? It's not really debatable. What I mean is, if she's known all this time, what's going to change? Are you worried she's going to find out that you know she knows? Is that going to change what she does about this horrible secret?"

Tiny confused ripples gathered above Elyrra's brows, as she combed the grass with her fingers, looking for an answer. "I don't know . . ."

"I mean, in a way, you're in a great position. Because she's shown you her play, but I can see why you wouldn't want her to know you knew it, because then she might change it, right?"

"I . . . guess I didn't think about that."

"So really, all you have to make sure of is that she doesn't find out you know she knows. That way you have time to work out what to do next."

As they sat there, in a lengthy silence, Riley could feel an impression forming. At school, Elyrra was meek, largely mute, seemed always to be writing in her book. At one time, Riley had glossed over all the details she couldn't fathom about Elyrra Glasse, by assuming there was nothing deep about her. Like she was just a hole in space that walked and whispered. Now, however, Riley was beginning to think that Elyrra was actually brimming with complexity and thoughts, but had no idea how to set them free.

She tried again, this time searching for something a little more profound, a little more foundational—it was something her dad had said to her and Riley couldn't imagine how it couldn't make as great an impact here. "How long are you going to let other people turn simple math into magic, huh?"

Elyrra blinked. "What?"

"Math is just facts, objects. They have to balance and equalize. If something is an unknown, it's given a letter or a symbol, and then it gets balanced too, until we can figure out what it actually means. But magic looks at those unknowns and substitutes all sorts of weird shit, makes all these assumptions about the missing pieces that basically screw with the ability to put in real info. Turns a simple equation into miracles and demons and whatnot. Takes understanding out of human hands, you know?"

Riley hugged her knees as Elyrra processed this. Eventually, the girl's voice snuck out between her pursed lips. "I'm not sure I understand what you mean. How . . . how does that apply to my situation?"

"Everyone has facts they know about themselves—things that don't change, *won't* change. Even teenagers. I mean I know we're nervous balls of utter batshit rebelliousness, or whatever, but we still have that core in us, and we know what sort of people we want to be." She tilted her head at the girl. "You're quiet, that's a fact, but what does it *mean*? To me, it means you think about things all the time, which is good. Like, maybe if you were in a different environment, it wouldn't be shyness, but strength, but that's an unknown variable and my opinion doesn't matter. Are you going to let other people interpret those in crazy ways, or are you going to take charge and tell people how they're *allowed* to think of you?"

Even dumbfounded, Elyrra was pretty. She was nothing like her older sister—Miss Superficiality—who had bleached hair for days and a perpetual vagueness to her expression. She was nothing so brittle as her mother, who had a face of sharp edges she dulled with the three B's: botox, booze, and bibles. Elyrra was a contrast of ivory and jet and a complete mystery, probably even to herself.

Riley was a sucker for a good mystery.

"You know most kids think that their parents have control over them. And I mean yeah, they have *power*, because they get to decide consequences, but they don't have *control*. They don't get to tell you who you are."

"Okay."

Riley unfolded and sat up. She was going to have to go soon, or risk the wrath of Russel. Those were some fucked consequences, but the power balance was about to change.

"Nobody has control over you, but you. Everything else is magic. They interpret what they see of you and force you to live by it. They cast a spell. Maybe you need to just declare who you actually are."

"So . . ." It was faint, but there was a musical note of whimsy in that voice, all of a sudden. "What are the facts of Riley Vanator?"

With a snort, Riley grinned at her boots. "That's easy. I don't like when bad things happen. I get bored really easily. I'm stubborn. I'm nosy." She glanced backward and watched the blue eyes dip to the ground, but the rosy lips were smiling. "I have a temper, so I keep it under control by giving it things to do. I've got a handle on it. I've sort've figured out an important thing to help me with that."

The whisper was back, and lifted the hairs on Riley's neck as Elyrra asked after her discovery.

"This shit we're going through isn't about learning stuff. I mean, sure we learn a few skills here or there. Like last week, dude . . . in Chemistry, I learned how to make napalm!"

It happened so suddenly, Riley forgot what she was going to say—Elyrra laughed, and it wasn't the tinkling of glass she expected, but a low and smooth song that glided through her soul so easily it left only a ticklish feeling behind.

Hearing it once, Riley was addicted and grinning like a fool.

"I haven't decided yet how I am going to use this information, but I'm pretty sure it's valuable."

"A good graduation prank?"

"I'm pretty sure burning down graduation is a terrorist act."

"Deforestation?"

Riley let out a goofy chuckle. "I think I was making a point, here!"

Elyrra's laugh coughed to a halt. "I'm listening."

"I was saying that kids think they're in school, or scouts, or whatever, to learn facts, but they're not. We're learning how to *interpret* facts, the process, you know? We're learning how to think about truth, because truth is already there whether we know it or not. We find it, we pick it up, and we have to make sense out of it. See?"

"I really don't." She sounded confused, but she was still smiling in Riley's periphery, so it was all good.

"The hoops are all laid out, right? A person who jumps through all of them graduates, gets a merit badge, or wins the pageant. But life isn't about diplomas and crowns. It's about making sense of yourself and being happy in spite of the bullshit the world throws at you. So while kids think they're supposed to be learning all this useless knowledge, they're not seeing the bigger picture. They're not learning the most important thing."

"What is that?"

"That kids who jump through hoops have normal lives. Kids who set hoops on fire with napalm . . . have *interesting* lives."

Elyrra tipped forward, her palms pressed to the earth as she shook with laughter. Her face was hidden behind a black curtain, but she was happy, and that was what mattered.

Riley stood up and smiled down at her, finally managing to catch her in a shared look. "Outsmart magic by being clever. See what I mean?"

"Yes, I think I do."

"Good, because I'm not really sure what the hell I just said. Like talking to the sphinx."

The laugh evolved into a giggle, quavering slightly as Elyrra braced herself against the tree and got to her feet. "No, it was good."

Riley pointed at the grimoire of graffiti, peeking out from her bag. "Is it ghostly communication from the other side?"

The long hair swished back and forth. "It's not a spell book, I promise."

"So you're not a closet Wiccan?"

"I don't even know what that is."

"A girl who wears a lot of black and hangs in the broom cupboard, I guess?" Riley was granted a parting laugh and danced backward, her spine tingling. "Don't you tell anyone about my napalm, Elyrra!"

"I won't! And please . . . call me El."

She tossed the girl a casual thumbs-up, and jogged into the parlor, nearly tripping when she realized El was still watching her.

Russel glanced at the clock much too happily as she stopped to catch her breath. "You're five minutes late. I'll have to report it to Sam."

Riley let out a huff, and smiled with every microscopic trace of sweetness she could manufacture. "That's cool, Russ. You do that."

3

Prince Charming

Normally, El made full use of every second away from her mother to turn her notes into email drafts with a fervor that caused people to stare. Between school, in which cell phones were banned, and home, in which cell phones were confiscated until the next day, she only had so long, and Friday was the one day a week that bought her a few spare hours to sing Riley's praises to her salivating fans, but at the moment, the phone was a dead weight in her slack hand. She couldn't even use it to call Oscar and gain some of the comfort he offered.

Today was the end and beginning of the world, and El had no idea what to say.

Mama knew. She had known all this time, or suspected it. She'd told Reverend Williams. She'd arranged to have him ask the right questions and say the right things, to make El doubt herself and fear for her spiritual purity. Like some sort of expert interrogator, he had pulled the information from her, gained some of her trust, and all to betray her.

How much had he then told her mother? Had he shown Mama the camp, or had her mother enlisted *him*? Neither made sense. If Reverend Williams were working for her mother, why would she have mentioned the camp, instead of leaving it to him? If Mama were following Reverend Williams' instructions, then she still would have waited until after he'd mentioned it to convince El it was the spiritual path. They had to have come to it independently of one another.

Which meant that it was possible Reverend Williams had not shared any information with her mother. If that was true, she could still fix the situation before it spiraled out of control.

Riley, that snarky angel, had put her terror to rest in but a few moments, and finally El could concentrate without her mind running in circles.

She leaned back against the tree and stared up into the leaves. Why, of all days, had Riley chosen today to notice her? Why couldn't it have happened sooner? If it had, it likely wouldn't have mattered. El would have been too afraid to whisper one word, let alone have a conversation. It had to be today, the day her inhibitions were utterly crushed by the sheer immensity of her circumstances, or she would never have been desperate enough to open her mouth. It was today because she was falling to pieces and Riley enjoyed puzzles.

That much, El had observed. Dog-eared detective novels, metal knots hanging from keychains just waiting to be untied, the look in those brown eyes that could solve a problem before anyone noticed it existed. Colorful hair that confused others, makeup that defied an adult to tell her it was "too much," a kind of aesthetic that mysteriously turned Army surplus and denim into feminine couture. Riley had crafted herself to always be a cipher; that much El understood.

Compared to that, El was timid, bland, boring.

But Riley had called her pretty. As she baked in the warm air, she knew it had to be because Riley was the most amazing individual the earth had ever known, and was being kind. Mama had told her that more than once—that people complimented her to be polite, not because she'd earned praise.

El's spine jerked her upright with a surge of insubordination.

Wait a moment.

That was something *Mama* had said. Which meant it was more than likely a self-serving lie. When Mama felt threatened by another person's value, she just reinterpreted it. El wasn't allowed to be her own person, and if someone told her she was pretty or smart, it had to be twisted.

That was the magic Riley was talking about!

The spell could only work if El allowed it to. All she had to do was stop believing it. Stop believing anything Mama said. Stop reaching for love and praise that was never there, stop accepting conditions for care and protection. If El wanted the suffering to end, she'd have to resist her own blood, her own mental conditioning that screamed about how children had only their parents as advocates against the world. It may be true for many, but nothing was universal.

Her mother was the enemy. El could not allow the witch to usurp her feelings anymore. If she did, it would eventually kill her.

The thought had physical consequences. Almost at once, El's stomach tossed with anxiety. Even as she remembered all the terrible things her mother had done, she wondered if it was possible to turn the magic around. Perhaps, if she worked at it, if she was clever, she could redeem her mother and help her be a good person. Perhaps if El could be patient, find a way to open up and discuss herself honestly, she could create a path into her mother's heart. They could heal and actually be friends. They could have that relationship other kids seemed to have with their parents.

As the idea burned and then dimmed, tears fell, because her body knew what her mind could not say—that the magic didn't work that way. The good could be overcome if they were too docile. The evil could only be overcome by themselves.

She dialed the church. Reverend Williams answered, sounding distracted.

"Reverend?"

"Elyrra! Are you all right?"

She cleared her throat. "I needed to think."

He let out a sigh. "I understand."

"Mama was already going to send me to that camp, but she didn't tell me what it was."

"I see. I had no idea."

This was the moment she began taking back her identity, in tiny deceits and ever-increasing increments of strength. "Please don't tell her I was so upset. She'd think I was being ungrateful. I don't want that."

To her relief, he agreed in a warm voice. "Will you come back to finish our session? We didn't get to say our prayers."

"I can't. She expects me to be with my boyfriend now. But I'll come next week, as usual."

"Okay. I'll see you then. Remember the Lord always comes to those who place their trials in His hands."

She thanked him, even as she knew that if she left it to anyone but herself, her fate would be decided against her best interests. If God existed, then she was as she was meant to be, and the only way to keep being that creation was to stop listening to the Bible and to the people who represented it. If God *didn't* exist . . . the same was true. Either way, she could not keep pretending to be someone she was not.

A person like Riley would *never* love or respect her if she didn't stand up for herself.

A text message summoned her to Jay's car. El gathered her things as the lump settled in her throat. Tonight would end the same as last time—in his heavy breathing and her cold compromise. She would drive to the river and get a little further from herself. It was the only way to subdue her mother and convince the world she was a normal teenager.

She came to a halt in the middle of the road, only vaguely aware that Jay's tires squealed to a stop at her very legs. Lost in a sudden epiphany, she didn't give the honking horn much thought.

Who decided "normal"?

It hadn't been her. El hadn't looked around and declared that the standard was everything she *wasn't*. She hadn't chosen to be an outsider. She was just being herself.

More magic . . . and she'd bought right into it!

"Elyrra! What the fuck are you doing?"

El turned and looked at the boy behind the wheel—this person she'd come to loathe. As she stared at him, he made faces at her, and while once she would have feared him, she now began to see that his power over her was that which she had given him.

She didn't owe him anything. If Mama was going to send her to a camp anyway, why even bother getting into the car?

Even as she asked the question, she knew the answer; she needed time to plan, and going with him would give her that time. Even so, she wondered what their date would be like if she simply refused to let him undermine her integrity, and decided she wasn't going to wonder. She was going to find out. Walking around the car and opening the door, she told herself that tonight would end on her terms.

"Are you retarded or something?"

"I don't like that word. Don't use it again."

He blinked. "The hell?"

"You heard me. I don't like that word. If you use it again, this date is over."

He let out a snort. El ignored him and gazed out the window at the ice cream parlor. Riley was in her classy turn-of-the-century uniform, giving it a rakish quality it could not have had on its own. Hat cocked at an angle, sleeves rolled up to reveal her rubber bracelets and compass rose tattoo, the girl chatted at her customers irrespective of their age. It brought a smile to El's lips and gave her confidence like nothing else.

Jay had been talking, but she wasn't paying any attention. At last, he pulled away from the park, ending El's moment of peace. He took them to the drive-in restaurant, all the while carrying on. When her name followed something sounding like it might have been a question, El drifted back to this reality.

El blinked at him. "I wasn't listening to you."

"What is wrong with you? You're in my car! If you're in my car, you listen to me."

"Why should I? All you ever talk about is the team, what stupid, cruel thing you're going to do next, and what I'm supposed to be doing to make you happy. I don't care about any of that stuff."

The waitress's voice came over the ordering speaker, but was silenced by an irate boy. "The fuck did you just say to me?"

"You heard me."

"Why are you being such a bitch? Is it that time of the month?"

"To realize I dislike you to the point I don't actually want to date you anymore? Yes, I think it's that time of the month."

What could he do? Hit her? It wasn't as if she hadn't been hit before. Numb to all consequences, she stared straight ahead and waited to see what would come of her rebellion.

"Why are you being like this? What did I do to you?"

"I think the real question is, what have you done *for* me, because I can't think of a single time you've ever cared about what I want. Do you know that Tamara got flowers on her birthday? Matt took Kayla to Disneyworld with his family over Easter. All you do is order me around and call me names. Well, that and try to have sex with me whenever you can."

He looked so stupid with his mouth hanging open that she couldn't help but laugh. In a moment, his face had turned crimson, his brows knitted together, and something in his eye changed. They'd been dating for almost a year, and it was the first time she'd ever seen thoughts register on his features. My, how they trudged through that muddy gaze, coated in mental muck by the time he muttered, "Do you want a hamburger or a hotdog?"

"I don't want anything, thank you."

"This is dinner," he spat. "If you don't eat this, you don't eat."

She had to suppress her smile as she calmly pointed out that she had a refrigerator and a cook at home. "I'll be just fine. Take care of yourself. You do anyway."

"I'm getting sick of this. I wonder what your mom would think of how you're acting."

In the past, that threat would have frightened her. It still did, truthfully, but the fear was secondary to a greater purpose. "Are you going to tell her? Because I'm happy to just break up with you right now and get it over with."

The car lurched away from the stall. In seconds, Jay was steering away from town toward the forest. As the buildings grew farther apart and his speed picked up, a nagging doubt pricked at El's courage, threatening to burst that bubble before it ever even had a chance to float skyward.

"You want to go on a trip? Let's go on a trip! I was going to use my money to get a new stereo for Heather." Jay loved his sports car almost as much as he loved himself. It was like an extension of his anatomy, and El was fairly certain she could identify the exact body part.

"What money? You don't have a job."

"I do too." He stifled whatever he was about to say. His hands were gripping the wheel as if to bend it, and his eyes kept flicking to her in a weird kind of rhythm. "Let's go on a trip! Where do you want to go?"

"With you? Nowhere."

"You said you wanted to go somewhere!" He was shouting now, and the car was beginning the winding ascent through the range. El's pulse picked up speed with every quarter mile.

"This isn't about a vacation, Jay. I don't like you! You don't like anything about me. I don't understand why you even want to date me!"

The car swerved off the main road onto an old logging trail and came to a dead stop in a patch of cool shade. Out of insults with which to goad him, she undid her seat belt and waited, her muscles tense. Jay stroked the wheel and took measured breaths, though she wasn't sure she understood what was upsetting him. He had never acted like this before, but then again, she'd never challenged him.

"I'm sorry," he said at last, though his voice was strained. "You're right. I haven't been a very good boyfriend."

Stunned, El turned to get a better look at him. Something was off. Jay never apologized.

"I promise I'll be better. It's just that ..." Suddenly, he was a perfect rendering of contrition, his knee braced against the steering column, his face twisted in anguish. "I never know what you're thinking. I can't figure you out. I can't tell if anything I'm doing is right."

Unsettled, El could not form words. Even her thoughts were a nonsense of incongruous impressions and half-framed realities.

"I really do want to make this work, because I really do like you!" He carried on inexplicably. "I mean, I want to talk to you more, and get to know you better! I don't even know your favorite color! We've been dating a year, and I don't know what kind of music you like. You're so pretty, Elyrra, and you get amazing grades. But you're like some kind of sphinx."

That was the second time she'd heard that word today, and yet it sounded so different. As she stared at him, El knew that this sort of act might have worked on other girls, but she was completely immune. Firstly, because he held no attraction for her, and secondly, because where she came from, compliments said in that tone were always weapons.

"Why would you ask me out? Why would you even want to date me?"

It had been so awkward. He'd come to her lunch table one day, after a fresh breakup with Claire, a girl he'd been dating off and on for years, and just insinuated himself into her day. Then all of a sudden, he was offering to take her on a date and wouldn't accept no for an answer. He'd even shown up on her doorstep to formally request becoming a suitor in antebellum fashion. She wouldn't have gone out with him at all, if not for her mother's encouragement that "he seemed like a clean-cut, blue-blooded American boy" that any girl would be lucky to snatch up . . .

El's body went painfully cold, her limbs cramping with the magnitude of the realization as if she'd awoken to an icy blizzard raging around her.

Her mother had always known her secret. Jay made eyes at Claire, but took El out on dates. And any time there was a moment of doubt about dating Jay, her mother did all she could to pacify or threaten El into staying with a boy she'd never even wanted to know. Jay had spending money, but no job.

"Oh god . . ." she whispered.

"I'm being serious, Elyrra. Look, I won't have much time this summer, what with the internship, to spend with you, but I don't want it to ruin things. I know I'm an asshole, and I'm trying to get better, but I need help. I need you!"

The internship—how could she have forgotten that? The elite position of working for a senator in his final year of high school was an opportunity an ambitious young man like Jay might do anything to have. Anything. Like covering for said Senator's amoral, homosexual daughter.

She'd assumed it had been arranged because he was her boyfriend, but what if it was just part of the payment?

Could it be a mistake? Could Mama have done it to protect her from being made fun of or picked on? El thought backward on all the times her mother had openly humiliated her and knew there was no way Mama had done it for her. Mama only ever did things for herself.

El brought her hands to her face, but they were shaking so badly, she couldn't blot out the green-filtered light. All this time, Jay had been working for Mama! That meant their few sexual encounters had all been setups. She'd been sold to him. She'd been trapped, and hadn't even known to fight her way out. She'd just taken it . . . thinking she was doing something to protect herself, when in fact it was being done *to* her.

Every breath became a shudder. Despite all the tears she'd already shed, her soul found them anew.

"Don't cry, baby," Jay murmured. His hand settled on her knee and moved upward as he tipped over the console and pressed his face to her neck. "Come here. Let me make you feel better."

El's heart stammered as he nibbled at her ear, and then slammed itself back to a ferocious cadence. With coursing rage, El shoved at him. Her voice, sounding like it had come from the darkest, oldest part of her brain, commanded him to stop. And when he gave no sign that he would listen . . .

Her fist broke the spell.

Something hot spattered her face. He let out a howl like a wounded dog and tumbled back. Her fumbling hands could make no sense of the door. Her bag was forgotten. In a tumult of swearing and wrath, Jay started the car and threw it in reverse.

"You fucking dyke. I'm bleeding!"

The car was rolling, but it was no longer about declaring herself. It was about survival. Her fingers caught the handle and tugged. The door swung outward just as he skidded onto the road. The tires bumped, she tipped outward, and a moment later collided with the blurred ground.

She lay there dazed, as the racing stripes on the door came into focus. Certain he'd come after her, El forced herself upright, but the boy was huddled inside the car, clutching his nose and gurgling. Clambering up, she realized one of her shoes had been torn from her foot and had vanished. Her bag was just there, inside the open car door. In it was her cell phone, but most importantly, her book.

She took a tentative step. As if he could sense her, Jay hurled himself toward the door, his face a brilliant shade of purple. With a glare the likes of which she'd never seen, he slammed the door shut and flipped a perilous one-eighty across the double yellow line.

Coming level with her, he rolled down his window. "Walk your ass home then. Maybe by the time you get there, you'll have stomped some fucking sense into your head and realized how much better your life is with me in it."

The car roared down the road, leaving El beneath the trees. The adrenaline flowed into her legs, making every joint ache and the very skin sore. Unable to stand, she sank to the dirt and sobbed.

4
Shining Armor

As she worked, Riley took the liberty of arranging her sweet revenge. This involved putting tape across the back door latch and positioning her laptop on the filing cabinet so that it had a lovely view of the manager's desk.

Russel was his usual charming self, which of course meant he was a complete prick to her, but she took every passive-aggressive comment in stride, delivering ice cream to patrons with a perfect smile. Not surprisingly, the secret flavor did not sell well, but on her break, Riley was in such a good mood, she gave it a second try.

It failed.

While Russel hovered around her, obtrusively trying to read what she was writing, Riley gave her review for Sam, their elderly shopkeep. He could make a custard base as smooth as silk, but Riley was convinced he was losing his sense of smell. Any man, however, who gave his employees free ice cream deserved eternal loyalty as far as she was concerned.

She clocked out precisely half an hour before closing, just like Russel always scheduled it. She removed her uniform and tucked it into her locker, checked on the computer, and set up the camera to record to a remote hard drive using the wi-fi.

Russel watched her walk out the front door. She took her usual route, for once thanking the city council for passing the noise ordinance that made it mandatory for her to walk her bike out of the downtown area after business hours. She'd been habitually obeying it, and vocally lamenting it, just so that the nerdy creep would be off his guard. Parking in the alley behind the shop, she waited. With the signal relayed to her phone, she watched. When the sleight of hand

and fuzzy math were at an end, Riley slipped in the back and made sure her knife was ready, just in case.

"So lemme run something by you, okay?"

Russel leapt from the chair. "Holy shit, Riley! You scared me! How did you get in here?"

Riley kept her hands in her pockets, but leaned her backside against the safe. "I dialed the latch while you were putting the chairs up."

Suddenly, he couldn't seem to make his eyes work properly. They wandered all over the place. "What? Why would you do that?"

"I'll get to that. Just let me do this right."

"Do what?" He scowled suddenly. "Disabling locks is vandalism—"

"Russel," she said in her customer service voice, as she drew her knife from her pocket and set it on the safe. "I'm gonna tell you what this is, and you're gonna listen."

"Are you . . . are you robbing us?"

Riley let out a *ha*, removed her phone from her pocket, and showed him what was on the screen. "Hey, Fuckwits . . . Sit down and shut up. You can't rob a robber. That's called *returning stolen property* and it's what we're going to do tonight, get me?"

His face was so white, his blemishes looked like fresh blood, as if all of a sudden, he'd acquired a deadly disease and his organs were seeping out of his pores. "What are you talking about?"

"I'm talking about the twenty bucks in your pocket."

His knees gave way. He hit the chair with such force it rolled backward a few inches. Riley crossed her arms and released a long, bedeviled sigh.

"Tyler's fourth birthday party, last month—you remember that, right? Spoiled brat who pegged you with a slingshot? Like twenty screaming toddlers and one of them dropped a sundae on the ground? Anyway, the next day, Tyler's mom came back and wanted another copy of her receipt. You were off that day. So I went in here to look for it. Only . . . I found something odd. Five voided cash transactions, totaling about thirty dollars. Except those transactions were mine. I know they got their ice creams and shakes, so why were the transactions voided in the system? And why was the money gone? Being the lowly employee that I am . . . I can't void transactions and I certainly didn't take the money."

Russel looked as if he was about to toss his ice cream cookie sandwiches all over his regulation shoes. He said nothing as she pulled a piece of paper from her pocket. It was one of about thirty, all photocopies of the voided receipts. The amounts were tallied nicely, and she was about to drop math on his head like a fucking piano.

"Every day you've worked, for the past month at least, you've been voiding about twenty to thirty dollars' worth of transactions, or writing off waste, or ringing up less than what people actually order. You've been skimming the till. For how much? I have no idea. I can only track what I can see, what I can prove, and I've crunched those fucking numbers into powder."

Russel pitched forward, burying his face in his hands. She liked him that way. It suited him.

She picked up the knife and opened it idly, tapping her chin with the blade. "I can prove that you've taken about thirty dollars a day for almost an entire month, which . . . I think, is about nine hundred dollars, right?"

"Come on, man . . ." he whimpered. His voice was honestly terrified. He looked up at her with fear in his eyes, and she knew he'd probably never done this before. He was a terrible thief because he lacked experience.

"Let me tell you how the law interprets these facts, Russel, because I feel like you need to know. Our state defines the receiving of stolen property in value of one thousand dollars or more to be larceny, which is a class H felony here. You know what that means?"

He sniveled like a child throwing a tantrum fueled by bubblegum swirl and began to rock in place. "Oh man . . . oh man . . . oh man."

"That's right! It means prison! You are so *smart*, Russel. I can see why you're the manager."

"Please don't tell."

"Oh, I'm not going to. I'm not a snitch."

She grinned, wider and wider as the silence stretched open. He had all the horrifying space he needed to fall in over his head.

"I don't have the money. I spent it all."

Riley's smile remained at full wattage. "Oh, I know! On that awesome big screen and that new Xbox your bros are always panting over!"

"Yeah, so . . ." His voice squeaked. "So I can't pay it back."

She waved a hand in good-natured dismissal and shoved it into her pocket. "Don't worry! It's fine! See, I know people!"

With a toss, he was holding a roll of what looked like twenty-dollar bills; in actuality, it was a roll of ones surrounded by a couple twenties. For an instant only, his eyes gleamed in feral lust, but then the look was gone. He was learning. That was good.

"What is this?"

"A loan! From a really nice guy back in New York. See, he steals identities for the Russian Mafia, and it pays super well. He's totally cool and was more than happy to dish out a small loan on behalf of one Russel Stilles from—"

"No! No, it's okay! I will put the money back. I'll put it back!"

Riley licked her lips. This was easier than she thought it would be.

"Well, I don't see how you're going to do that. I mean it's a lot of money, Russel. Let my friend help you out. Of course, the interest is pretty high, and he *will* cut off your feet if you don't pay him back."

"Oh my god . . ."

"But it's totally fine! I mean, you'll have like what? Three months? Maybe a little less? Before he breaks out the saw. If you're nice, I'm sure you can make up at least half of it in tips. Maybe get another part-time—"

"No, I swear! Give it back to him. You can do that, right? I swear I will put it back. I'll just not pay myself for two hours every day, but work the same shift. See? It's cool." He held the roll out to her.

She gave it a long look of consideration and hesitated dramatically. "You're sure?"

"Yes!" He seemed all too happy to be rid of the money, hands up as if in prayer. "I will put it back myself. I'll do it."

"Well, okay, if you say so. But I'll keep this money on standby, and let my friend know that you're still thinking it over, okay?" He was shaking his head constantly, a human metronome of absurd groveling. "Let's move on to my second condition."

He finally took off his little hat of authority and clutched it in his white-knuckled hand. "Okay. What?"

"You're going to be nice to me. And I'm not going to make that a vague statement, because I know how much you like rules. So what I mean by nice is, you're going to move on as soon as you've finished paying back the money. After that, you're going to recommend I replace you. And if I need you to cover for me, or look the other way while I take a small vacation or two this summer, you're going to. Does that make sense?"

He was nodding, and she could see his visions of a college education had gone behind bars. Riley had to force herself not to break character.

This little scheme of his was stupid, because the first time that Sam's accountant took one look at the books, they'd see exactly what she had. What the hell had he been thinking?

His idiocy, her peace of mind.

She picked up her computer and propped it on her lap so that he could see the active video feed. "If these things are not carried out to my satisfaction, I will give this recording to the police. My father is getting a copy. You've met my father, right? He's that giant dude who came in here before. Ate a whole tub of Butter Pecan."

Russel made a sound that was something like a cross between hiccuping and moaning. Riley leaned forward and looked into his eyes, malevolent joy sparkling in her own reflected gaze.

"Did you like his knuckle ink? He got that in prison."

Russel tipped forward and puked. She had just enough time to jump backward before her boots got covered in the stuff. It was the color of butter and stank like a carnival disaster. Riley collected her laptop and closed the knife.

"I think the regulations say the floors cannot be wet, or it poses a hazard. Jesus . . . Sam isn't gonna be happy when I tell him it looked as good coming out as it did in the tin."

She left the way she entered, feeling considerably lighter. The computer went into her pack, an abnormal load to carry, but light as air. Nothing could pin her down tonight!

Riley revved the engine three extra times, and then sped through the summer sunset on the long way home. The air was becoming tolerable and the fireflies were out, winking on and off like Christmas lights. Spirits soaring, she nearly sped by the pale shape that loomed out of the inky tree line. Hitting the brake so hard she almost capsized, Riley swung the bike around.

El was staring into her headlight like a doe, transfixed, her whole body trembling. Her cardigan sweater was smeared with blood, and she was missing one of her ballet flats.

Riley took her jacket off in one breath, and tossed it over the girl as if she were on fire. "El . . . what the hell are you doing out here? What happened to you?"

Her long lashes were heavy with little droplets. She'd been crying all day, it seemed, and that filled Riley with sorrow and more than a little rage.

"I'm fine. Everything's fine."

"No, it fucking is not!" Riley walked her back from the road and examined every inch of flesh she could see. "Where did this blood come from? Are you hurt?"

"No," the girl whispered, "but he is."

"Do I need to call an ambulance?"

"No. It's okay. He tried to touch me. I think . . ." El looked blindly into the twinkling air. "I think I broke his nose. I fell out of the car, and he drove away."

Holding her at arm's length, Riley opened and closed her mouth several times. "Who are we talking about?"

"Jay."

"Your boyfriend?"

"He's *not* my boyfriend," El hissed.

Riley made a face. "Well, he sure as hell isn't anymore. Wait. What!? The. Hell. You fell out of the car? Are you sure you're okay?"

El nodded, her face slack.

"You were just going to walk home?" Riley's mind was skipping over reality, picking up only bits and pieces, but her heart was beginning to slow. No immediate threats. No emergency situations.

"Yes."

"With one shoe . . . that many miles?"

The girl turned in place, still ostensibly suffering from some kind of trauma, and proceeded to do just that, shuffling like a zombie. Riley caught her by the arm and gently halted her.

"I'll drive you home."

"Mama wouldn't like that."

Her voice was completely devoid of emotion, and somehow that was more terrifying than anything else.

"If you want, I can drop you a little ways from your house and you can walk in, but it's too far for you with one shoe. Okay? Will you let me do that?"

As if tendons had been suddenly severed, El slipped toward the ground. Clutching her, Riley half dragged, half carried her to a guard rail and propped her upright like a life-sized plaything.

"Hey, come on! Don't faint on me, okay? I know first aid, but holy shit I do not make it a policy to kiss girls via CPR!"

Tears were glittering in the glow cast by the headlamp, but El's face was completely blank and emotionless. Compulsively, Riley swept the moisture away with a thumb and gathered the dark hair up off El's sweaty neck. With one of her elastic bracelets, she secured it in a knot and fanned the girl.

"Breathe, okay? Can you hear me talking to you?"

"Yes. My ears work perfectly."

"Oh good, because we'll need to check your software later. Your expressions protocol apparently crashed when you hit the deck."

Riley massaged the girl's arms and legs, just to make sure that nothing was broken. El wasn't too badly scuffed, so Jay hadn't pushed her from a fast-moving car, but she was definitely in some kind of shock.

"Riley, will you . . . if I . . . I . . ."

Riley looked up. The girl was watching her hands as if they were doing some kind of magic, the trace of a bemused smile on her mouth.

"What? What do you need? Tell me."

Suddenly, the mask shifted, and El was bawling. Before she really knew what she was doing, Riley was holding her, shushing her, petting her back and telling her it was going to be all right. But how could it be all right? Riley didn't even know what was wrong.

"It's okay. We can just stand like this. Let it out. I'm not going anywhere. Relax."

El wept like an avalanche, slumping forward until they were both balled up on the ground. Riley was silent, as she tried to make sense and couldn't, tried to craft a clever response and failed. This vulnerability and complete ineffectual helplessness . . . she hated it. Logic, action, plans—those were her default. She deflected, she fought back, she pushed harder, but there was no force that could overcome despair like this. It had to be received, absorbed, shared. She could only help if she could be passive, and that was so uncomfortable it gave her a stomach ache.

"Can you tell me anything? It will help, I promise. You just have to trust me."

El pushed her away gently, her face streaked with dirt and blood. "I'm just angry. I'm angry and hopeless and . . ."

Riley breathed a sigh of relief. Anger was something she knew. She could outline its uses easily. "Okay, let's start there. *Why* are you angry?"

"It's like you said earlier. Everyone wants to control me, define me, and to do that they're doing all sorts of terrible things."

"Okay . . . that makes sense to me. Who *do* you want to be, by the way? Because if you were aiming for the *Walking Dead* aesthetic, you're there. You're lucky I didn't bring Matilda with me."

El frowned and stared at her vaguely. "Who's Matilda . . . is she . . . your girlfriend?"

"She's my rifle."

The laugh had returned, sharp and uneven, snagging the air, but at least El had stopped crying. "Of *course*, you have a rifle."

"So, what are you going to do about how angry you feel? Don't get me wrong, I'm all for clocking uppity dude-bros in the puss, but you need more than that, or you're just gonna get arrested. You need to make things *happen* for you, the way you want them."

The girl was once again staring into the distance as if listening to something very far away. "I can't fight her. She's bigger and stronger than me. I can't go that route."

"That sounds legit." Riley carefully coaxed her to her feet and guided her slowly to the side of the bike, the hand fitting warmly in hers. "But sometimes the best way to fight is to bend."

"Bend?"

Taking the helmet from the ground where she'd dropped it, Riley held it up. "Your mom is rigid. The world is obviously way bigger and more complex than she is willing to accept, and so she tries to force it into submission, shout it down." El seemed to be wholly mesmerized by this notion, such that she didn't even appear to notice the head gear dropped on top of her. Riley tucked her skinny arms into the sleeves of the protective leather coat. "Because of that she has to fight the *whole* world, *all* the time, but you're flexible. You have loads of options, because you can think in a way that she can't, and you only have the one enemy. Her."

The sound of the zipper awakened the girl from hypnosis. "But . . . if I wear this, you won't have one."

"I'm good. I was conceived on a bike."

"What?"

"Yeah, no shit. Lemme tell you—how they did it, I don't know, because the kickstands aren't that sturdy, but my dad swears it's true. I have a baby picture of him wearing me in one of those papoose things, sitting on a hog."

"A . . . a hog? That . . . that's a motorcycle, right?"

Riley snorted. "Yeah."

The waif in her dark armor looked comically small, her eyes huge in astonishment. "But that's not safe!"

Taking hold of the shiny orb, Riley dipped her forehead to the faceplate and stared into El's saucer eyes. The girl went absolutely still, her lips parted as if to gasp.

"I am going to be okay. Now please get on. Just put your leg over."

"That's unladylike."

"Your mama tell you that?" Riley started the bike in a blast of sound. "Then yeah, I certainly fucking hope so."

All the way to the neighborhood of rolling grass and miniature castles, El clutched Riley around the middle. Worried the bike ride would only damage the traumatized girl even further, Riley prepared to comfort her as soon as they stopped, but at the corner El indicated, the helmet was removed, and the girl was grinning broadly.

Riley felt a wave of relief pass over her. Bikes were another fact of her existence. If El had been afraid, she wasn't sure she could continue to call her a friend or anything else. Unzipping the coat, she winked at the slowly reviving mannequin. "Now see? You've cheered up!"

"That was . . . fun. Scary! But fun."

"Like flying."

El nodded and shrugged out of the coat. Her hands found their way back to each other and continued their constant fidgeting. The eyes returned to her one naked foot. "Thank you for bringing me home. I'm sorry it had to . . . happen this way. I won't get in your way . . . anymore."

She began to leave, and perhaps Riley should have let her, but she wanted to keep this . . . whatever it was. She wanted to encourage the poor girl. She wanted a few more moments. She wanted something else.

Because something about El felt . . . really nice.

"I've been thinking about your problem."

El turned. In the streetlamp she lit up in a weird golden haze. "Which one?"

"Your mom. Her finding out about your secret. You should figure out *how* she found out. That's the weakness in your defenses, see?" Riley put down the kickstand and set the helmet on the seat. "You need to act as if everything is completely normal, so that she doesn't know you know she knows, but you gotta find out how she knew. Wow . . . that sounded really stupid."

The girl granted her a sleepy smile. "I understand."

"So for now, business as usual, while we solve the problem. I mean, it would help if I knew what we're talking about, because I'm pretty good with this sort of thing. The whole scheming thing."

"No!"

Riley cringed. They'd only just begun speaking, and she'd already invaded El's privacy and said something really bossy.

"Yeah, sorry, I'm nosy, remember?"

But El was already backing away. "It's not like that. It's just . . . you don't know my mother. If she knew you were involved, she'd hurt you too. I don't want anything bad to happen to you."

Those words had a promise to them, as depressing as they were. Riley tilted her head and couldn't help an off-kilter grin. "Your mom doesn't scare me."

As El vanished into the shadows draping over a stone wall, she chuckled. "Nothing scares you, Riley."

"That's not true. Have you ever seen a hairless cat? Those things look like they were pinched off the Devil's ballsack! It's unnatural."

The low music of El's laugh carried through the night and congratulated Riley on a mission well accomplished.

5
Mirror Mirror

All Saturday morning, El sat on the foot of her pink bed, in her rosy room, and waited for the world to end in a blush-colored haze. Her mind could not hold tightly to any one thought, flitting nervously from the dire politics of the house, to the feeling of holding Riley, to the shout Jay had made as he saw his own blood, to the smell of rainbow-colored hair. She twisted her hands and listened for her mother's familiar footfalls, twisted her skirt and held her breath.

She twisted her heart and her mind and still couldn't fit in.

Any moment, her mother would arrive outside her door and demand to know why she had punched Jay in the face, and she'd have to talk about sex. Her mother would know she was not being truthful, but she would have to pretend as if she had no idea. How could she do that, when all she wanted was to scream and demand to know why her mother couldn't love her?

Around noon, El heard her name echoing off every smooth, uncluttered surface. Certain it was the death knell, she clung to the last image in her mind, of Riley grinning in the darkness with a twinkle in her eye.

She felt it then, as she trudged down the stairs to the parlor—that specific pang that heralded one of her online venting sessions. She needed to talk about last night. She wanted so badly to tell the world how the girl had touched her, that Riley was intelligent and funny, that there was even more beauty up close than there was from a distance, but El would never have that chance. It was impossible.

"Don't drag your feet!"

Swallowing, El watched the platform sandals dance across the shining floor as Mama gathered items into a bag. The woman was gussied up, wearing her best pearls and a vintage revival dress. A person could have cut her out of this decade and put her back in the fifties with only a single dilemma—the smartphone in her hand.

"Yes, Mama?" El hazarded.

"Speak up! Why are you always mumbling?"

El didn't bother to comment that if she spoke in her normal voice, her mother either told her it was too deep or too loud. She often settled on not speaking at all, but this meant she was accused of being secretive or shy. If she talked about banal things, she was flighty, and if about meaningful things, she was being unladylike or impractically intellectual. It took more energy than El ever had to do everything right.

Not for the first time, she wished she could be normal, or whatever it was her mother wanted her to be, just so that it would all stop, and she could finally rest. She was just so tired.

But that magic, if possible, would come at a cost. She wouldn't feel what she felt when she looked at Riley, and that was simply unacceptable.

Exhaustion it was.

"Your sister's gonna be here any minute. We're goin' over to McKayla's for cake tasting. I would invite you, but you're not exactly the sort."

Torn between wondering what that meant and feeling overjoyed that Jay wasn't mentioned, El settled for, "I eat cake."

Her mother made a face as if smelling something disgusting. "We're not goin' to *eat* cake. We are goin' to *taste* cake. Your sister wants five tiers and plain *white*, but I swear that girl never did have an aesthetic eye. I told her, 'Your colors are lavender and turquoise, not *white*! You oughtta have somethin' . . . I dunno, airbrushed or somethin'.' And I am absolutely right. Everything is gonna be too *white*."

Mama always pronounced the *h* of *wh* words like it was the most important part. It made questions and discussions of color as uncomfortable as she intended. Like she couldn't stand when her privileges were questioned or when things remained silent. If there was some layer of subtlety, she'd reduce it, and if there was a tiny secret to be had, Mama would suss it out and turn it into torture.

"I read somewhere . . . that edible flowers are really popular, and maybe McKayla can make the frosting lavender or maybe rose flavored to play with her name . . . you know?"

Her mother stopped abruptly in her tracks. For a moment, El waited for the "artistic" axe to fall.

"When did you start learnin' about cakes?"

"When Rose got engaged." She shrugged. "I thought it might help if I knew things, since she wants me to be in the wedding and all."

She made no mention of her tiny, impersonal role in the ceremony, or the hideous dress, or that she hated everyone who would be there, or that it was all just an excuse to spend a lot of money, impress important people, and ignore the fact that Rose and Tom would be trying to hire hitmen within the decade. Instead, El put on her usual vague smile and fondled one of ten cake toppers from the table.

The woman frowned. Not the light frown of introspection, but the scowl of judgment. "I don't think she will need your help with that sort of thing, sugar. I have that covered. You just focus on learnin' how to walk in your high heels and not spillin' all over yourself when you eat."

El bowed her head, grateful she'd taken the time to toss her ruined cardigan into the garbage can before she snuck back in last night. Her mother inventoried her clothes, but she could easily say it was at school somewhere.

"Anyway, damn it, where is my head?" Mama looked around and finally spotted her wallet among the paraphernalia on the settee. "Your sister and I are gonna do that, and then we are comin' back here. We are gonna have a nice brunch, and then all three of us are going for our mani-pedis."

She snatched El's hand before she could evade, and clutched until El's fingers were sore, looking over the sparkling polish scathingly.

"Honestly, Elyrra, you are so clumsy. How do they get this chipped? *What* are you doin'? Is Liz makin' you do the dishes for her, because that is *what* I pay her to do."

There was that *h* again. She marveled that one small accent could trigger so much anxiety in her.

"It was because of our science class. We had to work with this chemical that dissolves things, and it ate the polish."

Mama dropped her hand as if trying to bounce it off the floor. "I don't see *why* they need to teach you things like that. It ain't as if you are goin' to be an engineer. Honestly. I've half a mind to put you in a private school."

El's stomach tightened as she strategized on the fly. It had to be business as usual. Reverend Williams hadn't told, and it seemed as she may have gotten away with her altercation with Jay as well.

"If you did that, I wouldn't get to see my friends! Or Jay."

Mama plopped down onto the sofa impatiently and swung her foot in the air. El saw the minuscule tell, as her mother avoided eye contact. She couldn't believe she hadn't seen it before, but then again, Mama was always plotting, and the tiny ticks and blinks of her duplicity were a commonplace thing. It was impossible to differentiate all of them.

"I thought you didn't like Jay."

"He is a stupid boy."

"All men are stupid boys."

"Exactly." El tilted her head. It was something her mother always said, and if she made it seem that the wisdom had finally penetrated, she might be able to gain some ground. In reality, her best friend, her *only* real friend was a boy. It didn't matter that she'd never actually met him; she knew Oscar wasn't stupid.

"How was your date last night? Did he try to make a move on you?"

That confirmed it. Jay hadn't tattled. Of course he wouldn't. His link to El was the only ticket into whatever life he saw himself living, and he'd never risk disappointing Mama. El had worried herself over nothing.

Relief was a few moments of reprieve from the constant battle.

"He did. I managed to convince him that we should be chaste."

"And how did you do that? By not brushin' your teeth?"

"I made an argument he couldn't resist." With a fist.

The doorbell rang. Even though Rose was a member of the family, she still had to ring the bell and be ushered in by the maid like a stranger. El stared at the ground while the mother-daughter reunion carried on in a series of shrill noises and superficial compliments. She found herself wondering what Riley's house must be like, if there even was a doorbell. If El turned up on the porch, would Riley throw the door open and smirk at her? She would probably say something like, "Well la-dee-da, who's this pretty young thing?"

The image brought color to her cheek that was immediately fodder for mockery.

"Elyrra did you try to put makeup on *again*? I told you to let me help you do it right, so it looks like a natural blush!" Rose tussled her up into a stiff and painful embrace, and then tossed her back. "Come on, Mama, we're gonna be late."

"Oh Hell's bells, Rose, you're the bride, you are never late." Mama collected their items and left her commandments, never missing the chance to sound like she would beat the small housekeeper if her instructions weren't obeyed to the letter. "Elyrra, keep an eye on Liz and make sure she folds those linens properly. I swear she doesn't understand a thing I say!"

And they were out the door, her mother still ranting about how it was impossible to find help that wasn't foreign, how the borders should be closed, how much she yearned for a maid who was *white* . . .

But what really needed to be pronounced was that her mother had worked with extra diligence to find a *black* maid, because this was Mama's South, and in her circles, it was still considered a mark of status. Racism was alive and well, and both her parents' supporters wore their red hats and confederate flags with pride.

El shut the door and leaned her forehead against it. "She understands you just fine, you're loud enough about it, you ignorant bitch."

Behind her, Lizabet giggled. "Don't give away my secrets. At least not while she's sober."

Following the maid into the kitchen, El sat at the counter and helped her prepare the brunch tray. "Liz, this may be a weird question, but has Mama ever said anything around you about Jay?"

"What do you mean?"

"Has he ever called here to talk to her?" She took a deep breath and folded her arms. Liz was the last in a long string of housekeepers, but she was by far El's favorite. In the two years since she'd arrived, Liz had been more like a sister to El than Rose, working with her to make both their lives easier. Even so, she had to be careful. If Mama caught wind that Liz and she were friends, the unspoken alliance would be crushed with terrible consequences. If Mama fired someone, they most often had to move away, or change occupations, because no one else would hire them. "I think Mama is paying him to date me."

Liz was at the sink, washing beans. The tap was turned off and the hands rubbed on her apron far past dryness. At long last, she turned.

"Yeah . . . I was beginning to think the same."

To her own surprise, El was relieved to hear that. It meant she wasn't going crazy, that she wasn't so deep into the rules of this prison that she was paranoid and seeing spies where there were none.

She sighed. "What should I do, Lizzy?"

A uniformed shoulder lifted and fell in slow motion. "You know your mama best. Everything got to be the way she says it's got to be. If it was me, I'd be on a plane to Alaska, before I'd marry that bully."

Nodding, El slid down from the stool and gave her a hug. Lizabet's face was soft and warm when she smiled. Seeing it every morning and every night brought calm to her in this horrible place. She would be the one person besides Riley that El would hate to disappoint.

Not for the first time, she considered confiding in the woman. If she just came out and said it, maybe there would be compassion, understanding. She opened her mouth to speak and then clenched her teeth together. There was an equal chance of rejection, disgust. Lizabet was a religious woman, and most of the religious people in El's experience were fond of reading the Old Testament with an eye for the literal. El had no way of knowing her beliefs on the subject without giving herself away.

She just couldn't be sure.

That was the anguish of being different. It was so solitary. Even if she met someone she thought might understand, their reaction would be completely unpredictable. How they treated her after she confessed was assumed to be entirely her responsibility, her confession something she inflicted on them. *She* didn't change, but telling someone she loved a girl counted as a betrayal. It was the only truth that really mattered to her, but to confess it was to inflict herself on others.

What a warped and hateful way to live. She could see that now—the bleak, dark poison that was seeping into every corner of her life. If not for Riley . . . she might already have succumbed.

"Would you be mad at me, if I left?"

"Where you going?" Lizabet held her around the waist as if they were dancing and then twirled her away. "You mean like college?"

"Whatever. If I left, would you be okay with it? You wouldn't hate me?"

"Praise the Lord! Girl, you *gotta* get out of this place! Shoot, if I had a car, I'd give you a ride. She is gonna kill you if you don't get out."

El swallowed hard. It was the first time they'd ever talked so openly about it, but knowing Liz agreed with her made her feel that much more confident. "Please tell me you're not staying here either."

Lizabet's face drew up sardonically. "Oh no! I threw down my apron as soon as your daddy decided to run for office again. Ain't no way in hell I'm gonna fold up his boxer briefs or cook his damn dinner. He wanna ruin this country, then he can mind his own damn house first. And that woman can make her own highballs."

"What about references?"

"Oh please. How do you think I got this job? I got references of polished gold and my old bosses love me so much they ask me to come back all the time. Only took this job because I thought it was a step up. Should've known your mama wouldn't settle for less than the best, so that she can make herself feel better by tearing them down." She turned, shaking her head. "Don't tell her. I can't get fired before I have everything lined up. I got bills to pay."

"I promise I won't say a thing. Not that she lets me talk anyway."

Pecking that darling cheek with a kiss, El dashed into the hall. Cake *tasting* would likely take hours. Rose was one of the most indecisive humans on the planet, and she never missed a chance to have sweets, if there was an excuse for it. Probably because she'd been on a model's diet since the age of five.

It would give El plenty of time to post her entries and check her replies.

She was giddy with the anticipation, but as she sat down and began her usual series of web-based warding rituals, her thoughts became tangled in memories and questions.

She had never given an inch in her demeanor, never even glanced at a girl in her mother's company. So how had Mama found her out? It had to have something to do with @loveunderglass, but just thinking that made her sick.

Her secret and now infamous online persona had had a humble origin.

It all began with a spiral composite book and a fuzzy pen. In it she had written all about her long life of ten years, her mother, her feelings of isolation. Into those pages, she had poured her pain and been granted some reprieve. She'd thought it well hidden in the crawlspace beneath the stairs, but her mother had found it. Two things had been made clear while she knelt, bare-kneed, for hours on rough clay tile, saying prayers of punishment—firstly, she absolutely *needed* a diary, because it was the only time she felt any sense of internal peace, and secondly, she could never afford to write legibly again.

That was when the code was assembled, and she had burned the protocol into her soul. It wasn't merely a standard cipher, substituting symbols for individual letters. It also replaced whole words with symbols, and rotated using a random number generator. Twenty-six letters, twenty-six shapes or symbols—every couple of days she generated a random number for both columns and matched the letter to its symbol. There would be absolutely no way her mother could read it.

Having that, she felt free to express all that she was, from lust to fantasy. Then one fateful day, she'd heard about a social media platform that allowed a user to create a blog, and talk to their readers. Now the @loveunderglass blog had thousands of followers, and Riley, an invisible club of lovesick fangirls.

That kind of popularity gave her support, but it meant even more precautions.

Her written journal could never be out of her sight long enough for her mother to take a crack at it. For the last ten hours it had been sitting in her bag in the back of Jay's car, and she felt naked without it, but it caused her no particular anxiety. Not only was Jay not smart enough, he had already accused her of being a lesbian and made the decision not to involve her mother.

She stared at the computer screen and frowned, knowing that there was no way her mother had discovered her secret from her journal.

But the culprit also couldn't be her phone, because she almost never used it. It was only allowed to be on her when she left the house. All the phones were on a shared plan and all of them used the same Apple ID to download apps, so of course, she didn't download any, especially the ones for her social media. She only ever communicated with Oscar and her other online friends using an email she would access via her phone's built-in email feature, deleting the account entirely every single afternoon on her way home.

All that left was the computer.

There was only one computer in the entire house. It did not have a password. This made it a perfect trap. El had always suspected that her mother checked the browser history and had a keystroke recorder. Consequently, El never traveled directly to her site. She'd long ago discovered a free conferencing webpage that allowed people to share the same screen and browser. She could surf the entire internet, and the only website that ever appeared in the history was the conference service. She would obscure her passwords and logins from the keystroke tracker by opening two or three different windows and moving between them while typing, so that the letters were randomized.

Her @loveunderglass entries were typed on her phone in her breaks at school, saved to her email draft box, accessed at home via the conferencing site, and cut and pasted into the blog text box. That was how she managed to type out long essays on love, with almost no key strokes, no downloads, no IP addresses—no traces of any kind.

It was almost impossible to imagine that somehow her mother had managed to get behind all these defenses.

Like Riley had said, Mama had forced El to set fire to all the hoops and live the interesting life of a CIA counterintelligence specialist. It was tolerable, so long as she had her outlet, and could be free for a few hours, but the things people needed were their greatest weaknesses.

She could see that now. Now that she knew her mother for the enemy, she could see how the woman thought, without her emotions getting in the way. The facts were clear, and unknown variables could be balanced without a thousand impressions and hopes clouding her judgment.

How had Mama done it? It couldn't be complicated, because while the woman could install a program, she didn't have that much technical savvy.

A camera?

No, there was no way. Her father would never allow such a thing. He was a senator. If any of his communications or business were recorded, it could be used against him. He was incredibly vocal about his feelings of privacy, which was ironic, given how much freedom he allowed his wife to revoke all privacy from El. There were only three cameras on the entire property, and they recorded only the exits of the home.

Then again, this was a recording studio.

This was where her mother made all her videos, her podcasts, gave interviews.

She looked up at the Thomas Kinkaid backdrop and the mounted digital camera. The thing had always made her nervous, it was true, but it was pointed at an angle, and turned off.

Or was it?

As if headed to her mother's small fridge near the sound stage, El strolled past the recorder and glanced at it from the corner of her eye. Sure enough, the recording light had been covered with a tiny piece of black electrical tape. El opened a soda she had no intention of drinking and turned until she could see the camera's angles. It was pointed at her mother's large swiveling makeup mirror . . .

Which was aimed directly at the mirror behind the desk.

With all her cunning, defeat had come down to smoke and mirrors. All this time, her mother had been recording the desk whenever she left, just waiting to see if El would arrive at the computer. She'd been piecing together bits until she could identify what was on the monitor screen. Once she had the name of the blog, it would be easy enough to locate and read.

Her mother was one of her followers.

El comprehended all of this in one frightful second. Her stomach lurched and quaked. Her skin went cold, then numb. Most importantly, her heart felt as if it was being clamped in a vice and wrung out like a bloody cloth.

This was how much her mother despised her. This was the extent to which she would go to make El miserable.

Business as usual.

El took a shaky breath, returned to the computer, opened the conferencing site, and got to work.

Rose—Colored Glass

The noise that heralded their homecoming was shrill and slurred. Cake *tasting* obviously meant also drinking an entire bottle of champagne each and driving home anyway. El logged off her extensive research, tucked her coded checklist into her bra, and allowed the stiff muscles of her back to uncoil. Sitting for several hours to obscure the camera was a small price to pay for the peace of mind she was slowly developing.

As Riley had said, there was a fact she knew about herself, regardless of the things that might be less definite: she preferred women. It wasn't going to change. Her mother could call her young, indecisive, worthless, ignorant, demonic, lazy, or any of the other things she wanted, but that was not up for interpretation. There was no magic to fix it, because it didn't need fixing.

That was a belief she now held close to her heart.

She was not going to that camp. No matter what it took. El was done trying to be what they told her she should. El was going to be El. Her mother wasn't unbeatable. Her mother was a stupid human being who wanted to turn the world as ugly as she was, and El wasn't going to stand for it. For the first time in her life, she was making a decision, and it was a decision her mother wouldn't be able to stop.

Of that, she would make sure.

As she listened to her sister retell a story from last week's "Wedding Arguments With Tom" at garish volume, she walked calmly into the hall. Her sister's handbag had been tossed onto the entry table, its contents spilling out. The jeweled phone was too good an opportunity to pass up.

Walking calmly to the back garden, El hid the device by tucking it into her armpit. In the corner beside the pool house, there was no camera coverage, because of the changing rooms. Suddenly glad Rose was always asking her to text Tom as she drove, El dialed a number.

Oscar answered within two rings. "El?"

"How did you know?"

His laugh was so soothing—low and soft. She loved it at once. "The area code. What's happening? Your entry was so generic, and then I saw the tag. That was the code, right? 'Or well,' like the writer? I've been clutching the phone ever since, just waiting."

"Yes. Thank you . . . for giving me your number."

"Oh my god . . . the witch found it." He took a deep breath. "Are you okay? What can I do? Do you want me to message the others? What's she going to do to you? How do you have a phone right now?"

His concern overwhelmed her. In an instant, she was weeping again. She had never done anything to deserve these people, and yet they were there. She'd loved, and these angels had come out of the woodwork to watch her do it. Here they were, on her side, even though she couldn't touch them.

"Shh . . . it's okay. Just let it out."

"I don't have time. Oscar . . . she's known for almost a year, I think."

"What?"

"She's known all this time. She's one of my readers. She has to be."

"Oh fuck. Oh my god." There was the sound of something clattering as he no doubt dropped whatever piece of artistic glory he was assembling. "This is so fucked. What do we do?"

"She's going to send me . . . to one of those places . . . those places where they—"

"Pray the gay away?" She sniffled to the sound of his multilingual string of swear words. "Why? Why do they hate us so much? What have we ever done besides make their lives better? I don't understand this at all!"

His anxiety triggered hers. Her breathing turned to gasps. Tachycardia set in, causing spasms of existential terror. She pressed her face to the cold stone wall and tried with every remaining vestige of will to hold on to the problem, and solve it as Riley would. "Oscar, I can't let her take me there. I can't keep pretending. I'm so tired."

His feelings were cast aside at once for a soothing mantra of whispered support. "Leave. Just leave. Come here. We will figure it out together."

Hearing him say it made it seem so much realer to her, then. Was it that simple? Just run away? She wasn't sure it was something she could do. The world was dangerous, and she wasn't strong enough. But the alternative . . .

"But you don't have any money. I can't stay at your house. You have roommates!"

"We'll figure it out. El, I want you safe!"

"Is there another way?" she breathed.

"Can you refuse to go?"

Just walk in and refuse her mother, just like that. Only if she wanted to lose the phone, the computer, and every ounce of freedom she had for the next six months.

Six months. She'd be eighteen in six months. Her mother couldn't keep her hostage then. She'd be an adult. An adult . . .

An adult her mother could manipulate with adult consequences just as she did Rose.

How many times had Mama brought up the courts, the judges she knew? There were veiled threats assuring her that if the phone bill looked wrong, she'd be arrested for theft, that if El rode home with someone else, she'd be reported as missing, that if she behaved in any way that differed from her mother's opinions on what was a good life, Mama would do whatever it took to see to it she ate her mistakes.

If she ran . . . she'd be a criminal in Mama's eyes, and Mama would treat it just like that. But if she stayed, she was a criminal anyway, already condemned to rehabilitation, with her mother as the sole deputy.

"No . . . I can't. That won't work with her. Then I really won't have any options."

Oscar huffed. To him, people who couldn't be bothered to undo their prejudices didn't deserve to have opinions considered. To him, Nazis were self-proclaimed idiots, anti-LGBTQ were self-identified monsters. To Oscar, the injustice was that society gave such people rights and rules in their favor. The first time she had messaged back and forth with him, he'd told her his coming-out story and it ended with a fist fight. Just like Riley, he was strong, brave, self-aware.

Maybe that was why she loved him so dearly.

"What about R? Can you go to her? I mean you don't have to tell her you are wicked insane in love with her, just that you need help."

El let out a whimper. That thought had occurred to her nearly a hundred times in the past two days, but if Mama ever discovered she'd spoken to Riley outside of school . . . it was a sure bet some police officer would find something they shouldn't in her father's repair shop, and his parole would be revoked, probably on the advice of an anonymous tip from a reliable source. That was just how Mama worked.

"I want to . . . God, I want to . . . but if my mother found out, she'd destroy her family."

He let out a sigh. "Then there really is only one way. I swear to you, I'm good for it. Please let me help."

Her tears spattered the thirsty concrete and evaporated almost at once. "But Oscar, I don't know how to . . . to do anything! My mother never lets me do anything! I don't know how to live."

"And you think that's going to change if you spend one more year in high school? It's gonna magically be better after six months of aging? El, princess, I am twenty-two. I still have no fucking idea how to balance a checkbook. It's why I eat my neighbor's avocados that fall in my yard. Free food is free food, bitches."

Her sob was stopped up by his practicality. Of course, the world was dangerous. Of course, age wouldn't suddenly make her more capable, but it would put the law on her side. How could she possibly get across the country without the legal right to leave her parents? She didn't have any identification—no driver's license, not even a library card.

But Rose did.

Her sister was taller than her, with blonde hair. But that could all be fudged. What couldn't was the face. Rose was a beauty queen, El was a house mouse.

Or was that just more magic?

It was her mother who had always told her that she wasn't like her sister, but Liz always told her how beautiful she was. Even Riley . . . that goddess of all things gorgeous, had called her pretty. Though he was vile, Jay found her attractive enough to dry hump her leg whenever the mood struck him. And really, a person could do amazing things with makeup. She knew that much from watching her sister transform into her crown-catching alter ego.

Mama was a horrible person. Her opinion was the worst possible one to accept. The spell had to break.

"Oscar . . . How hard is it to go blonde?"

He snickered. "What color is your hair?"

"Black."

"Shit. Well . . . do you care about keeping the hair?"

Reaching up, she ran her fingers through it. It was long, shimmered all sorts of colors, from purple to blue. It was soft. But it was also that thing her mother had raked with a brush as she snarled about how she hated it. It was the thing her mother grabbed to tug her to her room. It was the thing Jay liked to use to hold her fast. It was always in the way, always setting her apart from her sister—the good girl.

"No."

"Then it's pretty easy. You buy a bleaching powder and a peroxide developer at a beauty supply store. You mix, you apply, and you wait. And then if you want it to look somewhat natural, you come back in with a blonde dye."

"How much is all that stuff?"

"Twenty, thirty bucks."

That, she could manage. "Is it something I could do anywhere?"

"You'd need water to wash the hair, but yeah . . . I guess, if you have a couple of hours." She heard his chair creak and his cat meow. It sounded as if he was bounding through the house and suddenly his voice wasn't echoing off of anything. He was outside and pacing over grass. "Are you going to do it? Are you going to run?"

Her stomach, always sore, always churning with suffering, suddenly calmed. Her toes went warm, her heart fell into a normal rhythm.

"Yes, I think I am."

He let out a whoop of joy. But the delight was short-lived. In a heartbeat, he was back on the ground, and the real plotting began. By the time she was finished, she had a destination and all she had to do was get there.

Easier said than done.

In the house, El replaced Rose's phone and stood at the table for long moments as a kind of weird euphoria bubbled up from within. With a remarkably steady hand, she tugged the wallet free, removed the driver's license, several checks from the back of the book, and the least used credit card. Where once she would have been terrified, looking over her shoulder in a fit of paranoia, El was caught up in a trancelike calm.

If they were going to call her a criminal, call her a freak, then what was the harm in living up to their expectations?

The voices in the living room had fallen silent. Tiptoeing in, El found Mama lying on the sofa; another empty glass of wine was beside her slack hand; she was passed out cold. El thanked the universe for merciful favors. Rose was going through packages they'd somehow acquired, and didn't notice her until she cleared her throat. "How was cake tasting?"

"Well . . . I think I ate just about ten pounds of cake! Oh my Lord, there was so much—butter cream, raspberry, ganache, lemon curd—I just about died. But then Mama had a great idea! She said, 'Why don't we do like a filling that has flowers in it?' You know, like lavender and roses and orange blossoms!"

El clenched her teeth behind a wan smile.

"So McKayla is going to whip up some new things, and we're going back next week!"

"Guess it wore her out, huh?" She tilted her chin at the sleeping demon.

Rose spared her but a glance and a nervous laugh. Best not to talk about the woman while she was in the room. They both knew she might be faking. "Well, that's what happens when you have almost two bottles of wine. I think we should let her nap a bit before we have brunch."

The conversation collapsed. Not that they ever could manage to build much with so little in common. There was their parentage and what it took to survive it, certainly, but that was a negative. Friendship couldn't be built on negatives. It seemed laughable and preposterous to think, but El knew her mother, and she was fairly certain that was precisely the intention. Mama didn't want her two children to overpower her, and so they must be separated.

Rose was more easily pleased, distracted by aesthetics. She was flighty, free-spirited, and forgetful. While El had always been "willful," as her mother said, and introspective. Mama could control Rose, while El posed a tremendous problem.

"I've been thinking about what you said."

Rose's confusion was as lovely as her happiness. She shook her head and wrinkled her nose in that adorable way that always got her through the more difficult pageant questions. "What I said? What did I say? I drank too much wine today, sissy. You gotta remind me."

"About makeup. I'm going to be a senior this year. There's the wedding, homecoming, prom, all sorts of things ... senior photos ... and I don't know anything about makeup."

To El's relief, it seemed she'd said the magic words. Instantly, Rose's misgivings were gone. This was a subject she could go on about for hours to anyone. Makeup was the *lingua franca* of her world, the math of her universe.

"Oh sure! There's all sorts of things coming up for you! You gotta learn!"

"We have time ..." This was the key to her escape, and she smiled on it invitingly. "Can you teach me now? Maybe just the basics, and how you get your eyes to look like that every day?"

As if God above had given Rose an opportunity to at last fill in all the weak and empty parts of her life, she showed off every one of her pearly white veneers. "I would *love* to! Oh my god, I've been carrying all my makeup with me, because of all this wedding stuff! I have everything here!"

She squealed softly and skittered across the stone floor at full speed, snagging El's body with the force of a beauty queen possessed. Paying attention as she never had before, El dutifully washed, moisturized, and primed her face, allowed her sister to pluck, pinch and otherwise groom her. Within the hour, she was sure she understood technique, even if the actual execution might need practice.

Side by side in the mirror, she looked more like her sister than she'd ever dreamed she could. This realization lifted her spirits in countless imprecise ways. It wasn't about being pretty. Pretty didn't mean anything to her. It was about being confident, taking ownership of her body. People always used the word "self-possession" to describe a bossy person, but at that moment, as she looked on her face in the mirror, she felt the word would have new meaning for her. It was as if every curse her mother had thrown was being undone and she had control over herself again.

She was now a master of disguise.

"You look fabulous! I wish I had your dark hair!"

"Why do you bleach yours?"

Rose distracted herself with her products. "Well, because Mama said blonde was the color of winning. And she was right, you know. All three of the last Miss North Carolinas were blonde."

All of them blonde by the bottle alone.

Mama always called pageants "scholarship programs" which annoyed El on several levels. In the first place, Mama only condoned college education for girls if they intended to become nurses or school teachers. And secondly, no scholarship El had ever heard of cared about what a person looked like in a bikini. They cared about grades and expertise. Rose had Miss America coming up—the pageant to win all pageants—and after that, she'd retire and probably see not a single day of college past that point. It had to be tedious, always playing the fresh face preparing to start a life . . . without ever actually living one.

El leaned forward, examining herself in the mirror for the slightest discrepancy. "You should go to school for cosmetology, or maybe become a chemist and make your own makeup line. If you win Miss America, I bet that might happen for you."

Rose blushed prettily. "Oh, I don't know. I don't think I'd want to do that professionally."

"What would you do?"

She shrugged. "I love singing. I'd probably try to do it, you know, get a singing deal like Vanessa Williams. But you know what Mama would say if I talked about working, especially in music."

Did she ever. To hear Mama tell it, a woman's only purpose in life was to support her husband and surrender her body for his pleasure and the replication of his genes. To watch Mama live it, a woman's only source of amusement was tormenting her children and running the home like a penitentiary. That hardly seemed any way to exist.

"Are you and Tom going to have children?"

Her sister had a very good poker face, but it was meant to be viewed from the stage, not two feet away. "Oh, I don't know. The doctor wants me to stay on the birth control because of my cramps and headaches, you know."

"Of course!" Reassured that Rose had at least learned to excuse herself from compromising her individuality by getting a doctor's note, El dusted her face with the fluffy soft powder brush. "Thank you, Rose, I really appreciate the help. I guess I'll need to buy all this stuff."

Rose made another of her photogenically emotive faces. "Please, sissy. You keep this. People just keep giving me stuff because of the position and all. This way I can make sure you get the right kind of makeup instead of that cheap stuff. Some of it's good, but it always made my skin just break *out*!"

El heard the footfalls and had just enough time to prepare herself for the immediate shift in the air that preceded their matron. As soon as Mama's reflection appeared, bleary and a little disheveled, Rose's smile dimmed, her eye contact severed at once. As if caught stealing, Rose's hand fell from El's shoulder, and when she spoke, her voice shook.

"Look Mama! Isn't Elyrra pretty? I did her up just like me!"

Mama narrowed her eyes and turned away dismissively. "It's a bit much, isn't it? Wipe it off so we can go."

Rose's reflection paled beneath her expertly applied foundation, and her usually icy eyes began to melt as she stared at the spot where Mama had been. That was an insult to both of them, to El for daring to be anything other than a dull girl, and to Rose for practicing artistry.

After several swallows, her sister collected a few tissues from the box.

"Sorry, sissy," she whispered, crushing what of El's heart had thus far survived unbroken.

"It's okay. I'm used to it."

Their eyes met in a single breath, so charged with information that it sent a current through her, raising gooseflesh on her arms and legs. A sympathetic kiss crowned her and then Rose had gone, dabbing at her mascara.

All this time, it had seemed Rose had it so much easier than her, that Mama had been far kinder to her, that the pageants and public appearances had all been privileges granted simply for existing, El was now certain none of that was true.

Being a bully was a fact about Mama that would not change, and she'd probably spent hours working her sister over. As much as everyone complimented Rose's beauty, El could now recall every single instant their mother had denied the girl any agency, any autonomy, any opinions of any kind. Rose could only speak in aesthetics because that was the language she'd been taught. Mama had convinced the world, but more importantly, the girl herself, that pretty Rose Glasse was nothing but a doll whose mind was blank and whose identity was manufactured and endowed by her admirers. She was a statue only brought to life when someone wanted to objectify her.

As El swiped the makeup remover over her face, she became certain that her sister wasn't marrying the man of her dreams. She was escaping.

They were both running away.

7

A Damsel in Distress

"I don't understand the issue."

That didn't surprise Riley one bit. It also didn't matter to her. "There isn't an issue."

"Then why won't you register?"

On the desk between them were half a dozen letters. They were the only marks of approval society had ever really shown her, and to Riley they meant almost nothing. She leaned back in the uncomfortable chair and let out a long sigh. It was clear from the oblivious look on the guidance counselor's face that this was just the first round of impromptu meetings designed to intimidate her into having a life identical to every other infant shit out by this society.

"Riley . . ." Ms. Sweet wore thick glasses, and in them her eyes were magnified, displaying her absolute shock in badly applied mascara. "This is your future we're talking about."

"Yeah."

"You've been *accepted*! All you have to do is send back the papers and register!"

"No."

"But *why*?" Her voice had pitched upward sickeningly. Riley couldn't help but chuckle.

"Why would I?"

"Because . . . because you need an education to get a job!"

"No. I need a diploma to get a job. A diploma isn't a guarantee I learned anything. It just says I paid the money and passed some of the classes. It also doesn't ensure aptitude. Look at the President. But don't worry, if I want a job that requires a diploma, I'll get the diploma."

"That's—"

"Correct. I don't have money for this, which means loans. I'm sorry, but I am not going to sign away my soul as soon as I have a legally binding signature. Though I'm sure that would make everyone concerned very happy. Can't have demons like me running around without *controls*!"

The woman's face was pinching together in a slow-motion frown of increasing exasperation. "The longer you wait, the more difficult it will be to do."

"Uh-huh, because all those forty-somethings getting their PhDs are a great example of why it's important to stay in school for literally half their lives. I guess it *is* better to start young so that when you finish, you still have some life left!"

She crossed her arms. It wasn't worth the effort. Her point was that the system was broken, that academia was built as a binary: either you did the bullshit classes to get a job that paid slightly better than McDonald's, or you went full bore into some serious avenue of study that would theoretically pay more, if not for the crippling debt you incurred to get it. Even then, there was competition for funding, cutthroat admissions, finding a job in one's field . . .

"School is essential, Riley."

She understood that school taught things. She liked learning things, but no one should ever do something because it was easy, or less frightening, or just what one *did*. *Especially* getting an education, because if a person tried to get one in those circumstances, it wouldn't end well. Education came from passion. If a person lacked passion, they needed to find it first or they'd burn out. Then they'd have the debt and the failure to crush them into the service job they'd have gotten anyway, even with their diploma.

"Ms. Sweet, what are the dropout rates in these schools?"

"I . . ." She looked at her hands and hurriedly shuffled papers. "I don't know, I'd have to—"

"For the programs I'd want to attend it's over half. Half of the freshman class drop out. Why? Same reason half of marriages split up. People see something new and shiny, society tells them to buy it to be complete, and they compromise everything to have it, only to realize it isn't what they wanted, takes more stamina than they have, is way more complicated than they thought, and that they really aren't the sort of person to live up to it."

Her mouth was open, but everyone knew Ms. Sweet had been married three times, and was engaged to a fourth man who would probably go out like the previous three. Marriage was clearly not something that her personality could handle, but there she was, still trying to shove herself into that mold that everyone told her she should want. Four white dresses, each one more ironic than the last.

"I've just spent thirteen years in school because the law said I had to. I don't want to be forced to take Music Theory to fulfill some stupid prerequisite because I need to be 'well-rounded.' I want to take a break, figure out what fits me, then I'll get back into touch with one of the universities and see about the paperwork. I may figure out that I never want to go to college. I may decide on trade craft, which by the way, makes bank these days."

There was a gasp. "But that is . . . You can't! Your future depends on—"

"No. The future *you* want me to have depends on it. I know why you say that. I know you want me to be accomplished and successful, but there are other definitions of success, just like there are different ways to learn. I don't know what I need to learn yet or how. I'll figure that out."

"This is about your father, isn't it?"

The words pushed a pin through her buoyant mood. Why did everything have to come back to her father? She loved him with all her heart, but his past didn't have to be the measure for her entire existence. It was like everyone wanted to rescue her from that, but she'd never felt more at home than in the workshop with him.

Truth was, they weren't listening to her when she told them she was happy. To them, it was one more kid with promise succumbing to a lack of ambition, but Riley had ambition in every cell, right alongside her mitochondria, being tapped as a fuel source for any and everything she did. Yeah, she was still a "kid," but if they were going to expect her to be an adult, hadn't they better start honoring her decisions?

"What's that supposed to mean?"

Ms. Sweet shoved the papers away. "I know you're thinking that if you leave, you'll be hurting him, leaving him here. You're worried he'll fall back into old patterns, aren't you?"

Riley could feel her face slackening until the apathy was suddenly leaking out of her ears. If there was one way to lose an argument with her, it was to suggest that any part of her identity was codependent.

"My dad can take care of himself."

"I'm afraid for you, Riley. I'll be blunt. You get bored too easily. If you don't go to college, I'm terrified you'll end up—"

"Like him?" She sat forward, elbows on her knees, insides boiling with fierce and sudden rage. "Was that what you were about to say?"

"Yes, frankly."

She got to her feet, but her temper was not ready to leave. It took hold of her fist and bounced it lightly off the desk in an aggressive tattoo, as if knocking to be set free. "Like that man who was in the wrong place with the wrong people when someone got killed, lived every day with remorse, and then reformed despite the fact that his whole family and everyone he knew were sucking him back in? That man who went to a trade school, who owns his own business, who married an amazing woman, who single-handedly took care of her when she was dying, and who raised his daughter alone and in grief? Like that asshole? Yeah . . . I can see why that might fucking terrify you."

"Riley, that's not—"

"Ms. Sweet, hear what I am saying to you. This is my life. Officially. I'm taking it from all you assholes. It's mine now. I am going to find my own way through it. If I feel like college is going to be good for me, I'll go, but there's a hell of a lot of self-analysis I need to do to find the university that will fit me, and it's going to happen on my terms." The counselor made to interrupt her, but she was pretty much finished with the part of her life that involved swallowing her tongue because the adult in the room didn't want to acknowledge her. "I'd appreciate it if you'd mind your own business and not bring up my father, ever again. You do that, and I won't tell you why I think you should have gone back to college for a different credential. Agreed?"

She didn't wait to be dismissed. If the woman wanted to hit her with a referral for detention, she could do that without Riley standing there to take it. It wasn't as if calling her father would do a damn thing, as they'd learned in her first few weeks there. One week left of school, and she couldn't really care less what they did, but the day was ruined, regardless. She had a PE class full of pricks, a period of something they called Civics that was really an exploration of the War of Northern Aggression, and a shift of Russel the Cowardly Bastard to look forward to. Luckily, it was football day, which promised to make getting her aggression out a hell of a lot easier.

Walking toward her locker, her ear caught a shriek among the usual noise of the crowded corridors. It was a sound so incongruous that it poisoned the air and muffled all else. As Riley rounded the corner, a clump of teens obscured the unfolding drama. She was about to walk away, but there was a more insistent and frightened call.

"Stop it! Let me *go*!"

It was El's voice, and all at once, Riley's body was a mass of quivering action contained in a girlish shape. Dividing the crowd with two elbows, she forced the scene to open for her. El was pinned against the lockers, her bag on the floor. Jay was grasping each of her wrists in a white-knuckled hand. His shoulders were vibrating with the force and he was so furious he spit as he talked.

"You fucking cunt! Is that how you think this is gonna go? You don't break up with me. That's not how this works."

In a glance, Riley assured herself that there was not a person in the circle who was as prepared to bleed and draw blood as she.

With all her strength, she swung her heavy book bag at the spot right between Jay's shoulder blades. As he was thrown forward, she did a flying leap at his back, knees raised, slamming him face first into the metal, smashing his already flattened nose. Blood spattered out from his face in a halo as Riley snaked her arms around his neck and clamped down. Jay spun in a wide arc, arms flailing, but as he did, Riley got her legs around his waist, and hung on like a vicious rabid koala. He clawed at her head, tried to dislodge her by crushing her against the lockers, but she was an immovable object, about to choke out this varsity wrestler with all the hell-fury she had been storing in her uterus.

Spinning, she was aware of only one thing: that El was leaning against the wall, her face covered in tears and her mouth hanging open in reverence.

Riley grinned and squeezed even harder.

The boy's neck was ropey, but she had her right hand hooked firmly around her left elbow, utilizing an entire life of nerves and muscles tuned to the throttle of her bike. His struggle began to weaken. He slumped against the wall, slapping it with his hand as if there were an umpire, but Riley didn't fight to win.

She fought to end shit, because that's what it took.

Jay hit his knees, probably intending to roll her like a crocodile, but she unwrapped her legs and wedged a boot against the ground. Finally, Jay fell forward onto his face. Only then did she release. He drew air with a loud, sucking gasp, his face mottled. Riley undid her belt in one move and gathered his hands behind his back. Drawing them together, she snared them with a loop and then pulled up an ankle. Securing the belt end through the buckle had this pig fully hog-tied, for her fleeting glory, his eternal shame, and El's immediate safety.

The crowd had grown and was heckling. Riley pressed her knee into the boy's back and put her mouth to his ear. "Touch her like that again and see what happens."

He coughed. "Bitch."

"Uh-huh. Tell me you're gonna press your luck." She dug her knee in farther and tugged up on his arms. He let out a whimper. "I've already been pushed to my limit by you fucking rejects, but now I catch you slapping up a girl. That's a hurricane in a bottle, Jay, and you just dropped it from the third floor."

"Get off me."

She sat up with a laugh. Looking at all the smug, cackling faces. "But you told me you liked being tied up!"

"I did not!"

"You mean you didn't try to hit on me last year for like two months? You didn't tell me all these sexually explicit secrets about yourself? I'm pretty sure you did. I think I even still have the text messages!" She drew her phone out of her coat pocket and scrolled through. Her seat humped up and down like a whale, but Riley had been waiting for the right moment for almost a year, and she was positive it wouldn't get much better than this. If she was right, the teachers were in the lounge on the other side of the school, and they wouldn't know to come unless someone went to get them.

Who would do that, considering what Jay was, and how hilarious she was about to make this?

She had all the time she needed to ruin him forever.

Holding up the phone, she began to read through the old text messages. "*Hey there sexy. Lemme lick your twat.*"

The teens let out catcalls. Riley rode the struggle beneath her as if sitting on her bike on a mountain trail, grin as hard as armor.

"*'Who the fuck is this?' 'I'm your hard daddy, gonna show you what it feels like to be with a man.'* Lemme scroll down here. There's a lot of text about . . . you know . . . the kinky stuff he likes—"

"Fuck you, that's not true!"

"Here we go. This is me, *'But don't worry about it, asshole, I've already run this number through an online reverse directory.'* Oh look, here! It's his dick! He sent me a picture of his wrinkly penis just before I called him out!"

With a flourish, she swiped the phone through the air, allowing every young lady to take a giggling gander as every boy dove backward in guffaws.

"Oh my god, that is his phone number!" a spectator sang with glee.

Her adversary went still. There was no point in fighting anymore. The tiny high school pond had just run out of oxygen for this big-ass fish.

Most importantly, Riley was now his first target, not El.

She got up and for good measure, kicked him in the side, hard enough to wind him. "You're a coward and a sleaze, Jay, and now everyone knows it. Now everyone knows, especially these girls, that when you want sex and the girl says no, you treat her like shit. You throw her out of a moving car, you follow her through school and attack her, or you call her a dyke and tell her you can make her straight, when honestly, you've basically made me glad to be a lesbian. You're a disgrace, and if you argue with me, I will send every girl in this school that picture of your shriveled little pinky prick, you disgusting psychopath."

She turned her back on him to a chorus of low whistles and mockery. The onlookers parted for her, giving her a wide berth as she retrieved her bag and El's. As delicately but quickly as possible,

Riley ushered the girl out the front door to the parking lot. Under her favorite tree, she could finally stop to assess the damage.

El was staring into space as she had been that night in the woods, but her pupils were tracking movement and reacting to the light. Riley gently touched her chin, turning the face this way and that. She could see no marks. The wrists were different, though. They were already turning purple.

As Riley watched the bruises form, she expected her anger to melt away, but it didn't. Why hadn't El fought back? Why had she just stood there and let that piece of shit . . .

She took a deep breath. "Did he hit you?"

El's voice was husky and garbled. "No. He just shoved me."

"Okay."

"I asked him to give me back my bag, but then he tried to kiss me. I told him no. I made him angry."

It was all Riley could do to keep from punching the tree. She succeeded by telling herself it would frighten El and hurt one of her favorite life forms. Instead, she shoved her fists into her coat pockets and controlled her breathing.

"You didn't *make* him angry, El. He *got* angry because he has no concept of empathy and is a classic narcissist. Don't ever apologize for saying no. You're allowed to, even if you're a girl, even if he was your boyfriend, even if the rest of the fucking world wants to argue with you on it. You're *always* allowed to say no."

El stared at the ground, eyes the color of a swimming pool and just as refreshing. She sniffled, but she wasn't crying. In fact, it seemed as if the entire experience had settled something for her. A more resolute expression was lifted.

"After school today . . . will you do me a favor?"

Running her hands through her hair, Riley took a step back. Whatever tension there was now was easing back, as if the warm breeze and a good sigh could blow it all away. "Of course! What do you need?"

"Help shopping for camping stuff. Do you know about that . . . camping?"

Crossing her arms, Riley examined the girl more closely for signs of shock. She looked fine—calm, composed, her tears drying and her gaze steady. It seemed like a non sequitur, but to El, the odd request was apparently natural.

"Seriously? Your ex just tried to beat you up in front of a crowd of people who were going to let him, and you want to go *shopping*?"

El looked away, for a moment shivering as if all her focus and energy were almost spent, and at any second, she'd spit out a gear or something. "Camp starts soon. I need supplies, but I don't know what to get."

Suddenly, it clicked. Of course El would want to look for tents and sleeping bags! She wanted the hell out of this fucking town! She probably found it comforting, thinking she was about to be far away from everyone she knew so that it could all spend a few months cooling off. And here she was asking for Riley to participate.

That was . . . like a compliment.

"I know about that stuff. I can help you."

"Thank you."

"Why don't we go now? I could use a break from this bullshit."

El blinked at her. "That would be ditching."

"Yeah, so?"

"If Mama found out—"

"If anyone asks where you were, just tell them you were freaked out by Jay and sat in the bathroom the rest of the day. There are about fifty witnesses."

"Mama would blame me, anyway."

Riley scowled involuntarily. "She'd blame you for him beating you up?"

El seemed to swallow her pride and chased it with a nod. "I'm f . . . fucked either way."

"Your mom . . . is a piece of work. You really going to let her teach you to be afraid, to roll over, to just let people kick you constantly? If you're fucked either way, why not have a little fun?"

El shook her dark head. "*You'd* get into trouble too."

"I don't really care. Jay can sic a lawyer on me, but then he'd have to tell everyone how the fight started. And I don't think he wants to do that. Especially after the dick pics get sent to his mother."

She won a tremulous smile. El closed her eyes on it and relaxed against the tree. "I meant with the school."

Riley waved a hand. "Naw! They don't care about me. I've ditched like twenty times this year, and I sorta just called Ms. Sweet an idiotic, nosy bitch. They just shake their heads and say, 'There goes Riley Vanator the delinquent who'll end up just like her daddy.' And I just flip them off and move on."

As Riley pulled the girl toward the bike with a charismatic smile alone, El ran her hands nervously over her injured wrists as if she could feel the restraints. She was following, but she still seemed terrified. It made Riley sad to think that the world must be so dangerous to her, that everything appeared perilous, probably because everything always had been. Did El even have a safe place?

She did. Right here, with Riley. The decision made itself before she could even think it. Riley Vanator, vanguard champion of the oppressed damsel. Her dad would smirk beneath his beard.

El shook her head. "Doesn't it bother you, that people talk about you like that? How do you come away from that so confident? It would kill me. It *does* kill me."

Riley handed her the helmet and tossed a wry glance after it. "Why the fuck do *they* matter? I know who I am, and I'm not going to let them convince me their opinion matters more than mine. You shouldn't either. We deal with facts here, not magic. Remember?"

As she waited for El to mount the bike, Riley watched a transformation take place. In the tiny twitches of a body unwinding from years of anxiety and self-loathing, El came to life. There was color in her face, softness in her expression. She lifted her smile to the sky and when she'd finished her salutation to the sunlight, she was actually happy.

"I've wasted a lot of time."

Riley held out her hand. "Let's make up for it."

Suddenly, the girl was giggling, and climbing onto the bike, her arms slipping comfortably around Riley's waist. Giddy with a feeling she'd never had, Riley turned the engine over in an anthem of noise.

8

Firebrand

E l looked into Riley's sparkling, smoky eyes and felt like laughing and weeping at once. That smile was something she had never witnessed before—so free, so filled with delight. To think it might be her doing flustered El to no end. Emotions bubbled and churned within her, until nothing made sense. She wanted to leap with happiness and shake with terror, but more than anything else, she wanted so badly to sit in silence and run her fingers through the girl's bouncy hot pink tresses.

With a wicked smirk, Riley shoved the cart conveyance to the end of an aisle, swinging it around so violently that El had to fight to keep her footing on the metal bars.

"Do you always drive like you're escaping?" she giggled.

Riley screeched to a halt at the metal shelving with a cackle. "No! I always *live* like I'm running out of time."

El fought to keep the smile on her face, but it faded as her mind let go and began to wander. A new tragedy was brewing, because these were the moments for which she'd hoped with an absolute fixation . . . and she would never be able to talk about them. She could never turn back to her devout audience and give proof of just how perfect a creature Riley was, teaching her things she'd never known she was missing. She could never defend Riley's reputation or give joy to the readers who were watching, waiting, hoping. She could never reassure the people like her that she *had* breached the divide and found friendship, that her story was an example to follow. Not now.

One more thing Mama had stolen from her.

That frustration knew no outlet and had no cure.

The store smeared in a watercolor of bright hues as she stared blankly into space, but warm hands landed on her shoulders, and gently traced the back of her neck. In one instant, El was shivering, and had forgotten she was ever sad.

Riley glanced at her with a soft smile, her gaze so warm it was almost hypnotic. "Keep crying, and I'm going to start tickling you."

"I'm—"

"And no apologizing either! Yeesh! Your mother has you cringing like a scared but ridiculously cute puppy. Knock it off! It's killing me."

Her expression twisted comically, and she didn't wait for an acknowledgement. Gesturing broadly to the shelves before them, Riley performed a bow. Thousands of little cloth squares in every color of the rainbow were neatly folded and stacked.

"Now!" Riley cleared her throat and crossed her arms. "This is a serious matter. A bandana is a must-have."

"Really?" El pulled one free and opened it. She'd always wondered why people wore them. It seemed so odd and her mother had always called them "White trash attire." They weren't even allowed at school because of supposed gang affiliations. "Are they to keep the sun off your head?"

She draped the scarf over her hair and made a face.

Riley shrugged and plucked a rainbow tie-dyed one for herself, demonstrating each of its many uses with helpful pantomiming. "Well, yeah, if you want. They're like, multifunctional. They can keep you warm, they can keep smog or dust from getting up your nose, they can carry stuff, they can tie stuff down. You can even knot them to stuff so you can see it better or use it as a washcloth. A bandana is an important camping tool."

El looked back at the cart, full of an assortment of Riley's choicest picks. The expense was adding up, but she wasn't packing to save money. She was packing to run for her life. Besides, her sister would never even notice a few hundred dollars gone missing.

"What color should I get?"

Riley held a few up to her, assessing her so closely that her breath caught in her throat in anticipation. "Well, what's your favorite?"

She swallowed hard. "I don't know."

"What?" Strands of neon coral were blown out of Riley's eyes. "You're shitting me, right?"

"No. I don't know. I like lots of colors, but I guess . . . I just never thought about it."

At an obvious loss, Riley flailed in impotent fury. "Why, though? It's a color! It's easy. It's like . . . It's like knowing if something tastes good! Like, why wouldn't you ever think about your favorite color?"

Her body ached yet again with that painful realization that her way of life had always been a sham, an outlier, a horror no one should ever endure. All this time she'd spent afraid, living day to day, never realizing how much of her existence was just coping. She didn't even know her own favorite color. And why? Because Mama bought all her clothes and crushed every opinion that deviated from hers. Normal kids knew their favorite colors and foods and music. If she didn't know anything about herself, then how could she be real?

How could El protect a life that had no substance to it?

All El had was this baffled and ferocious girl standing next to her, and she couldn't even spit out what she'd always dreamed of saying! It was ridiculous! It was stupid! And it hurt, so, so much.

"Hey, I'm sorry."

Riley grappled her into an embrace. She went willingly and suffered through every painful breath of it. Riley's hair smelled like grape popsicles. The skin of her neck was soft beneath El's flushed face and even the spiked choker didn't bother her. In a dull agony, El wondered what Riley would do, if she just brushed the flesh with a kiss, but it was pointless to consider, because it couldn't happen.

El could never be that selfish. She could never play risky games when it came to Riley's safety. She may not know her favorite color, but she knew that much about herself.

"Look, it's cool if you don't know which color you like best! Lots of people don't have favorite colors! Look at me! I can't even decide what color hair I should have! I've dyed it four times this month!"

Riley's tone tugged a moist laugh from her. "Okay."

"Do you like blue?" The girl held El out at arm's length and stared narrowly into her eyes as if trying to read her mind in her gaze. "What about purple? No. No purple, okay. What about green?"

Wiping her face, El managed to nod. She was released and in a flurry of movement, Riley had snatched down every shade of green and was modeling them like a couture clown. In an exaggerated accent, Riley discussed the various attributes of each tone, furiously dismissing the lime-colored one when it dared to clash too harshly with El's eyes. Before long, El was laughing again, and Riley had narrowed down their choices to a single bandana.

"What do you think? Is this the bandana?"

"Yes. Definitely."

"Good, because I am pretty sure that is the last thing you absolutely have to have for a survival trip in the woods." She looked into the cart and whistled low. "This is a lot of stuff. Your mom gonna be okay with this?"

El shrugged, but her nerves were acting up again. As they wheeled the cart to the register, she tallied up the bill, clutching the card in her hand. If it didn't work, she wasn't sure what she would do, but she hadn't heard anything from Rose about cards going missing, and that seemed the sort of thing that would have gotten back to her, if her sister had noticed.

While the clerk rang up and bagged the items, Riley carried on a conversation with him about hunting knives. He jabbered, ignoring El as she ran the card through the machine. As if it were choreographed, he didn't even look twice at the person committing credit card fraud, instead laughing at Riley's jokes and asking about her dad as he handed off the receipt reflexively. Forging the signature, El tried to quantify Riley's easy and engaging demeanor with science.

Surely, with all the attention she'd paid, she could mimic Riley's confidence.

The idea soothed her like magic, weaving a warm image of wearing the memory like armor or a mask, passing through the world clothed in every aspect of her affection, without needing to make a single confession.

Adrenaline seeping from every pore, she followed Riley to the parking lot with a bemused smile. She was officially a criminal now. There was no going back, but in some strange way, that too was comforting.

As light as air and on the brink of hysterical laughter, El knew that her path was what she had made it. Finally, she was her own master and her future was going to be of her own making, because there were consequences for what she'd just done.

Mama couldn't hide her from the world anymore, because she'd gone against the world.

Opening the purchases, she and Riley secured them into pockets and spaces in the new backpack, throwing the cardboard and plastic ties into the dumpster. When the fasteners were too strong to rip apart, Riley produced her knife and flicked it open casually, cutting things with its gunmetal edge as she made jokes about nothing and everything.

"Does your knife have a name?" El wondered aloud. When Riley looked at her in astonishment, she could feel her face run hot. "I mean . . . Because you named the rifle."

Grinning as if she'd been discovered in some sort of prank, the girl handed off the knife. "I like to name things that are useful to me. Tools are important. They're what make us human, so I guess I kinda feel like by naming them, I'm treating them with respect? Is that weird?"

"No." El turned the knife over and over. Folded up, it was only about five inches long and unembellished, but the deep charcoal of the handle and blade absorbed light as if breathing it in. Heavy like nothing she'd ever held, it seemed to resonate with function and purpose. It whispered in the air with the curved teeth of a shark and opened with a smooth flick as if waiting. This knife was probably the most basic of tools, the sort of thing a person like Riley would own, but something about it was warm and alive.

It *deserved* a name.

"*Tizóna*. It's the name of a famous sword. I guess it means 'firebrand.' Which is what my dad called my mom."

The words woke her from her trance. Licking her lips, El held out the knife with all due reverence. She *knew* it was a relic of some kind, definitely something she had no right to hold.

"*Tizóna*. She's beautiful."

To her surprise, Riley pushed it back. The carefree smile was gone, and Riley was blinking furiously. "Keep it. I can buy another one. They won't sell you a knife, because you're a minor, but you'll need one."

"I . . . I can't keep this!" El protested so quietly, she could barely hear herself. "This is—"

"It's okay. She'll take care of you."

The corner of her mouth twitched, but Riley wasn't happy. The unspoken was looming over them, colder than any shade. El had always longed to know, but there had never been a time to ask before this stolen moment.

"Where . . . Where is she? Your mother, I mean."

Riley's eyes were cast to the ground, her blackened lashes sweeping her lightly freckled cheeks. "She died when I was little. I never really knew her. It's just been me and Dad all this time."

All this time . . . while El complained about her mother, Riley had never had one. Regretting her unthinking cruelty in a single gasp, El stepped forward to comfort. When Riley's arms came up around her, her entire body reacted with a jolt. Clutching the knife, El searched for words that weren't a useless apology. The girl in her arms deserved more than that. Finally, Riley freed her, and El could breathe again, but she still had no idea what to say.

Riley smudged the kohl under her eye. "Like I said, *Tizóna* will take care of you. I want you to have her."

"Thank you," she whispered. "I'll take good care of her too. I promise."

In an instant, Riley dashed the sadness aside and found her smile again. "So what are we doing with all this stuff?"

El had been pondering that explanation since she'd straddled the bike at Riley's back. She was already a spy and a thief, why not become a liar too? The next few days were going to be full of such things. She ought to get used to it.

With a look at her phone, she put on a smile. "I'm going to call my sister. She'll take me home since she is on the way to my house anyway. You need to get to work, don't you?"

"Yeah, I guess." But Riley continued to stand there, as if there was more to be said. She was chewing a purple lip and tapping every surface with her gaze, in the most adorable display of awkwardness El had ever seen.

"What?"

Riley ran her chipped nails through her hair and let out a huff. "Yeah, okay, I'm just going to say it, even if it sounds weird. Okay?"

El's stomach tightened involuntarily. "Okay."

"Even when you're laughing," she said quietly, her hands outstretched, "it seems like you're about to cry and it really bothers me."

"I'm—"

"Don't apologize! I'm not telling you it's your fault. I'm telling you that I know that it isn't you. I'm telling you that I want to help you, because I want it to stop."

Though the air shimmered with heat, El trembled. The knife was still clutched in her hand, burning the palm in the sunshine. She moved her fingers around and around, squeezing it for all her strength, just to keep her self-control. If she didn't remember that she was in this body, standing in this moment, her mind would be propelled from the atmosphere by this bittersweet joy.

It took a long time for her to clear her throat, while Riley looked on expectantly. "It's okay. You are helping. I know this is something I have to fix and that some of it isn't my responsibility. I do know that. You don't have to worry. I'm going to do better."

Riley threw up her hands. "You don't have to do better, El! You are just fine! You have to tell *them* to shut the fuck up! You have to protect yourself!"

The multicolored frustration on her behalf was both charming and inspiring. El couldn't help a chuckle as she held up *Tizóna* in a solemn vow.

"I swear to you, I get it. I understand. You are right, and I am going to take your advice."

Riley's palms jangled together in a prayer. "Thank you. And I am here for you, any time you need help. Just ask me. Anything! I am telling you, there's nothing your mother could ever do to me that I could give a fuck about."

El's smile faltered yet again. There was no way to focus on what she wanted to express when she was so anxious about things she couldn't predict. The longer they stood there, the more it stung.

"That's because you don't know what she's capable of, but thank you. I'll remember."

"You're sure?" Riley's askance was made sassy by the curve of a tilted hip, the crook of strong fingers at a pointed chin, just below a full plum mouth.

El's tongue seemed to swell as she contemplated how truly stunning Riley was and that their time together was at an end.

She could only nod.

Backing away, Riley shot at her with finger guns. "See you tomorrow!"

When the motorcycle roared from the parking lot, El put *Tizóna* into a zippered pouch on the outside of the backpack. Shouldering the burden with a sniff, she cut a path to the church that took side streets. At the back of the sanctuary, there was a row of classrooms used for Bible study. The key was hidden on a specific ledge near the back steps. Retrieving it, El stowed her pack beneath the counter in the tiny bathroom. To it, she pinned a note indicating that the luggage was being held for a parishioner. Locking the door, she knew it would be safe there for a few days.

A few days were all she needed.

When she turned on her phone, it was to find nearly thirty text messages. Scanning them, all her misgivings were confirmed. Jay had done precisely as she knew he would, sharing his version of events with his employer and in typical fashion, the witch had decided the fault lay with El. El, however, was finished accepting blame for the weaknesses of others.

Tucking the phone into her schoolbag, she set out on the long walk home, giving the ice cream parlor a wide berth.

Soon, she would be free from everything that had ever plagued her. It would be the most difficult thing she'd ever done, but also the most important. It would cost her everything she loved, but she could always learn to love new things.

It was time to discover who and what she was.

9

Letters

Riley looked up at the parlor window. There stood the girl, positively gaunt and laboring beneath a heavy pack. It took her a moment to recognize the enormous eyes and small stature, because Elyrra Glasse was wearing clothes more fit for hiking. As she took off her apron and rounded the counter, it occurred to Riley that she'd never actually seen the doll in anything but dresses, even in the winter. What would Mama Glasse think of flannel and denim?

She could feel that sea-colored gaze following her as usual, only this time it beckoned with an intense insistence. Riley collected the serving tray and made as if to clean up the outdoor seating area, glancing sharply at Russel as if to hex him if he dared to stop her.

El backed away from the window and for a moment, looked as if she might just turn tail and run.

Riley halted a few feet away, one boot on point behind her, and wondered what to say. "So . . . you changing the time of our usual date, or . . . ?"

"I wanted . . ." The girl took a deep breath and scoured the pavement for words. Her voice fragile and hesitant, and she looked as if a gust of hot wind might knock her over. "I wanted to come by and say something . . . to you."

Riley propped a hip on the railing and tried very hard not to grin, succeeding only slightly. "A *whole* something? Well, shit! What will I do with that? Been surviving on a few words here and there all this time. Didn't even know you had a whole something in you."

The girl coughed out a laugh, partially calming the ache Riley felt at seeing her. Wherever this was going, she wasn't sure she could really stop it, even if she wanted to. She could hear it just in the tone of El's voice, that tremor of bittersweet confusion and sorrow.

"I wanna say," El spat out with a fading smile, "thank you!"

For a moment, Riley wondered if she'd heard the words properly. She blinked at the two customers sitting at a table and licked her lips. "Uh . . . for what? That thing the other day? That's nothing. I make it a policy to kick ass on a routine basis—"

El cleared her throat, and for the first time, looked Riley directly in the face. "No . . . just . . . for existing, I guess."

Woefully off her game, Riley tried to frame a word, but realized that for all her affected gallantry, she didn't have one. There was only one person who ever thanked her for existing and only one yearly celebration of the fact. Those two things weren't scheduled to align for another two days, so what the hell was this?

She didn't have a moment to ask, as El sped through the rest of her whole something. "I mean, because I just wanted you to know that I appreciate you being here, and that I really feel like you add to my life in a positive way, and so I just wanted to say that, so that you know. Because everyone should hear that, and also because I feel like you are picked on a lot, but you never let it get to you, and that deserves recognition."

The girl took in a lungful of oxygen and clutched the straps of her pack. Riley's cheeks were burning; tongue-tied, she managed to nod.

El appeared to shiver. "Okay. I have to go."

All at once, the world returned to full volume. Roused from her surprise, Riley stood up straight. "Wait, what? You're gonna miss today's flavor! It smells like peanut brittle."

El, however, was already retreating, and something about the look on her face said there would be no more new flavors to try. There was pain there, and loss, two things Riley knew with absolute perfection, no matter who wore them.

"Goodbye, Riley Vanator."

Frowning, she set down the tray. That was too definite for her liking. "Where are you going? Is it Camp Day?"

The girl let out a shuddering sigh and walked away. In the close air, Riley stared at the spot where she had been standing and felt as if every sinew and nerve was pitched in that direction, all waiting to catch more.

There wasn't any more. Elyrra Glasse was gone.

The rest of the day hummed and buzzed with routine, and as usual, her heart wasn't in it. Her thoughts wandered constantly. Every time she opened the cooler, a chill went through her. She was glad to clock out and anxious to get home. If there was one thing she needed, it was a Papa Bear Hug.

The trailer was silent when she returned, but the metal lunchbox was open on the kitchen table, its carefully filed contents arranged in neat little piles around a new addition: her stack of University acceptance letters. She checked the fridge. Three light beers were missing from the weekly six pack. When she glanced out the back window, the warm glow of the shop lamp was like wrapping herself up in a big blanket.

"Hey there!"

He wasn't working, just perched on his steel stool staring at the car guts in front of him with the beer sweating in his hand. He shook himself, and she could see the puffiness in his face, even though his beard was fluffed.

"Hey, Rye-baby."

"Saw the box. You okay?"

Behind him was one of the beers, unopened. He cracked it and offered it to her. Well, that was good. A two-beer night instead of three. She took it just to keep it out of his hand.

"Yeah . . . just been . . . thinking."

"You wanna talk about it?"

His gaze sparkled and swam. Riley leaned against the car body and swigged. As long as they were both drinking, doing the same thing at the same time, equals, he could convince himself to open up. The only way was to remind him that there was another person in this with him.

"She would'a been so proud of you . . ." His voice broke. He wiped greasy hands over his face, making matters worse.

Riley found a cleanish shop towel and smeared some of the grease away. There was a time she'd been too small to comfort his bulk, but she'd sprouted, and now she could lean over him, wrap her arms around his wide neck and puff warm kisses on his whiskers.

"Maybe, but you know, she didn't raise me. You did. And if she was still here, I might have been different." She shrugged, but kept her hands on his shoulders. "I probably would have been less badass, you know?"

"Naw. Your momma was a chili pepper." He sniffed, mustache twitching like an annoyed ginger caterpillar. "Hell, I dunno. Maybe so. Still needs saying."

"Okay."

"I been thinking about your birthday. Gotta celebrate you being alive. Whatcha wanna do?"

Suddenly, she was leaning against a railing, watching a sweet, lost girl say goodbye, and something about it didn't sit right. In fact, it was downright worrisome. But there was nothing she could do now, and the giant in front of her, covered in tattoos and battle scars, was still sniffling like a huge baby.

That was something she could fix.

"Dad . . . when did you know? I mean, like, when was the moment that you said, 'Hey, this woman has her shit together. I gotta grovel at her feet until she takes pity on me.' Or was there a moment?"

With a chuckle that sounded like someone pounding an empty barrel, he shifted his weight and beckoned her toward the house with his beer. "That's easy. Yeah, there was a moment."

"Really? That sudden? Just like that?" She trailed in his shadow, like always, only now she could keep up. She was old enough, wise enough, had paid enough attention. Dad didn't say much, unless it was about his Heavenly Angel, and then it would go on like an opera she never tired of hearing.

He didn't even look at the table as he selected a yellowed piece of paper. It was dog-eared, by far and away the most often read. As he began to read, the gravel rolling around in his throat got heavier, and he sagged into a chair.

"'People always say that being good isn't easy. That's simply not true. It's the easiest thing in the world, Jerry. It's as easy as deciding that the hardship you face doesn't matter to you, that you're willing to take the roughest road. That's all. How many times have you already been down that road? You know it so well it's like it's written on your eyelids. You know what it means to starve, to be hated, to be beaten, and most importantly to regret what you have done. You know that road. So why does it bother you so much? Why are you so afraid of it that you'd fight it? Why would you hurt someone, kill someone to escape, when you have it in you to be strong? You are strong, Jerry. So you can easily be good. Easily.'"

He wasn't reading the gorgeous cursive; he was reciting from memory. There was a long silence. Riley said not one word and dared not even breathe.

"Your mom . . ." The rumble became a purr. "Your momma saw me for who I *could* be. She knew me from day one and the things she wrote always made sense of shit I'd never even tried to understand. No one else did that for me. Not even me."

Riley let out her sigh. "And you knew?"

"Well hell!" He waved as if to vanish the whole table with a magic trick. "I mean here she is, this soulful, brilliant woman and she's writing to me! I already been rejected, my whole damn life! Knew that road real well. Decided the hardship didn't matter to me. Took a risk and asked her if she'd mind if I thought romantically on her."

"You send her a picture first, you ogre?"

With a snort like a wild boar, he tipped back into a full laugh. Wiping his face and tugging on his beard, he shed that old familiar sadness and came back to Riley in one mountainous heap.

"She came to see me the very next week. Dark hair, curves, singing in tongues and looking like she could rip out my guts while putting on lipstick. About shit my jumpsuit when I saw her."

"If you had shit yourself, there woulda been hell. Probably only had the one in your size." Riley sipped the beer, using the green glass to pin down her knowing smirk. "She quake with fear?"

"Sidled right up to me, shook my hand like I wasn't about to eat a goat from under a bridge, and started grilling me about my ink, all in the same breath. Your mom . . . she was a spitfire."

"I guess I had to get it from somewhere."

He drained the beer and cracked his painted knuckles. "But come on! What about your birthday? You wanna go to the junkyard or maybe go over to the park and have a barbecue?"

"Actually . . . yeah! That sounds rad. Can we take the bikes?"

"It's your day!" He got to his feet, and began puttering around the galley kitchen for a plate and cutlery. "Hey, have some dinner! I think I finally got it right. It took me two hours to cut everything up like she used to."

An oven-mitt-sized hand lifted a wooden spoon to her lips and dispensed the tamale sauce. Riley nodded in approval.

"Oh yeah, Dad. That's perfect!"

It's what she always said, no matter how different the tamales were from week to week. How could she know what they were meant to taste like? Abuela's tasted better, but she had decades on Riley's father. She took her seat at their tiny two-top and watched as he saw to every detail of presentation like a bear rifling through a beehive. It was a miracle his fat fingers could even wrap the corn husks properly.

Riley's hands began automatically reorganizing the letters into their time capsule. Looking over the frail leaves, a kind of bittersweet sorrow washed through her veins.

He was going to wear them out. They'd fall apart and he'd be even deeper into the hole without a way to climb free.

"Hey, Dad?"

"Yeah?"

"You mind if I borrow these? I promise I'll bring them back in mint condition."

He seemed to give the notion of being without them a moment's stern thought, and then his face broke like a mischievous Santa Claus in Highland colors. "Sure thing! Your mom had the prettiest handwriting."

"She really did."

That night, Riley laid them out on her bed and began the painstaking process of positioning and lighting each tinted paper, each swirl of faded pencil, each crease. Once in position, she took a set of triplicate photos with a phone app, converting the missives into PDF. First, she grouped them into an album and zipped them, then she put them on the Cloud, then she uploaded them to the nearest print shop's online platform and ordered a bound volume, and finally, she emailed them to her herself.

In a few hours, her parents' romance was preserved for all time, and she could sit quietly at her machine and scan them into her own memory to fill the space that was shaped like her mother. They joined a hazy image of long dark hair sweeping over Riley's face and a sensation of happiness and safety, a kind of unspecified joy. These letters were all that was left of her mother's more tangible qualities and wisdom, but they were extremely rich sources of information. Riley picked and pored, and didn't stop until her eyes ached and her face was wet.

Leaning back in the harsh lamp light, she wondered why she had waited so long. She was about to turn eighteen, and this was the first time she'd done this close reading. But wiping her cheeks, she knew it wasn't really a mystery.

Fear had kept her from it.

If she knew her mother at all, then the Heavenly Angel would be something human, something that made mistakes, and most importantly, something that had died.

Riley got to her feet, and in those cooler wee hours, wandered away from the tiny house, out behind the garage, to the tree stump that was her favorite thinking place. The sky was turning the green that was somewhere between twilight and gold. She hugged her knees and let herself cry.

She'd never really seen much point in sorrow, being firmly of the mindset that handling the problem was the quickest way out. Complaining and carrying on just slowed her down, but every now and again, she would find a hiding place—in the park behind their old apartment, the back of the pickup, or this stump—and let out every tiny emotion that action couldn't repair.

It was that or explode.

Dealing with her dad's past, new schools, bullies, keeping her focus on her grades, ignoring all the frivolous things that sucked most teenagers in . . . took resolve. It took guts. It took a stubborn, disciplined calm, and if there was anything her life had been, calm was not it.

Tires churned the quarry that was their driveway. In the growing light, Riley turned to see the front end of a silver Lexus SUV crawl to a stop, gleaming palest violet. When Mama Glasse tumbled out of the driver's seat looking irate and spitting obscenities, Riley forgot her private anguish and snuck around behind the automobile.

The woman stood, arms drawn close to her body, looking around as if the rusted chassis and tractor parts might come to life in this eerie patch of woods and pounce on her. Even this early in the morning, Mama Glasse was perfectly coiffed, made up, pastel and prim. It would have seemed impressive, if Riley could forget the haunted look on El's face and the rumpled, unloved look of her girly clothes.

With a mischievous swelling of her heart, Riley smacked the SUV's fat ass and let out a whoop. "Well, hell! I ain't seen a car this purdy in all my life! Lemme get a gander under that skirt!"

Mama Glasse almost leapt out of her heels. Riley met her astonishment with a wicked smile and lounged against the vehicle like Athena at the Parthenon, surrounded by her semi-naked virginal attendants.

After a few moments of fidgeting and trying to regain composure, Mama Glasse cleared her throat. "You must be Riley."

No one had ever made her name sound less lovely.

"Do I have to be? Sometimes I think it might be better if I'm not."

Mama's nose went up, and Riley knew exactly what she was dealing with. Bullies were never difficult. From the sex-addled minds of teenage boys who couldn't make sense of their mingled desire and frustration with her blanket rejection, to middle-aged women who wouldn't place value on human life until they were correctly appraised by divinity experts—bullies did it to assert dominance. They wanted to break people apart into rubble, and then climb that shifting pile to the top. They wanted control in a chaotic universe. They wanted to feed their ego-god with blood sacrifices. The only way to handle it was to figure out what the *specific* bully needed, and deny it.

"You think you're funny, huh missy?"

"Don't call me that." Riley stood up straight and was grateful she still looked the part of the terrifying biker bitch from *Sons of Anarchy* hell. Crossing her arms, she gave Mama a once-over and put a look of disdain firmly on her face. "Nobody calls me names on *my* property, because I have a solution for that, and its name is Matilda. That make sense to you?"

"You have no respect."

"Respect is earned. For now, I tolerate you."

There was silence, as Mama considered how to proceed. In the interim, Riley had a chance to center herself, wonder *why* the woman had come, and realize that she wasn't at all surprised to see her. She could still hear the emotion in El's voice when she said "goodbye." The memory itched like a healing engine burn or a mosquito bite.

"Where's my daughter?"

In a blink, all earthly mysteries condensed into that single one, but oddly, didn't ruffle Riley at all.

So Elyrra Glasse *had* run away? It took a special stripe of character to up and vanish from such a cushy life. As soon as Riley thought that however, the pride was doused by worry. El was small, timid, pretty, and frail. Then again . . . she *had* broken Jay's nose. She'd needed help to buy equipment, advice on how to be independent, but she'd been sensible enough to come to Riley for it.

Pride and a sense of responsibility mingled awkwardly.

"Shouldn't you know where your daughter is?"

"She never went to her meeting with our minister. She was supposed to go there and then go to the ice cream parlor to be picked up. That's the way we always do it."

Ear pitched to every rise and fall of Mrs. Glasse's voice, Riley listened for fear, for anxiety, for any trace of concern. She found them, but there was something off about her cool demeanor. Once, Riley had seen an interview with her on some religious television program, and had marveled that the waterworks were switched on and off with absolute precision. It was nearly impossible to see Mama Glasse as anything but a robotic salesman.

"Yeah . . . El came to the parlor, but earlier than usual." Her eye flicked to the woman's fingers, loosely folded around her elbow. They didn't clench or flinch at the revelation. "She was wearing a backpack and hiking boots. Like she was off to summer camp."

That rigid face spun her way as if on some kind of demonic mechanized ratchet. "What did she tell you?"

Not *What did she say*? Not *Did she talk to you*? Just *What did she tell you*? Which meant that Mama assumed El would speak to Riley, and that whatever she said was somehow a threat to Mama.

How odd . . . and tantalizing.

El's voice played through her mind in the exact inflection of resignation and grief, and Riley knew there was more to this story than a girl and a mother failing to get along. She should have followed El. She should have made certain the girl was okay. Why hadn't she done that?

"She just thanked me for existing, which was weird."

Mama took a step toward her, but seemed to think better of squaring off. Her arms fell, and the sweater knotted over her shoulders sagged.

"You expect me to believe you don't know where she is?"

"Why the fuck would she tell me where she was going?"

There was an inelegant snort, then the woman wrenched open the car door and collected a tablet that had been sitting on the center console. It was already displaying a blog page titled "Love Under Glass", the whole thing a moody palette of green and gray. Riley tipped forward and examined the smaller print, and suddenly Mama was shoving it into her hands.

"You don't know about this? With the way you kids are these days? Carrying on with gossip and posting your lives all over the internet."

Riley peered from the tablet to the woman's grimace. If Mama Glasse got any louder, Dad would wake up. "I'm not gonna talk to you if you shriek at me, lady. Just so you know. I'm not your daughter, and that shit doesn't work on me."

"Whateva."

With a curious finger, Riley poked the webpage. A description popped up, and as her gaze swept over it, her pulse went topsy-turvy.

Call me Snow. 17; She/her pronouns, please. This blog is a confession I can never speak. It's meant for her—the girl I love—but she will never read it. I want to stop hiding, but it isn't safe, so I write to get these thoughts out of my skull. I watch her all day long, waiting for every opportunity to be close to her, to know her, to wish and hope, but she never even notices. I want to charm her or give her something to admire, but I fall short.

No surprise in that, because R is aloof and strong and beautiful. Someone braver than I will make her very happy. She deserves that.

There are no reblogs here. Every entry is original material. Tags include #R #Poems #mylife and #asks

Mouth hanging open, blood raging, Riley scrolled through a few of the most recent entries and realized what she was looking at. The whole thing, every single bit of it, was dedicated to this dream girl—R—who sassed bullies, rode a motorcycle, and worked at an ice cream parlor . . .

"What . . . the *fuck* is this?"

"It's a sick love letter to you, obviously!" Mama Glasse snatched the tablet from her. "She's been writing it down in that stupid book an' copyin' it here somehow. You're tellin' me you didn't know about it?"

Riley blinked, her mind spinning around wasted moments and kicking itself in a drunken spiral. "If I did, don't you think I would have hit on her at least once?"

The medically preserved face flooded with blotchy color, somehow inhumanly pink cast in dawn colors. "Why on earth would you do that?"

Riley frowned. What kind of mother asked that sort of question? She didn't have much experience with moms, but she was fairly certain that fuzzy euphoria was supposed to overlap all things that moms did. They were supposed to talk their kids up, not down.

"Uh. Because she's smart and hot, and I like that sort of thing?"

Mrs. Glasse issued a sound of disgust and climbed back into her metallic behemoth. "As if I'd ever let such sin into my family."

"Hey, lady . . ." Riley shut her door, not as careful as she should have been about slamming it on the white-clad chicken legs. "Sounds like it's already in, no matter what you do. Maybe you should rethink your life strategy. Try not being such a bitch and maybe loving the kid the way God obviously made her?"

The engine turned over, and to her surprise, the woman took hold of her wrist and leaned through the window to glare at her. "If I find out that you or your ex-con daddy know anything about where Elyrra's gone and you haven't told me, I will make your lives a living hell. Believe that."

In the face of battle, Riley never could resist a grin.

"Wow . . . hard to see why she left!"

As the car spat pebbles, she blew a kiss to the rearview. The moment the SUV turned the tree-lined corner, Riley dashed back to her computer.

10
Transformation

"Now, see here, missy," Mama began with a sharp nail pointed to her nose. "I will pick you up here in *one hour*. And you will *stay* here and wait for me, do you understand me?"

Another screaming lecture about the behavior of ladies toward their men and the evils of ditching school, combined with a sleepless night of nervous energy, had left El drained, but the profound feeling of resolution was a steadying force. She ignored the finger and looked the woman in the eye. This would be, if she was lucky, the last time she would ever lay eyes on Mama, and though she had expected to feel regret, all she felt was relief.

"After that *stunt* you pulled, you're not going one damn inch without me watching you like a hawk! Apparently, that's something you need. And at seventeen years old! Your sister was going to all her pageant rehearsals alone by this age, and you don't see her getting into fights in front of the whole town or punching her boyfriend in the face! I won't have it! I won't have you turning into a hoodlum from the slums."

"Why do you think you have any control over who I am as a person?"

Mama's eyes flew wide. For a moment, her mouth hung open in astonishment.

"I'm not your pet, you know. I'm a human being, but you've only ever treated Rose and me like inconveniences you tolerate if they pay off. We're purse dogs trained not to bite or bark." El opened the car door when her mother made no reply and stood looking at her in the chilling gusts from the air conditioner. She needed to say her piece, but it couldn't sound like a goodbye, because if it did, her mother would move too quickly to stop her. "I want you to know that I don't like you. I never have. I never will. And I think you are a tremendous hypocrite who should be ashamed of herself."

At last, her mother's mute awe shriveled up into encyclopedic contempt. It was clear she already had a number of choice words lined up like a row of soldiers, but as she fired the first, El slammed the door in her face.

Her heart beating with furious elation, El ignored the shrieking from the window. As usual, she cut around the sanctuary to the office door and ducked into the covered breezeway. Mama's SUV sat there for a long while, and the speakers and shouting were so loud, El could hear her mother making an incensed phone call. As if on cue, the phone inside her backpack began to buzz, but last night had been the last time she'd be summoned to account, made to stand and listen to a tyrant spit venom at her because they needed an outlet.

Turning off the device, El popped open the cartridge and removed the SIM chip. With it out, Mama could not track her, but she would keep it, just in case it ever came to a Prodigal necessity. Making her way to the classrooms at the back, she liberated her pack and changed clothes. The SIM was secured in a tiny pouch meant for medications. When the phone came back to life, El tested the internet, finding that it would link with the church's wi-fi and allow her to log into her accounts.

She sent one coded email to Oscar. A few apps were checked, calculations made, plans set in reservation numbers and email receipts, and her journey began.

There was only one thing left to do.

At the ice cream parlor, she took one last, long look through the plate glass window, her chest so cramped with emotions that she could scarcely breathe. As their eyes met and Riley's face lit up, El withered a little. This moment alone seemed to reawaken all the pessimism she'd tried so hard to stifle. Words spilled out, but made no sense, and her thoughts were too addled to correct her. Riley's brow furrowed in concern, crushing El's nerve in a single tick. El turned on her heel, and with one backward glance, said the thing she'd prayed for years she would never have to say.

"Goodbye, Riley Vanator."

Riley shouted after her, but El's misery ran over. Sneaking around the building, she dropped her pack on the ground and pressed her fingers into her eye sockets. She wanted to sob, but it felt so wrong. If Riley knew what El was doing, she would want her to be strong, and most importantly, Riley would never want to be the reason for sadness. El controlled her heart with measured breathing and regulated her feelings with the recitation of all the dates and times of her escape. Within a minute, she could stand up straight again and lift her burden.

For the fourth day in a row, El tapped her bank account for the full daily withdrawal amount. With the transaction complete, she stood staring at the card. It was a tether to her past and she hated it. Even the thought of keeping it for security made her cringe.

Taking a deposit envelope, she stuck the card inside and dropped it in the night slot.

That was the end of that.

Twelve hundred dollars had to see her across the country and into her new life. She had never existed within any kind of financial limitations. The very concept of it was foreign and unnerving, the anxiety compelling her to snatch up the coupons as she stepped into the department store. Walking through the aisles, reading each tiny square carefully, she worked her way through non-perishable foods, found a bar of soap and a cheap roll of toilet paper. A reloadable Visa card for her cash, a first aid kit, a pair of cheap sunglasses. The electronics department had a contract-free smartphone for a reasonable price. Chewing on her thumbnail in the cosmetics department, El selected a bleaching and a dying kit.

Her train didn't leave until midnight. Mama would be looking for her, but wouldn't come to the Walmart to check until closer to bedtime. That would be more than enough time to transform into a less glamorous version of her sister, one who was making a cross-country trip alone, one who was running from emotional agony and was tired to her core.

Purchases made, she retreated to the restroom and read through all the instructions. It seemed simple enough, but something profoundly embarrassing hit her as she sat on the toilet trying to plan her next move: she couldn't wash her hair in a Walmart sink.

Too many people would see her! They might even complain to the management! She'd have to stand there and be criticized by someone barely older than her. It might even get her thrown out, and there was no telling if the police might get involved or her mother called.

How did homeless people do this?

El sat frowning in consternation at the open box, certain she was doomed. There was no way a spoiled, privileged girl like her could ever accomplish what she was attempting! She lacked the ingenuity, the survival instincts. She couldn't even swear without apologizing. How was she going to learn how to bathe in a sink without being ashamed?

Stuffing everything into her bag, El wandered back out into the store, her numb mind looking over shelves without seeing them. She ate a meager dinner in the sandwich shop, gazing out over the brightly lit commerce with increasing worry. There was only so much time, and it would take her at least an hour to walk back to the station. She couldn't return to the church, because the alarm would be set by now, but there weren't any other places between here and the station with a restroom friendly to such things.

El had no choice. She was just going to have to do it, and that must be the secret really. She just had to see her own success as being more important than anyone's opinion of her. Necessity demanded she compromise her ego, so that was what she would do.

Riley would scoff and use some choice words. Perhaps she'd tell a story about all the fascinating ways she'd done bizarre things to her own unruly hair. But above all, Riley would encourage her to be brave.

Mind made up, El cut back through the store and into the restroom. The bleach was easily applied inside the stall. She spent the forty minutes setting up her new phone and docking it with the store's wi-fi.

Texting Oscar to ask if he got her itineraries, she got a confused emoji as a reply.

?

Why did you break up your trip like this? Why not just fly here?

El used the camera to check her hair. It was a patchy orange color and her scalp was beginning to burn. This would certainly be interesting.

I had to. Flights were $800+. This is half that and if I know my mom, she will check the airport first, bc she doesn't think I can handle myself. This way, I move around the country in smaller increments too difficult for her to track, paying for everything in cash.

Oscar sent a voice message howling with laughter and calling her the most dyed-in-the-wool spy he'd ever met.

Not dyed just yet. Wool is still curing.

Is it even close to yellow?

She listened to the room and when it was empty, snuck out to get a better look at herself in the mirror. Parts of it had indeed gone bright orange-yellow, but not all of it.

Does it matter if it's not all the way white?

Not really. The dye will do some of the work. It might look like shit, but you're not trying to be a beauty queen.

Snorting, El tucked the phone into her pocket.

It might have been a better idea to use a little more of her reserves, or risk using Rose's card again at a salon, just to have this done right. As she stared into her own eyes, however, she knew there was no way. Everyone in this town knew her sister. She could never get away with that farce.

A Walmart sink it was.

Mama would laugh and call her white trash. Riley would tell her to rock on.

The door opened. A woman burned her with an askance as she stepped into an available stall, expression twisting into scorn as she took in El's rugged clothes and the caked tresses. Hands on the sink, El clenched her teeth and swallowed her feelings.

This was going to keep happening. For the foreseeable future, she was going to be judged. She was going to be talked down to. She was going to be cast out and laughed at and called a host of names. She was going to feel picked on, bullied, desperate. That was just how it was going to be.

But ... how was that different from every other day in her life? So it came from strangers. That was in many ways better than it coming from her own family.

The blue eyes in the mirror were haunted by that long-fought sorrow. She could look into them and see her own story so easily.

Her life had been nothing but ridicule and torture, the constant chipping and picking that ate a person down into dust. And yet, here she was, still standing.

Suddenly, it didn't seem so impossible. Suddenly, she didn't give a good goddamn about the woman in the stall behind her, or the staff of the store, or her mother's mean-spirited abuse.

Tipping forward, she rinsed the pale blue foam out of her hair, massaging it carefully. Her scalp thanked her, and when she stood up, it was much lighter than she'd expected, though by no means perfect.

Strangers came and went, saying nothing aloud. A clerk in a blue smock entered and departed with nothing more than a sniff as El dutifully cleaned the mess with a handful of paper towels. No one commented as she dumped a bottle of golden chemicals onto her crown and worked them through the damp mane.

As she twisted the lathered knot up and clipped it into place for its half hour of processing, an ancient old woman with coke-bottle glasses stared at her like an insect blinking back disbelief.

"What color are you doing?"

Surprised, El took a moment to remember how to speak. "Blonde."

The wrinkled face split into a warm smile. "I was blonde once! It was fine, I think, but my favorite color was black. Oh, I worked so hard to get jet-black, but I never could. My hair was just too orange. It always faded into green. Of course, that could have been because I was doing it in my girlfriend's backyard with a bottle of ink."

El's emotions were so raw that the image was painfully amusing. Though her laugh echoed around her, tears had begun to spill down her face.

"Why ink?"

"All I had. Mama wouldn't let me get dye. Course, then my daughter started doing hers with powdered drinks, do you believe that? Who puts Kool-Aid in their hair? Smelled good, though." She patted her own snow-white curls. "Now my great-granddaughter wants me to put pink in it. She says the white will make it easy. I think it'd look like cotton candy. What do you think?"

El dabbed her face dry and nodded. "I know a girl with pink hair. I think it looks really pretty."

The crone cackled. "Oh my, what would the girls at the club say! They'd be so shocked! But who cares what they think? They're gonna be dead in six months anyway. They better be anyway. I have a bet to win."

While El fought her giggles for breath, the old woman stroked her arm and bade her a gentle farewell. A glimmer in her enormous eyes said she knew exactly what she'd done for El, and El had no trouble thanking her.

She applied her costume in makeshift layers, toasting her hair beneath the hand dryer, pulling it up into a haphazard bun, applying cosmetics with her fingers and a pocket mirror. The makeup was a bit easier, because she'd been watching Rose do it for years and practicing every day for a week. It was a little too much or too little here and there, but all in all, it was as good as she could get it.

On her way out the door, she snapped a photo for Oscar.

Holy shit. You look really different.

Yeah but do I look like my sister . . . who duh, IS a beauty queen.

The ellipsis was on the screen for a long while before he came back on with one of Rose's pageant pictures, cut into a side-by-side comparison.

OMG I did not know! Goddamn! But that's ok, because it means regular people won't know who she is either.

That was difficult to imagine. *She is always put together tho, and I look messy.*

Gurl, it's close enough for an ID check. Now you just have to behave like an adult.

How do I do that?

Stop giving a fuck. Act like every single thing you have to do is annoying as balls and you need a drink.

Doable. She'd observed her father and mother run a religious and political fiefdom on copious amounts of liquor and aggravation for her entire life.

Do I look older?

Oscar sent her two thumbs-up.

I'm gonna walk back to the station now. There's wi-fi on the train. I'll tell you when I'm on board.

For an instant, she wished she'd thought to get Riley's phone number. It would have been easy to do, but she hadn't thought of it. As she berated herself for that stupidity, she already knew her subconscious had been working on her behalf.

To transform and walk away, she had to cut ties entirely. She could reflect on what Riley had meant to her, but she didn't dare hope for more. That would be too difficult to endure, and the temptation to reach out would be too great, increasing the risk and giving her mother more opportunities to find her.

It had to be this way.

The phone buzzed. *I love you, Snowy. Stay safe, okay?*

El chewed her lip. *Tell me I can do this.*

You can do this.

But can I?

What would happen if you walked out right now and went home? Oscar remarked sagely.

Okay, you win. I'll text from the train.

She put the backpack on and clipped it into place. The green bandana tickled her neck, tied as it was to her strap. With a smile, she pulled it loose and secured it around her topknot.

"Green is my favorite color," she whispered.

Whirlwind

No matter how far she scrolled, the words kept coming. There had to be thousands of entries, paragraph after paragraph of constant admiration. For a moment, Riley sat staring at the sheer magnitude of this outpouring of feeling and was in awe.

Practically since the moment they'd met, an entry or five a day, all beneath Mama Glasse's gaze, all without the object of affection ever even noticing?

"This is . . ." Her voice faltered. It was reckless, incomprehensible, shocking, embarrassing, a bit unsettling, and so, so magical.

Her face on fire, she rolled past all the tempting titles and settled on "She Isn't a Girl." Half expecting the sappiest, fangirliest love poem ever written, she took a deep breath, and even though it felt like some kind of crime, read on.

A girl is a thing still forming. A girl is incorporating tolerance through the slow crush of expectations, saturated with that pressure which makes her a gem amongst the rocks. A girl learns her place, which is nowhere she wants to be. A girl crosses her ankles and bows her head and contorts herself into the shape they want to see. A girl is forced into patience because no one is listening. A girl speaks when spoken to. A girl does this because she doesn't know any better, and she is still being educated, still waiting to see how long she will be called a girl. Will it be until she is eighteen, or will she be in her hospital bed, while a nurse whispers "Atta girl," as she shovels in the last meal? Will she be a girl until she wears her first bra, or until she removes it for her first lover? Will she be a girl

raising another girl? An endless line of girls. A girl is receptive and makes no choices, because a girl is a girl, and her body is built to receive, to hold, to constantly begin, but never mature until the world has nothing else it requires from her. And then, she is a sack of bones, a sack they call "girl."

R is not a girl and anyone who names her one will learn why she is not. I have never met someone quite as sure of themselves. I have never seen someone so calm in the face of turbulence. But R is a storm of her own making, a whirlwind, a sublime tempest. She smiles, and somehow, that is the only thing that will ever move in reply to a man. Everything else about her body is still and composed, hers and no one else's, though her mind and her spirit are swirling inside and flickering in that knowing smile.

R is simply perfection, in that way that is so complete, she does not even acknowledge her own grace. I wonder sometimes . . . Caught in her life and all the tiny details I can never know, she must look in the mirror and see how gorgeous she is, how her confidence is a life-giving force for me. It can't escape her, can it? Can anything?

I don't know. I don't know if when she looks in the mirror, she sees a girl looking back at her. If she does . . . I am both fascinated and frightened. If R is now a girl to herself, what will she be when she declares herself at last a woman?

With a sucking gasp, Riley laid the laptop aside. For long moments, she stared at nothing in particular, her ears ringing and her flesh a vulnerable mass of impressions and senses. Sounds seemed louder, but somehow farther away. Her skin brushed her blankets and felt as if it had raked across dry ice. Her stomach was a tangle of butterflies.

No one . . . how could anyone ever say such things of her? It was all bravado. It was all a facade. She wore armor so that when she fell and skidded over asphalt, it wouldn't take off her skin. It still hurt like hell when it happened, when people called her a freak, when they tried to put hands on her, when they made fun of the wonderful man who raised her. But Dad had always said that knowing how to fall was what determined who lived and who turned to jelly on the side of the road.

Sniffling, Riley squeezed her hands into fists.

Always fighting, always being strong, always projecting confidence even when inside she was shrinking. All her life, always pushing back so that she couldn't get hurt. Constant force, all the time, draining her energy until she had to find ways to cope and replenish, but there weren't any that could fully replace what she lost. That was why she'd been counting days until she could escape.

And someone had found beauty in that, meaning, perfection? Someone had been inspired to rebellion by her struggle? How? Someone saw her as more than she'd ever seen of herself. But was it an illusion, or was she capable of that? Could Riley Vanator be that kind of goddess, that kind of hero, or was it magic?

The energy built inside, until at last, she had to move. If she didn't move, she would die.

She thought about the slamming door only after she was down the driveway. Running and running, she made the great circuit through the trees and down the road. Across the creek, leaping logs, down the hill, around again, past the great towering tree, and upward. Boots thumping, heart pounding, thoughts beating a constant rhythm, so monotonous it seemed like buzzing. She ran until the blood swelled into her limbs, but left her stomach aching.

At the stump, she collapsed, breathing in great huffs. There should be words in her mind, she should be able to make sense. Say something. Finish a sentence. But no. All she could see was that long dark hair, those huge blue eyes, the glow of the sun on her face as she smiled and said, "I've wasted too much time."

Riley's hand was shaking as she lifted it to her face. Astonished, she watched it, because never in her life could she remember such a thing happening. A hand so steady, she'd been servicing transmissions since she was a toddler—she never shook, even when she was cold. The shiver would wash over her like a bucket of ice water, and as it reached her toes and draped her with gooseflesh, she would focus her eyes on a point, tell her body to be still, and still it would be. Now, sitting like this in the dawn . . .

She couldn't make it stop.

El was gone, on her own. She could be lost. She could be in danger. She could get hurt, terribly. Or worse . . . she could vanish forever.

"No."

The trip back to the house was swift but perilous, as she bumped into every possible obstacle and tripped over every crack. Her memory had been wiped and her eyes shut off, and she was kicking at the ground in a body lighter than air.

Her father was standing at the window. As she tumbled through the door, he caught her, and held her out, examining her with such intensity, she found she couldn't quite look him in the eye. All those feelings were new and raw and didn't have a place behind the armor. She had no defenses.

"What's wrong?"

Even as he asked it, she knew that somehow all at once, nothing was wrong, and everything was. Someone . . . someone loved her. And that someone was gone.

"Dad . . . I . . ."

"Was there a car here a while ago? Did you go somewhere?"

All she could do was fall into a chair.

Head in hands, her mind made a list of all the horrifying things that could happen to El, wandering with a bag of stupidly chosen camping equipment. Riley had talked her into strike steel and a water filter, but what she needed was an attitude and the willingness to defend herself. She needed confidence. She needed armor.

"Jesus Christ, what did I do?"

"Rye-baby, talk to me. You're scaring me."

"She ran away. She took everything I said, what I was . . . and she ran away. All because of me. She's alone, Dad. She's alone, and it's all my fault."

He squatted down, his hand warming her shoulder as he chafed her back. "Who are we talking about?"

"El . . . this girl . . . she—" No matter how many times she swallowed or cleared her throat, everything sounded wrong. "She ran away from home, because I told her to stop letting her mother push her around. She listened to me, Dad, because . . . because she . . . Go look at my computer. I can't."

He was gone a long time. Riley stared at the clock and waited for him to make some joke that put it all into perspective and made it easy to handle. When he returned, he carried the laptop in one hand.

Setting it beside the microwave, he filled a huge mug with fresh coffee and then added to it from a bottle in the cupboard. It *thunked* down at her elbow like a gavel.

"You haven't slept yet, have you?"

She shook her head. He nudged the mug toward her.

"Calm down. Drink it. Warm up your hands."

The drink was hot in more ways than one, but as it slid down her throat, it coated her insides with liquid tranquility, until the stuff moved through her limbs and loosened her muscles enough to allow a deep breath. She listened to his finger tap, as he read through entry after entry with an impassive face.

The cup was empty; he sat back and crossed his arms, his facial hair wiggling as his opinions flexed his rigid face.

"What do I do, Dad?"

"What do you *want* to do? I mean, what's your first reaction?"

Riley looked at her hands, clinging to the mug so hard her palms burned. She wasn't sure if it mattered what she wanted. What mattered was that El was safe. No, it was more than that. El *deserved* to be safe and loved. She *deserved* to be cared for by somebody. She *deserved* to be happy and have her wishes come true.

Her father refilled the mug from the pot and let out a sigh that could fill the Grand Canyon. "You don't owe her anything. She's pretty smart, and I bet that that's why she never said anything. She didn't want to pressure you, especially here, where people are jackasses. She felt what she felt . . . and that was on her."

Riley's body was suddenly heavy. She slid lower into the chair and stared at the ceiling. "El was protecting me from her mother. If it was just one-sided, Mama Glasse wouldn't come after me. If it was a relationship, we'd both be fucked."

"Yeah . . . that too." He nodded and continued nodding, as if the act kept the thoughts coming. "She's got good taste. I think I like this girl."

"She's top of her class."

"Yeah, but does that matter?"

"To me? Yeah, but not the way people think."

"What else matters?"

She could feel that ancient medicine doing its work, calming the physical so that her mind could work through the logic. For the first time in her life, she gave a thought to that thing that seemed so impossible it was pointless to consider. For once, she envisioned what it might be like not to be alone. If there was a Heavenly Angel for her father and they could find each other across states and cultures and through iron bars, surely it was possible that there might be one for her.

"She *has* everything that matters."

"Then what do you want to do?"

Riley licked the coffee from her lips, tasting the smoky whisky in it. She wanted to track El down, tackle her onto a soft surface, scold her for frightening the shit out of her, and then give her a night she wouldn't forget, but that was not something she could say to her dad, even though she was pretty sure he could already see it written on her face.

"I have to find her."

"Can you?"

She looked at the computer and knew, almost as if the strategy were divinely inspired, that yes, she could. She could lay a trap because she knew the bait better than anyone.

She knew what she saw when she looked in the mirror.

"I can. But if I want to keep her safe, I have to go."

She met his eye. His nod came to a slow halt. He massaged and groomed his beard with a hand. "That sudden, huh? Just like that? One minute you're all *Screw this* and now you read this and it's that fast?"

Riley looked at the metal lunchbox sitting where she'd left it. "Yeah. Sometimes it's just like that."

His chin ticked downward. "You'll miss graduation."

"I earned the diploma. It's done."

"I've been waiting eighteen years to take that picture."

She could hear the humor there and was already filling with relief. "You really think I'd be caught dead in that getup?"

"Hell, I expected you to at least decorate the cap. Maybe with rockers and a flaming skull or some shit."

She smiled, but then it hit her: what would her mother think? Riley had never lived for anyone else. She'd never been that girl, because she'd existed without a mother, without a woman to watch.

"Do you think . . . would mom be okay with it?"

"Rye-baby . . . your mom would go batshit crazy if she thought for one second you weren't going to go after that girl."

A laugh and a cry became confused and fell out at the same instant. "Yeah, but we can't afford it."

"Been down that road, Riley. Know it well. Needed to go on a diet anyway, seeing as how you ain't gonna be here to take care of me forever." He pulled himself up from the table and nudged his head to the back door. "Come on, I got something to show you."

She followed him around the back of the house. The sun was already turning the entire landscape into a sauna. He led them out to the old shed and lined up the numbers on the padlock. Just inside was a white canvas tarp.

"Me and Mike been working on this for a few months now while you was at school. I was gonna give it to you at graduation, but . . . I like this idea better. Go on!"

Confused, Riley gave the tarp a tug, and hissed as it fell away.

There before her, a massive touring bike of black, chrome, and power. Matte charcoal sculpted scales into the fuel tank, saddlebags, and fenders, transforming the whole thing into a sleek lizard with reflective horns, bright LED eyes, and fiery red nostrils. Four speakers, USB port, navigation, a full tour pack, Streetglide seats, and heated grips. She stood in reverence and felt all her exhaustion drain away.

"Dad . . ."

"I know, right? It's a 2017, Milwaukee 8, 107-cubic-inch. 103 pounds of torque. Twin cooled, six-gallon tank—which should get you about 200 with good driving. Renegade twenty-one-inch front and seventeen-inch back. It's got a couple mod kits, and I got you two brain buckets with the matching headsets."

She shook her head, her hands slowly churning the dusty air. He was rocking on his heels, his face rosy with pride and joy. The more she stared at it, the more she wanted to tame it.

Putting her leg over, she tested the backrest, felt the grips and flipped the switches. This was a far cry from her janky sport bike assembled from spare parts—that labor they'd shared—her father's teaching aid and her touchpoint with him. She spent so much time pitched forward on that thing, it sometimes hurt to stand up straight. This was a bike meant to cruise. This was a bike to go on long treks. This was the Shire horse of rides, and it cost more than anything she'd ever owned.

"Dad, this is too much . . ."

He made a face. "Don't be stupid. I been saving up for this since you was born, and I been keeping my eye on everything trying to pick the perfect chassis. I was gonna give you something meant for handling, but I had this feeling . . . 'Jerry,' I said, 'She is gonna want to explore. She is gonna ride from one coast to another and sleep under the stars and kill anyone who gets in her way. She's gonna roam and she needs a dragon, not a pony.' And here you are, and my instincts were right."

All of a sudden, tears and snot were flowing out of her face like someone had turned on a faucet. Wails turned to hiccups, and her shirt was coated in mascara in seconds. He put his arm around her and petted her head.

"Come on, Rye, you're okay. I been planning this all along. This is all I know, so . . . I did the best I could for you."

"Thanks. I love it . . . so much. This week has been . . . really crazy."

"Yeah, and it looks like it isn't gonna let up."

She pressed her face into his chest. "No, I don't think it is."

"What are you going to name her?"

The name manifested itself in her head so quickly it was like the bike was whispering what it wanted to be called. She had seen it once in a library when she'd been writing a paper about the Amazons.

"Aella. The whirlwind."

12

Into the Woods

El scanned all the roads near the tracks and whittled down her fingernails with her teeth. If she knew her mother, the woman would be in the midst of calling the banks and credit card companies, or trying to track her phone via the service provider. El didn't know what resources a Senator really had for this kind of situation. Mama could even have the FBI scouring footage, or the Secret Service reviewing her website.

Every shadow was a threat. Every person who took too long a look at her was a villain. Every time the door between the cars opened, El anticipated confrontation. Twisted up on herself in her seat, muscles rigid, the burner phone nearly frightened her out of her skin as it rang.

"Hey, Snowy."

Her veins ached with the sudden change in blood pressure. "Oscar. Oh my god, I am so . . . Fucked up right now."

His voice was sleepy, as if he'd set an alarm to check in with her and was trying not to doze off. "You're safe, though, right?"

"I think so."

"Are you almost there?"

"Yes." The conductor smiled her way as he passed. Instinctively, El furtively tucked the phone to her ear. "I am so bad at this."

"Go get a drink. Remember, you're a grown-up?"

"Are you saying adults are drunks?"

"No, I'm saying adults don't feel anxious about showing their ID. If you're going to pretend to be one, you gotta get used to it."

It occurred to El then that she was breathing in tiny gasps, coiled up so tightly that her head was beginning to throb. She was so caught up in the flight, her skeleton almost refused to budge as she unfolded. The languorous stretch was at a sloth's pace. Fully wrung of adrenaline, she sucked back a yawn.

"You are gonna keel over if you don't get some rest."

"I've been too keyed up."

Oscar's amusement had a sardonic ring to it. "Don't worry. You'll get good at sleeping when you can."

A voice came over the PA and announced their arrival into DC Union Station. El looked out the window on an already sweltering day. Her reflection was sunken and pale, her frizzy, singed hair hanging in damp strings despite the air-conditioning. She'd have to touch up the makeup before switching trains.

Oscar's voice was muzzy. "Text me from the next leg."

"Go back to sleep."

He was already on his way and mumbled a farewell.

El's pack felt unreasonably heavy as she shoved her arms into the straps and hefted it. She was definitely going to have to sleep at some point, before she collapsed in sheer exhaustion, but that meant she needed to do something to combat this nervous energy. If she kept flinching at every sound, she'd draw attention to herself, and if she kept behaving as if she was ready to bolt, someone would give her a reason.

There had to be a way to seem confident, even if she wasn't. Perhaps she just needed to pretend she had a legitimate reason to be where she was. If she could convince herself that she was not doing something wrong . . .

She came to a halt on the platform. Her jangling nerves suddenly went still, and the weight of the pack no longer mattered.

More magic. El had bought into *their* version of reality. She *had* a legitimate reason to be where she was! She *had* a right to leave the care of someone who had done what her mother had. She had feared for her safety! If society couldn't help her, then why should she care what it said was permissible? She was shrinking, terrified—withdrawing into her own head and her fear—all because the world refused to support her. The world had no right to ask her to obey.

With her eyes closed, El could see Riley's defiant grin clearly, and it gave her strength.

The terminal opened up around her in turn-of-the-century opulence. The arched ceiling of warm carved stone, the statuary in the galleries, the shuffle of men and women in fine suits all rendered her speechless. Columns and marble floors, potted palms of bright green and polished ornate wood—the single room was huge and decadent with such lofty heights that the sound was dampened.

El ducked into the restroom and stood at a sink. She looked like a bedraggled wretch, distinctly out of place. Brushing her hair furiously, she put it back up into a neater bun. Her face got a fresh dusting. She removed the flannel shirt and tucked it into the pack, pulling free a cardigan sweater she'd decided to bring at the last minute. Her clutch wallet was an expensive brand and the backpack was brand new and still clean. Like this, she could pass for an adult on vacation, she was fairly certain. She just had to keep her justification firmly in the front of her mind.

Cutting across the foot traffic with her head held high, she proceeded to the nearest ticketing counter and purchased her next ticket with cash. The agent didn't even look at her ID.

As her tickets were being printed, El thought back on Oscar's advice. Adults did adult things without fear of disapproval, but it was more than that. They had an entire culture built up around their age and all the difficulties included in it. It was a shared understanding. There wasn't a line she had to cross to be an adult. There was only a sense of sameness she had to relax into.

Every adult she'd ever met had been so quick to tell her why being an adult was terrible, but El couldn't decide if that was because they hated being grown, or wanted to keep her a child. Either way, she'd already dealt with more stress than most of the adults she knew. Living with Mama was like every tale of a controlling boss, every story of a bad relationship, and every joke about a social interaction rolled into one. She may still technically be a child, but it seemed to her that her life absolutely entitled her to adult culture.

"May I ask, sir . . . I know it's early, but is there a . . . a bar serving drinks at the moment?"

To her tremendous relief, the agent's face split into a wry smile. "It's not that early. Besides, it's five o'clock somewhere, right?"

El tugged her lip from between her teeth and stood up straight. In one breath, she was Riley at the counter of the sporting goods store, chatting amiably about things kids shouldn't know. "In my time zone it sure as heck is."

He laughed. "Oh-drink-thirty, am I right? Liquor Standard Time? Check out the Sugar Factory over there." He nudged his chin and handed her the travel documents. "It's a bit pricey, but they make a bunch of sweet cocktails. A decent Cosmo."

She wasn't quite sure what a "Cosmo" was, but that was something she was just going to have to figure out as she went, the same way adults did. Halfway there, her nerves manifested one more concern. If her stolen ID wasn't honored, she had no idea what the consequences would be. Could underage people be arrested for trying to get alcohol?

Hovering at the door, she reasoned her way through it, finally refusing to buckle beneath the angst. If the rules were that strict, then there'd be a more sophisticated way of checking identifications—some sort of scanner or a police officer at the door. There wouldn't be a gussied-up bartender who looked like she'd been there all night. If they didn't like her ID, they'd probably ask her to leave. If she was really and truly the adult on the card, she'd be upset about it within measure, but she'd go.

That was that. If it wasn't . . . well, she'd have to figure that out when the time came.

"No excuses, El," she whispered to herself as she took a seat at the bar. "I'd like a drink."

"Here's the menu."

That simple. El couldn't help a quiet snort of disbelief.

The entire place had the 1950's aesthetic of a candy shop or a soda fountain, as if there should be children running through with sticky fingers. It was a unique kind of irony, that as a child playing an adult, she was sneaking her first alcoholic drink in a place designed to give adults a nostalgic fix.

Reading the brightly colored cocktail menu, her breath caught in her throat. Fourteen dollars? For a glass of juice and rum? Adults couldn't *really* be that desperate to dull their minds, could they? But her memory had a tally of the wine bottles in her recycling bins, and as she stared over the drinks listed, she knew that in her parents' pantry were enough bottles to reproduce many of the cocktails.

With a somber sigh, she closed the list. This experiment, while it served a purpose, would have to be something she repeated very seldom. It was something she knew about herself, though she'd only just come to that realization.

"What would you like me to get started for you?"

El cleared her throat and leaned her elbows on the polished green marble. "I don't drink very often, but I'm exhausted, and the ticketing agent said you have an excellent Cosmo."

The bartender gave her a cheerful nod. "That we do! Cotton Candy Cosmo!"

Cotton candy. El was fairly certain she'd never heard of that being used in a drink before. Most alcohol smelled terrible and burned the nose going in. "Sounds good, thank you."

"And may I see your ID?"

El's knees clamped on the stool as she opened her wallet. All at once, her mind was back to one of her few outings with Rose, when she'd bought wine at the grocery store.

"Well, aren't you sweet? I haven't been carded all spring!"

The card was held up and a facial comparison made, while the bartender smiled absently. "That bad a spring, huh?"

It took El a moment to respond to the joke, she was so happy to be included in it. "You wouldn't believe it if I told you."

"This is DC. I doubt that very much." Her card was handed back with a friendly nod. "I'll get that Cosmo going."

"Appreciate it."

And with that, the hurdle was overcome. El relaxed on the swiveling stool, allowing herself to finally feel the excitement of her situation.

She had escaped. She had gotten loose from Mama's stranglehold. Even if tomorrow she made a mistake and was caught, she was free for now. Every time she had a success like this one, when she accomplished something adult in spite of her lack of experience, she needed to celebrate. No one did anything perfectly, including adults, but these triumphs might be just enough to get her through failures to come.

When the drink arrived, she knew she hated it at once, but smiled approvingly at the woman for all the showmanship that went into it. The liquor was strong, neon pink, with an altogether obnoxious sweetness and a garnish of fluffy cotton that melted into the glass. El forced it down, wondering why for fourteen dollars they couldn't make it taste more like a dream of youth instead of a nightmare of regrets. Soon, however, the warmth in her throat began to spread, and her toes stopped cramping.

For the first time in days, she wanted to write. She reached for the notebook, but caught herself. No more spy games. No more encryption. She could link the new phone directly to wi-fi and blog all she wanted, and there wasn't one goddamned thing her mother could do about it.

The ecstasy of that went right to her head. With a tiny giggle, she flagged the waitress and asked after wi-fi, and then she was on her own site, thumbs well lubricated by the spirits. A blog entry came into shape, outlining her feelings toward her mother, pouring all her sorrows into the page. Her adoration of Riley, so pivotal to her self-discovery, was a crime, and El made her ferocious disgust as evident as she could. The monologue stretched with each moment, transforming into an argument against bigotry, sexism, and all the other things she had silently endured. It ended abruptly in a single assurance that she had finally run and that her readers would hear from her when it was safe.

Scheduling the entry to publish in a few days' time, when she was already off the east coast, El swiped away her tears and looked at the time.

With a gasp, she shot out of the stool. Her train should already be boarding!

Taking some bills from her wallet, she tossed them onto the bar and tipped the last half of the glass upward. The sickly sweet stuff slid down her throat without trouble, but burned all the way down. She threw an offhand wave to the bartender and beat a hasty retreat. Huffing and with moments to spare, El jumped aboard her train. As it left the station, she was caught in a tangle of other passengers all moving through the aisles with their luggage in tow. When at last she found her seat in one of the first cars, El was ready to drop.

Dragging the heavy pack, her limbs partially numb and sluggish with the alcohol, El shoved the bag into a narrow space and found her way back to her seat.

In twenty-four hours, she'd be in Chicago and the next leg of the trip would begin. She sent Oscar a quick text using the train's wi-fi, and then dozed off to the clacking of the rails.

El woke abruptly, sitting bolt upright. It took a few moments of gasping to remember she was aboard the train, that it was stopped at a different station, and that she was miles away from home. But even as she reassured herself of this, she became gradually aware that something was not right.

The other passengers were clustered on one side of the car, some wearing looks of concern. A few of them let out little noises of wonder, having hushed conversations about something unfolding outside the window.

El's limbs tingled and every hair rose. Stumbling up, still groggy and recovering from her fishbowl-sized brush with adulthood, she squeezed in at a rosy window and peered out. The station house was a quaint mustard-colored building adorned with white filigree, the platform around it so small that there weren't even overhangs to shield from the summer sun. Spread out around the tiny building were a group of men all clad in dark suits. They wore earpieces like the ones El had seen at her father's campaign events, and two of them weren't shy about the leather slings beneath their coats.

El's soul crystallized in cold fear. It was all she could do to count them, to survey their faces for familiarity, to clear her throat. "What's happening?"

A woman seated station-side peeled her nose off the window. "I think they're FBI. Maybe they want to search the train. Probably terrorists or something."

El didn't wait to hear any more speculation. Moving silently down the aisle, she stood beside the luggage rack and craned her neck into the vestibule. The external door to the car was open, but the conductor was blocking it. Slipping along the control panel, El pressed herself into the protected space and listened.

It was definitely an argument. The furious tones of voice were enough to convince her that these men in suits were not the FBI, and they were meeting with unexpected but justified opposition from the Amtrak staff.

"All you have to do is take a look at the fucking picture and search the train for yourself. We're talking about a young girl, traveling alone. She could be—"

"So why don't you have the State Troopers meet us at the next station? Why didn't they meet us here? She could have gotten on or off any—"

"Look at the picture! She got on in DC. Blonde."

"Show me some ID."

A third person lifted their voice above the other two, bargaining for one man to pay to board the train and search while it got underway, but El was already moving. Tugging her bag onto her shoulders, she sped along the gallery. Opening doors with a booted foot to the kickplate, El cut a path through the sleeping cars.

At the last car, she met a dead end and finally had to stop and think. She had spent hundreds on this train ride. If she disembarked now, she'd have no way to afford an additional ticket. But if those men spotted her, she'd be dragged off it anyway.

The one way to keep her freedom was to get off this train. It had to be done without any witnesses. Instinctively, El tugged on the exterior door handle. The panel didn't budge. She tried pushing buttons or searching the perimeter for a lever, but found no way to release the lock. The door apparently required a conductor with a key to open it.

Trapped, blinking back desperate tears, El staggered into the aisle and pressed herself against a wall.

She'd gotten so far, but it didn't matter. Her parents would always track her down, employing professionals who knew how to think while she kept making naive mistakes. Running had been her greatest transgression. If captured, she'd be a prisoner until the end of time. They'd lock her in a room, force her to see doctors, or worse, have her prosecuted for the theft of her sister's identity. She'd be cut off from everyone and everything but the Bible and prayer. Mama would force her to marry some terrible man, and then he'd keep her in a tower with the blessing of the church.

The backpack slipped to the ground, and El collapsed beside it. A sob escaped her, but even as her emotions began to spiral out of control, something steadied her.

"They don't have power unless you give it to them."

Something Riley might say, but this time, in her own shaky voice.

El opened her eyes. The vestibule was dim, one whole wall of the car devoted to sleeping compartments and the other curtained against the late summer sun. She clambered up and looked out a window. The men were still arguing with a growing cluster of train company personnel, and for the first time, El could see why the conductor hadn't ended the discussion and gotten back underway. A large SUV was parked in front of the train, directly across the tracks.

What was Mama paying for *that* kind of service? She also knew then that they weren't law enforcement of any kind. What would such men do to her if they got ahold of her?

El had to get off the train, and even if the door wouldn't open, the windows were equipped with emergency locks.

Her fingers found the red handles and gripped them for dear life. For a moment, she considered what might happen if she opened it. Maybe the train would suddenly erupt in alarms and flashing lights. Maybe they'd come storming after her and she'd be arrested.

El tugged anyway.

With a sickening static sound, the entire segment of glass flipped in at her. It was thick and heavy, but she braced a foot against the wall and pulled it free. It rested on the ankle of her boot and then tipped to the side, clattering heavily against the wall. With a single glance around to see if anyone was going to attempt to apprehend her, El hefted her bag through the hole. Only as it hit the ground with a thud did she consider that there was something of a drop to the gravel below.

It was too late to worry about such things.

Swinging her legs into the opening, she scooted off the sharp sill and landed with a crunch beside the bag. She was off the train and safe. Now all she had to do was make sure she could outrun her pursuers. They were good enough to track her onto this particular train, but apparently stupid enough to provide her with the perfect distraction to make a getaway.

Hugging the train, El ducked below all the windows, moving at top speed for the SUV parked in front of the engine. She barely noticed the smattering of stately homes on either side of the tracks, or the grand river that ran beside the road. All she could see was the nose of the vehicle sticking out from in front of the train and its empty driver's side seat.

Coming level with the engine, El set the bag down and took every step as if creeping out of her room to use the computer while her mother was asleep. In the car's side mirror, El could see that the driver may have gotten out, but he was hovering near the rear bumper, looking down the platform to his colleagues. The loud rumbling of the engine covered every sound as El carefully pulled the passenger door handle, but it couldn't compare to the terrible rushing of her own blood in her ears.

Slinking up into the seat, El reached across the console and tugged the keys from the ignition, tossing them beneath the engine. In one breath, she was out of the car and had slung her pack over her shoulder. Back down the train she ran, barely thinking to duck below the windows as her boots chewed the gravel. Her lungs felt soaked in acid and her legs ached, as she beelined for the bridge, but she didn't stop running until she'd crossed the river and was safe inside the gas station.

Wheezing, El stared out the window.

"Can I help you?" asked the clerk, propped on her elbows with a sleepy look.

Startled, El pushed a few strands of hair out of her sweaty face. She must look terrible, like the sort of person who would curl Mama's lip.

What else was new?

"Yes, thank you. Can you tell me . . . where I am?"

Huntress

R iley cleared a spot on her cosmetics-cluttered desk and put her feet up. Tugging the computer into her lap, she moved between webpages. With the shades drawn and her screen at full brightness, time was illusory, measured only by each tap of the Refresh button.

Had it been the right question?

The @hellonaunicycle profile was a mask she'd painstakingly designed over the course of several hours to be the perfect bait. Average user, eighteen, in love with the story of Snow and R, with just a dash of extra original posts, like beautiful stock images from around the world or quotes that Riley found particularly appropriate to El's situation. No reblogs from sites other than El's, no content to link it to any other site on the net except @loveunderglass, no way anyone else would stumble onto it in the thousands of lives on display, except by meticulously scanning the notes on El's entries. It was perfectly innocuous, but Riley considered that El might be too savvy to get online or fall for such a slipshod trap. The girl was at least clever enough to evade Mama Glasse, and with familial political ties, the woman had to have every agency in the world on top of the disappearance by now.

Surely El wouldn't . . . but if she didn't, then Riley would have no way to track her down, something that gave her a cold chill and a full-body ache.

The Statshunter window reloaded, and the result was so surprising it took several seconds for Riley to realize anything had changed. She must have let out a sound. Her father appeared in the doorway to watch her fingers tap as she switched programs, and entered the IP address into the tracker.

"How does this work?"

"I made an account on El's blogging site with a tracking program embedded in the code. I built the profile to be innocent, but interesting to one specific person. Then I asked that *one person* a question."

"And that *one person* decided to research your fake profile before answering?" He crossed his arms. "And you can use that to track her?"

"Exactly. I can track any IP address who comes to my profile page."

"It could be the wicked witch," he grumbled, "checkin' up on anyone who'd help El."

"She'd have to hack the account to see the question."

"Wouldn't put it past her."

"Yeah, but if she had hacked El's account, she'd probably know where El was going. I agree, though . . . Mama Glasse is more than capable." The map constituted itself from the grid on the screen, and Riley zoomed out. Whoever the person was, the IP ping had not come from this state. "Well, unless the woman is using a VPN to reroute her IP, it isn't her."

"Could it be another fan who noticed your page?"

"Maybe, but I've been pretty obscure. There are at least ten fan blogs. I've looked through all of them. El's been careful to keep the notes neutral and the contacts she's had in DM, but I'm pretty sure none of them are combing her notes to find other fans."

He leaned forward and used his stubby finger to move the mouse across the screen, tracing the interstates. "Look. This is right along the railroad tracks. I just saw this town . . . Alderson, on the news! Someone parked a car right in front of a train and tried to board it."

Riley began to pace, her thoughts exploding in every direction. El had been on foot when Riley saw her at the parlor. Without a car, there was no other way for El to escape but to take the train. Could someone have tried to block her train in West Virginia to capture her?

He pulled up the news story and scrolled through to find an image of two State Troopers looking perplexed by the black SUV parked before a locomotive just itching to pull out of the station. "That's a rental car."

"How can you tell?"

He glanced at her sardonically. "The license frame and the air freshener."

"What happened to the guys?"

"All arrested. Their car got towed away, because I guess they couldn't find the keys."

Riley took back the laptop and shuffled maps with ticketing information. "If she caught the train and they figured it out, they'd intercept it, so of course she would have to ditch early. But then, who's *they?*"

Her father stood up and stretched, easily capable of grazing the ceiling with his knuckles. "So what? This crack team of stupids park a car across the tracks so they'd have time to search the train? Or did she do it to strand them there while she made a getaway? Newswoman didn't say anything about the guys looking for someone."

Riley stared at her own frowning reflection in the wall mirror and wondered if El had that kind of subterfuge in her. If so . . . she was one hell of a chick.

To look at her website, El had to be connected to a network. She wouldn't be stupid enough to do that with her own phone, since her mother would definitely be able to use that to find her. Yet the tracker program indicated that the user had logged in from a smartphone. This meant El had to have a secondary device like a pay-as-you-go phone purchased with cash, but those had limited cell data, and it would make sense that El would conserve it. She had to have logged in on someone else's wi-fi, which would tie her to a location.

Mama Glasse would never be able to follow that, but Riley could.

She returned to a Google street view and tapped the arrows until she could estimate approximately where on the avenue the user had been. As the signs came into focus, Riley's face split into a smile. She jumped up from the table and snatched her motorcycle coat from the bed. Flinging herself at his bulk, she slapped her dad's beard with a kiss. Then she was gone.

On the road, she had to remind herself to pay attention, and that traffic laws weren't just theories, but indicated consequences. Aella growled through the streets, drawing stares and head shakes. With careful maneuvering of the large bike, she swam upstream, and it wasn't long before she had freed herself from the tangle of traffic. Soon the streets widened, the houses grew fatter, and the gates more imposing.

White stone and columns, giant trees and palatial estates. Riley scanned the brass numbers for the one she remembered from the night she'd given El a ride.

Riley should have known something was terribly wrong. She should have known to give El another hug, or reassure her that she could divulge any secret without betrayal. She should have given off a vibe, or kissed El's cheek, or anything other than act like a stupid, awkward tomboy.

If she *had* kissed El, would the girl still have run away?

Her heart skipped, and she almost didn't see the bronze plaque embedded in brick. Riley stopped the bike so hard it screeched, and looked up at the house. Yup, the one that looked like a fucking plantation.

She punched the buzzer.

"Hello?"

"Uh . . . I'm here to talk to Mama Glasse. She home?"

It was a practiced customer service voice who replied. "May I ask who this is?"

"Tell her it's R."

"Like the letter?"

"Yup."

"One moment." The intercom went dead with a brisk pop. Riley picked her teeth beneath the lifted visor and looked up at the security cameras. The place was like a goddamn prison. El really had executed an escape worthy of any criminal. If Mama Glasse ever found her daughter, she'd likely install a moat and alligators so that the next breakout saw El swimming for her life or building a raft out of shower curtains.

With the squeaking of metal pulleys, the gate slid aside for her. As slowly as she could without falling over, Riley rolled Aella down the lane. She'd expected to see conspicuously unmarked cars, men wearing nondescript suits, or at least some sign that a girl was missing and that the authorities cared, but the manicured lawn and well-maintained shrubs were unassailed.

Riley sat for a moment on the silent bike. She'd always been an apt pupil, and aside from idolizing her father, she'd also learned a great deal about the criminal element. All it would take were a few timed comments composed of specific phrases, a general disregard for authority, a cautious negotiation style, and Riley could appear to be a budding, avaricious miscreant willing to break the law. Tiny threads began to weave, and Riley's plan took shape. It was a web, all right, but it was one she was fairly certain she could navigate, if she was careful and trusted no one.

Especially Mama Glasse.

She took her phone from her pocket and flicked through a few apps, then let the thing lock.

A lady in a tacky maid's uniform answered the door, shoulders hunched in exhaustion and face sunken from worry. She ushered Riley to a large sitting room with a whispered, "Let me go get Mrs. Glasse."

Fairly certain her entire house could fit into this one room and completely disgusted by that fact, Riley walked to the couch that was about where her bed might be and took a cue, stretching herself out, muddy boots and all. The whole room was done up in hunter green and pink pastels. Inset paneling and white shutters spoke to the time before the war they deserved to lose, and the Victorian furniture and ornate scrollwork made the place look like a museum. The air was cold like a mall and every shoe clicking across the tiled floor carried through the entire estate.

Riley grinned.

"*What* are you doin'!"

The shrill voice echoed, enough to rouse anyone with a conscience, but Riley made full use of her delinquent genes. "Some lady told me I lacked respect. I think it's cuz it's fucking tiring. So I thought I'd take a nap. Save up my strength."

Mama Glasse wheeled around the couch and glared down at her. She was wearing twice as much makeup as usual and the dark circles still showed. "*What* do you want?"

Picking at her tasseled zipper, Riley shrugged. "Your daughter is missing..."

The woman crossed her arms and scowled. "I'm aware of that."

"I don't see any cops, no signs you're out looking for her. But someone like you ... I mean, you gotta be curious."

The eyes glazed over, less a dewy motherly concern and more a malevolent sheen of reptilian reasoning. "I'm not sure I take your point."

Riley sat up. "What's she gonna do? Out there, all by herself, knowing what she knows about what hurts you? I wonder if her coming of age story would damage your husband's reelection campaign."

In a blink, Mama Glasse was bristling, quivering as if about to linguistically backhand her with a perfect southern drawl.

"You're implying *what*?"

The H in the word was heavy, like a sledgehammer.

"Just that you might want her back... and that you might not want the world to ever know she was gone." Standing up, Riley was about an inch taller than the woman. It filled her with accomplishment when her host was forced to her full height and had to lift her pointy chin just to reassert control. To needle her, Riley put on an exaggerated accent and shook her head woefully. "What *did* you tell the othuh ladies at church this mornin', Mama? I gotta wonder. 'El's at home, so sick she just can't *move*, the po' *baby*!'"

"Get out of my home," the woman spat back.

Chuckling, Riley raised a gloved hand. "Whatever you say, lady... just thought you might want someone to *actually* find her, instead of getting stranded on the railroad tracks."

Her gambit was rewarded with a sharp intake of breath. "How did you ..."

With a smoky glance, Riley clucked her tongue and cast the whole mess into the realms of the mysterious. "What would you say if I told you I not only know *how* to find El ... but that I'm probably the *only one* who can?"

"Her name is Elyrra, and I'd call you a liar."

Riley let out a snort. "That's not very nice! Where's that Southern charm I've heard so much about?"

"And how are you gonna do it?" The woman tilted a hip and was the very picture of impatience. "If you think you're just gonna call her cell phone, you're an idiot. She must've turned it off and taken out the SIM. Neither I nor the phone company can track it. I've tried."

Riley looked around the room and raised a brow. The whole place gave her the creeps, and the itchy sofa, hives. "Look ... I could go into all the details, but I'm pretty sure you don't want me to. I mean, my daddy is an ex-con, after all, your old man's a politician, and there's this thing called 'plausible deniability,' so ..."

In actuality, nothing she was doing was in any way illegal, but if she tipped her hand at all, this witch would just pay someone else to do what she was doing. Better to let her think it might tarnish the Glasse name, and make her comfortable with the idea of hiring an expendable teenaged girl from the wrong side of the tracks.

Mama Glasse eyed her, and Riley could almost smell the Coco Mademoiselle baking off her flesh as the skin gave a promising flush.

"Come with me," she said finally, and turned crisply toward the receiving hall.

Led into the depths of the place, Riley took a journey through time, as each successive room became more modern. Finally, at the back of the house, she was practically shoved into a doorway that opened onto a state-of-the-art studio. Canned lighting and reflective umbrellas, computer equipment and sound mixers—this must be where all Mama Glasse's famous vlog posts were created. As she scanned the room, Riley recognized the backdrop and gave a tiny shake of her head.

The acoustics were fucking perfect in the belly of the beast.

"So what, precisely, are you offerin' me, sugar?"

"Now I'm your sugar, huh, Mama?"

The smile didn't even try to look human. "You're willin' to break the law to protect my baby girl. You're sweetness and light and everythin' right."

Riley had a moment then, in between heartbeats, to give this all a second thought. Looking into those feline eyes and feeling like the canary in a gilded cage, Riley's soul ached for El. It was sudden and strong, and it nearly wrecked her Mercenary-AF persona. Riley forced down the urge to punch the woman in the nose and made as if to check the time on her phone.

The app was working perfectly.

"I can track her down. The only proof I'll give you of that is the fact that I knew about the car." She set her helmet down on the prop table and put her phone beside it. "What jokers *did* you hire, because that's a rookie fucking mistake. I'm a teenager, and I know that."

The lines around Mama's mouth ticked. "Well, it hardly seems fair to tell you about your competition. They've signed NDAs after all."

Nondisclosure agreements? Jesus, she was thorough. "Huh. Hope you didn't put down too big a deposit."

"I'm paying them each three a day plus expenses . . . *including* legal.*"

Riley coughed out her shock. "For real? Shit. I'd do it for two and never get caught."

Mrs. Glasse's scathing appraisal came to an abrupt halt. Either Riley had convinced her, or she was too desperate to care. She slid into the desk chair and removed a thick wallet from a drawer.

"You still haven't told me what your plan is."

"I plan to find her. That's all you need to know. Once I do . . ." She shrugged. "You don't care what I tell her to get her to come back, yeah?"

The French twist tilted to one shoulder. "Not a bit."

"It's like that, then." Riley propped herself against the wall, slouched in comfort with such shady dealings. "But uh . . . I might have to, you know . . ." She licked her lips suggestively.

Mama's face shriveled up on itself in disgust, but in spite of that, she didn't object. "Whatever it takes."

Riley's gut clenched down on her disdain, but her voice had to come out just right, or Mama would know she was playing a game. "I want two hundred per day, plus expenses, and five to kit my bike."

"How long do you think it'll take?"

Riley looked at the backdrop, recalling the several videos she'd seen while researching this woman's online presence. To her ear, every single artfully constructed word was obviously backward, insane propaganda designed to instill fear and teach people to hate others. To her ear, it sounded like cartoon super villainy, either completely unaware of its own hypocrisy or not concerned with it in the least. To Riley, this woman was a manifestation of everything she hated about the world, all the phobias and prejudices that had darkened her days.

But here she was, about to shake hands with it.

Then again . . . Riley had heard it all before, had it all thrown in her face in brawls. She was either too dark-skinned or too gay, not respectful enough or from an untouchable family, a "wetback" or "white trash." She'd been down that road. In that moment, she decided the hardship didn't matter to her.

"Let's say a week at first, but that might change if I can't pin her down."

Mama filled out a check, tore it with a flourish, and held it out to her. "This is the deposit. But for the day-to-day, I have an idea."

Riley looked at the check's memo bar. It read "Housekeeping." Her muscles shivered with rage-induced chemicals, but she moved not a bit.

The woman took something small from a pocket and held it out. It was an ATM card. "This is Elyrra's. She drained the account and left the card when she ran. The PIN is our address. Every day, I will deposit two . . . oh . . . let's say two hundred eighty into the account. You can use the card to buy anything else you need, or make hotel reservations. Every day, you can remove the cash on your end."

Riley gave the card a stern look. Just like this house and everything in it, the sparkly plastic was a jeweled restraint. This woman would be waiting to see the transaction records. She'd track Riley's movements and know precisely where she was. Which meant that if Riley wanted to obscure her location, she'd have to stop using the account. On the other hand, if she did stop using it, Mama would know.

This was going to make things a little more difficult.

With a deep breath, Riley reached out her hand, only to grasp at empty air.

The woman tucked the card to her breast as if reading her mind. "If you stop taking the money outta the account . . . if I don't hear from you . . . I will march my prim little butt into the police department and report that you stole this card along with several other valuables, while you were here cleaning my house, and that I know you have gone across state lines with my property. Do you understand me, sugar?"

A jeweled leash . . . ending in a choke chain.

Riley held out her hand. "Whatever you say, lady."

The card was bestowed. Mama brought her machines to life and triggered the printer. As it hummed and whispered, Riley watched the austere face. It remained emotionless. Either the woman was a Class-A psychopath, or she was highly medicated, and Riley couldn't decide which was the more palatable option.

"I want a progress call every single day."

"Uh, I don't even call my dad that often."

"We aren't family, honey," came the sarcastic reply. "This is work. You're a professional, now."

"A professional what? Housekeeper?" She feigned a chuckle. "Seductress? Enchantress?"

There was an easy hitch of one shoulder. "Huntress."

Riley looked down. Her phone screen was still glowing. It had only been a few minutes, but it felt like she'd been standing there for ages. El had lived in this for almost eighteen years. The thought sickened Riley. No wonder the poor girl had always looked as if she'd go airborne if someone made too loud a noise.

"Fine. One call per day to give you my progress."

"And the first group to find Elyrra gets a bonus."

"You mean you're keeping those jackasses? Did you have to bail them out or could they do that on their own?" That was another problem. A serious problem, because if they were private detectives, they were probably former 5-0, and packing. Then again, they'd already been evaded by a scared girl with no driver's license. "Don't you think they've kinda lost the contract?"

"Competition will keep you sharp. Let's say five grand to the winner. That's enough for you to buy a pretty new bike, or a new dye job for that mop, or a coat made outta real leather, at least."

It was a goad, to see what she'd do. Criminals fought for status and respect. Angry teenagers wanted acceptance. It didn't matter that the money wasn't important, and Riley didn't give a shit, she'd have to react with the proper amount of ire. All this, Riley calculated in an instant, and lifted her eyebrow.

"Bitch . . . this *is* real leather. It was my mother's coat. And my bike cost about five times that. If I win this, I'm gonna use the money to move back to New York."

"Uh-huh . . . whateva' you say." Mama smiled then, as if she were holding a plate of super thick fudge and ice-cold juleps. Instead, it was a newly printed NDA with Riley's name on it. "You're an adult right, sugar?"

"As of today, Mama," she murmured. "As of this very moment."

"Well, then just put your little old initials on all the lines, and sign the last page!"

The saccharine quality of that voice was damn near intolerable, like being boiled alive in honey. Riley flicked the pen across the paper a dozen or so times and counted the seconds until she could get the hell out.

The bargain struck, Mama reclined on her black throne and smiled. "When do you leave, sugar?"

"Tomorrow."

The chair swiveled in dismissal. "You know the way out, I'm sure."

14

Tracks

"Nearest place with public wi-fi's probably the library, but it's closed now. This town is so sleepy it might as well never open its eyes." The cashier executed a blink so long, she seemed as if she'd dozed off.

El's heart sank in front of the window and watched the kerfuffle across the river. The police had shown up and called the Troopers. Lights were flashing into the fiery sky. All four of her pursuers had been detained, which meant her escape from the train might have been too hasty, but she told herself it was still justified, because there was no way to know what those men would have done, or whether or not the State Troopers would believe them and search the train too. The SUV had been shoved from the tracks by a group of large men and it appeared that no one had noticed the window pane missing from the last car. Whatever levity there was in seeing that vanished as she realized she had no idea what to do next.

Letting out a breath she hadn't realized she'd been holding, El looked around herself, searching for answers. She couldn't afford to spend one more penny on travel than what she'd budgeted—not if she wanted to get to California with enough money to . . . well, to do whatever it was she was going to do.

Her eyes burned. Tears dropped. When she rubbed them away, her fingers were smudged with black mascara.

The clerk yawned. "Why do you need it?"

El looked around in surprise. "What?"

"The wi-fi."

"To message a friend so they don't worry."

The woman cast her bored gaze outside at all the flashing lights. The train let out a whistle. It was getting underway again. As the clerk turned back to El, she wore a knowing expression beneath her dropping lids.

"If you buy something, I'll let you use the wi-fi."

Blinking furiously, El couldn't help a smile. Normally, she'd refuse help and try to work it through herself, but it was life or death now. She didn't have that option. "Thank you."

She paced the several tiny aisles, looking for something to stock up on. She hadn't eaten since the sandwich at the Walmart, almost a full day ago, but the idea of putting anything in her stomach sounded disgusting. El knew she needed to eat to keep up her strength, but she was queasy with nervous exhaustion.

Dispassionately picking out a package of beef jerky and some trail mix, El returned to the counter, wiping her smudged makeup on her sleeve.

The clerk checked her items in slow motion and took her preloaded visa, never making eye contact. "You okay?"

"Honestly, no," El murmured.

The bathroom key was pushed across the counter, attached to a set of streamers. Without a word, El took a moment to clean herself up. In the bad lighting and cracked mirror, she looked exactly as she felt: small and terrified. Nowhere to sleep, no transportation, no money for either, in a town too small to have a bus depot. She could hitchhike. The very idea of climbing into a stranger's car horrified her, but it was the only way, unless she planned to . . .

El frowned at herself.

Walk. All the way to Chicago? That was hundreds of miles, but she'd intended to switch to Greyhound when she got there. Perhaps there was a city a bit closer that was large enough to have a bus depot with routes toward the west coast. If so, it might be as close as fifty or sixty miles away. El did a swift calculation based on her PE class fitness markers. She knew she could walk three miles an hour. If she walked all day, say twelve hours, that was thirty-six miles a day. West Virginia, Kentucky, southern Ohio . . . they were all wildernesses, and she had enough camping gear in her pack to make spending the night in the woods completely feasible.

But she'd never camped in her life. Mama had the RV, of course, and they'd go out to the lake occasionally to show it off, but that was like having a slightly smaller house containing the same, and even some extra, amenities. Riley would scoff at such luxury and poke fun at her, El was sure, and there was no argument she could make against her "glamping" past. El Glasse had no experience with the Great Outdoors.

Maybe it was time to improve her skills.

Who was the girl in the mirror? What sort of person was she? The sort who was going to learn constantly, work hard, do everything the tough way if that was how it was going to be. She could do that, because she had already done it. Besides, everything was frightening the first time, and if she didn't mess up, then she'd never needed to learn it in the first place.

El was going to be journeyman.

When she returned to the register, the clerk had written down a password on a sticky note. She appeared to be napping as she handed it off without opening an eye. "Feeling better?"

"Much. Thank you. May I ask you something?"

"Sure."

"Do you know what's the nearest town that has a Greyhound station?"

"Hmm." The clerk chewed a bright pink lip, still leaning partway over the counter. "Beckley, I think."

El couldn't keep logging into cell towers just to calculate her location and screen capturing a map seemed too inaccurate. There were too many possible routes and too much potential for error. Then again . . . the train had only one path, and much of it was sheltered from other kinds of traffic.

"Is Beckley along the train route?"

"Nope. Highway. Fifty miles or so. Nearest along the train is probably Charleston."

"And how far away is that?"

"'Bout a hundred miles."

One hundred miles. For an instant, that felt insurmountable, but El knew that if she pushed herself, she could do it in three to four days. That wasn't so bad at all, she told herself. The tracks dropped into a number of tiny towns she could use to restock, it kept her along a clear route, but shielded from observation from the road. If it was good enough to travel in the locomotive, it was good enough on foot.

"Thanks. I think I might buy a few more things before I go."

"I'm here all night. In fact . . . I'm here almost every night. I don't sleep, except on the job."

El logged into the wi-fi, wondering what she could say that wouldn't worry Oscar. All she could think to do was outline the story briefly and give him her plan of action.

His reply was immediate. *WHAT THE FUCK DO YOU THINK YOU'RE DOING? ARE YOU CRAZY?*

There's no other way. I cannot afford another ticket to Chicago, and now that they know I've taken a train, they'll be on the trains looking. They already knew I changed my hair!

He sent a series of emojis. *But how will I know you're safe?*

El thought swiftly. Her phone had a prepaid amount of data, texts, and cell minutes, but the amounts were so small, she could not afford to use them unless there was an emergency. At all other times, the cell data was turned off, and the phone was unusable unless it was logged into wi-fi.

I'll text you every few hours. Let's do 8 a.m., 12, 4 and 9 p.m. Does that work?

OMG You're going to give me a heart attack. I swear if you're one fucking minute late, I am calling the National Guard.

El couldn't help but giggle gratefully, imagining him pacing through his tiny shared apartment, watching the seconds tick by on his clock.

Thanks for caring, O. It means so much to me.

No prob, Snowy. Text me tonight at 9 p.m. your time.

Will do.

She glanced up at the clerk. The woman was dozing on her stool, her head propped against a display case. El logged into her blog app and checked her contacts. There were about fifty messages from different readers and to her surprise, about twenty questions asked of her. There was the usual nonsense of anonymous people being rude, the friendly well-wishes espousing hopes for her relationship with R, but one ask caught her eye.

If R is the person you say she is, it sounds like she'd be the type to give your mama a run for her money and enjoy it. So my question is, why won't you let her? You say you worry about her safety, but could it be that you worry you're not worth it? That is a lie your mama taught you to believe. I hope someday when you look in the mirror, you see a woman looking back who is worth every single struggle or fight R might meet. Have faith in this person you admire so much—she might see something inside you that you can't and want to come along for the ride.

Be safe.

Strangely unsettled, El leaned against the freezer unit, reviewing the message again and again. She couldn't put her finger on it, but something about it was uncanny. It was provocative while still being constructive, oddly knowing, but it could all be in how she was reading it. It felt like a warning, but that was probably just because she was so anxious. She hadn't yet told her readers about her escape, so none of them could possibly be commenting on anything current.

El's first instinct was always to suspect her mother of subterfuge, but this person gave their username willingly. She tracked it back to the blog, scrolling for a few pages of her own posts that had been recycled. The description of the user was bland. The only thing on the blog that appeared to be original was a series of motivational quotes.

"There are two mistakes one can make along the road to truth . . . not going all the way, and not starting," she read aloud in a soft voice.

It was oddly applicable, but that could all be a coincidence.

Perhaps it *was* a real user, and this @hellonaunicycle was just some side-blog used to track her story. She hoped it was, because more than any other question she'd received in recent weeks, this one caught her attention. El followed the blog and tapped the Notification button, so that she'd receive an alert whenever @hellonaunicycle posted anything.

She couldn't answer the question just yet, but it did give her something to think about. There were miles yet to walk before dark, and nothing else to do.

A few more items were added to her pack and after a last goodbye to Oscar, El set out.

Waiting to cross the river again until she was well past the train depot, El dropped back onto the tracks with a swift survey of the surrounding yards and street. There didn't appear to be anyone interested in stopping her, and no signs warning her off the rails. The only difficulty she encountered was a southward ninety-degree turn just outside of town that took her practically the opposite direction of her destination. It occurred to her then that the railroad might meander, tracking the river's natural path rather than a direct route. That sort of thing would add time to her trek, but when she considered deviating, it was still preferable to being the target of some maniac with a car or the group of men her mother had apparently hired.

El adjusted her pack, clasping every cross belt to redistribute the weight. Her shoulders were unbearably sore already, but there wasn't time to worry about it. It might be summer, and the sunsets long and late, but that didn't mean anything if she didn't make any progress. She had about three hours before pitch dark descended, and the animals started to circle. In that time, she could make it ten miles, but that meant pushing herself hard.

At first, her eyes would obsessively scan the land for threats, but by the end of the first hour, she had fixed her blurry gaze on the rails. The pack wasn't really that heavy, but it felt like it weighed as much as a car, its unweathered edges abrasive. Her new boots were rubbing against the back of her heels. Her knees were aching in a way she'd never felt.

The town blended into a rail yard outside of what looked to be a prison—high walls, watch towers, razor wire fences—El stopped at the base of the great retainer wall and contemplated life within.

El could already feel her recently acquired self-assurance waning. She was tired, sore. The worse it got, the less her own justifications would matter. At some point, she'd get too hungry, too tired, and she'd be tempted to pick up a phone and call for help. Everything had to be set into perspective and held there. Her convictions had to be absolute.

She needed a mantra.

At home, El had worn what Mama told her to—a drab and unflattering uniform of girlhood. El ate what was made—her portions controlled by a woman so afraid of weight gain that she starved her daughter. El slept and rose when instructed—seven hours per night with no naps. There were even bars on El's windows, because her mother had once suspected she was sneaking out at night, simply because some items had supposedly been moved around in her car. Constant abuse, neglect, silence, or vitriol. Put-downs, insults, and religious dogma shoved down her throat. Prison was probably just like that. It wasn't too much of a stretch, or too naive of El to think of that house in a similar way.

"Mama needs a victim. Mama will keep you there forever if she can. You are escaping." She repeated this again and again and left the prison in her dust.

But no amount of emotional buoyancy could keep her head up. She began to sag with the sun, her feet to shuffle, her pace too slow. Yet, the wilderness she'd been counting on had yet to appear. Alderson apparently abutted several smaller towns that clung to the tracks like debris cast to the sides during its construction. There was nowhere to rest.

With the sky a pale lavender, El knew a decision had to be made. If she didn't stop and use what daylight she had left to set up a camp, there would be less guarantee of safety. Just as she was sure she'd reached her limit and would have to sleep in a ditch, the ground around her vanished. It took her fully a minute to realize that she had stepped out onto a trestle bridge.

El gave a sleepy blink and then gasped as both the danger and potential benefits of her position hit her simultaneously.

Standing on a bridge with no idea if a freight train was coming was likely unwise. The last thing she wanted to have to deal with was a sudden leap into the river. Then again, at the base of the structure, the foliage created a dark and shielded nook. Roofs poked above the treetops all around, and it was likely that these banks were on private property, but as long as she was gone by the time the home owners began to stir, there was no harm, surely.

El trudged across the bridge at top speed. On the other side, she leaped from the leveled mound and dropped her entire body beneath the trestle. The soil was a mire of green gook and silt, but fifty feet up the bank, a cluster of large growth created what seemed to be a perfectly acceptable campsite. Shedding her bag in relief, El peered through the branches at the nearest home. It was a large one, with manicured lawn, a few chandeliers, and probably a sophisticated alarm system, but it was most definitely far enough away that she would probably not have to worry about being seen, so long as she kept her flashlight use to a minimum.

Collapsing in the dirt, El stared into the viridescent river. If she had been at home right about now, she'd have eaten her dinner and been sent upstairs to chew her dental pill. Then she'd spend the next twenty minutes trying to get every trace of red dye off her teeth, her mother checking in every few minutes to assess her progress, squeezing her cheeks as if she were a horse at auction. Next would be pajamas and the obligatory reading of the Bible. Her mother would sit there beside the bed and work her somnolent way through untold chapters and verses, sipping her wine all the while. Then sleep until El shot awake the next morning with her heart hammering.

But she wasn't at home. It was time for a new routine.

El opened her pack and removed the tent Riley had chosen. It was camouflage print and supposed to pop up like magic. At the time, El could not see a reason for it, but had purchased it to keep up appearances. Now she was grateful for it. It slid out of the bag and with a good shake, sprang out of her hand, fully assembled, its walls framed with rigid wires that unfurled. Only one side had an opening, and this could be completely sealed with Velcro. Her bedroll and sleeping bag came next, so tightly wound that she had to press them to the floor of the tent to get them to uncurl.

At the waterside, El ate a meal of gas station junk food and brushed her teeth with bottled water. She removed her boots and washed her blistered feet with a bar of soap, rubbing the sore bits with ointment from her first aid kit. The alarm on her phone went off just as she finished dressing for the next day's hike.

She turned on the data and checked her location. She hadn't come as far as she would have liked, but it was good enough.

Oscar dispatched a phalanx of messages. El shared her location with him to appease him and then bid him a good night.

Text me if you need anything.

Lying on the hard ground, uncomfortable and sticky with perspiration even though the night had finally fallen, El found herself chuckling. What she *needed* was not to be camping next to a river in midsummer, listening to the insects buzz as if hankering for her blood. What she *needed* was to wear two pairs of socks and buy new Band-Aids. What she *needed* was not to have pooped so close to her tent.

Everything had its learning curve.

She plugged the phone into the emergency power bank and curled up on top of the sleeping bag.

Dozing in and out, she contemplated the unanswered question: had she turned away from Riley's help because she didn't trust her? No, it couldn't be. Riley would never breathe a word of any secret, El was sure. So why hadn't she run to the girl and confessed everything? Given her current position, that would have been much easier, and Riley might have had some ideas El could never have come up with on her own. Was it because she was afraid Riley wouldn't return her sentiments? A bit, she had to admit, but the closer she'd come to leaving, the more she'd thought there might have been a bond between them greater than her fantasies.

The actual answer presented itself as she drifted off to sleep, when her guard was down.

El wasn't sure of anything. If she ever looked into Riley's eyes again, she wanted no doubts to cloud her thoughts. She wanted the purity that only came from having her resolve tested.

That was what Riley deserved, anyway.

15
Invisible

R iley packed with her mind on absolute utility and the need to get to El before anyone else could. Three of the five-hundred-dollar advance for supplies went directly into her own rainy-day account. Her father checked out the bike and made sure everything was in tip-top shape. At dawn, Riley got out of bed and showered, her jaw clamped so tightly she nearly snapped her toothbrush in half.

In her armor and brain bucket, she looked mean, scary even, and that was exactly how she felt. Her rage on El's behalf was rooted in her own experiences, and while El might luck out, while nothing bad might happen to her, there was no way to know for sure. El needed protection more than anything, and that was one thing Riley was more than capable of offering. Her temper was formidable, even if everything else about her might be a mess most of the time.

As Riley snugged her fingers into the gloves and tightened a squeaky fist, she imagined it going through Mama's Escalade window and wringing her spray-tanned neck. If Mama were being strangled to death, would her paralyzed face be able to form expressions? Riley doubted it and something about that pleased her.

Her father was remarkably quiet as he bid her farewell. Gathering her up, he lifted Riley fully off the ground, swinging her legs from side to side like a Newfoundland with a rag doll. She remained limp, her head crooked over his shoulder. When he put her back on her feet, she expected to find him blubbering.

He was stony. "Go get her. Keep her safe. Call me if you need me. Any time, day or night, for anything."

Somehow, she hadn't pictured it going this way. Riley was positive she'd have to convince him one last time, but he seemed as determined as she. Her father was confident in her, because she'd proven herself. Knowing he felt that way, however, made leaving difficult, because she suddenly felt closer to him than ever before. In a way, if he'd struggled, it might have made this easier for her, because she was used to leaving people in a furious storm.

Riley took a step back, pausing as she lifted the helmet. "I have to do this. It has to be me."

He gave a single nod. "Yeah. It does."

Suddenly, the butterflies in her gut settled. The snarling, wayward temper was pacified for the time being. Her father was the only person on earth whose opinion had ever mattered to her. If he said it was so, then it was so, and she was doing exactly what was right. Misgivings, hesitation, anything in her that might pull her from this course, be damned.

Riley slid the helmet into place and straddled the bike. "I'll call you when I get to Alderson. Should take about five and a half hours."

"You're already a day behind her. Get moving."

She started the bike, revved it a few times, and shot out of the drive without a parting word.

On the road, her mind wouldn't stop running over all the scenarios that El faced. The girl had absolutely no street smarts of any kind. She could be secretive and clever—that much was obvious from her website—but struggling to keep her sexuality hidden from her parents was something completely different from outrunning the cops . . . or the commandos hired to find her.

What had El done last night? Where had she gone? When darkness had fallen, was El safe? Riley prayed to the universe that El had been sensible enough to pack the tent, that she'd taken the water filter, that she'd remembered to buy food. She hoped that El had enough money to get by, until Riley could track her down and shake some intelligence into her.

Riding at top speed, she found herself glad it was a straight shot northward on a divided interstate. It wasn't her first long tour on a bike, but it was her first on Aella, and they were still bonding. Not having to worry about sharp turns or oncoming traffic gave her time to really listen to the workings and get a feel for the beast. From the stereo equipped helmets to the acceleration, it really was perfect for her. With Aella, Riley felt more confident than ever before.

And then there was that empty second seat and the helmet to match it—for her, the promise that her life would one day expand and bring some kind of connection.

Before she could block it out, a rendering of El flickered briefly in sunlight across her mind. She shook it away with a mutter.

Riley barely saw the tall trees and slopes around her. The line in the road hypnotized her, releasing all the memories of El's gaze. With hindsight's perfect lens, Riley could see the longing.

The practical half of her mind told her it was stupid to make plans based on poetry. Relationships were complex things. She only knew what her father had told her, but if he was right, then the other person had to have something she was missing, and that list was longer than any other person should ever have to check. There was a great deal of chaos to Riley that she kept hidden. El was under no obligation to help her make sense of any of it. El's devotions were the naive fantasies of a girl sheltered from the world, a kind of mental exercise to keep hope alive. They didn't mean anything, and Riley had no right to see more in them.

Besides, if El had run, perhaps it was because she didn't actually want their relationship to evolve. El might grow out of Riley. That was just the way it was. El needed help. She needed someone to run interference between her trail and the shrew in the McMansion. Riley's primary focus had to be giving El whatever she needed, because it was the right thing to do, even if it excluded her.

If Riley was on this mission just to see what might happen, or to selfishly steal El's heart, then she should turn around and go home.

She kept her nose pointed north, because it was the right thing to do.

Riley finally reached the tiny hamlet of Alderson in the afternoon. It was a quaint place spanning the river, with a waterside gazebo, Victorian homes, and bucolic charm. Riley had eyes for none of it. She went directly to the filling station and sat outside on the bike wondering how to go about interrogating people.

If she came in with guns blazing, as she wanted to, she'd get nowhere. Things like this took finesse, something Riley didn't keep on her person in large supply. Thankfully, there was a teenaged boy behind the counter who wasn't likely to be suspicious or ask her for some kind of badge.

Riley smiled sweetly at him. "Howdy."

"Hi." He pointed to her head with a grin. "Like the hair."

"Thanks! I'm wondering . . . my friend was in here last night. She moved on, but she knew I was going to be passing through. She says she thinks she may have left her wallet here."

He stepped back and looked down behind the counter. Picking up a lost and found box, he presented it to her. Riley made a show of looking through it.

"Is it there?"

"Nope. Hmm . . . She was in here at about five or six o'clock last night. Were you here then?"

He shook his head. "Not me and Sonny may not have noticed."

"He would have noticed my friend."

"She fell asleep twice on the job last year. It's kind of a joke."

"Well, shit." Riley looked around. She needed to find that clerk. There was no way to get the particulars on the events or El's state of mind without speaking to Sonny directly, but asking for her address would be overstepping the boundary. "She's going to be really upset if I can't find that stupid thing."

"Well, Sonny is back on at four. Till midnight. You can come back then."

Two hours, killing time in this village, while twiddling her thumbs? Two more hours of El wandering alone. Two more hours she had to allow such a thing to happen. It sounded horrible, but Riley hadn't eaten, and there was no reason not to refuel if she had to wait anyway.

"Anywhere around here to get a burger?"

"Sure!" He pointed up the road, and Riley was gone with a promise to return.

At the restaurant, Riley asked for a table out of the way. Seated in her corner, she connected her laptop to her phone's hotspot. Picking over her food, she read through a few more of El's entries, the ache in her heart expanding as she confronted the unimaginable reverence in which El seemed to hold her.

All her life, Riley had been stared at—children who were looking for someone different to punish for their own flaws, racist shitheads who saw her dark tan skin and her father's ginger beard and wore their contempt on their faces, drooling men who objectified her curvy figure, women who wanted her to conform to their standards of presentation—a whole gallery of expressions pointed at her in judgment. Then Riley had realized the only way to fight the intrusion was to take ownership of it. If people were going to gawk anyway, she might as well give them a show, because when she was the performer, she could leave the stage any time she liked.

But someone had been trying to see beyond those illusions to find who she was at her core, and it astonished Riley. That she had not felt how different El was from the others crushed her with regret.

The chip on her shoulder had finally caught her in the jugular, just like everyone always said it would. Now, Riley was thinking over a lot of the advice she'd blown off and wondering if it had untold applications too.

She stopped scrolling at an entry from several months previous, her eyes tearing up, even as she tried to sit back and disconnect from the emotions there.

I'm invisible.

The capabilities of the human race are measured in peaks and valleys. Here I am, sitting on one slope or another, but never an example. I'm one of those tiny details lost in averaging. That isn't who I want to be, but I can't compete and I'm not allowed to fail, and so I end up this way.

But I suppose, being invisible is a power. I can haunt this place and walk through every secret, because no one sees any reason to keep them from me.

I notice things about R. I can't tell what caused them, but I can imagine.

She's lonely. Not the way most people are, not even the way I am. She's lonely because she's complicated and exceptional. She's on the peak, you see, at the very tippy-top, where only one person can be at a time. Other kids our age can't even conceive of what her life has been, and they don't bother to put together the details she does share. They find her off-putting, because she is always so unforgiving and real. They think she's an unqualified snob, because surely they're better than her, and so she hasn't any right to ignore them! They're the "cool kids." People should let them have their illusions of grandeur and oh my, what a bitch she is for denying them their make believe.

They don't realize that she's already seen some truly terrible things, but that's because they don't even know how truly terrible it can get. She's the cool one, the true Big Fish. She's that, but she never even bothers to mention it to them, because she's seen horror and she doesn't want to frighten them.

How do I know?

Because I'm invisible. I see it when they repeat their parents' politics and her face hardens, or when they won't shut up about "having fun" with someone and her dark eyes turn to stone, or when sexual assault is casually mentioned, and she breathes like she's just finished a marathon. I'm allowed to see it, because I am not someone who concerns her. I'm not a threat, because I don't exist.

Irony, isn't it? That the person she cannot see is the one who sees the most of her? I'm not sure I'd have it any other way, to be honest. I can't imagine what I'd feel inside if every time I looked at her, she tried to hide. I think I'd die if one day, she gave me that same fake smile she gives to others, when she's tired of entertaining them, and just wants them to vanish.

I'd rather notice that her fists clench when she hears racial slurs, as if she is building the strength to one day crush their faces. Or that when she is disengaged from a conversation she finds disgusting, she tucks her chin to her chest. Most people look up when they are trying to dismiss someone, as if looking for permission from God. I don't know why, but R looks down at her shoes or her crossed arms. It's like she's commanding her body to be still, because she is the one who sanctions her actions. I'd rather notice that she rolls her tongue piercing against the back of her teeth when she's being lectured, as if she wants to bite the speaker so badly, that she has to give her mouth something better to do. Or that when a boy thinks he can sexualize her, for a small moment, before she emasculates him, there's a spark of fear in her eye.

Or that sometimes . . . she disappears.

Where does she go?

I wondered myself, until I realized she was trying to be invisible like me. She's terrible at it. Being invisible is something you're born to.

We unseen children know the best places in our school to feel relaxed in our anonymity. We pass each other going to and from like ghosts. We never even look at one another on our way, and no one ever divulges the secret. Who would we tell?

I found R behind the maintenance shed. She was just breathing, her face tipped up to the sun and her eyes closed. But this little meditation had the ring of ritual to it—something in how she opened and closed her hands, tilted her head back and forth. This was like some kind of exercise to clear her thoughts, to get through another hour. Then she was back out again, scattering idiots left and right, engaging in every fight the way she always does.

It made me very happy to witness this. It gives me hope. If she needs to be invisible for a little while to calm down, then maybe being invisible isn't so bad after all.

"Come on, El," Riley whispered, shutting the laptop. "You're killing me."

The best protection was the kind that no one could see, and Riley had spent a long time carving hers out of pure bitterness, certain it was completely perfect and that no one would ever know there was a person underneath who could be harmed. But pain was pain.

Abuela had once told Riley that if she ate through good sense to fight the world, one day she was going to realize she was starving and alone. It had been said in a moment of uncharacteristic frustration from the old woman, during their spat when Riley announced she was going to flee New York with her father. Riley hadn't known what it meant at the time.

Suddenly, she did. It was El who'd taught her.

"Goddamn it, El."

How was it possible that a person could become more substantial by vanishing? The contradiction made no sense to Riley, and when things made no sense, she wanted to destroy them and build something more logical.

She wanted to find El and convince her that she had just as much value when she was visible.

When Sonny came on shift, Riley was waiting in the convenience store, sucking down a Slushee with her leather coat unzipped. She was running so hot that even an ice cream headache dare not trouble her. The boy behind the counter had begun to shrivel up beneath her gaze. He tossed his relief a warning glance.

Sonny's eyebrows went up, so finely plucked, her round face looked precisely like the emoji for surprise, if that emoji had ingested tranquilizers. "Can I help you?"

Riley bottomed out the drink like a shop vac picking up lug nuts. "My friend was in here yesterday around five or six. She had a backpack?"

Recognition slowly dawned on the clerk's face as she yawned. "Yeah, I remember her. Blonde. Seemed upset."

Blonde? Couldn't be. El had hair so dark it gleamed blue in the sunlight. Then again, both Mama and Rose had gone blonde. Suddenly, Riley knew exactly why this change might have happened. El was a minor.

She'd stolen Rose's identity.

"Yeah. There was a whole thing . . . on the train?" Riley dropped her cup in the trash can and sauntered toward the counter. Once there, she picked out a lighter from the rack and rolled it around in her fingers. "Did she tell you about it?"

Sonny frowned. "No. You the friend she messaged?"

Riley's teeth clamped down on what would have been a shout of happiness—El *did* have help! Knowing that there might be a plan, that there was perhaps a more experienced person guiding El, relieved her somewhat. But the truth was, Riley trusted no one but her father. She couldn't be sure that El was getting the right advice, unless it came from her.

"That's me! The friend! She didn't want me to worry, but . . . I worried."

Sonny chuckled. "I'd worry too. Girl looked frazzled. Mascara smeared all over her nose."

Riley nodded with a worldly frown, but her stomach was tightening. She wanted to know what on earth had transpired on that train. If any of those men had put hands on El . . .

"Now I'm trying to find her, but she didn't tell me what her new plans were before radio silence. She was supposed to stay on the train, but . . . well, that didn't work out."

Sonny shrugged and looked around with a slothful stare. "She asked about Greyhound stations. I told her the nearest town that had one was Beckley."

Springing up to her full height, Riley tried not to leap out the door before the clerk finished talking. "Where's Beckley?"

"About fifty miles southwest."

"Thanks!"

Riley was out the door in an instant. Aella's GPS determined the quickest driving route was to loop northeast and take the highway, but El wouldn't have backtracked. On foot, she could have walked straight across via Hinton on what seemed to be a two-lane road. It would give her better cover, more forests and terrain to camp in. There would have been no way to reach Beckley by nightfall.

Unless she hitchhiked.

"Oh god, El, please tell me you didn't hitchhike," she murmured, staring at the map.

If Riley drove the route, she could intercept the girl. If that wasn't the right path, she could double back via the other route and scour it. That circle made for about two hours of travel.

Two more hours of El walking alone. Two hours closer to darkness.

Riley put on the helmet. It was time to get moving.

16
In Sheep's Clothing

In as long as El could recall, she'd never needed an alarm clock, because the fear of Mama's intransigent meanness woke her in advance of every assault.

This morning, she opened her leaden eyelids to the sounds of birds. Sunlight dappled the walls of the tent, dancing in the wind in a dazzling display. She lay looking up at it, smiling at the rush of elation she felt. She had survived. Better than that . . . she was free, because if she could sleep in the wild and pass unscathed, then she was mistress of her own fate.

Her mother's warding and spells were completely undone, because the world no longer seemed quite so frightening.

Joy warmed her through and through.

Then she tried to move and remembered that everything came at a cost.

El had been smart to dress for the next day, because as she failed to sit up and crawl out of the tent, she knew she wouldn't have had the strength to do it now. Every single muscle in her back was either made of pure concrete, or had the elasticity of jello. Her skin was feverish and somehow hurt. Her joints were swollen to the point that it was almost impossible to bend her knees. She needed to stretch, but lacked the stamina to even move to do so.

And to top it all off, her stomach was completely empty. After twenty minutes of writhing and careful breathing, El managed to rifle through her pack for sustenance. She found some fruit leather, some freeze-dried veggies, and a pack of salami. At some point in the night, she'd slurped up all that was left in her bottle from the gas station. She would need fresh water and more food very soon.

El tucked the filtration unit and her bottles beneath her arms and made her way to the water's edge on her hands and knees. The instructions—when she could read the words blurring in and out of focus—said that for optimal results, she should filter it twice, and if fearing other contaminants, boil the results.

Looking around the area at all the signs of habitation she could see, she knew she could not start a fire, even though she had the things to do it.

Maybe she could just filter it a couple extra times?

The water looked like a thick pea soup. The whole area was mining country. She read the filtration instructions again, praying it could handle all the heavy metals she was about to put through it.

Finally able to stand, El walked out into the water. While the filter dripped, she reached for the sky, brought the clouds to meet the earth, performed every ballet pose she'd been taught, contorted and cracked herself in slow motion. Dizziness and darkened vision came and went. The blood began to move again, and the soreness to recede a bit. By the time she'd finished stocking up her water, she could walk without wincing.

El took a long while to figure out how to flatten the belligerent tent. The bedroll and sleeping bag were wound tight. She even made certain the area was free from every sign of her before she again lashed the pack to her back and climbed up to the railroad.

She turned on the cell's data and texted Oscar. He praised the gods that she was all right.

This is actually pretty easy. I'm really sore, but otherwise, it's working great to do things this way, but it might take me longer than I thought.

Girl, I would be like, where's the fucking Holiday Inn? You are the man.

By noon, however, El was truly rethinking her life. The heat was unbelievable. After dipping the handkerchief in the river and tying it around her neck to keep it cool, she finally resorted to taking off her shirt and wetting it. The water she'd bottled tasted like pond scum, even though it was mostly clear. Waves of hungry nausea were growing stronger by the mile. Her body hurt so badly that she'd had two pain relievers before she'd even finished her modest snack.

Oscar rolled his eyes at her with an emoji, when at last she checked in. *Why don't you just strip down and go for a swim?*

What if someone sees me?

OMG Snow . . . your bathing suit covers less than your underwear.

That's not true! My mother only ever let me wear a one piece with a skirt.

WTF? Is she scandalized by table legs too? Do we need to have a locksmith come when you get here to remove the fucking chastity belt?

She laughed in spite of her agony. *NO. But I'd take a therapist.*

Done and done! Get your skinny ass here so that I can fatten you up with free avocados, cheap whiskey, and give you all my stored-up hugs.

I need hugs. I think. There's not a lot of hugging in the Glasse household, but humans like that sort of thing, right?

Oscar called her. The conversation was full of soothing tones and comforting words. Somehow, he'd known she needed contact and was making it happen. Even after she'd hung up and stripped down, she was thanking providence that she'd managed to find such a wonderful friend.

Floating in the water was exactly what she needed. Her legs touched more than one undulating form she would rather not think about, but the loss of gravity and the cold was divine. She'd never gone into the pool much at home. Somehow in her mind it was linked to being the wrong shape or too pale, her sister's lengthy physical training, or her mother's lavish summer binge-drinking parties. This was something completely different. She rolled onto her back and closed her eyes, content to drift in the current for a bit.

What did it matter how fast she moved? No one was timing her. She was in just as much danger here as at Oscar's house. The warmth of the day ate through the tension in her shoulders. Her head began to clear. She used the water's drag to help her work the vigor back into her frame, and when she'd finally gotten her body under control, she redressed and went back to walking.

It was mindless, in a landscape that hardly ever changed. At the first town, she ducked off and wandered as far from the rails as she dared, buying fresh supplies at the nearest store. By the next check-in, her limbs felt human and though she was weak, she was fed and moving at an excellent pace.

"Send me pictures! I wanna see this fucking state," he said when she called him later to check in. When he received them, Oscar let out a whistle. "It's like really green!"

"Yeah, but there's all these abandoned buildings and stuff. I've seen about ten people wandering the tracks like me, most of them missing teeth."

"Mmm... Snowy, you better fuck yourself up a bit before they do."

El frowned. "What does that mean?"

"Like, smear dirt on yourself. Mess up your hair. Look strung out. Get the backpack a bit grubby. You gotta look like you've got nothing, or someone is gonna target you."

She halted abruptly. That hadn't occurred to her. She'd been walking this whole way in brand-new everything, newly bleached hair, white teeth and perfectly manicured nails because her mind had been trained to see always looking perfect as the best option. Mama had drilled it into her, that to get what she wanted in life, she had to *look respectable.* But in this environment, she was not a tramp and it was far too obvious.

"Oh, my gosh."

"You mean, Oh fuck, right?" Oscar chuckled.

"Oh... fuck. You're right. Wow. I'm so bad at this!"

"Stop changing clothes. Get dirty. Fuck the people who look sideways at you. Girl, you gotta be mean! You gotta look like you're on a trek into destruction, not a fucking cake walk."

She tossed her pack down, sure to roll it in as much gravel as she could. Plopping down beside it, she leaned back against a tree. "Riley would have told me to scowl more."

Oscar let out a gasp. "Is that her name? Is it Riley? Oh my god, I have to tell my boyfriend."

El snorted. His excitement was adorable. She still couldn't come to terms with the idea that she was important to anyone, let alone that she might be somewhat famous in some circles for who she was, not for her last name.

"Yeah... her name is Riley."

"She sounds like a bad bitch. I imagine her like... as an Amazon, you know? Like strong and lean. With a bared breast and like... a headdress."

Riley's grinning face and wicked glimmering gaze filled her thoughts. She closed her eyes on the image and sighed happily. "Riley is . . . Not that tall, actually. A little taller than me. Curvier than me . . . just . . . gorgeous. She's got dark auburn hair that she dyes all these colors. Her skin looks like . . . like . . . I don't know, like sandalwood. She has freckles all over her face and the backs of her arms. Oscar . . ."

"Girl, you are so in love."

Suddenly, her heart fluttered. "Oh my god, I just realized something."

"What?"

"I've never said it aloud. I've never said what I think of her with my own voice."

"Sing it, girl."

"I love her. She is the most amazing person I've ever met. She's brave. She's funny. She pushes through things that would petrify me. She's unbelievably smart. She's complicated and strong. She's just . . . she's just . . ." El threw up her hands and let them fall. "Amazing."

Oscar was giggling. "Now that is the kind of preaching I can handle. Come on, Snow. Keep marching."

"You're right. Okay, I'm up." She took in a deep breath and held it until her mind began to float. Finally, she let it out in a giddy chuckle. "Oscar . . . thank you for being my friend. Without you, this wasn't possible."

"Shut up. You got this. I'm just here to feed you guacamole."

Laughing until tears fell, El bid him goodbye.

Somewhere, about a mile outside of the nearest town, El knew she had to make camp. The sun had sunk below the hills, the sky was draped in twilight and mauve clouds. This time, she refilled the water and took twice as much ibuprofen, anticipating tomorrow's aches and pains. With the oath that the next day would begin with a swim, she crawled into her tent and was unconscious before she could blink.

In the dead of night, she startled awake. A bright light was punching through the dark and stabbing at her bleary eyes. El scrabbled upright as a man's voice silenced the nearby cicadas.

"Hello? Hello in there!"

El swallowed hard, her mind reviewing every scenario she'd contemplated for some inkling of what to do.

"This is private property. Can you come out, please?"

The accent had a patina to it. El put the age as being greater than her own. Her heart beating fiercely, she stuck her head out of the tent flap. A flashlight pointed right at her eyes, blinding her in a painful burst.

"I didn't realize. I'm sorry." She blinked furiously and shielded her gaze with a hand. Against the pitch of the woods, a large figure could be seen. Bits and pieces came into focus—a beard, a pair of large boots. "I'll pack up."

"Well, miss . . ." The man ran a hand over his face and seemed to be considering her. "I've already called the police."

El's blood turned to ice in her veins. "Oh, no! Please don't! I'm so sorry! I'll leave! You don't have to report me!"

He grumbled, but it seemed as if she might be able to persuade him. "Are you alone?"

"Yes. I'm sorry. I was just tired. I can go."

"No . . . hell . . . no. It's okay. Look . . . the cops are gonna come whatever, so . . . Why don't you come back to my house? You can talk to them there. Maybe we can clear this up. I know most of them anyway."

El crawled out of the tent. He dropped the light as if he'd just realized it bothered her. Finally, she could make him out—overalls and a ball cap, a utility belt and workman's boots. From head to toe, he was every inch the blue-collar sort. His brown beard and hair were shot through with gray, and a pack of cigarettes peeped out from the bib at his chest.

"I don't want to cause trouble."

"What's your name?"

El began to say her own name, but at the last instant, remembered herself. "Rose."

"Are you a runaway?"

Her eyes fell to her feet, her mantra a whisper against the prospect of dealing with the police. She was chasing freedom, not running away. She had to keep hold of that. "No. I just . . . I like to wander."

He chewed his lip and then ticked the torch in a gesture. "Come on. I'll get you a drink. You can talk to the deputy and sort this out."

El wondered if she could just leave now. He couldn't stop her legally, could he? But if he told the police she'd run, they would surely go looking for her. She knew they had jurisdictions, and that she might be able to make it to a county line, but she had no idea where those lines were, and the authorities had radios.

To her sleepy mind and sore body, the only reasonable option was to explain.

The man began to walk back into the brush. She took one step, before she thought of her bag and grabbed for it. The tent and sleeping stuff she could come back for if she managed her way out of this, but the bag had her life in it. It couldn't leave her body.

As she followed her guide back into the woods, she wondered if she'd hidden her true identification well enough. She didn't know if the police were allowed to search her pack, but she'd done as was suggested on the websites she'd found, folding her birth certificate, her passport, her ID all up inside of plastic sleeves, and stuffing them into a metal water bottle. If they found these items, everyone would know she wasn't actually an adult, and most importantly, they'd call her parents.

The flashlight fell on a fallen tree. The man held out a hand for her. "You gotta climb over top. Sorry."

Without thinking, she took his hand. The fingers closed on her wrist tightly. She had an instant only, to look up at him in question and see the hunger there. With a single blink, he yanked her arm nearly out of the socket. Gravity caught her. She hit her knees, one colliding with something very sharp. A shriek was pulled from her, but then he had hold of her pack, and a hand around her face.

El's thoughts had no substance to them, no words or reason. Without them, she could do nothing but react. At once, her arms and legs were numb, her ears deaf to practically every sound but his haggard breathing.

"Move!" he growled.

Hurled into the dark, her knee refused to take her weight. The pack made her top heavy and sent her end over end down an incline. At the bottom, she staggered, but the leg was worse than she'd realized, and the man was much too fast.

Suddenly, she was back on her feet, lifted bodily by her pack straps. Jostled on, she searched the night for any way out, her mind fighting in broken reason and frantic patterns. The woods were a wall all around her, the white glow of the flashlight darting about like a menacing crowd. She tripped, finding a set of steps. It was a building of some kind. The doorway was black as oil inside, but he seemed to know exactly where they were going.

Like a clap of thunder, the words returned. Sense spiked through her entire frame like a shock. Life came back to her muscles.

He took hold of her again, and lifted her bodily. El knew that if she went inside, she might never come back out again. With a shriek, she kicked her legs out, bracing her feet against the doorjamb. The wood was soft beneath her boots, and her leg, bloody from knee to ankle, could not hold them in stasis for long.

With a ferocious snarl, he tugged her backward and threw her into the darkness. El hit the ground and skidded into a pile of garbage. She gasped for air, then lay still. His boots came closer across the planking, thumping in a self-congratulatory swagger.

"You sure look pretty," he crooned.

El closed her eyes. For some reason, she could see Riley leaning against the wall of the maintenance shed, her face upward in sunlight, her fists like steel clamps, her teeth grinding whatever grist the stupid boys had given her. What had she been doing? Why had she wandered off alone so many times a day? Riley was pulling the machinery back from chaos, assembling plans to undo magic. To her, anger was just fuel. Fear was raw energy that had to be channeled.

When he laughed, it was like a goad. Her perfect rendering of Riley opened dark eyes and stared right at her in command.

The nausea intensified, but her muscles coiled.

He thrust out a foot and kicked El onto her side. A bright light flashed and flashed, picking at her retinas. Blinded again, her other senses came to the fore. As he knelt down beside her and fumbled lustily with the clips at her chest, El could smell his stink, judge his distance by the eager warmth coming off him.

El's fingers were roaming too, and as it had been in the bright glow of high noon, Tizóna was hot to the touch.

17

Fated

When Mama Glasse answered the phone, she sounded as if she'd already had a few cocktails. Riley had a bit of difficulty wading through the accent turned to molasses by a thick tongue.

"Consider this your progress call."

"Well?"

Well? That was all she had to say? Not *Is my daughter dead*? Not *Please say you've found her*! Just *Well*? Riley's temper was itching at her eyelids as she sat breathing, her chin tucked to her chest.

"I have leads and I'm working on them, but I need a photo of El."

"Her name is El-ear-uh. Say it right, you twit."

Riley narrowed her eyes at the pavement. This was going to be complicated—playing Mama's assumptions out while still doing what she needed to do. "I don't have time or energy to pronounce that stupid fucking name. I'm R. She's L. Now are you gonna listen to me, or do I need to just ride home?"

The silence was a heavy one. At last, the woman seemed to sober up a bit. "I have a few school pictures. I'll email them to you."

"Send a few of Rose too."

Mama let out an undignified snort. "I beg your pardon?"

"Something tells me you don't know what that phrase actually means."

"I don't know *what* kind of trashy—"

"Don't finish that sentence."

Why was it, that once people found out she was a lesbian, her entire existence spun in the orbit of deviant sex addiction? The idea that lesbians, or gays, or bi people, or trans people thought about sex any more often than a cis-het person was ridiculous. And if they did, it was because the rest of the world made it such a big deal that they had to constantly think about it. Their entire existence and character were suddenly distilled down into their sexuality, and they were denied any identity outside of that. It was the worst thing to do to a person, but folks did it without a moment's thought and insisted that members of the community play along.

That was some fucked-up magical thinking.

"Look, lady—" Riley squeezed the grip and torqued her wrist "—can we not address your obsession with gay sex? I don't have time to reeducate you on what *queer* actually means, you ignorant hillbilly *twit*."

"*What* did you just say to me?"

Oh no . . . the dreaded *H* of perdition. Riley rolled her eyes, but knew it was time to dial it back a bit.

"I told you I'd find your daughter. I didn't say I'd take your bullshit. You want the job done, you call the person who can do it. You don't call someone to roll on their back while you kick them. So either you behave like a professional, or the contract terminates. I may not be as rich as you, but I'm not so poor that I need your money."

She could practically hear Mama grinding her teeth. "Tell me *why* you want the pictures of Rose."

This could be dangerous, but Riley had to give if she expected to take. Chances were, if those men had tracked El to the train, they knew she had changed her hair. They might have gotten the tip from the station attendant or CCTV footage. "I think El might have changed her appearance. I need one with makeup and blonde hair."

To her surprise, Mama let out a chuckle that she drowned in a glass of ice cubes. "Well, they were right then. I wondered why she all of a sudden wanted Rose to teach her about cosmetics. God, people are going to think she's a street walker."

Riley's mouth fell open. This woman had coached Rose through every one of her beauty pageants. If El had decided to look like her sister . . . was Mama suggesting Rose looked like a prostitute, or that El did for trying? Either way, it was fucked up. It seemed unbelievable a mother would say such things out loud.

She checked her phone. All her apps were running.

"Rethinking the objectification of your daughter for the sake of a cash prize, eh Mama?"

"Watch it! Without those scholarship programs, Rose wouldn't be able to go to college."

"You guys are rich enough to afford college, but yeah, keep telling yourself that you're totally *not* backing a culture that teaches women their only ticket to the good life is their tits."

"Rose is a communications major. She's not curing cancer."

For the first time, it occurred to Riley that perhaps Rose had *given* El the idea to impersonate her. If she had, maybe she was in on the plan. If that was true, then Riley might worry even less, because she would be assured that El had a safety net.

The glass clinked as Mama mulled her wine with muddled thoughts. "I'll email you the pictures."

"Good."

"So what lead are you chasing, then?"

Riley couldn't contain her sarcasm as she dismounted the bike and switched to the handset. "Sure, I'm gonna tell you, and you're gonna pass it to the other guy, because you'd rather *they* win, right? Because fuck that dyke, right?"

Mama took the high road in a long-suffering tone so lofty it sent Riley's eyes skyward. "I'm sorry you have that opinion. I don't hate gays. You're living in sin. It's my spiritual duty to tell you that."

"How benevolent of you." Riley ran her tongue over the inside of her teeth. That any person could apply a negative judgment to someone else's life and then say it *wasn't* being used to discriminate was completely batshit. Doing that was the opposite of coexistence, and coexistence was what had made laws and rules about morality necessary in the first place. It was irrational! She was five minutes from ending this entire thing in one string of swear words.

Mama was oblivious. "Elyrra *believes* she's a lesbian. The more I think about it, the more I agree that you might be just the . . . uh . . . *dyke* to do the job. Not to mention, that if *you* bring her back, she might rethink trusting *you people*."

Skin crawling, Riley stowed the helmet on the chain and locked her bike in place. "So it's fine that I'm living in sin as long as it gets you what you want, huh?"

"I'm praying for you too."

"I'm good, thanks. Your god can pretty much kiss my ass if *you people* are the welcoming committee."

Mama began to speak, but Riley was finally at the end of her tether. There hadn't been any clause in their contract that told her she would be dismissed for being a jerk, so why not live by the letter of the arrangement?

"Send me those pictures, because I need to use them before this place closes. I'll email you in a couple hours with more news."

She hung up. It took a few minutes to calm her nerves. People always commented on how absolutely stoic and severe she looked in a fight. They didn't see the aftermath, when her knees went weak. They didn't see the turmoil inside or the rage that just kept getting in the way of all logical thought. To everyone else, she was a badass, but really, that stillness just came from the PTSD of learning to recede inward when someone was trying to hurt her.

Her phone let out a bing, and she jumped nearly five inches. The pictures went directly into her photos file.

Beckley's Greyhound station belied the town's smallness—modern glass and a lofted ceiling. Riley heckled the agent only for a moment. The man said he'd never seen the girl, nor checked in anyone going by the name Rose Glasse. When he asked to see her ID, she walked away.

The whole way into town, Riley had scanned the roadside for signs of El. At a few steep inclines, she'd even stopped and looked down, just to be certain. Either El had not taken this route, or she'd already gotten on a bus.

Riley sat on a retainer wall and thought for a moment. She could wait here and see if El showed up, or she could drive back to the last place she knew the girl had been, via the other route. If El had already made it to Beckley and was waiting somewhere in town to board a later bus, they'd miss each other, but if she was still en route, their paths would cross.

It came down to El's safety. She was in less danger on the bus than on the street. So if they missed each other now, at least Riley could follow in her wake, assured she was with people who would call the cops if something happened.

As she drove back to Alderson, however, and found no trace of El, Riley began to question her thought process. By the time she made it back to the gas station, the sun was nearing the horizon. The idea of El having to spend one more night alone drove Riley to distraction. She parked the bike and didn't even bother to lock it up.

To her astonishment, a different clerk sat behind the counter. Flustered, Riley took a few moments to get over her confusion.

"Wasn't . . . wasn't Sonny supposed to be working right now?"

The man shook his head. "Took off early for her daughter's graduation. She'll probably sleep through it though, knowing her."

Graduation. Her own graduation was in a week. One more normal thing in which Riley had no interest. It seemed such a silly tradition. She had to stop herself from being annoyed that anyone would halt her progress to attend a bunch of boring speeches and watch someone get a meaningless piece of paper. She couldn't blame anyone for sleeping through that.

"Do you know if she'll be back on tomorrow?"

"Yup. We switched. She's on at eight."

Riley left the station and stood staring out at the river. She felt adrift. Usually, plans just sort of sprang out at her, but nothing presented itself. She was missing something, pacing in the parking lot, uselessly churning up gravel.

Walking across the bridge, Riley went to the gazebo and put her elbows on the railing. Reading through the several articles written about the train fiasco, she tried to piece together what she knew. The train had been stopped, and El must have been terrified. She somehow escaped, disabled the SUV, and then made her way to the gas station. She'd asked about buses, but if those men had found her on the train, surely they'd also be looking on the buses.

Well . . . once they got out of jail.

If *Riley* were on the run, she'd have asked the clerk all the wrong questions, just to divert anyone who followed behind, interrogating the people she'd met.

Maybe El hadn't gone to the bus station at all. But if not the station, then what was her plan?

Riley watched the sky shift through the rainbow and felt her spirits sinking with the sun. There was no way she'd locate El before sundown. Defeat pressed her to the concrete. She put her face in her hands.

Her phone beeped. It was a text message from her father asking why she hadn't called. Riley tapped the Call button and put it on speaker.

"Hi, Dad."

"You don't sound too good, Rye-baby. Haven't found her, huh?"

"No. I have some ideas, but . . . I have to wait for someone to come back on shift. This is killing me, Dad. It's getting dark."

"I hear you. You can only do what you can do. So go do that like a boss. Eat some dinner. Get some rest. Try to get your head on straight so you can do right by her."

Tears welled in Riley's eyes. She fought them back. She'd been alone before, but this was different. Someone might be depending on her, and she was failing. If anyone understood that feeling, it was her father, and she could hear it so easily in his deep voice.

"What if something happens to her, Dad?"

"Then you deal with that. Come on, Rye. Calm down. Prepare. Ducks in a row so you can shoot 'em all down."

She nodded to herself. One good sigh helped compress the emotion. "You're right. I'm just . . . really tired."

"And you know you're really close, but you still can't reach her."

"That too." Riley rubbed her temples where the new helmet pressed in. "I also have this terrible feeling like I need to find her *now*. You know? Like something bad has happened."

He let out a noise. "It did. She's probably camped out in the bushes by the side of the road wishing she'd thought this through a little better. Go get a hotel room. Take a shower. You can't ride safely if you're sore, *Tizóna*. You know that."

"Yeah. I do."

"Talk to me about how you're feeling."

She sniffled. "About what?"

He made a sardonic noise. "I've been reading that website same as you. I agree with everything she's said, but that's because to me, you're the most beautiful thing in the world. But how do you feel about it?"

Riley tipped back and pinched the bridge of her nose. "It doesn't mean anything, dad. It's just . . . it's just a girl daydreaming about a life bigger than the one she has. Once her life grows, you know . . . she'll forget all about it."

"You really don't have a good gauge of how you seem to others, do you?"

"What's that mean? I'm a bitch. I come off like a bitch."

"Rye . . . *mija* . . . you don't have resting bitch face. You have resting warrior face. The only people who would call you a bitch are the boys too stupid to know they're about to swallow some teeth."

She couldn't help but laugh, but it wasn't true. None of it was true. "Dad . . . That's not the real me."

"Yes, it is. You just haven't figured out who the enemy is and why you're so angry with them. You'll get there. Warriors have fear too. They just keep going in spite of it. I think—"

"Dad—"

"Listen to me. I think that you should give this girl some credit, because she may think the armor is . . . uh . . . sexy, but I think she can see exactly what you're protecting and why you're hurting. You need someone who can get into those places with you, someone you'll let in."

Tears were freshly wandering down her face, but she was smiling. Anyone who ever looked at her father and saw an ignorant hillbilly was scum, because to her, there was no wiser philosopher in the world.

"You don't think it's unfair to dump my shit at her door?"

He chuckled. "Is it any more unfair than scaring the shit outta you by running away?"

"That's square. I'll think about it."

"Happy Birthday, sweetheart. I never imagined you becoming an adult like this, but yeah . . . I guess I should have. I love you."

Most of the night, she tossed and turned on her cheap hotel mattress, staring into a popcorn ceiling, looking for patterns. She sought insight in reading El's website, but that only made the anxiety worse, because more and more she saw the beauty in El's mind and how tragic it would be to lose that. Riley could not escape the sense that some danger would befall El, and that it would all be her fault, for not being fast enough, or smart enough, or strong enough.

At six in the morning, she awoke from a horrible nightmare, her pillow wet with tears and perspiration. She'd been in the hospital room again, sitting on that maroon chair that was so uncomfortable, watching her mother slip away, not fully understanding why she could not be fixed.

Some things cannot be fixed, they would say to her. Some things cannot be prevented. Some things just have to happen, and because they "have to happen," they must be fated. Meant to be.

Riley got out of bed and stood in the humid breeze of the ancient air conditioner, staring down at the railroad tracks—a reliable path carved out of the ground, static and unchanging for a century and a half. El had taken this route because it was tried and true, and one of the few courses open to her. One mishap threw her off that track, and now, she truly was gone.

As much as Riley hated the idea of fate, she had to admit, it made things a hell of a lot easier.

At eight o'clock, she was back at the gas station, occupying the space between the door and the padlocked ice cooler. When Sonny spotted her, she looked as if she'd been startled awake and hated the idea.

"Not in Beckley, huh?"

Riley shook her head. She hadn't put on makeup this morning. She wanted the woman to see the dark circles. "I've been up all night trying to find her."

Sonny shifted on her feet and searched the horizon line, clutching a huge energy drink in one hand. "I hope she's okay."

"I'm sorry to bother you again, but I have to ask if there's anything I'm missing."

She nodded and unlocked the station door. "After you left, I thought of something. Figured if you didn't come back, it wasn't important."

Riley followed her inside, arms crossed. "Here I am."

"Here you are." Sonny went about a few small tasks as she talked, her tone a laconic drawl that made Riley want to take a pack of the wakefulness pills and shove them down her throat. "I think, maybe, she might have decided to turn hobo. You know? Walk the tracks and catch the freight trains as they move through the curves. They have to slow down then, because of safety and all that. We used to hop on them all the time when I was a kid. Man, I miss having that kind of energy."

The epiphany sent her bolt upright. El hadn't left the tracks! She'd just taken them in a different way. But where the hell had she been going?

"Any idea which way she was going?"

"Mmm . . . Charleston, I think. I told her that was the nearest bus depot along the train route. I think she said she was looking for something along the train. Sorry, I have a toddler. I don't sleep much, and my memory is pretty shitty."

Adrenaline titrated her blood for action. This time, before Riley went after any more wild geese, she made sure to ask after Sonny's contact information.

"If you don't hear from me, everything is fine." She pulled a Red Bull from the cooler and paid for it in cash, meeting the woman's eye with a grim stare. "If *anyone* else comes by, like say . . . maybe some guys who look a bit hard?"

The half-asleep surprised emoji face returned. "Yeah?"

"Tell them she went to Beckley. Tell them . . . I don't know, lie?"

"Who are they?"

"The guys who blocked the train."

Riley left her with her mouth hanging open. A quick scan of the regional map showed a triple stripe of railroad tracks, river, and road, running more or less parallel for miles and miles. Riley directed Aella slowly, casting her eyes to the tracks every few seconds.

On foot, El could have made it about ten miles the first night, and possibly about twenty-five or thirty the second day, if she could manage that. At the ten-mile mark, Riley exited the road, and just after a trestle bridge, brought her bike directly onto the track.

Keeping her attention divided between safety and the search, Riley counted miles. Worry set in as she neared the twenty-mile mark. All at once, an olive-colored shape formed in the greenery. A shape rather like a dome.

Letting out a yelp, Riley shoved the bike up and over the rail. Skidding to a halt on the gravel incline, the bike wouldn't stand upright and had to be propped against a tree. Calling out for El, she crashed through the bushes. The tent was wide open, sleeping bag still in it. No other trace of the girl could be found.

As the true horror cast its shadow over her, Riley's knees buckled. El wouldn't have gone without packing these things. Even a slow-moving train and a finite window to jump aboard wouldn't induce that kind of stupidity in someone as circumspect as El.

No, this was a sign that Riley had been right. Something *had* happened. The worse part was that she had no idea how to proceed. Her genius was tapped out, and El was nowhere to be found.

Riley finally bowed her head and cried.

18
Unanswered Questions

"**S**top it," she said to herself. Riley repeated it over and over, her entire torso bobbing back and forth over her drawn up knees. But the tears wouldn't stop coming and shudders hit her in intense waves. "Stop it! Fucking stop! Focus. Focus, Riley. Focus!"

She pinched the skin around her wrists as hard as she could. The sharp pain drew her thoughts inward. Riley closed her eyes on the tent.

"Think. Six questions. Answer all of the ones you can."

Whatever had happened to El had happened *after* she'd camped, but *before* she'd risen fully, or she would have packed the tent. That put the *when* in the last eleven hours.

Riley got onto her hands and knees and slowly combed the area around the tent in increasingly large circles. Finally, her eyes fell upon some flattened leaves and snapped twigs—signs of foot traffic. The tent was immaculate, no rips, tears, or signs of struggle. Even the sleeping bag was neatly laid out as if El hadn't yet crawled in. If she'd been removed by force, the kidnapper would have come back for the tent, to make sure all proof of her existence was erased. All this combined with the missing pack led Riley to believe that El had walked out of the camp under her own power.

The very thought chilled Riley so fully that she instinctively tugged her motorcycle jacket closer around her.

She'd answered the *when* and the *how*. Now for the *where*. Crouching over the almost invisible trail, she followed it for as far as she could. It terminated abruptly in a fallen tree, as if El had been forced over the log. Orienting herself against the river, Riley formed a mental gridwork. During search and rescue operations on TV, the authorities always searched in a systematic pattern. She was going to have to follow suit, even though her hands were again shaking, and her mind was frantic.

Bugs whined around her head. Perspiration dripped from her face as she clambered around the fallen tree searching for the trail. Mud and moss and cobwebs caked her leathers as she knelt looking for footprints. Her hair was plastered to her face and decorated with bits of lichen. After almost thirty minutes, she gave up.

El had to have been *going* somewhere.

But there was nothing for at least a mile—no city, no tiny town, not even a gas station. Fanning outward, Riley moved away from the water, and back toward the tracks. About two hundred yards in the direction she'd ridden, Riley's boot struck a large rock. Shaky limbs could not hold her. She tumbled forward with an oath, putting a gloved hand out to stop herself. What she clutched was a block of chiseled sandstone.

No town. No buildings. But here was an entire pile of precut stone, growing saplings in the woods.

Her head snapped up. All at once, Riley was back on her feet, prowling around the pile in concentric arcs. Cutting through a particularly dense wall of brush, Riley shoved an entire branch the thickness of her arm aside. To her absolute shock, she was looking at a chimney stack, crusted in greenery.

Ducking beneath the foliage, Riley followed what she could now see was an ancient wall. The jungle opened up as she crept around the building—someone had been clearing the area around the small A-frame. Piles of brush and shriveled vine had been collected and cast aside. Rotten lumber was stacked beneath a shattered window, while a fresh pile of timber sat beneath a tarp. A new set of wooden stairs were propped up to the front door, though no actual door hung in the jamb.

But there, at eye level, was a small, muddy boot print.

Riley's organs squirmed and goose bumps rose. If this was the *where* of El's latest vanishing act, it had the instant creep-factor that put all of her instincts on alert.

She stepped back. It was dark inside and though she could see the shady forest through the window across from the portal, there was no telling what dangers existed. Taking her phone from its holster at her waist, Riley called up the camera. With her back to the wall, she fired a few flash pictures up through the windows and door.

The pictures revealed a vacant space with external walls of laid stone. What walls had not begun to crumble were covered with graffiti. The ground was littered with debris and stripped down to the sub-flooring. Garbage was in piles, some of it—like the box of washing powder—apparently dating from as far back as the fifties. An ancient skirt front kitchen sink was against the far wall, and a pile of tools rested beside a hole in the floor. Strangely incongruous, a perfectly serviceable table and metal bedstead sat in one corner.

Riley's heart beat so fast that her necklace swung in the air like a pendulum. It dipped forward and back as if to coax her in, reading her body and the map as if scrying.

Inching up the stairs, she swiped the phone's glow from left to right. Riley searched the detritus on the ground, pushing bits of plaster caked wallpaper and tin cans to the side with a careful toe. Something glittered in the corner of her eye. Riley brought the light around swiftly.

Beneath the leg of the table was a dull gunmetal sheen against the plywood subfloor. She knew that shape at once, but even as she bent down to retrieve the knife, she wanted it not to be real.

From point to hinge, *Tizóna* was smeared with oxidized blood.

Riley's mind fell silent.

From the top of her head to the tip of her toes, a painful tingling began. Tunnel vision set in as she stared at the blade. Muscles locked in place as her body went through the stages of terror. Riley could not focus her eyes on the brown smudges or the blurred droplets of goo that spattered the ground around her feet. Every creak of the ancient structure became a shout. The hot summer wind in the trees outside was suddenly roaring. The cold shadows burned like ice.

Intuition let free a surge of painful sensations as a tiny shuffling filled her ears. Riley turned, limbs aching, but eyes cutting through the dark.

A male shape blocked the doorway—weary from an apparently sleepless night, his overalls stained with a dozen shades of rust. His pallor was bad, his eyes were sunken and furtive, his breathing was ragged. Around his upper arm was a wad of scarlet fabric, tied with a handkerchief of deep green.

El's favorite color.

Their eyes connected in an instant of electric fire. Riley knew him for what he was, and he knew she did. Her weight shifted and daylight gleamed off the weapon in her hand. Before her right leg could sweep back, he was hurling his bulk through the portal at her. She had only a heartbeat to ground herself.

Everything slowed. Each tiny movement of his seemed exaggerated. He tilted his head as he lunged, his nostrils flaring as he glared at her. He was tipped forward, his balance off. He wanted to take out her legs. Once he had her on her back, he'd try to pin her.

Without an instant to spare, Riley propped her boot on the edge of the metal bed frame and jumped upward. He crashed full speed into the table, knocking it into the far wall. Spinning, she dropped onto his back and lifted the knife, but she had underestimated the strength of his temper. He rolled, tossing her easily to one side. *Tizóna* flew from her grip and skittered to the pile of tools, but she didn't focus on it. Riley kicked away as he grabbed for her, and staggering up, found the first thing that would fit in her hand. She swung it with all her might.

The sound of the small shovel smacking him across the face was like a bell ringing. He toppled, letting out a grunt. His bulk hit the floor so hard the planking quivered beneath her boots. Riley heard a shriek of fury and realized only as she fell on him with blow after blow, that it was she who had made it.

The tool leaped from her fingers. It wasn't enough. She cast around for the knife. With it in her hand again, she approached the body, kicking it in the legs for good measure. Fingers like steel cords, she grabbed the handkerchief around his arm and yanked it free. The blood that had seeped through it had turned the hunter green into a deep burgundy. There was no denying it—it *was* El's scarf, the one Riley had helped her choose.

Her glove squeaked as she clenched the knife. Her breath came in hisses through clenched teeth. Her hips and shoulders squared, Riley dared him to test her. His body was completely still, a deep gash oozing crimson at his brow. Riley put a foot on his hand and stepped down. He remained senseless.

If El was hurt . . .

Wrath twisted in her flesh. Fury like none she'd ever felt possessed her. This person, whoever he was, had dared to touch El and he was going to pay for it. No one would miss him. She could leave him there to rot and no one would ever know she'd been there.

Riley lifted the knife. Even as the idea formed in her mind, she knew it had been the truth of her last few days—she wanted the promise of El, and without her, her life had no direction to it. Without El, she didn't really care what happened to her. She planted her boot in the small of his back and put the knife to his throat.

A shrill mechanical chord sang out, shattering Riley's state of mind like the most fragile of things. In an instant, *Tizóna* was forgotten for her phone, resting on the disgusting mattress. The words danced as Riley scanned them. It was the answer she'd needed far more than any other.

I trust R. I know that she would fight and she would probably win, because that is what the world has built her to do, but I don't want that for her. I want her to find as much peace in me as I find in her. I want her to have the chance to fight for everyone, not just some stupid girl whose mother is a monster.

That's what I want for her. Until I can give her that, I'll keep working. Until I am a person who can fight for her, I'll get stronger.

A sob echoed in the tiny room. Riley looked at the shallowly breathing body sprawled beside her. It stank like the swamp and rancid meat, dark circles colored the shirt beneath the armpits, a layer of mud coated the cuffs of the pant legs.

Everything about him disgusted her, because looking at him, Riley was uncertain if she had really ever known herself fully.

His wallet was a large bulk in his back pocket. Riley liberated it and the phone on the other hip. The driver's license gave what appeared to be a local address. The ancient smartphone was protected only by the birthday of its owner. She rifled through his life, from his banking information to his text messages. As the latest picture he'd taken appeared on the screen, Riley's thoughts again collapsed on themselves beneath the weight of her rage.

It was El's face, covered with tears, dirt, and absolute dread.

The next thing Riley knew, she was gasping in the doorway, blinded by sunlight. Her leg hurt so badly she could barely walk, and she knew she had kicked the unconscious man several more times.

A phone in each hand, Riley stumbled away from the building and into the tree line. A choice in each hand, she dropped to her knees.

"Oh, my god," she whispered, scrolling through his pictures as if watching countless horror movies unfold. El's wasn't the only face—women, a teenaged boy—and prominent in the background of every image was the abandoned building. "Oh, holy shit. Oh, fuck."

Riley dropped the device as if bitten. She'd always known such people existed. She'd practically grown up knowing it, but it had always been tempered by all the good she'd seen. In that moment, beauty was overshadowed. The world was a horrible, malicious place, full of disgusting people who clawed at each other to get what they wanted. Hungers and lusts drove society. There was nothing at all redeemable about any of it.

She lifted her phone to her ear. When she heard her father's low voice, the barriers broke and everything she'd been holding within burst free. It was haphazard, the facts pieced together in a collage of atrocities and outrage. He interrupted seldom, understanding her slurred speech without much effort.

"Dad . . . No one will care! No one would even know!" Her voice sounded alien to her, so high-pitched and hysterical. "Oh, my god, her face! Dad please. Jesus, what the fuck did he do? I can't—"

"Stop," he commanded. The word was sharp, steely in a way it never had been. "Right now. Stop. Breathe."

A wave of shivers wracked her. Her teeth were chattering, and nausea was threatening to punctuate their conversation. She did as she was told, sucking down air and shoving it back out again.

"Are you *physically* hurt?"

"No. I'm fine. I knocked him out."

"Where is El?"

Riley sobbed, her words garbled. "I don't know, but she's safe."

"How can you be sure?"

"She just answered my message on the blog."

"Could that be timed?"

"No. It doesn't work that way. Dad, he doesn't deserve to live. I'm going to—"

"You're going to listen to me, do you understand?"

The shaking stopped. Her throat sore, Riley knew she couldn't speak even if she wanted to.

"I know you, Riley. I *know* you." There was desperation there, but this was the voice of a man who had stared down his own demons. He wasn't afraid of hers. Her father was never afraid. He would say what she needed to hear. "I know how angry you are, because I feel it too, but that's not how we handle anger. Anger is blind, it's deaf, it's senseless. You know that, baby. Say you know it."

Tears slid off her chin. "I . . . know it."

"There are pictures, you said. On his phone."

"Yeah. A few different people. Dad, they're all so afraid—"

He let out a growl. "Send them to your email. Right now."

"Dad, I have to stop him!"

"No, you *don't*! That is *not* your job. You have *one* goal right now, and that is staying safe so that you can find that girl! Think of how afraid she is. Think of what she's been through. You have to find her. That is who you are."

"But—"

"No! *Tizóna* . . ." Emotions flooded his throat until his voice was barely treading above the misery. "I know you don't want to make the same mistakes as me. Don't let this person you don't even know tell you who you're going to be for the rest of your life. This isn't about who or what he is. This moment is yours. His came and went. He made his decision as soon as he put hands on another person."

She sniffed, wiping snot across her face. She'd never wanted to ever disappoint him, but there it was, in the soft undertone of his bearlike rumble.

"I'm . . . I'm sorry, Dad."

"Honey, no . . . I'm the sorry one. I'm not with you and I should be. I should be."

She shook her head and gathered enough strength to get to her feet. She wasn't a child. She didn't need him to fight her battles for her. She had grown out of that a long time ago, and every individual who got in her way was going to learn that. They were going to regret the person they'd made when they stepped to this bitch.

"No, Dad. This is mine. I *will* figure it out." The steps thumped as her attacker reeled stupidly over them out of the ramshackle house. "Hang on."

Silent and shielded from his view by the tangled branches, Riley took his picture. A grimy hand was gripping the wall for support as he appeared to have trouble breathing. Her boots had steel toes—she'd probably broken a few of his ribs. He'd be in the hospital by nightfall if he had any sense of self-preservation. Like a drunken man, covered in dirt and blood, he teetered off in the direction of the tracks. A few moments later, Riley heard a car door slam and tires tear down a gravel road.

"You there?"

"Yeah. The fucker just tucked and ducked."

Her father breathed a sigh of relief. "You gotta get out of there."

"I know. I will," Riley said, but she was already hesitating.

"Riley," he warned.

"I've got it, Dad! I promise. I'm okay now. Thank you."

He grumbled incoherently, but didn't bother to argue. Once she made her mind up, it was difficult to change, and aiming for two corrections in one conversation was ambitious.

"Call me when you're finished."

Tapping the red button, Riley began to photograph the entire scene. Outside and inside the house, she patrolled. Recovering the knife, she captured the blood stains on it, on the floor. While she was documenting the bedstead, her mind constructing one repugnant scenario after another, the sledgehammer caught her eye.

Time to tear it all down.

Riley flexed her hands around the handle, hefting it up to shoulder height. Anger might be blind and deaf, but goddamn, it was strong. One swing put the ten-pound head through the wall. Another took out a block of bricks. Dirt flew, filling the air like smoke. Wood splintered in sickening sounds. Riley attacked the steel bed frame, broke the edge off the sink, pummeled the stone and mortar until she could no longer feel her fingers. The air she gulped itched at her lungs until she spit what tasted like lyme. Exhausted to her core, she dropped the hammer and looked around.

The dust settled and though she'd used every ounce of strength, the horrible place was still standing.

Her shoulders sagged. She let go of the sledgehammer. Force wasn't going to be enough, as satisfying as it was. Then again, she'd never been the type to win a fight with brute strength alone.

Her eyes fell on a series of long, sturdy lengths of steel pipe. One of them had been attached to wood planks at either end with some plumbing fixtures, though it had yet to be wedged into service.

A smile tugged her face.

Fifteen minutes later, Aella was backed up to the front door, a rope threaded around the trailer hitch her dad had so judiciously installed. The other end was tied to two of these makeshift supports, which appeared to be bracing the entire structure upright. Her father's Harley could tow a three-hundred-pound trailer.

The dragon ought to be more than capable.

Riley put on her helmet and brought Aella to life. It shot forward to a loud crack. Before the steel pipes had even stopped keening, the roof shifted. In an avalanche of noise, the whole structure caved in, taking the remaining external walls with it. Riley let out a whoop, her fist in the air as the chimney came tumbling down in her rearview.

At the intersection with the main road, Riley stopped to tie El's blood-soaked handkerchief around her wrist. A mushroom cloud of debris filled the sky, some ten or twelve feet higher than the tallest tree. Birds had scattered and were swooping around it in circles.

Riley grinned. "I'll huff and I'll puff."

That ought to teach at least one pig a lesson.

Bash

E l ran blindly, his outraged scream echoing all around her. Tearing through the brambles and overgrown brush, she misjudged her footing in the dark. The injured leg went out from beneath her. He bellowed at her back and a rush of air from his outstretched arm brushed her face as she tumbled into the small ravine. Finding his shape against the moon and stars, El knew that the universe was with her. While he prowled the edge, looking for a safe way down, she was already off and under cover. Her legs scraped branches, her hands warded off limbs. She aimed for the patch of pale gravel reflecting the moonlight and the loud clattering of a passing freight train.

Breath caught in her searing lungs, El could hear him cutting through the dark in a string of swear words and snapping twigs. He was gaining on her. She pushed harder, tugging free of the tree line in a stagger, only to realize that the train had narrowed her escape to two possible paths, both completely obvious to her pursuer.

El looked right and then left, Charleston was left, but if the man couldn't find her, he'd go back to the tent which had to be somewhere that direction. In a snap decision, El ran to the right, the train cars speeding by her. A movement caught her eye just ahead. The man was emerging from the trees.

She lurched to a halt, her knee sending a sharp pain all the way to her hip. Spotting her, the man squared off, a malevolent grin in place.

"Where you going, huh?" he shouted over the cacophony.

El's thoughts scattered in fear as she watched the blood drip from his arm. His hands were covered in it and that . . . was because of her. She felt a surge of confidence and anger, and looked on the passing train completely differently.

In a single stride, she'd spun around. Her stumble turned to a swift hop and skip as she came level with the slow-moving cargo car. Metal rigging gleamed and flashed. Knowing it was dangerous did nothing to stop her, because if she stayed where she was, the end was a certainty.

El threw out a hand and stuck. The train jerked her along, forcing her into a run, though her knee would not bend. With a savage shriek, she swung her other arm around and latched on. Feet dragging in the gravel, she wrapped her arms through the bars in a death grip.

Despite her attacker's heat, he could not keep up, and his labored breathing and heavy footfalls fell farther and farther away.

Tears streaming down her face, El could not see to find footing on the side of the car. Her arms were growing tired, and only the physics of her elbow joints were keeping her on the train at all. Clinging and kicking at air, she shoved her face into her sleeves and finally cleared her vision.

To her left were a series of large hitches, joining metal chassis together in a creaking tangle of metal just large enough for her to sit on safely. It took six tries to swing her good leg over to it. The pack dragged at her shoulders, but El managed to take hold of a split in the facing on the outside of the railcar. With the last of her strength and adrenaline, El pulled herself aboard and wedged her body into position.

The world became a smear of navy and hunter green as she allowed herself to weep. Her hands shook terribly, her skin went ice cold and full-body tremors set in until the only way to stay straddling the rigging, was to wrap herself up in a loose chain. She locked her eyes on the rust-colored metal, the scent of grease and dynamic brakes oddly comforting.

El was safe on this giant squeaking machine. All she had to do was hold on. It didn't matter where it took her, because the plan was the same no matter where she ended up. She was escaping. She was defending herself. She had a right to this path.

Eventually, the shivering stopped, and her heart became sluggish. Her mind was a blank. She looked around at her perch and found that it was larger than she'd thought, but when she tried to scoot along the metal grating to settle in more comfortably, not a single muscle in her body would take on the burden. The exhaustion was overwhelming, but there was no choice. She had to move to be safe.

The effort of dragging herself to the platform at the end of the car took an eternity and put her close to passing out. Her right pant leg was scarlet with blood and the leg already swelling, she was covered from head to toe in brush and fine limestone dust. Thankfully though, the pack containing her life and most of her supplies was still strapped to her back. From what she could see, all the items in the outer pockets were still in place. She'd lost the tent, the sleeping bag and the bedroll, but those were a fine sacrifice to her safety. What couldn't be replaced was *Tizóna*.

As soon as she thought it, her heart ached anew. She'd sworn to keep it safe. The knife had done *its* job, and for that, she'd abandoned it in that terrible place where it would probably be used against the next girl.

It was like walking away from Riley all over again. Ashamed, she squeezed her eyes shut and prayed. Not to God, but to the Universe at large—a little poem of faith that things would align to protect everyone she cared about and undo those who would harm them. She prayed the knife would find its way back to someone who would know it on sight and gain strength from it.

The vibration of the car, the constant rhythm of the rails lulled her. Her lids drooped. She dozed, rousing only when the sound shifted so drastically that something instinctual tugged her back to reality. The train was high off the ground, her feet dangling over a precipitous drop. Between the beams of the trestle bridge, El could see the river far below, glinting with pale fire. The view over the valley was astonishing. It was the highest El could ever remember being without a pane of glass between herself and certain death.

From normal girl to death-defying daredevil.

All at once, she could see him standing over her again, licking his chapped lips in anticipation as he reached to unbuckle her pack and strip her of her life. The shine on the water became the glint of the flashlight on *Tizóna*. She'd stabbed a man.

She was a violent offender too.

Heart pounding, she shook her head fiercely and pushed her fingers into her eyes until the memory was beaten back. She would *not* give him that place in her mind! He had *no right* to stay there! His power *ended* the moment she was free!

"You're safe now. You made yourself safe."

If El had been the child her mother wanted to create, she would probably have cowered. She would have frozen. She would have let his lust determine her future, because obedience would have been so much a part of her. But she wasn't that child and her mother didn't want her. She was her own person, and that person was prepared to fight.

That person was strong enough.

She leaned back against the car, suddenly so calm and centered that every misgiving and worry faded away. When her ride began to slow and the tracks divided again and again, El knew they had to be nearing the end of the line. Trains were slotted side by side and a few cranes laced the sky, prepared to shift cargo as soon as their operators clocked in. She freed herself from her position with some difficulty, finally falling from the giant hitch in a bedraggled pile. Every muscle hurt as she got to her feet and walking was more difficult than she'd ever known it could be. In a small shed, she found cover, finally freeing herself from the backpack.

Her leg was stuck to the inside of her jeans. If she wanted to treat it, she'd have to cut them off, it seemed. She needed a bathroom with a sink and fresh running water, but the likelihood that any business would let her walk in looking like this was slim. She'd have to just make do, something she was getting very good at.

"Uh . . . Hello? You can't be in there. This is private property."

El's heart dropped into the dirt yet again. The voice was coming from beside the door, the speaker just out of sight. Fear, frustration, and fatigue finally took their toll. The very thought of moving again, of being forced to run, sent a shockwave through her. Sobs welled up from within and unleashed a tide of fresh tears.

A face peeked around the edge of the doorway, eyes cast at the ground. It was a young man, probably a little older than El, with a buzzcut and hazel eyes. His expression was blank, and as he stood there looking at her boots, she could see him rocking slightly in place.

"Are you okay, because there's all kinds of blood on you. I can call you an ambulance. I have a radio."

El's nerves began to recover. Whoever he was, he didn't seem to want to hurt her, and even though he had every right to tell her to get out, he wasn't pushing.

She cleared her throat, but somehow still sounded like she had bronchitis. "I . . . I fell and cut my knee. I can walk, I just need minute to get sorted."

"My boss is going to be coming by here soon on his rounds," he warned. "He doesn't like when hobos come in. He has them arrested. Yes, he does. He says this is private property and even if you're leaving, it's trespassing. If he finds you here, he's going to be mad at you, but also me. I'm not supposed to let people come in."

So she was trespassing too. The list of criminal complaints was growing, shoving her further and further away from any kind of average existence. It was almost difficult to care anymore or bother with rules, and maybe Riley would tell her that bad rules did more harm than good, but El did care. Everyone, everywhere, just wanted to live their lives and be accepted. Laws were the way society accepted people. If she couldn't exist without breaking the law, then it meant the world really didn't have a place for her.

El struggled up, leaning against the paneling. The young man's gaze remained affixed to the gravel, and though he wore a smile, it was somewhat practiced and masklike. She slung the pack over her shoulder. "I'm sorry. I'll go. You only have to show me the way. I don't want you to get into trouble."

"I can do that." Without warning, he spun on his heel and cut off through the rail yard in a straight line. "You came in on the freight from New York. You must have, because you weren't here an hour ago and that's the only train that comes in right now. I know. I have all the schedules memorized, and we get updates all the time."

Hobbling after him, El could barely keep up. "Yes. I caught the train in West Virginia, I think."

"It's right on the line," he confirmed with a nod. "Well, I hope you were aiming for Ohio, because you're in Ohio. This is Cincinnati. You know that, right? Is that where you wanted to go?"

Cincinnati! Somehow, El had gotten farther west than she'd realized, but so much the better. If she could find a bus station, she could be back on schedule in no time.

"That's perfect actually. I was hoping to make it to a Greyhound station."

"We have those here. Yeah. I can tell you how to use the buses. I know all the lines by heart too. I can get anywhere on the bus. I even know the timetables. I'm not allowed to drive, because I'm not good at that kind of stuff, because I can't do lots of things at once, but I can definitely do buses. You just get on and off them. The only bad thing about buses is that they're always late and that's annoying. Why have a schedule if you don't obey it?"

Understanding dawned for El and her nervousness ebbed. All his body language and the lack of eye contact made sense and no longer spoke of threat. In fact, she felt safer than she had in the last four days. "I hate that too. They should just say that it comes every ten minutes or so and leave it at that, right?"

He smiled at the dirt, his pace slowing a bit. "My name is Bash. Well, no, it's not my name. It's a nickname, you know? Well, I guess it's kind of a nickname. People think I'm shy. I'm not shy, I'm not really, but people say that, so they call me Bashful, but I'm not shy."

Despite her situation, El smiled. "So you shortened it. Makes sense."

"Yeah, I don't know. It makes me sound mean. Like I break things. Like they call a group of rhinos a *crash*. Like a *bash* of me's. I'm not mean, though. I'm nice, but I do sometimes get angry. Even then though, I try not to break stuff."

"Everyone gets angry and frustrated."

"Yeah. Do you have a name? Of course you have a name. Everyone has a name, but what's yours?"

"Call me Snow. It's a nickname too."

He glanced at her. "How come? Do you just like winter, or something? I don't like winter."

"My real name means snow. Snow's just easier."

Nodding, he stepped across some tracks and over the rigging of a parked train. He waited on the other side with his back turned as she clambered over them in an ungainly tumble.

"Are you homeless?" he asked suddenly. "Is that why you were riding the trains?"

"Yeah." El swung her bad leg over a car hitch with a wince. "I ran away from home."

"How come?"

El's body refused to budge. She tried again, but it was no good. She needed to rest. "I'm sorry. I need to stop for a minute. I guess I'm just worse off than I thought."

"That's okay. I can wait. I'm not supposed to check in yet. Sorry, I don't mean to ask things like that if it bothers you. I'm bad with people." He sat down beside her, poking his toes into the loose stones and shoving them around. "It's okay to tell me if I mess up. I don't mind. Everyone else tells me."

That was something she knew well, that feeling of always getting it wrong no matter what she did, that embarrassment that no one seemed to notice, that helplessness when everyone around her took the liberty of advising her whether she liked it or not. It was disgusting. It felt horrible.

"No, Bash, I think you're doing really well. You're being really nice to me, when you didn't have to be. Thank you for that."

"I shouldn't have asked why you ran away. My mom says that I ask too many questions and it makes people uncomfortable, and my boss says that if I wasn't a retard, he would have fired me."

El's mouth fell open. "That's a horrible thing for him to say! I hate that word!"

"I mean, yeah, I hate it too obviously. But I don't get lots of things, because I'm not normal, I guess."

Forgetting the pain in her leg, El stomped her foot. "Who decides what is normal? If you decided that you were the normal one, then everybody else would look different."

"They'd look really weird," Bash admitted with a smirk. "Because why do they say things like *How are you*? If they're not going to wait to find out? I like asking questions and getting answers for them, because why else would I ask if I didn't want to know! I don't ask *anything* unless I want to know."

"Exactly!" El took a deep breath. "Well, I'm not *normal* either, so you don't have to worry about that stuff with me. I don't think you're doing anything wrong. You're just fine how you are. So you can just be yourself, okay, and I won't be upset."

"Okay. You really look messed up."

Her giggle surprised her. "Yeah?"

"I should have said that differently."

"No, you're right. I do."

"Does it hurt bad?"

"Yes, and I need to clean it up. I have no idea what I fell on. I think it might have been a rock."

Bash sat silently on the hitch, but his rocking returned. Then he began to pat his hands on his knees in a rhythm. El had once read that autistic people had coping behaviors to help them manage stressful situations. Maybe she was making him nervous, or he just didn't like sitting still.

El shifted her weight to limp on. "Do you want to keep walking? I can get up now."

"No, it's okay. I was thinking I would ask you something, but I don't know how you feel about me, so I don't know."

"Ask."

He titled his head and looked at the space between them. "I have to go home in a little while, because my shift is over, but I'd feel bad if something happened to you. I can hide you somewhere until it's time for me to go, and then you can come with me and I can take you to the Greyhound station if you want me to. You seem really nice. I know I don't know you, but I promise I'm a good person. I'll even take you to my favorite place to eat, and you can clean up there. I know everyone there, so no one will bother you, because you're with me and everything and they know I'm weird, and so they never get upset."

His speech collided with silence at top speed. El's face warmed with the reminder that though she may have seen the worst of people, in the same day, she was seeing the best of them too. What an odd thing, and so very perfect. Suddenly grateful to the point of shivering, El accepted his invitation.

"I don't want you to get into trouble."

"No, it's okay, I know a place no one ever goes but me. I'll take you there. I like it because it's quiet and I can listen to the trains come. It's my secret place where I am invisible."

Eyes stinging, El hobbled after him. "Thanks, Bash, it sounds perfect."

20

Vengeance

Somewhere outside of Charleston, Riley paid in cash to use a computer connected to a printer. She stuffed a padded envelope addressed to the West Virginia State Troopers with a series of terrible images, a wallet, a phone, and a note.

This man attacked the minor in the photos in the abandoned property indicated on the enclosed map. I have in my possession physical evidence of the crime. The phone's code is 0827. You'll find the photographs were pulled directly from it and date throughout the last two years. Do something about him, because if you don't, I am going to doxx him and make sure he's on every sexual predator list from here to the arctic.

Riley opened her IP tracking program to find a great deal more traffic on her website. Apparently, El's reply to her question had drawn thousands of views and she had hundreds of new followers. None of the IP addresses, however, were nearby. With a sickened feeling, her worst suspicions were confirmed—the blogging website funneled questions and answers back and forth with no IP information. If she wanted to follow El, she had to find a way to tempt her back to @hellonaunicycle to trigger the tracking program again.

If she just messaged directly and revealed who she was, Riley wondered if El would reciprocate, or would she be more likely to turn away? Everything in her told her to reach out, to offer herself up like a bodyguard and take El wherever it was she wanted to go. Now, later, until she got bored. Who cared? But El was on her own journey. Who was to say she wasn't running from Riley too, from an obsession she'd had because there was no other avenue? Who was to say that with the world open to her, El wouldn't find she needed a new love to be with the new individual she would become?

Uncertainty and doubt were not emotions Riley was accustomed to feeling, and so a coping mechanism did not exist in her repertoire.

She sat staring at the timer on her computer session. She wanted so badly to speak to El and heal what injuries had been done. She knew that fear very well—how noises and smells could trigger the memories, how the events would play behind one's eyelids, over and over, the words exchanged repeating on an endless loop of misery. El had to be suffering, locked in a mental model of the abandoned house, trying to free herself even though there wasn't a door to keep her in.

But no . . .

She stopped the spin of her office chair and sat up.

Reviewing El's reply, she saw that it was poised. It was eloquent. It existed—something Riley could not even comprehend. Long ago, when those older boys had so helpfully shoved Riley down in that alley to *straighten* her out, her entire life had fallen apart. It had taken weeks to recover, a year to fight her way out of depression and paralysis. Even now, she was still the person that experience had made her.

Here was El . . . calmly back at the helm of her tiny empire, silencing Riley's fears like the queen that she was.

"One hell of a chick," she whispered.

If El was cogent enough to write, perhaps she was capable of more than that.

Riley returned to her notifications feed and scrolled. She sifted the data until she found the alert that El had liked one of her motivational quotes that had been scheduled to drop in the early hours of the morning. This gave her an idea of what time El had logged on. Cracking her knuckles, Riley flipped to the trace program and weeded through every single IP that had ever pinged on that entry, collating it to the time of day.

The nearest one wasn't in West Virginia. It was in Cincinnati. When the map de-pixelated, sheer relief filled her up to bursting. It had to be El! The only public location in the vicinity was a restaurant and hotel near a rail yard. The anonymous kind of place a girl might end up, in the dead of night, after she'd somehow jumped on board the first freight train to pass by.

Riley dropped her envelope in the mail slot and hit the road. She could clear the two hundred miles in three hours on Aella, especially if she treated the lanes as suggestions and the speed limits as technicalities. It was when she stopped to refill her gas tank that she realized it would do no good to rush. El had apparently last been online hours ago, and there was no way she would just hang around in one place. Not with those men from the train chasing her. Cafés and bars were like the tides, taking people in and spitting them out in a rhythm, so even if Riley got to the place as swiftly as she could, she'd likely be in the same predicament as she was in Alderson.

The very thought of being patient felt like a knife to all the major nerve clusters, but it seemed the universe was going to shove it down Riley's throat whether she wanted it or not. There was nothing she could do but find that café and pace the terrain around it, check into the adjacent motel, and plan her next move.

She took an icy shower. She looked over her latest group of bruises and popped some pain killers. She scheduled more content on the blog, this time choosing the most provocative things she could find. She inventoried all her gear. She even used the coin-op laundry machine to smell like synthetic flowers.

And that was just the first hour.

For dinner, she jogged across the parking lot to the café and planted her backside in a booth, eating a sirloin steak while she became acquainted with the place. For good measure, she confirmed her suspicion that the night shift rolled over into the early morning—the staff she was looking for arrived at two in the morning and stayed until ten.

The night passed slowly, but sometime around midnight, her mind could no longer circle around El. Eventually, Riley just became too exhausted to stay vigilant, too much of a failure to read any more entries praising her beauty or grace, too weary to fantasize. Her eyes closed and when they opened again, the sun was checking on her through the privacy curtain. Riding soreness had set in. The skin of her back was tender to the touch and every muscle was like a steel cable dragging beneath her skin. In desperate need of coffee and more Tylenol, she looked out the window at the café and felt every fiber of her being slam awake in a painful jolt of adrenaline.

A black SUV was parked at the restaurant.

"Fuck."

Riley packed in record time and checked out by throwing her keys on the floor. From the sidewalk, she could see the air freshener dangling in the windscreen.

So they'd gotten out of jail. Riley tucked her chin to her sternum as ideas manifested in a wrathful surge of exactly how to make them regret their freedom.

The nearest electronics store was only a mile away. She was in and out in fifteen minutes, part of her day's expense account well spent. The new smartphone took five minutes to set up and claimed a full battery charge. Riley adjusted it to the power conservation mode and downloaded an app.

Squatting on the asphalt at the back of the SUV, she rang home. "Hey, Dad!"

"You sound chipper. Sleep well?"

"Naw, like shit, but . . . you're never gonna guess what I turned up."

"You found her?"

Riley couldn't help but giggle at his enthusiasm. "No, but I found the SUV dudes. Remember when you told me that story about that guy . . . what was his name? Scabies? The one who did that thing with the phone."

"Scabs? Oh . . . shit, yes! Are you—"

Riley tore the duct tape with her teeth and reached below the back bumper. "Yup. Pull up FindMyPhone, will you?"

She listened to him smash through the house to his computer while Riley made damn sure that no matter what kind of terrain they went over, the phone would never come loose. With it in place, Riley relayed the new phone number and listened to her father go through the screens.

"Cincinnati? By a Motel Six?"

"You got it! Thanks, Dad."

"Play nice."

Riley dragged herself upright and carefully obscured her movements behind the other cars in the lot. "Really?"

"I was joking."

"You had me worried there for a second. Call you from the road."

Riley dashed around the building and in the front door. The entire circular restaurant wrapped around a central kitchen. If she kept herself beside the register, she was directly opposite the only table occupied by a group scary enough to be the "assailants" from the train. She peered through the heat lamps on the service passthrough and wondered how the hell they'd tracked El. They must have a more sophisticated way than she did. If so, she needed to learn what it was, or she'd never be able to outpace them.

Riley stuck her head around the curve.

Something was off. Four men as rigid as she'd envisioned, but seated in the booth with them was a young guy a little older than her. The body language was all wrong—they were leaning into the kid, their voices low, but he was staring at his lap as if being scolded, pale and silent.

A waitress approached with a taut smile.

"I'm not here to eat." Phone in hand, she flashed the picture of Rose. "I'm looking for a girl, and I'm guessing that those guys are too."

The woman's face dropped every pretense. "What did she do?"

"Not a damn thing."

Her mouth fell open. "But then, why is everyone—"

Riley scanned her name tag. "Look, Chelsea, it's a long story, but *I'm* the good guy. *They're* shit-eating kidnapper fucks. No idea who the kid is."

"That's Bash." Chelsea glanced back at the four men and took hold of Riley's arm. In two steps, they were out of the line of sight, hidden behind the coffee machines. "His mom works here. He comes in every day. Yesterday morning, with that girl. She looked like she'd been through hell. She was covered in blood. She cleaned up in the bathroom, paid for his breakfast."

Riley's stomach bottomed out. "What happened to her after she was here?"

"I don't know. Bash got on the bus with her." Chelsea wrung her hands and then covered her mouth. "Did *they* do that to her?"

The truth wouldn't get Riley what she wanted, but really, it was *entirely* their fault that El had been attacked. It would be easy to make them look like complete assholes—they were slowly wrapping around Bash as the regretful Samaritan shrank even lower in his seat.

"Yes, and if they don't get what they want, they'll hurt him too."

Chelsea was beside herself. "He's a good boy! He's just like a little kid in his mind, you know? He gets taken advantage of a lot. I thought she was—"

"She wasn't. He was helping her." Riley thought swiftly. Somehow, she needed to get Bash away from them and convince him to talk to her instead. "I have a plan."

Chelsea managed a hard swallow. "They have guns. I thought they were cops."

In reply, Riley's face split into a cocky grin. "Don't worry."

"What do you want me to do?"

Picking up a menu, Riley dialed the restaurant's phone number. "Answer like normal. Let them see you do it. Then go over to the table and tell Bash his mother is on the phone. Be casual. Smile. Refill their coffees."

Chelsea chewed her lip. "I don't know . . . if they're as dangerous as you say—"

Riley threw down the menu with a snap that made the waitress jump. "Look . . . I'm going to go over and talk to them. When I do, call the police. Got it?"

Riley didn't wait for an answer, but hit the Dial button on her cell. The café phone summoned the woman to bravery. Despite an ornery glance, Chelsea picked up a coffee pot and role-played a few moments of false conversation. Moving back around the breakfast bar, Riley took up position beside the stack of extra chairs and watched the exchange in a polished water pitcher. Chelsea waved a hand. Bash shot up out of his seat. One of the men tried to grab for him, but the one sitting across from the kid gave a subtle shake of his head.

Bash made it to the phone unscathed. Riley cleared her throat.

"Hello Bash, this *isn't* your mother, but I can help you get away from those guys. They are *not* nice."

To her surprise, he let out a sardonic noise. "Yeah, duh. I knew that. Nice guys don't threaten to kill your family."

Riley slid back toward the register. "The girl you met yesterday, the one who was covered in blood?"

"Snow? Yeah, she was hurt—"

Riley wanted to hear more, but it had to wait. "I know. They're asking about her, right?"

"Yeah. I know how to play dumb, though. I'm not a snitch."

"That is perfect! I have a plan. Tell them you need to use the bathroom, but then go out the back door instead. I will meet you outside."

"I don't know who you are," he said softly.

Riley came up level with him. He was staring at his shoes, his body bobbing back and forth. He wore a shirt that said "Security" and had a belt with a radio and a flashlight. Riley put two and two together and couldn't help a smile. El must have made friends with him in the rail yard.

"My name is Riley. I'm Snow's friend," she whispered.

His eyes ticked upward, found her chin, and then swept back to his shoes. Without being instructed to, he kept the phone to his ear, though the call had ended. "You have pink hair."

"Yup! Do you think you can help me fuck with these guys?"

He frowned at the counter. "Yeah. I know all about spies. I've seen every detective movie and I read all the books too."

"Awesome! Me too! We'll make a good team."

"Okay, bye." Bash hung up the phone and turned on his heel. Returning to the table, he shuffled his feet and excused himself to the bathroom. Again, the man who'd been sitting beside him moved as if to escort him, but once more, the apparent leader shook his head.

As soon as Bash was up from the table, Riley stepped out from cover and swooped in as a distraction. She should be scared of these guys. Somehow, though, she was right at home. As she sauntered to their booth, Riley's eyes flicked over the ink on their forearms. Not for the first time, she was grateful that she'd spent so many hours in tattoo parlors learning the codes. Abuela had said it was no place for a child, but it was exactly the sort of place to craft an avenging angel.

Without a care in the world, Riley plopped down in Bash's empty seat and stole a piece of bacon from the man who'd been so eager to keep him in it.

"Hey there, guys! I'm thrilled we finally get to meet!"

It took a chew for them to get over their astonishment. She knew the leader was a former Devil Dog before he ever bothered to spit out the word "Ma'am," but it was nevertheless funny to hear it applied to herself.

"Ma'am. Who might you be?"

"Your competition!" Riley grinned at him and wedged her knee against the table. "Mama Glasse *did* tell you she hired someone else after you bozos got arrested, right? How'd that work out, anyway? Isn't impeding a train like a terrorist offense? They let you post and then tell you not to leave town, or what? Are you even supposed to *be* traveling right now?"

He crossed his ropey arms with a glance to the man beside her. "We're fine. And yes, she told us."

"What a bitch, am I right?" Riley tongued the bacon, her ear pitched so as to capture every vocalization, her eyes cemented to his impassive features.

"We don't discuss our clients."

Riley arched a brow. They could be part of some kind of security firm. Each one of them had hip holsters and polo shirts that looked about two sizes too small, but something about that seemed off. She counted one convict, one Marine, and one Army. The fourth man was older than the others, no ink, and less fit—possibly ex FBI or homicide. But why would they ever agree to this? Taking a child across state lines was kidnapping, even if the girl was a runaway and the kidnappers were acting on the guardian's approval. They had to be walking a fine line, some kind of desperation. They might even be some of Mama's zealots.

She licked her fingers and leaned forward, plucking a piece of toast from a plate. "Man, you guys are so professional. That must be how you got here this morning, yeah? Too bad she isn't here."

"How do you know that?"

"I've been here all night."

The man beside her shifted on the bench. "Bullshit."

She graced him with an eye roll.

"Doesn't matter who gets where first," the leader said with a tiny shrug. "The point is who gets the girl."

From the corner of her eye, Riley could see Chelsea clutching the telephone and whispering furiously. She would have to speed it up.

"Honey . . ." Standing, Riley executed a lithe stretch, careful to show off every leather-clad curve. "I always get the girl. Never send a straight man to do a lesbian's job."

They exchanged looks. The eager one slid closer to her along the empty bench. "Who do you work for?"

"I didn't come here to chat about business. I just wanted to say hello, be gentlemanly. Spirit of the hunt." She gestured with the toast. "All that shit. Thought I'd thank you for the entertainment, because it's been fucking funny as hell watching you struggle."

If there was one thing at which Riley excelled, it was shit-talking. She'd attended Tio Tito's School of Billiards, Betting, and Bullshit, and had watched him run quite a few games just by picking away at the confidence of grown-ass men. She'd learned that at their core, most adults were still children and playground psychology never went out of fashion.

"Struggle? We're doing just fine. We—"

The leader silenced his cohort by picking up his coffee. The guy was robotic in his movements, his face indecipherable. "Happy to entertain you. See you at the finish line."

He was calling her out. Riley either had to leave, or she had to have a better reason to stay. It would take the cops a few minutes to arrive if Chelsea sounded terrified enough. Riley needed to keep them focused on her for as long as possible.

Lifting the leader's fork, Riley chewed his eggs thoughtfully and waved the utensil as if conducting.

"Okay . . . you got me. I am actually *really* surprised to see you here. I mean, I have a foolproof system, so when I see you pull up, I'm thinking to myself, how the fuck did those asshats get all the way from Alderson to Ohio? I mean, I know they probably went to Beckley, right? But then how do they get from there all the way to a shitty café in Cincinnati? I am just dying to know. It's the *friend*, right?"

Her vague hook caught big fish, as the antsy member of the group squirmed in his seat. Riley strung a few facts onto the line of reasoning and wove a bit more colorful bait.

"The one she's been calling, right? I've been wondering if there was a way to get to her on that end, but I don't know who it is. Like seriously . . . How are you doing it? She's using a burner!"

"Yeah, but *he* isn't," spat the newb.

So it was a "he." And *he* was talking to El from his own phone. They had to have a phone number on him. There was no other way.

"Goddamn! She called him from her house?" One glance corrected her as their body language spelled out the truth in a series of tells. Her mind hopscotched through possibilities. "The cell? No! Oh, wow! The *sister*!"

The leader sat his coffee down with a clack. The conversation was clearly over. He turned a dismissive smile on her and silently warned her to walk away.

For spite, Riley cracked her neck. "See you at the finish line, boys. It's been hilarious."

With as much swagger as possible, Riley made for the front door, shooting Chelsea a conspiratorial look. Once outside, she dashed to Aella, and bailed, pausing just long enough to convince Bash to climb on. The sirens rolling up to the restaurant may not result in anything but a brief delay for the other hunters, but it was long enough to escape.

21
What Ails You

El stared at the message, her mind blank from the numbing horror of it. Thoughts met that fear and were poisoned until all logic withered.

They know who your friend is. Do NOT go to him. Find another place.

El leaned back against the bus window. Her legs were stretched across the seats like pale sticks from her khaki shorts, her rainbow-colored knee so swollen she couldn't bend it. Pressure was building in her chest, but the characters on the bus with her were each intimidating in their right, and she couldn't risk breaking down in front of them. The two tattooed men seated a few rows behind her had already tried to talk to her more than once, the larger of the two tracking her with his eyes every time she hobbled to the bathroom. If she let the mask slip and became the lost little girl, the wolves would circle.

She took a shaky breath, tears welling in her eyes.

It didn't matter how they knew about Oscar. She was sure they had ways. They'd found her on the train even though she'd bought the ticket in cash and changed her hair. The more important question was . . . who was @hellonaunicycle and how did this person know what was happening?

Even that was pointless to think about, because the truth was, her escape was cut off. She had nowhere to run and now it was even possible that her friend, the one who'd been beside her the whole time, would get into trouble. El wasn't sure, but it seemed possible that helping a minor run away from home was some kind of crime.

She'd made him an accomplice to her delinquency.

The bus pulled into a truck stop for the dinner break. El gathered her wallet and phone and hopped off, staying beside the door until all the other passengers had gone inside the store. The two large men smiled at her yet again, but El kept her eyes down at her feet. When she was certain the driver had locked the bus, she limped after him.

In one of the unisex bathrooms, she dialed Oscar and sat sobbing on the toilet. He shushed her, the constant voice of calm in her ear, even though she told him about the mysterious message and what it meant to her.

"It's okay. It's fine. Look . . ." He let out a sigh and a few noises as if his mind still hadn't thought things through yet. "Fuck this place. I don't like my roommates enough to stay here, anyway."

"They're your best friends, you liar."

"Yeah but . . . look, I can't leave you hanging. Let's run away together! My boyfriend and I can get an apartment somewhere and—"

"Oscar! You have school! Don't." El scoured her face with the scratchy paper towels. "I just need to find another way. I don't know . . . I have no idea what to do."

When he sniffled, she realized he was crying too. "I'm sorry, Snow. This is all my fault."

"No . . . no. It was *my* half-assed plan. I should have done more research, woken up sooner, planned a bit longer. I should have figured it all out. I'm sorry. I have to go. I can't call you anymore for now. I don't know how safe that is for you, but I'll be on my site. Message me through that, okay?"

He tried to object. She hung up and sobbed, her entire body heaving with the effort. Shaking, she washed her face and brushed her teeth. She looked a unique shade of green, and knew that she was still recovering from the shock of the attack. She'd lost blood and that had to have some kind of physical effect.

In the shop, she stocked up on foods that seemed healthy— nuts, meat, fruit juice. She bought more pain medication and an ace bandage. In the restaurant, she ordered a steak sandwich and carried it outside to the picnic tables.

The men from the bus were sitting at one. El chose the table farthest from theirs and watched them from the corner of her eye. The larger man was talking softly in his deep voice, his dark skin glowing in the pink sunset when he shook his head in dismay. His companion, whose bare arms were covered in graphic tattoos, seemed to be in a terrible state, sneezing every few words. He refused the hot sauce bottle that was set before him.

"Man, fuck that! I already have a runny nose, Doc." He dabbed at his watering eyes and nose with a disintegrating napkin. "I don't need that shit!"

"I'm telling you, it'll help."

"That's some hoodoo shit."

"My granny may have been a wrinkled swamp hag, but she knew her remedies! How the hell you think I ain't die in that stupid desert?"

"Hexes."

"Cayenne pepper, motherfucker, and garlic, and sugar."

"Yeah, well, I'll stick with my antibiotics and nasal spray, not hit the sauce like your bug-eyed granny. Lookin' like a shriveled-up bat..."

Someone tapped her shoulder. El couldn't help but flinch, her head swiveling so fast, it made her dizzy. A man stood grinning at her. He looked to be a trucker, with button-up shirt over a tank top and a cap seated on his balding head. He smelled like cigarettes and cheap aftershave and the look on his face put El's teeth on edge.

"How much?" he asked with a wink.

El frowned. Was he talking about the sandwich? She looked around. The two men had halted their conversation and were watching her again. Her eyes darted over the parking lot, but no one else was nearby.

The trucker tucked himself into the bench across from her and leaned over her food. He had a twisted grin and a glimmer in his eye that was eerily familiar. "How much, baby? I got about fifteen minutes."

El's emotions, still raw and bloody, were dragged to the ground by her stomach. Her mouth fell open as she realized fully what he was asking her. Her fingers lost the ability to clench and the sandwich fell onto the plate. The man watched the dawning humiliation with a patient smile.

"Come on, girl. It's cheap, right?" He reached out and tried to touch her hair. El recoiled as if burned, but he didn't seem to mind. "You ain't pretty enough for even a hundred, I think."

El looked back at the restaurant. The driver was inside at a table. Her pulse skipped as it tried to amp back up into the cadence that was quickly becoming the norm. This was just how it was going to be from now on. She was going to have to deal with this kind of person constantly.

And all because she was a lonely female.

Why did they think they had this right? She didn't need to ask it, because she knew. All the sermons she'd heard about a woman's place and all the lectures her mother had used to torment her. She was a girl, she would always be a girl. She would always be someone's property, someone's responsibility, someone's maid or plaything. She was doomed to always be an extension of someone else and she'd have to suffer whatever shame they chose to give her, because that was their right. That was what the world was telling her.

El picked up her fountain drink.

The world could fuck off.

As he priced all the hanky-panky they could get up to in the cab of his truck, El's ears went deaf. She popped the lid from the cup and got shakily to her feet. He grinned in triumph, until she dumped the entire sweet tea over his smug face.

"Cool down, fuckwits."

He sprang up from the table, spitting venom, until a shadow fell across the puddle and a low voice apparently disabled every one of his nerves.

"Take a walk. Better yet, go jerk off in that cab of yours for free, instead of gifting women your moist pocket change, slime ball. Look like you could use the money, anyway."

The trucker looked as if he wanted to start a fight, but at her back, El heard a sneeze. It was two against one and both of these men were bigger, stronger, and far rougher looking.

"The lady—" the tattooed man sneezed again "—said no. Do you need me to say it in another language, because—" He punctuated it with another sneeze. "—I know three more ways I can call you a perverted asshole."

"I don't know," said his friend, suppressing a smile. "I'm pretty sure the lady did fine on her own."

The trucker spat on the ground. "Fuck you. And fuck this slut."

Of a sudden, the larger man took hold of the damp flannel collar. Lifting the trucker in the air, he hurled him about ten feet. "Kiss your mother with that mouth? She give it up to every man who threw a twenty at her? You know your daddy, son?"

The trucker's features were beet red and deformed with rage, but he backed away, retreating around the building muttering impotent curses. In the silence that followed, El's body had no opportunity to recover. These two men may have rescued her from one threat, but that didn't make them saints.

As if he could read it on her face, the larger man shook his head. "It's okay. We aren't gonna bite. Promise."

The sneezing man went back to his food and this time, he dumped half the bottle of hot sauce onto it before he took a bite.

His friend watched this with a growing smirk. "Oh, now you listen to me. Dumbass."

"Can't be tough when my nose is running. What's this shit supposed to do?"

El's fragile nerves and emotional state collapsed, sending her back to the bench. She just couldn't fight anymore, with everything coming down around her ears. She was too tired. She needed to rest.

To her relief, the large man went back to his seat and stared down at his friend with a long-suffering grin. "Flushes out all the allergens, then stuffs you back up. No more sneezing. If you were smart, you'd buy some of that allergy medicine in the shop."

"Knocks me out."

"Good! Then I don't have to listen to your ass! Jesus, all you do is complain!"

El sat staring at her food, her appetite gone. She wanted to curl up in a ball on the matted bus seat and close her eyes. She didn't want to think about disgusting men, her mysterious protector, what she was going to do once she got to California. She wanted to be unconscious for however long it took to just . . . wake up someone else. In a new life.

"Miss?"

El looked at him blankly. His expression was honest, forehead wrinkles and drawn mouth speaking to his concern.

"Hmm?"

"Are you okay? He didn't bother you too much—"

"I'm fine."

He ran a huge hand over his shaved head as if debating what to say next. His friend glanced over from his hot sauce with a side of beef, his face covered in slime and pink as a sunburn.

"Look, I know it's fucked up that women need to be protected, but I don't mind if you sit with us. I have a daughter about your age, I think. I'd be worried sick if I thought she was traveling alone."

El sniffed and tried to sit up straighter. Her back was too sore from carrying the pack and she immediately winced. "I'm fine alone. I'll be okay."

"Your leg is pretty bad," he remarked into his chili. "I used to be a medic. Let me at least take a look at it."

She weighed the risks. This was a public place. She didn't have any first aid knowledge but what she read on the internet. If she let the man look at her knee, it was probably fine as long as she didn't go anywhere with him. But where was he going to take her? They were getting on the same bus.

"Okay. Thanks."

He got up from his bench and she stretched the technicolor horror out for him. He prodded and poked, frowning over it with a precise gaze. Every time he adjusted his thick but gentle fingers, he found a new spot El didn't realize was sore.

"It needs to be cleaned out better. You're working on an infection. Looks like there's some gravel or something under the skin."

"Does it . . . Do I have to get stitches?"

He smiled. "No. It's not bleeding anymore. It will leave a nice scar, but otherwise it's fine. Doesn't look like you damaged the patella or the tendon. Just sliced the shit out of it."

Despite her anxiety, El felt better. He excused himself and ran inside the shop. The sneezing man sat smiling at her, sweat dripping off his face as he white-knuckled his way through the spices.

"Do you have allergies?" El asked finally, to make small talk.

"Happens every time we do this. Midwest is mostly stuff I'm allergic to, I guess."

"You do this a lot?"

"Yeah. It's our summer job. We drive cars out to people who move or order through small dealerships, you know, then we bus around to the next gig, and then drive another car. Lets us see the country, test out different cars. It's kind of like being on a long road trip."

"So . . ." El couldn't help but smile at his features, so contorted in agony that it gave him a comical aspect. "You guys are friends?"

"Practically brothers. We were in the Army together." He licked the sauce from his fingers and used a few wet wipes to clean his hands. "Sorry if we freaked you out. Doc kind of keeps an eye out for runaways. I guess because he ran away from home as a kid, it's like something he has to do."

El tucked her gaze to her lap, wondering if it was that obvious to everyone.

"Not that you're a runaway! It's just . . . well. With the leg and the backpack. And also, you do look a bit young. Sorry."

"Why'd he run away?" El whispered.

"My dad was an alcoholic," said the deep voice. El looked up and found Doc standing there with his arms full of hand sanitizer and wipes and all sorts of repurposed medical supplies. He dumped it all on the table and crouched back down, tending to her knee without a word about it. "He used to beat the shit out of me. I ran away. Got into some trouble. Got out of it. Got a GED. Went into the Army. So here I am."

El watched him work. Somehow the tiny hope that these men were safe and a resource was more painful than the idea of reliving her attack one more time. If she trusted them and they hurt her, there would be nothing she could do, since the numbers weren't in her favor. If she trusted them and they betrayed her, that was worse than anything she could imagine at that moment. Then again, she wasn't a naive girl anymore, and they were just sitting on a bus together.

"What's a GED?"

He smiled. "It's a high school equivalency. You just take a test and they give you basically what counts as a diploma. You can get into college with that. Doesn't matter what age you are either. You just pay for the test and take it."

Shocked, El blinked at the amber streetlights, slowly clicking on, finally roused by the hiss and squeal of truck hydraulics. "That's a thing? Like . . . that is a real thing that anyone can do?"

He seemed to find her surprise amusing. "Of course! Lots of people quit high school and they can't go back because they're too old, you know. I got my GED at nineteen! But you can get it early too."

El chewed her lip. "But . . . how do you do it?"

"You sign up online, go to a testing center, show your ID, and take the test."

Show her ID. Her *real* ID. If she did that, there might be a way her mother could track her. That was something El couldn't allow for another six months at least. Fine. In six months, when she was an adult, she'd walk into a testing center and take the GED exam. Maybe there was a book or something she could find to help her study.

The brief happiness subsided as it occurred to her she didn't have a place to be for six months. She didn't even have a tent to camp in.

Doc used an automotive tool to pull the tiny fragments of rock out of her knee, mopping the fresh blood with wet wipes. His voice had a soothing rumble to it as he dropped it to what seemed to be, for him, a whisper. "You know, there's lots of shelters for young people. I lived in one. Some have programs for GED too. Give you two meals, a place to shower. They even do health care if you need it. And most of the time you don't need identification. It's a great service for kids who have nowhere to go."

El swallowed. A huge knowing eye peeped at her knee through a magnifying glass.

"Thing is, some people were never meant to be parents. Sometimes they do it because they're bored. Sometimes to fix a marriage. Sometimes by accident. And sometimes they do it because they think they're supposed to."

She couldn't help the snort that erupted. When he winked at her, relief finally came. For the first time in a few hours, she took a lungful of fresh air and let it out slowly. "Sounds like you've met my mother."

"Yeah? She an alcoholic too?"

"Among other things. She's also a snob, a religious fanatic, a Tea Party member, a racist, and a homophobe."

He made a face and pasted her knee with Band-Aids. "I'm guessing she isn't your best buddy?"

"She's a terrible person."

El took his hand as he helped her to her feet. Testing her weight on it, the knee felt much better. Already it seemed less hot and the irritating itch had gone away completely. She hobbled in a circle and decided to take another risk. She was El the Daredevil, after all.

"If I'd stayed with my family, they would have sent me to a reeducation camp to learn how not to be a lesbian."

The sneezer let out a whistle. "That's fucked. Dude, you remember Sid from Boot? She said she got put in one of those, and they had a psych guy tell her she had some kind of mental disorder. Gave her Ritalin. Zonked her out like a heroin addict."

El wobbled, but Doc's hand shot out to steady her. "Yeah. I remember her. Isn't she married?"

"Yeah. Her wife's name is Carrie, I think."

"Good for her."

Feeling like a show pony being put through the paces, El let go of her trainer and sat down. The idea that in some parts of the world it was acceptable by law for her to marry like any other person, invite guests, eat cake, and have a certificate was just astonishing. Tired as she was, her thoughts were uninhibited and before long, she was imagining what Riley would look like wearing a white leather motorcycle coat.

Doc sat beside her and ate one of her french fries as if to poke fun at her. "So who's the girl? I mean, there's a girl, yeah? You have a look on your face."

Riley wasn't a girl. Riley was a demon. El's demon, possessing her heart so easily that it took barely a word to summon forth a memory, and from the memory spilled the devotional. What she felt, there was no containing, and for days she'd kept herself from her one outlet. Her miseries were piled up so high she'd been bricked off from the thought of how much she missed Riley Vanator.

"Where to begin," she murmured.

Doc smiled and pushed her plate toward her. "Start with *and then I saw her*. That's my favorite part."

22
Changeling

Riley kicked off her boots and collapsed backward onto the bed. The sheet-covered trampoline bounced her back off in a cloud of dust, but she stuck the landing and took it as a sign that there was no rest for the clever. Her body was so heavy she could barely trudge into the bathroom and peel off her armor. Instead of a shower, she soaked in the tiny, chipped bathtub that thankfully had water so hot it could brew tea. She ordered a pizza and set up her tech station, flipping through all the programs at the sluggish speed of the motel's tragic wi-fi.

El had replied to her warning exactly as expected. And she had no idea how to respond.

Who are you?

For her dad, she was a continuation of her mother's sacred legacy, handled with mingled joy, sorrow, and deference. For Abuela, she was the replacement daughter that somehow didn't match up because she was too much like her daddy. For everyone else, she was that obnoxious bitch who wouldn't leave things alone. But without all those people, without their ideas of her, she honestly wasn't really clear which parts of her were constants. She had a small list of irrevocable character traits, but ever since the start of senior year, she'd been wondering what would happen if she magically blipped into another universe where the rules were different. Would she have to suddenly learn to be nice, polite, less intense?

Everyone who'd been to it acted like college was one of those places where suddenly social dynamics went topsy turvy, and intellect was all that mattered. They talked as if a person could be unique or eccentric and it was just kind of taken in stride. People embraced fringe ideas, opened their minds a little, started using their newly acquired votes. People stopped picking on one another, jockeying for position, and started being peers.

All Riley's skills had to do with getting out of trouble or fucking with people, and that only applied to college if she wanted to be the resident forgery expert or a serial prankster.

When she looked in the mirror, Riley knew who she *had been*, but with all her unspoken words, El had changed everything. El said she wanted to know the girl who needed to take a deep breath in silence. She wanted to make a world that didn't put Riley in those corners and force her to kick her way out of them. She wanted to see who Riley *could* be if she had everything as she wanted it. It seemed like El wanted the same thing for Riley that Riley had entertained briefly before a summary dismissal. She wanted Riley to relax.

Riley wasn't exactly sure if she knew how to do that.

Who *was* she?

The phone rang. At a glance, all the uncoiled muscle torqued back into readiness. Setting up the apps on her phone, she answered the call on the laptop and let her fingers wander to Tizóna. Opening and closing that blood-streaked blade, she felt somehow stronger, more focused. She'd always seen her mind like a sharp edge she could release from a scabbard, embed into a problem, and slip out with only a whisper of a sign. Knowing that the knife had already saved El once, gave it even more power.

Riley answered the witch's call with a smile. "Well, hello! I was just about to call you for your debriefing. Wanted to make sure you weren't busy."

"Very funny."

"It wasn't a joke."

"Really? That's new. Aren't you always jokin'? Isn't that your . . . thing? Aren't you the one who thinks *everythin'* is a big fuckin' joke?"

Riley closed the blade and opened it again. Something wasn't right about the voice. Mama always had the tone of a pleasant tigress looking at the bars as if to calculate how much force had to be applied to eat every small, cooing child in the vicinity. At the moment, the woman seemed frantic and was cutting the edge of that anxiety with her usual medication.

A glass clinked against what sounded like a bottle. "Are you laughin' at me? Hmm? Did you read it and think I deserve it? Such *ungrateful... mindless... bitter* lies!"

Riley's brows went into her hot pink hairline. "I haven't read anything. I just now got to a hotel. Look at the card records, you can probably see the pending charge."

Without even bothering to fully finish her gulp, Mama launched into a fluid tirade between coughs. Every other sentence was a prayer to some deity Riley had never met or angels she hoped she never would. Gathering the gist together as if plucking lentils from cinders, she went to El's blog and within a few lines, let out a low whistle.

"Holy. Shit." Her grin was so huge it hurt. She skimmed over the absolute devastation that lay before her—the story of a girl held captive in a golden castle, her hands tied with ribbons and her body sold to princes. A young lady with a mind like razor wire, dulled with Bible verses and potions. A woman with passion and ferocity, bound by illusions of normalcy, but unafraid to finally and forever cut herself free of all of it. El's heart had bled pixels and the words were terrifyingly sharp. Sharp enough to cut down a witch, no matter how powerful she thought she was.

All that held this incantation in check was the name. One name could summon the assailant to account. Its absence echoed through the readers' comments on the entry. Who had done this? Who were Snow's parents? How could this be happening?

Didn't they say that to destroy a demon, you had to know its name?

Riley ran her tongue ring against her teeth and knew that whoever she had seemed in all those timid encounters, El had always been one hell of a chick.

"God*damn*, lady!"

"You see? You understand, don't you? She could ruin me, ruin us, ruin her sister! Oh my god, Rose's wedding! Oh, this is *horrible*! She just doesn't care about anyone but herself! She doesn't know what she's doing. She's gone insane!"

Riley let out an explosive cackle. "Guess you shouldn't have fucked with her, huh?"

The silence stretched and the wine glass was refilled in a succession of clinks. Riley kept count on the hotel notepad of how many times the bottle had touched the rim.

"You guttersnipe piece of *white*—"

The *H* hit Riley's nerves and got a knee-jerk interruption. "Latina, *¡Métetelo por el culo, Mamahuevo! Escuchame. La familia de mi mama son de Mexico, y hablo español también. Claro?*"

"Wetback, then."

Riley hissed. "Where are your people from, huh, Mama? You're white as herring, so you must be from Europe, right? Is that *nearer* or *farther* from the United States than Mexico? Before you answer, Mexico used to own half this country."

Mama snorted. "Oh, sure, but your people don't own it now."

"They do, actually, seeing as how we're citizens, but okay, keep up the racist rhetoric. That really helps me sympathize with you."

The line sang with the tinkling ice. A quiet sobbing began, dainty and ladylike. It put Riley's teeth on edge, but she let it continue and tallied another drink.

"All I've evuh done, was for my babies. I quit school to help their father get his law degree. I wined and dined his cronies! I told him to run for office! I did that! This *house*, the servants, the lifestyle, it's all me! I did this! And she throws it back in my face! I don't understand *what's wrong with her*!"

Riley tilted the chair and put her feet up on the table. "Not one damn thing. She's exactly how you made her."

"That is *not* my child. She is *not* what I made! The Devil took her from me!"

Riley sighed, all her ire suddenly anesthetized. It was an intractable situation—this woman would never be able to see the twisted logic at play, because logic wasn't real to her. "Or . . . the Devil took *you* long before she was born. That ever cross your mind? Would God really want you to hate your own child?"

"I don't *hate* my daughter."

"Yes, you do." Riley set *Tizóna* down and crossed her arms. "All these problems came from you trying to turn her into something you thought she should be, instead of just waiting to see. If you loved who and what she is, the thought of changing her would never occur to you. And to be honest—"

"She's *my*—"

"To be *honest*, you'd fight anyone who *wanted* to change her. But you didn't, did you? You let the world, you let the church, you let *God* tell you who your daughter should be without ever once listening to her!"

Mama gasped, but Riley wasn't going to apologize.

"You *made* a child, lady! She grew *inside* you. She came from *your* body, and you let other people tell you she was ugly. You had one fucking job—to defend her, to fight! And you failed! You let her down, and that was *before* you ever threw your derby hat into the enemy's ring. Once that happened you betrayed her again. Every day you're betraying your motherly duty."

The bottle hit the floor and bounced in a bell-like tone, rolling along the stone floor of Mama's castle. As Riley listened, another cork squeaked loose and freed a fresh batch of curses.

"You don't even *have* children. And where's *your* mother?"

"Dead."

"He kill her? Your jailbird father?"

Riley's hands clenched, but there on the screen, just below El's sorrowful autobiography, was the balm she needed—the first reply El had given her. El didn't want her to fight. That was why she'd set out to transform herself.

El trusted her.

"My mother died of cancer."

"So she didn't have to live to see *what* you turned into. Lucky her."

It had all begun with that ending. If her mother hadn't died, Riley would have been a different person altogether. Maybe a bit similar, but not as ready to hold a knife.

She picked up the pen and marked the count as Mama swam in her own desperation.

It was all true, but that wasn't the end of the story. She was bigger than a reaction to everything around her. She knew she was, and so Riley calmed her temper and got to the point.

"Did you really pay Jay to sleep with her?"

"Oh, puh-lease!"

"That's not an answer."

"I paid him to *date* her, because she was so fuckin' awkward not a single boy would touch her!"

"That's because she prefers women," Riley said softly. She wanted to be angry. She wanted to cuss the bitch out and hang up, but that wasn't her mission, and if she was honest with herself, she didn't have it in her. Finally, she understood why it was easier for El to run. Guilt and shame and backhanded apologies were the blood and bone of the abuser, and Mama was by every cell a monstrosity.

"How can she possibly know if she's a lesbian if she hasn't fucked a man? I mean, really!"

"The same way you knew you were straight, assuming of course you ever knew that about yourself."

Mama spat the wine with a sound like a gurgling jackal. "That is dis-*gust*-in'!"

"I'm a lesbian. To me, it's normal and completely understandable. You get that, right? If you came out to me, I'd be chill. Things would make sense actually, in a fucked-up way."

"Oh, you can put your painted ass right behind me, you harlot of Babylon."

Riley sighed and glanced at the seconds ticking down. "So was it just a bonus? I mean when Jay decided to pin her down, get a little nut on the side? Was that just like, added benefit, maybe help El realize she was actually straight?"

"She should be thankin' me!" Mama hiccuped and had to cough to regain her voice. "Think about it. She feels . . . *gay* or whateva. She can't be sure! She has sex with him and she suddenly is. Doesn't say much for him, but he's a teenager. When they get married, he'll get practice."

Riley would've facepalmed if it wouldn't have been audible. "The blog entry says that she didn't give consent, but held her tongue because she didn't want you to punish her. Is that the kind of situation you wanted her to be in?" Riley chose her words with the mind of a mechanic, piecing a machine together. One day that engine was going to turn on and convert Mama's life into exhaust. "I know Jay. He's a bully."

"Maybe to people like you."

Riley leaned back with a satisfied smile. "You mean people like your daughter, right? Lesbians."

"Jay is a good boy."

"Sure he is."

"Elyrra is so *selfish*. I cannot believe her!"

"Do you ever take responsibility for how you feel?"

Mama slurred. It took Riley a moment to understand her garbled, "What are you tryin' to say?"

"It's everyone else *but* you. At least that's what you say in every single one of your interviews and vlogs. It's the immigrants, it's the gays, it's the other party. Never you. Which helps you feel superior, sure, but it also makes you a nagging weight around people's necks."

"I don't pay you to be my therapist."

Still smiling, Riley shook her head. "Shit, I hope you pay *someone* to, 'cause you are one mint julep away from drinking mouthwash, lady."

"I'm just fine, thank you."

"Look, I have to get to sleep. Do you want me to tell you what I found, or not?"

The ice jangled in the glass as Riley imagined Mama waving her arm for emphasis. "Why do you think I called?"

"El was attacked. I think she may have been seriously injured." Her eyes went to her phone screen and watched the little readout as it jumped and leapt with each sound.

"Wouldn't have happened if she hadn't run away. Serves her right, really."

"You can press charges if you want. I know who he is, and he's an adult."

"Your *job* is to find my daughter, or are you incapable of focusin' on that task?"

"Oh, I think I'm doing fine. I've tracked her to Iowa."

"Iowa?" This seemed to surprise Mama. Her voice sharpened a bit, surfacing from the Southern drawl just long enough to hint at her partial Ivy League education. "The *other* team only got as far as Ohio."

With a chuckle, Riley flipped through her programs and found the cell phone. It was parked beside a highway in Indiana. She'd outpaced them by a state's width, but they had four drivers. They could easily catch back up. All she could hope was that El had figured out contacting her friend via phone was a bad idea. Unless they decided to simply drive straight through and try to beat El to her destination, they were probably following the same bus route Riley was.

"Yeah, I bumped into them. Nice guys even if they are a bit stupid. They bought me breakfast."

Mama sounded more like herself with sarcasm in her throat. "They told me you were extremely grateful."

"Waitress called the cops, not me. Do they even *have* CC permits in Ohio, because you know gun control is a very political issue these days? Boy howdy, their legal fees—"

"Shut up."

At long last, Riley could swallow her pain meds and crack her joints. Her muscles uncoiled. She yawned operatically. "Hey, I do have a pretty important question."

"*What's* that?"

Riley rolled her eyes and laid a new trap. "That was a pretty neat trick they pulled, with the kid's phone number, but see that's unfair, because you gave them more than you gave me. I was supposed to have the same footing."

"They asked."

"For Rose's phone records?"

"For *my* phone records. Who d'ya think *pays* for her phone?"

Riley popped each knuckle in turn, thinking of Rose's mask, painted up and plucked, her body trotted out on the stage for disgusting people to rate like prized pork. She may have found a different strategy for dealing with her mother, but Rose was just as much a prisoner as El. Riley was sure of that.

"You *do* realize that they can use a backward directory to find his address, right?"

"So?"

"So, if they do something criminal to him, it ties directly to you. You might want to make sure they don't. Just a thought."

"Oh, so now you're an attorney too, huh?"

"Ask your husband. Get something back for all the work you put into his education. I gotta go to sleep."

"My husband isn't part'a this. He has enough to think about." Mama poured another drink. It was like listening to a faucet, the way she guzzled it down. The hashes on the page multiplied. "You're gonna find her, aren't you?"

"Yes."

"You have to."

Riley picked up the knife. "I know."

"Somethin's gotta be done."

"*For* her or *to* her?"

"It's the same, sometimes," Mama whispered. "That's what love is. I love her."

"You love yourself and how she was supposed to fit into that. It's pretty sad you don't know the difference."

Riley hung up. For the next half hour, her phone lit up with misspelled text messages, every one an attempt to draw her back in. Berating to begging, pathos to promises, she ignored it. Without El, Mama had no one to use as her personal victim, so she was looking for a replacement.

She might be able to get one more day of use out of the ATM card, but this tenuous association with Mama Glasse was going to have to end.

Riley returned to the question El had asked of her and knew the answer.

Who was she?

Yours.

Shelter

El's companions exited the bus in Utah with promises to stay in touch. As she watched them retrieve their suitcases, the loneliness descended. She'd felt so comfortable and safe with them, something that made working through her attack even easier. These men, whom her Mama would have gasped to see her with, had paid attention to her in a way no adult had ever done, never once speaking down to her. When she began to talk about her abuse, they didn't offer advice, but sat and took in her feelings. When she described her online following, they were impressed and got their own accounts so that they could read her journal too.

It was the first time she'd ever felt proud of the blog, she realized, and if they left, she worried that feeling of accomplishment would vanish with them.

Doc drew El aside and wrapped her up in a hug. "You got this, sis. You are one of the smartest kids I ever met. You ain't got no problems. You just gotta stay safe and know when to fight."

She held back tears. "Thank you for talking with me. It helped a lot. I have a plan now."

He released her and stood back as if memorizing her face. "You getting off at the end of the line?"

"Yes."

He gave a thoughtful nod and looked out over the parking lot. "I know a guy in Berkeley at a shelter out there. Want me to call him and tell him you're on your way?"

"You can do that?"

"Sure can. I'll set you up. Least I can do. You'll call me, anytime, if you need anything? Even if it's money, right? I can help here and there."

El's lip trembled. She was mute, marveling that anyone could be so kind without any prompting. Doc was a religious man, and though she knew that those beliefs conflicted with her own, she didn't care, because unlike every other Christian she'd ever met, Doc actually embodied the principles of his teachings. It was a strange thing for her to contemplate—that goodness and decency weren't *dependent* upon faith. Rather faith seemed one method for delivering goodness to the world.

They said their goodbyes, though they stayed to wave at her as the bus pulled away. Feeling vulnerable, but somehow stronger overall, El wrote a multitude of entries, each one detailing a different instance or type of abuse she'd suffered at her parent's hands, because Doc had told her it was important to get it out of her mind and into the world. Each one was like a case study in her life and as she documented them from that objective viewpoint, things made complete sense. *Feeling* them, she'd never been able to *think* about them. Now looking in on her life, she could clearly detect the warning signs, the programming that she'd endured, the cycles of behavior. Everything she'd endured became somewhat formulaic, which helped her to distance herself even further from the pain in a way that was healthy, like pulling a sliver from her brain and letting it heal.

Once the oppressive sorrow left her, she returned to the reply from @hellonaunicycle.

"Yours," she whispered.

El entertained a number of possibilities, from creepy stalker who had somehow figured out who she was, to Jay, to her mother in disguise, playing another game to undermine her spirit. For almost two days, she pondered it and if it was prudent to continue the conversation.

Oscar even weighed in via direct message, though his idea was decidedly romantic and nonsensical. To him, only one possibility made any sense—her admirer was Riley, who had been following her blog all along, secretly trying to find a way to approach her. Not only was that silly, and at odds with events, it was impossible. Riley could never lie to her face like that, because she had too much inherent nobility. And even if Riley did know about the blog, there was no way she'd ever be interested in El. At most, Riley would make that adorable face of surprise and then say something like *Ain't that a fucking kick.*

El stared out the window as the forests of the Sierra Nevadas rolled by, daydreaming about the fierce beauty she'd left behind. Perhaps someday, when she was an adult and sure that her mother couldn't hurt Riley, El would contact her and tell her of the crush she'd harbored for years. Not expecting anything in return. Just to tell her that someone found her magical.

If there was anything El had learned, it was that acknowledgement was important.

Downtown Oakland was a strange mixture of art deco and 1960's aesthetic. The tall buildings cast forbidding shadows over many empty shop windows, security bars, graffiti. Walking just from the bus depot to the local transit station, El felt out of place. It was her first time wandering a densely populated area alone, and the Bay Area was far larger than any city she'd ever visited. There were dozens of homeless people along her route, people whose circumstances seemed far direr than her own. The closer she came to the shelter, the more nervous she was about accepting aid from anyone.

The BART train screamed through the tunnels. People seemed to be in their own worlds and no one made eye contact with her. Her misgivings grew as she walked toward the shelter and through a group of kids her own age just getting out of school. For the briefest instant, El was homesick, not for her mother or her cold mansion, but for the easily understood circumstances. She knew that life and how to handle it. Every day in this life was new and complex in ways she hadn't imagined.

The shelter was a series of buildings tucked behind a church. The large crucifix at first put her off. If it meant the same thing to these people as it meant to Mama, this may not be the safest place. Then again, Doc wouldn't do that to her and whatever they had was better than nothing.

The woman immediately recognized the name on her sister's ID. "I've been expecting you!"

El smiled, but as she stood there, she felt incredibly out of place. A cork board was covered in notices and local events. Looking them over was like seeing a collage of cultures she didn't recognize—free music and food events, local clothing drives, and a series of posts for people trying to find others. Mama would have taken a glance and then rolled her eyes, but El was drawn to them, reading each flier for a missing person with an eye for detail. She knew what it was to be lost. She wasn't sure what it felt like to be found.

The woman assembled a clipboard. "We have a lot of parents come and post them, just in case."

El nodded. So other people's parents didn't hire goon squads to hunt their children down. That was comforting and also unrecognizably odd.

Filling out the forms, El had to give a great deal of information she wasn't sure she wanted to. Before she could be admitted for a bed, she'd have to submit to having her bag searched for anything hazardous and go through a series of rules and regulations for the shelter. Meals were at specific times and consisted of the best the organization could afford. The bed was a twin-sized mat on the floor in a dormitory. The bathrooms were communal.

El initialed everything and signed—she was supposed to be at camp anyway. This wasn't too far off the mark, though the situation was anything but a holiday. But she would take the Camp of Hard Knocks over Fairest Meadows any day.

She was assigned a locker and a mat. Lunch was a peanut butter and jelly sandwich and canned green beans. El ate every bite. She'd been living on beef jerky and dried fruit for days and had gone far past the threshold of being emotionally invested in food. As she sat, paper napkin in her lap, sipping her Solo cup of fruit punch with her pinky out, she noticed two girls watching her. They weren't subtle about it, one scowling while the other whispered in her ear and set them both snickering.

In high school, El had never been picked on in the usual ways. Her mother's looming shadow was enough to secure her a silent seat at the cool kids table, but she was out of that darkness now and she'd have to stand the full light of a harsh sun.

As she sat there, breathing deeply, her hands clenching around her plastic fork, more of Riley came into focus for her. El had watched, mute and dejected, as Riley had been tormented by the bullies she used for protection—from food being thrown to threats. Riley somehow managed to turn it back around, transforming a conflict into an examination of the bullies themselves, and when that didn't work, she'd step right up to them. Riley could look at a social dynamic and see the weapons just lying there to be used.

But El had never been a fighter. She knew her way was different, even though she had no idea what it was.

Maybe it was time to figure that out.

Picking up her tray, El walked to their table and smiled down at them. The comedian had a shaved head and piercings up both ears, while her friend wore long braids, each one ended with a bauble of some kind, some sea shells, some beads, some little pieces of glass with string wrapped around them. They stood out beautifully against her skin and read like a kind of guide to her travels.

"I'm sorry to stare, but I just had to come over and say . . . I really like your hair. Did you do that yourself?"

"Naw. She went to this salon on the hill, got a nice massage at the same time. That's Boho Chic sea glass in genuine rawhide. And those plastic beads are on fleek." The girl with the shaved head rolled her eyes. "Of course she did it herself."

El shifted from foot to foot nervously. "I just meant I wondered if she had help with the back ones. I can't braid my hair at all. Working upside down and backwards doesn't make sense to my fingers. All I know how to do is put it into a ponytail. It keeps getting caught in my pack straps . . . Sorry to bother you. I just thought it was really unique and pretty."

Uncertain where to go, or how to diffuse the tension, El walked stiffly to the trash can and dropped her plate in. Without looking back, she went back into the dormitory and sat on her bed mat. Being lonely was nothing new to her, but being alone while lonely, that was a new feeling.

As she sat there, the two girls appeared. When they spotted her, they cut a path to the locker room, declaring her an outsider with dismissive glances over their shoulders. El logged into the wi-fi and texted Oscar, just to forget how uncomfortable she was.

In his usual way, he offered to come and meet her, but if @hellonaunicycle was right and the commandos knew about Oscar, they'd be following him. He confirmed there were no ominous vehicles outside his home, but El couldn't imagine what she'd feel if something happened to him.

What if we meet at like a crowded mall, it would work, right?

She smiled. *Maybe tomorrow. I haven't showered in a few days and I am really tired. They make us leave during the day, so I won't have anything else to do anyway.*

I have the perfect place!

Plans made, El disconnected the phone and tucked it into her pocket. When she looked up, the two girls had reemerged with their own backpacks and were on their way out. As if they couldn't believe how stupid she was, they laughed at El and shook their heads.

"This ain't no day spa. You want a nap, go sleep in a doorway."

Embarrassed, nervous, confused, El gathered her necessities for the day into a smaller sack.

If this was where she was going to be for the next few weeks, it might be a good idea to figure a few things out before the evening curfew. Signing out, she set an alarm on her phone so as to be sure to arrive before the doors locked for the night, and walked out into the city. She toured the busiest streets, located the library and got herself a library card so that she could use the free wi-fi. Seeing a sign for a junior college, she steeled herself and dropped in on the administration office. They gave her booklets of information on the exam she'd need and what she could do to get into a college after taking it. They even explained the loan system and taught her how to file for financial aid.

Feeling overwhelmed but happy, El wandered toward a patch of trees, realizing she'd found the local University. Its monolithic bell tower played an entire concerto as she sat beneath a redwood tree. She retrieved some employment applications from a few shops, watched some skateboarders perform tricks, and treated herself to a scoop of ice cream for a dollar. She felt accomplished by the time the alarm on her phone warned her to start back.

Halfway to the church, El's mood was knocked askew by a series of shrieks. As she passed a parking lot, she looked for the source of the noises and recognized the two girls from the shelter amidst a snarl of limbs. Above the screams of the brawlers, she could pick out the voice of the joker among them, crying out for everyone to chill.

Two people had a hold of the girl with the braids and were trying to rip her bag off her shoulders, while she fought back in spitting, hissing fury. The three collided into a metal dumpster. One of the strangers had a hand tangled in the braids and used the hold to smash the girl's head into the metal. Her friend tried to pull them off, but the aggressors seemed to be older and stronger.

El didn't know why, but she couldn't walk away. Her friendship with Doc and John had begun when they'd helped her and if she didn't take their example, she'd never embody what she admired. She dropped her ice cream cone and took to her heels. As she gained speed on her hobbled knee, a fuzzy thought came to El. All day long she'd felt as if she didn't deserve to take any charity, that her circumstances were so much better than most runaways. She'd filled up her time trying to think of *valuable* things to do to repay the debt she owed to society. But all the things she'd considered—going to school, getting a low-level job, trying to find a way to pay back the shelter—ignored the fact that she'd been forgotten in the first place. El didn't want to exist in a world that ignored the people who needed the most help.

Just as she had seen Riley do at school, El ran full force at one of the girls. At the last possible second, she jumped and brought her good knee up to chest height. She landed the blow right to the small of a back. In a loud shout, the attacker lost her grip on the girl with braids. In a sound like the bell tower, her forehead hit the edge of the dumpster. As they fell away from the main altercation, El got a leg around a flailing arm and tightened her hold. From the ground, she watched the girls from the shelter chase off the other attacker. It wasn't until the person vanished around the building that El realized she was restraining an unconscious body.

To her surprise, as she wriggled out from beneath, the girl with the shaved head offered her a hand. Huffing, her fists bloodied and her feet unsteady, the other girl nodded at her.

"We gotta go. Come on!"

El spared the body one glance to make certain she was breathing, and followed. They jogged down a backstreet toward the shelter. Every time a car passed them, they ducked behind trees. El mimicked them, uncertain what she'd just gotten herself into. Apparently, her way of making friends had a lot more in common with Riley's than she'd thought.

"Who were those women?" she hissed.

The victim shook her head. "Just some bitches from another shelter."

"You knew them?"

"One of them took my shit. I took it back and she tried to get me kicked out. She's got a thing for me. She hears voices. Thinks I'm in some kind of conspiracy."

El leaned against a tree and rubbed her knee. Blood stained her pants, but she wasn't sure if it was hers or someone else's. The pain was certainly intense.

The snarky girl ran her hands over her stubbled head. "We gotta clean up or they won't let us in."

"I have some wet wipes," El wheezed, digging through her bag. "I'm El."

The girl with the braids mopped blood from her forehead, her face screwed up in pain. "Maddy. And this is Risa."

Risa made a wry face. "Some introduction."

"I don't know." Finally catching her breath, El smiled. "Where I come from, we usually make friends while shooting plates with rifles."

With a snort, Risa shook her head. "You're not from around here, are you?"

"North Carolina."

"You guys scrap a lot down south? That was a nice move."

"No. My first girl fight, actually."

Maddy dropped the wad of bloody cloths into the trash can and donned a sweatshirt from her bag to cover the spattered clothing. "I coulda handled it."

Without missing a beat, Risa rolled her eyes. "Yeah, but did you want to have a skull afterward? Don't be a bitch, Mads. Just say thank you."

As if she couldn't stand the idea of owing anyone anything, Maddy crossed her arms. "Thanks. This doesn't make us friends."

"Sure as hell don't make us enemies," Risa remarked smartly. As they followed Maddy to the door, she leaned over and patted El on the back. "Don't mind her. She's always grumpy. Her situation is pretty shitty."

"And yours?"

"Also, pretty shitty, but I have a sense of humor."

"Mine is too."

Risa shot her a look. "No! You mean this isn't just something you do for fun?"

Poison Fruit

E l sat on the sectional sofa in the common room with her knees drawn up to her chest and tears in her eyes. Risa had framed her tale in a darkly comedic way, but it was too horrible to be funny. Her mother had become addicted to drugs and had turned to prostitution to pay for it, until she'd suddenly stopped coming home.

"I called her the invisible woman for about six weeks. Ate school lunches until they ran out. Then the landlord found out she'd gone AWOL and called CPS. I dunno. I didn't like the foster home. The woman made us do chores for food. And we weren't allowed to have stuff. You know? No personals."

El thought of her bag, full of nothing but the things Riley had helped her buy and a few scraps of paper. She thought of her bedroom full of all the things her mother thought she ought to own, none of it important to her. Her only personal possession was the blog and if anyone tried to take that from her . . .

"I couldn't tell anyone," El whispered. "My mom is . . . she's kind of famous and no one would believe me. The things she does . . . she keeps them hidden. Not even my sister would vouch for me, because we're treated differently."

Maddy had been silent, staring at the ground as if lost in her own thoughts. Suddenly, her eyes lifted, filled with righteous fury. "She didn't stand up for you?"

"She's . . ." El shrugged. "It's not her. My mom just decided I was the one she needed to break, I guess."

"Is she older than you?"

"Yes."

"Then she should have fucking stuck up for you."

A bit taken aback by her vehemence, El set her pillow aside. "My mom would tear her down too."

"So what?" Maddy crossed her arms. "She's your sister! That's what they're supposed to do!"

El took a deep breath and resolved something in that moment, as the words came out of her mouth. "Maybe . . . but to me it's fine. I'm stronger than her, I think. I'm the one protecting her from the worst of it. The age doesn't matter, I guess."

Maddy was shivering. "Older kids gotta do for the littler ones. That's how it's supposed to be!"

Risa shifted uncomfortably. "Maddy's mom is in the hospital. Her little brother is in foster care around here. They don't let her see him."

El's mouth fell open. "They can *do* that?"

Maddy shrugged angrily. "We don't have any rights! I don't have a lawyer to go in and ask for visitation. No judge would ever let me see him, since I ain't got a house or a job."

"But . . ." El looked up at the ceiling in astonishment. She'd never considered that children would be kept from each other. It was unthinkable. "Why . . . how did you two become separated?"

Maddy looked as if she was about to rip out her own braids. "What do you mean, how? They just come and take him, that's how!"

"It's okay, Mads. She doesn't know." Risa put a hand on her arm and squeezed. "Her mom can't take care of them. She's got moved to a hospital in LA. Maddy is too old for foster care. She doesn't have a high school diploma because she left to take care of him. Getting a job without one and living out of a shelter is almost impossible."

"There aren't . . . any programs?"

"Bitch!" Maddy strangled a pillow. "You think anybody is going to give me a chance? I don't know how to do any of that shit. Ain't no one sit down with me and teach me to read! The letters don't make any sense. My daddy in prison, my mom . . . dying! Nobody cares."

Risa sighed, her humor finally dried up. "She's waiting for her brother to age out."

"I walk him to school sometimes, when they ain't around to see us. We got it all planned out. He's gonna get that diploma, and then he's gonna go to college, and we gonna live together and help each other. I gotta just wait."

The horror of it all grew in El's mind until she could see others she knew experiencing it. Riley's life could so easily have been mapped onto this girl's. If things had been timed even a little differently, Riley could have been sleeping in places like this, eating peanut butter and waiting for clean socks to be donated.

"Your mother . . . does she know where you are?"

"She fucking sent me." Maddy wiped tears from her eyes. "I haven't talked to her in a long time. I don't even know if she's alive."

"She has some kind of liver thing," Risa muttered.

"You haven't . . . called her?"

"I don't know nobody with a phone. Shelter don't let us call long-distance."

Stricken mute, El stared at Maddy. This girl, whom she'd protected, who had become her friend and given her pointers on survival, was probably going to be trapped on the street forever. Judging by the look on Risa's face, she knew it too.

El's first day in a shelter and she'd already met one person whose life seemed impossibly stuck. Society had literally no place for Maddy and didn't even know she existed. If it was that easy to find one such person, then . . . how many were out there?

All through dinner, the betrayal El felt toward her parents grew. Not just for her mother, but now for her father too. He was someone who could have helped her and he'd ignored it, but he was also someone who could have helped girls like Maddy. The truth was, though, he was busy playing games. He didn't care about anyone like these people in this shelter. Once they stopped being useful, they stopped existing. And if they bothered to speak up, they were told to somehow make themselves useful first. She'd heard it a dozen times in the last year, at his campaign rallies, her mother nodding in agreement at his back.

In the locker room, El went through the employment applications. All of them required basic skills like making change, using a computer, reading. Some of the questions on them, upon reflection, seemed to be designed specifically to exclude people who didn't have their own cars, or who couldn't afford to clean a uniform every day. All of them asked for a social security number or a residential address.

Sitting on the long bench, El barely withstood a wave of hopelessness. She had what she needed to get her feet beneath her, but only because her family had been white, wealthy, privileged, putting on a show for their peers. But Maddy didn't even have that. Misery wasn't a competition, she knew, but El couldn't help reflect on the embarrassment of her riches, even as she sat there on her borrowed bed mat.

In her invisible moments, El could sense others moving past her, as if she could reach out in the haze and grab a hand. Whenever her mother railed about entitlement, whenever her father argued about welfare programs being a socialist scourge, they were creating more ghosts. Suddenly, what they'd done to her seemed merely the tip of an iceberg, and El could feel herself slipping into that frozen sea and understanding that she was perhaps the only person who saw what was coming. If someone in a position of power could hurt their own flesh and blood, imagine what they could do to the thousands of lives depending on them.

How many children like Maddy had paid for her sister's pageants? How many had been dispossessed to buy the possessions she'd just scorned? How many girls like her had been squeezed dry so that she could pay for her adventure?

El couldn't get warm, even when she stood under scalding water. Even when she slept fitfully twisted in her assigned blanket. Even when she left for the day to meet Oscar.

He was easy to pick out in the crowd, and when she smiled at him, his eyes lit up just as she'd imagined they would. He practically threw himself around her, and held her tightly. But still, she was numb with the chill.

"You're really here, like an actual person!"

Her laugh fell flat. El walked beside him, letting his string of words stand in for a conversation, while her thoughts continued to mull over possibilities. There had to be a way to help Maddy, to break the cycle. The more she thought about it, the more she realized she knew the answer, but it wasn't a good one.

Oscar walked her to a park with a huge waterfall. Beneath a tree, he spread out a blanket and began unpacking a small snack. Guacamole and chips, as promised.

"So . . . What's wrong with you?" He scooped up some dip on a chip and shoved it into her mouth as she attempted to answer. "You come all this way, and I *finally* get to hug you, and you look like you're about to cry."

El was hungry, but she couldn't pay attention to her appetite. Chewing had a mechanical feel to it and the food was tasteless. "You're going to think I've gone crazy."

He laughed. It was nice to hear that sound in person. It really did feel as if they'd known each other their entire lives. When he took her hand, she held his happily.

"Okay, so after everything you've told me in the past two weeks, what is going to make me think you're crazy? I mean really? Are you going to tell me you met a faith healer, or like, saw a ghost?"

"I . . ." El looked into his eyes and felt calm suddenly. He was her friend. She didn't need to put up the barricades, or try to pretend it made sense. The words toppled out with barely a shove. "I'm going to leave."

His jaw dropped. After a long while, he shook his head. "What are you talking about?"

When she'd finished explaining the situation to him, his expression hadn't much improved.

"She has to stay here, Oscar. She doesn't have a choice. And she needs to call her mom. I can't afford to give her my burner phone. I have to conserve every minute I can. But I can give her the iPhone on my mom's account."

"That makes no sense! If she uses it, your mom is going to know where you've been!" He let her go and sat back, waving his hands dramatically. "She'll send those assholes to the shelter! She'll follow you!"

"I know. That's why I'll leave."

"El . . . Come on! Think about this." He shook his head imploringly. "If you let her use that phone, your mom's just going to fuck with her too."

"Not if she sells it quickly. She can use it to buy a burner or something. She can get a few free calls off in the meantime. I'm going to call my friend Doc to help her. He will. I know he will. And I can get far away. I can keep moving."

"But you're *here*, El! You made it to the end! You don't have to keep going!"

With a sigh, she reclined on the blanket and stared up into the trees. "I don't have to, but I'm going to."

"Just give her your burner phone then and get a new one."

"I don't have any money left, Oscar. She panhandles. I know it's crazy to imagine, but there are people who can't afford cell phones."

"I'll buy you one!"

Smiling ruefully, she looked away. "You don't have any money either."

He fell silent. For a moment, she wondered if he was going to come back with another reason why she shouldn't be stubbornly set on this, but he didn't. Instead, He tipped back next to her and put his hands behind his head.

"A week ago," he said softly, "you were afraid of every step you took. Now you're telling me you want to keep going."

"She doesn't even know if her mother is alive, Oscar. I don't love my mama, but I can't imagine not knowing if Rose was alive, or wondering if Riley was okay. I can't imagine what it might feel like to wonder if you were buried in an unmarked grave by strangers."

When she looked at him, his eyes were closed. Droplets trimmed his lashes in glitter. She rolled and poked his nose with a finger.

"It's a tiny thing, I know, but I want to do it, and all it costs me is another move. That's it. I can do that. I can be gone in minutes. I get on a train and I vanish."

"And then what? You don't have any money!"

"I have legs. They work pretty well, I've discovered."

"I can get you a ride somewhere, okay? Just tell me where you want to go."

"Really?"

He nodded.

"North, I guess. One of the girls said that there were forests. I like forests on the beach. That sounds amazing."

"Okay. I'll take care of it. Just give me a day," he said quietly, though he sounded as if he was about to cry.

They spent the rest of the afternoon walking the city. From the waterfront to Chinatown, they roamed, making jokes and talking about life, until it was time for El to return to the shelter. At their parting, he gave her a long embrace and swore to visit her as soon as he was finished with exams.

As she sat on the subway, calmly contemplating her path ahead, a sound drew her to her phone. She'd forgotten about the wi-fi in the tunnels. It was a notification from the blog site telling her she had a new direct message. At the sight of the @hellonaunicycle handle, her stomach lurched.

If you're giving this Maddy girl the phone, make sure you reset it to factory settings first.

Lips parted in astonishment, El stared at the screen until it went dark. Then in a furious shake, she brought the device back to life and smashed out a reply.

Who are you and how do you know about the phone?

Your friend messaged me.

"Oh my god, Oscar, you doofus."

The next message appeared with a well-timed bloop. *He's a nice kid. Don't be hard on him.*

In a sudden panic, El looked around. The car was packed with commuters, but no one in particular was looking her way.

Don't worry. That was a lucky guess. I'm not psychic or anything. And I have no idea where you are, though I'm guessing it's on public transit, yeah?

How do you know these things?

Simple math, really.

Who are *you*? El fired back, a frown permanently etched on her forehead. *Why are you messaging me?*

If you meet me, I'll tell you.

An address appeared with a corresponding time.

El turned off her phone at once. The train operator announced her stop. El leaped up and practically ran for the escalator. Waiting for her to return from her face-to-face with some guy she'd met on the internet, Risa and Maddy were standing outside.

She slammed into them at full speed, almost breathless. "We have to go! Right now. I need to be in the shelter, now."

Risa made a face. "Ketchup meatloaf that big a favorite in North Carolina?"

But Maddy knew fear when she saw it, and didn't hesitate. She cut a path through a crowd of tourists, pulling El by the hand as if they were sisters. When they were safely behind the doors of the shelter, El went straight for her bed. Risa and Maddy insisted on sitting with her. They didn't even seem surprised when she pulled out a phone and returned to the blog site.

She obviously hadn't done enough research on the @hellonaunicycle profile. It had to be some kind of trick. A clever way of getting her to let her guard down, but she'd be damned if she did that.

Tell me who you are.

Meet me and I will. Face-to-face.

Why should I?

Because I've been following you long enough.

El's heart was pounding, but it was comforting to think this was just another fan. *Lots of people follow me. The blog is popular.*

That's not what I mean, Snow, and you know it. Meet me at that address as soon as you leave tomorrow. Give Maddy the phone first. I'd feel better if you didn't have it anymore anyway. Your mother is relentless.

El froze. For a brief instant, she dared to hope, but she'd gone a long time without such an emotion. It was almost impossible to remember what it felt like.

This could be a trick.

True. Although, Mama's more the 'hire a death squad' type, you know?

You could be the death squad.

I could be. El read the text bubble in a singsong voice, her skin tingling with goose bumps. *But I'm not.*

How do I know?

You're just going to have to trust me. I know where you are. If I wanted you caught, I'd just send someone to get you. But I want you safe. So eat. Sleep. Do your good deed. Then meet me. I'll be waiting. You want to see the forests? So let's ride.

25
Parlor Tricks

There El stood, within grasp, waiting in the ordering line. A few steps away. Even with the ice cream cones around her, El didn't seem the least bit clued in. This all began with El visiting Sam's parlor to stare at her and mutter incoherently. Now it seemed like it was going to come full circle, except that Riley was probably going to be tongue-tied.

All she had to do was move. She wanted to, her mind having done this dance so many times in the last few days it had every possible twirl mapped, but she couldn't. Her legs were numb, her mouth dry. She leaned her forehead against the window and watched El clutch her phone and scan the room.

"Come on, Riley! What the fuck!" she whispered to herself, but even with the encouragement, she couldn't move.

She'd been hooked. That fast. She couldn't escape it, but . . . what if it was magic?

Against the backdrop of her affection for El, played doubts she hadn't considered in the midst of her quest—these feelings they both had could be some kind of illusion, so that they didn't have to be alone. El admired Riley's way of dealing with challenges, and she admired El's depth, focus, and drive. El saw past her bravado and wanted more from her than that. She could see how much El had suffered and wanted her safe. They saw in each other something they wished they possessed, and knew that there were hidden meanings written in tears and scars, but was that enough?

Relationships built over years and never stopped, Riley understood, so would that be enough for a beginning?

Riley thought of her own mother and the tremendous risk she'd taken. Writing letters to violent convicts had to have been an unnerving prospect. But she must have lost her shit when Jimmy asked to think on her romantically! She had probably argued back and forth with herself about all the horror stories of naive girls being headhunted by monsters, all the dark roads such a relationship could traverse. Somehow, though, she'd seen his strength in his story. It was enough to keep her coming back to the prison to learn more about him. What she learned from those encounters was enough to put her at the gate when he was released. And how he handled the next phase of his life had been enough to make her say "yes."

When El's turn at the front of the queue came, she pointed at the flavor closest to her. She seemed so disappointed, but as Riley looked on, she lifted her face and took a deep breath, shouldering her pack with a determined expression.

Riley put her back to the wall just as El's gaze swiveled to the window.

Freedom was a tricky thing—open ground in all directions, the option to go anywhere, do anything, but with absolutely no protection from shitty weather or cataclysm. How a person handled freedom, how they behaved on the open road, was a good measure of who they were.

No matter where they went or what they learned.

Mom hadn't been afraid of Dad, because she could see he was done with the pack. He was a lone wolf who rode with caution. That had spoken to her more than any fumbling words Jerry O'Leary could smash together with ham-fisted, high school language skills.

Riley closed her eyes. She wasn't afraid of all the wonderful things she could imagine. She was afraid because of all the terrible things that could happen, what she could lose, what might occur if she took off the armor.

"Stupid." Riley clenched her jaw shut. El had faced every challenge to her freedom, from disrupted plans, to attackers, to the self-righteous vitriol of her own mother. El had spent years watching Riley in silence to protect her from the consequences. El had everything it would take and really, it was Riley who was lacking.

All she had to offer was rage.

Her dad would tell her that wasn't true, but he loved her more than life and without her having to earn it.

Riley lifted her phone and typed out half the message before she thought about the implications.

How did R earn your love?

Riley hit the Send button and then spent a good five minutes crouched beside the front door hating herself for doing something so childish. She'd jumped into fights with less thought than walking through this one goddamned door, but nope. This was too much. It turned out she was just that fucking fragile.

When the answer popped on screen with the sound of shuffling papers, Riley could barely read it for the full-body cringe.

She didn't have to earn it. I think she's exceptional, that's all. I just want to watch her exist, because she never disappoints. She does just fine without me, but we might have been even better together.

Riley hid her face in her knees.

Just fine without El? It was true. Riley had always done just fine never knowing about the girl in her shadow. If she had kept to her trajectory, moving from one cool experience to the next, she'd probably do just fine. She could handle anything bad that life threw at her. She would always be just fine.

Riley stood up and dusted herself off, checked her makeup, huffed a few lungsful of pure air.

Just fine wasn't good enough.

Riley Vanator had ambition. She had drive. Everything else be damned, Riley was never going to settle for "just fine."

Learning, evolving, growing—it all came down to being challenged, having something dropped right in the path that couldn't be ignored. Experience had taught her how to keep the vulnerable parts hidden, but she couldn't let go of a chance to learn what it meant to be seen. It wasn't a risk, so much as an opportunity.

"I cannot fucking *believe* you had to psyche yourself up! Like, how fucking old are you? *Five*? Jesus, Riley!" Her muttering caught a few looks as she danced angrily in place. "Come on! Fucking go in there! Ugh!"

Someone held the door for her with a raised brow. She slid inside and stood like an embarrassed idiot in the entryway, staring at El's back and fumbling for something suave to say. Her phone vibrated in her hand.

Where are you? I can't stay here for long.

Riley licked her lips and knew she'd crossed the threshold—it was now or never. Their positions were finally reversed. It was she who was writing from the shadows, Riley who had stepped behind the protections unnoticed.

Turn around.

El's phone clattered onto the table. Her back hardened into a wall of muscle as her fingers curled around the table edge. Over her left shoulder, a blue eye stared widely at the tiled floor.

Dad would call her impatient, but Riley put a booted foot right in the center of El's wonder. "Hey there, Snow."

As the gaze slid up her body, it triggered a shiver in Riley. Gone was the diffident little girl who couldn't bring herself to make eye contact. El's stare was now so penetrating it could probably gut Riley if she didn't move.

Legs a bit weak, Riley sank into the empty chair. Her habit was always to bring up a knee, lean back, do something to upset the dynamic of serious situations, but this wasn't a struggle for dominance. This was just the two of them sitting side by side, defenseless.

El's breathing was shallow and swift. Her expression demanded answers. Riley reached into her pocket and set *Tizóna* on the table. "You dropped this."

El's eyes squeezed shut, though nothing else about her face changed. "How did you find me?"

This wasn't playing out like her fantasy, but fair enough. Riley had deprived El of a clean getaway, so she just had to accept the consequences. "I'm pretty fucking clever."

Still as rigid as iron, El opened her eyes and stared Riley down. For the first time in the two years she'd known the girl, Riley saw confidence and strength. "If you found me, then they can too. My mother—"

"Who do you think she hired?"

El bit down on her lip as if to hold in a shriek. Tears glimmered as she seemed to piece a bleak story together. It was based in her life's experiences of human nature to date, and it was probably a pretty tragic fairy tale. As the flicker of betrayal stoked to life, Riley reached out and touched her pointed chin.

"I'm not here to bring you back, El."

"You're . . . You're not?"

"I'm here to join you . . ." Riley shrugged. "If you'll have me, I guess."

El's sun-kissed face went blank. Her lips parted as if to ask why, though not a word was spoken. Suddenly flustered and uncertain why she'd ever thought herself stronger than El, Riley tangled her fingers in her unruly hair and cast around for words.

"Your mom thinks so little of you that she'd rather believe you're just infatuated and naive and life is going to prove you wrong. Pisses me off. I mean, it's not like I think I'm the goddess you make me out to be, but I really am . . . You know . . . Honorable and all that shit."

A giggle erupted from El, pouring out of her until she was gasping for breath and the infection had spread to Riley. Face burning, tongue-tied, she laughed at herself more than anything else.

"Riley?"

She had to clear her throat, suddenly more sheepish than she'd ever been in her life. "Yeah?"

"How long have you known?"

"About the blog?"

El nodded with a sweep of her dark lashes.

"Since the day you vanished."

With a great sigh, El curled up on herself, forehead almost touching the table. "I'm so sorry if it made you feel uncomfortable. I know it was wrong to—"

"Are you kidding me?"

She couldn't stand it anymore. This was too excruciating. Riley hooked a steel toe beneath the rung of El's chair and tugged. The thing swiveled just enough for her to plant a hand on either side of El's hips and lean close.

Nose to nose, she dropped her voice to a whisper. "I keep asking myself . . . if I'd just kissed you any of the times I had a chance to, would you have run away? Would you have left me behind? We could have ditched that fucking place together—"

"It's not safe, not even now."

"Yeah?" El's eyes had fallen to her mouth. Riley caught the gaze again with a dip of her chin and a grin. "Because I strike you as the kind of person who gives a fuck about safety?"

"I know you. You give a fuck about mine."

Riley swallowed. "Of course."

"And you know I couldn't run if I thought you would be hurt standing up for me. I had to go alone. I'm sorry."

"Stop apologizing. It's killing me." She closed her eyes. She could smell the chocolate ice cream on El's lips. The skin on the tip of El's nose was soft as it traced a line along her cheekbone. A hand brushed her hair aside and sent a tingle down her spine.

The cacophony of the parlor was muted compared to the sound of El's breathing and the steady thumping of her own heart.

"Is this okay?" She didn't sound like herself at all, her voice was so ragged, but she couldn't waste energy on trying to be perfect when she was just trying to get it done. "If I kiss you now, are you gonna—"

El sat forward and sent a shockwave through her. Every muscle contracted at once—fingers tangled in the belt loops of El's jeans, toes curled in her boots, stomach clenched like she'd taken a blow. Somehow softer than she'd imagined, El's mouth swept along her bottom lip and left her breathless. The kiss tasted like peanut butter cups, and the sigh in El's throat was the finest sound.

"Come with me," El whispered.

Riley had to remember how to speak, something she'd never had to do in her entire existence. "Wha? Where?"

"Anywhere. Everywhere."

"How about my room at the Mission Hill Motorlodge?"

With a husky chuckle, El shoved her back. She had a goofy grin on her face, but before Riley could get too far, the chipped manicure dragged her back by the tassels on her jacket.

"One more for the road."

Giddy and uncoordinated, Riley managed not to trip over everything when they finally caught their breath and rose to leave. It felt suddenly like her clothes were too small and her shoes too large, but as long as she stayed tethered to El, nothing in the universe could possibly be wrong. They meandered along the crowded street, communicating in sidelong glances and laughter, hands clasped, going no particular direction until Riley spotted her bike.

"So, uh . . ." She slapped a hand down on the top box, airbrushed with quicksilver scales. "Allow me to introduce you to Aella, my steed."

"It's a dragon!" El stroked the handlebars in awe.

"It's a two-seater . . . with a hitch. Can pull a little tent trailer. Cozy bed for two, if you're interested."

Much to Riley's joy, El licked her lips. "Sounds comfortable."

Riley popped the clasp and tossed the girl her helmet. "Came with two of these too. Radio headset so we can talk or listen to music while we ride into the sunset."

"I love her."

"You'll need an outfit," Riley took the helmet back and crowned her, pulling the chin strap across and anchoring it. "Something leather and very sexy."

El raised the shaded visor to greet her with a wry look. "Is that mandatory?"

"No, I just know that you'll have a hard time finding anything made out of leather that doesn't inspire me to make out with you. If that's uncomfortable, you can always back out now. After this moment, you're gonna have a hard time getting rid of me, to be honest."

El had taken hold of her belt and brought their hips together with a tug. In the shade of her faceplate, she nipped at the tip of Riley's nose and tickled her soul. "I *literally* ran across country and you followed me."

"Yeah, okay, the line *may* have been crossed a while ago. Should have warned you. Sorry about that."

"Stop apologizing," El shot back, dropping the visor. "Let's ride."

Riley unhitched the chain and stored it, chuckling to herself. "Anyone ever tell you you're one hell of a chick?"

She took her seat. El's arms slid around her shoulders and a thumb stroked her pulse point. As she started the bike, two wonderful sensations collided.

A little voice crackled to life in her helmet. "Just you. Has anyone ever told you that you're the coolest?"

"Just you."

26
Yours

As they entered the hotel room, El knew she should be nervous. In this moment, where so many possibilities and desires thrashed around, a girl's hand shouldn't have the strength to keep order. But was that right, or was it what she'd been conditioned to believe? With her lips pressed to Riley's, El felt an incredible strength and an urge to get as close as flesh would allow. Not a drop of nervousness flowed in her veins.

Riley had defended her honor, outsmarted their enemies, and protected her ferociously, but was tame beneath her, with a sleepy gaze and a bemused smile. When they lay down together, El ran kisses over each curve and traced landmarks with fingertips. There was a map here to be learned and a journey to make, but she was an adventurer now.

She had what it took.

"Is it all right to say aloud? To you? I've wanted to for so long, but I never did and . . ." Her eyes stung. She squeezed them shut. "When I was on that freight train, dangling over the trestle bridge, I kept thinking it was the one thing I regretted. Everything else made me who I am, but that one thing . . . I wish I'd said it."

Riley gathered El's tragic mop of streaky hair and twisted it onto the crown of her head with a single admonishment from the clicking of her tongue ring. A rubber bracelet secured the strands off her neck, and bare skin was kneaded and caressed until El's back gave way. It was impossible to stop absorbing information, so she nibbled a studded ear and shook with the tiny tremor in Riley's throat when she spoke.

"Say what you want, El. No one will ever tell you to shut up again. Not while I'm here. Not if they want to keep their teeth, anyway."

Her giggle didn't stop the words from spilling out. "I love you. You need to know that. At least, I think you do. You go from one fight to another. In between, you should know someone is waiting."

Riley let out a hiss and sat up. Unsettled from her comfortable perch, El glanced up in time to see the tears Riley hid with lacquered fingertips.

"Fuck, you talk just like you write. I'm gonna look like a panda if you keep saying that shit."

"A really *sexy* panda."

"Maybe she's born with it . . ."

"Maybe it's mammalian?"

Riley's laugh was husky, and her skin glowed bronze and rose gold in the yellow lamplight. El brought the blanket up around her shoulders like a mantle and wrestled her lover back beneath her hips, pecking each freckle with a kiss.

"We barely know each other," Riley whispered. "I've done a lot of messed-up stuff in my life so far. I know that's stupid to say, because I'm only eighteen, but . . . I don't know. I feel a lot older sometimes."

El sat back, admiring Riley's naked body with a long stare. She had a grouping of flowers tattooed in the hollow beneath her left collarbone. They trailed into the cleft at her sternum. As if to counter, a skeleton's hand grasped the rib cage beneath her full breast, as if Death were coming from behind to seize her.

"It doesn't matter. I know who you are *now*. You can't hide who you are, Riley, it's not something you are capable of doing. You're like . . . you're a tuning fork. You strike and then stand, and the world just sort of . . . vibrates around you."

Riley's fuchsia hair was fading to bubblegum, but the dark roots had a purple sheen to them as she shook her head in obvious wonder. "Is this going to be how it is? You're just going to drop poems on me all the time."

"Someone should. You deserve them."

"How do you know?"

El sighed as she realized why Riley's tough exterior was always in order—she had a warm, voluptuously vulnerable core to protect. "Because. Everything you've seen or done, as terrible or painful as it may have been, is what made this person. I know this person. She has an old soul and a strong heart. There's nothing you could possibly tell me that would disappoint me. Not if it made this person here with me."

Riley bent a well-muscled leg against her backside and bucked. Toppled from her throne, El was tangled up and captured, suffering the coup with a smile.

"I don't handle compliments well," Riley grumbled.

"I have powerful magic if I can embarrass you."

"Yes, you do, you sorceress."

The hungry kiss pulled a moan from her. Bit by bit, the anxiety of the last week was worked from El, and in its place warmth and joy were spreading. When the girl beckoned, she rolled onto her stomach and offered up her back. Riley's fingers were incredibly precise, strengthened by years of bike and brawl, but perfected by tinkering. Eventually, El was dozing, her body a lump of jelly.

Riley's tongue swept up her spine. A kiss was planted at the nape of her neck. The girl's weight lifted from the bed and the shower rattled to life. As El listened, Riley began to sing a Spanish anthem in a low and soulful voice. This moment was perfect in every way, right down to the war she was fighting between peaceful sleep and a wakeful mind. If she rested, she'd lose the details. If she clung to the details, she'd be at the point of exhaustion.

El sat up and stretched.

Their clothes were scattered across the floor. She gathered them with a blush, retracing the steps of the dance, fueled by music only they had heard. Sneaking up behind Riley in the shower, she snatched the washcloth and took charge of scrubbing her champion.

There was another tattoo just above the swell of Riley's hip. It looked as if the flesh were peeled back and beneath it were scales like the ones on Aella. Tracing them, El found that part of the realism came from a scar along the edge of the folded skin. It was long and rough and when fresh, must have been deep.

"How did you get this?"

Riley's hands were braced on the wall. Her head drooped, face dripping. The look on it was one El had never seen on Riley before and the sadness there caught her off guard.

"I got jumped by a group of boys right after I came out. Neighborhood punks. I landed on top of some sheetmetal from a construction site."

El pressed her forehead to Riley's spine. The water flooded over her and washed her own recent memories away. They had no right to interfere with this. "Did they . . . ?"

"Yes."

She said nothing. Tears welled in her eyes. El had always suspected that this kind of toxic nettle was buried in Riley's body, but it had to work its way out. She couldn't force it. For two years she'd dissected Riley's tiniest word and deed, but only in the last two weeks could she clearly analyze any of them. The shame and powerlessness Riley had to have endured were now extremely clear to El.

She wanted to apologize, or tell Riley that she'd risen from ashes, but both of those were insulting. One implied Riley was weak to begin with and required sympathy to get by, the other implied her strength came from the assault. In fact, Riley was born brave, born to act when others said nothing, because it needed to be done.

"Riley . . . you are a perfect creature."

"Thank you," Riley murmured. "For not caring, I mean."

Mystified, El wrapped her arms around Riley and laid her hands on the smooth tummy. "I do care. But only about you. Were they punished?"

Riley nodded. "My dad made a call. And then he left New York and left me with my grandmother."

"But you followed?"

Riley heaved a sigh and turned. "I couldn't take it. Abuela wanted me to go to church and forgive. I don't forgive. People earn forgiveness. They don't take it like they took everything else. My dad understands. He teaches me how to control what I feel, how to use it, because that's what he learned in prison."

Her makeup was gone, the deep tan of her skin and the dark rose of her lips so beautiful El couldn't help but kiss them. There were other terrible things she had to ask, and every kiss was a promise that none of it would be begrudged.

"Riley, how did you find *Tizóna*?"

The muscles of Riley's jaw flexed as a black eye stared malevolently into space. "I took care of it."

"What did you do?"

"I should be getting a call any day now from the State Troopers. We can handle that when the time comes."

"Then you met him."

"I know his address. And if I don't hear from them by the time you turn eighteen, I'll be sure everyone else does too."

"I love you."

To her relief, Riley smiled, and the darkness was forgotten. "I called Jay yesterday."

El blinked back in surprise at the confession. It had been days since she'd even thought about Jay. It seemed like an eternity since he'd tossed her from the car. Something about the memory of his face had turned almost comical in its childish lines. "Why?"

"I wanted to hear it for myself. Hear him gloat about how well he'd tricked you. How stupid you were." Riley brought their noses together. The hotel soap smelled like mint and citrus. "I'll handle him too, if you let me. I've been itching to fuck him up since day one and I have a pretty good idea how to do it."

"I'm going to have to do things for myself, you know."

"Yeah, but you have bigger fish to fry, and boy I hope you fry that meapilas."

"Mama?"

"Yeah."

El had never considered getting even with her mother. Now that Riley said it, however, it sounded right, but she had no idea what that would even mean. She was a child, a runaway, a lesbian. In her mother's circles, it would be her word against Mama's, and no one would believe her, because she was a "degenerate."

"That blog is a platform that reaches exactly the right people," Riley whispered as if she could follow El's thoughts. "And then there's your writing. These people are a cancer. They're killing this country. The way you write, you could speak for so many. Make them visible again."

"Like you?"

The corner of Riley's mouth ticked upward. "Yeah, me. I don't know if you caught this while we were going at it, but I like girls and I fucking suck with words. Actions, though . . . Major turn-on."

"Well . . . then I guess it's worth it," she chuckled.

Riley spun her around slowly and poured a bottle of shampoo over El's head. As she worked the lather, she made clucking noises with her tongue. "This is seriously the worst dye job I've ever seen. Like, what were you doing? Using a garden hose?"

"Walmart sink."

"Shit. I can go down to the Seven Eleven and get enough stuff to do this right. You wanna stay blonde or do something fun?"

El looked back at the girl over her shoulder. "What did you have in mind?"

"I like the black, to be honest, but for now, till the blonde grows out, why not do a color?"

"Pink."

Riley seemed surprised. "Pink? I thought you were a fan of green."

"I am, but . . . I think it needs to be pink."

"Your mom will be happy with that! It's such a girlish color!"

El laughed and sputtered as the water cascaded over her face. "No, she won't. She'll be furious."

"Ah. Okay, I get it. This is like a *what's wrong, I thought you* liked *pink*, yeah?"

"Exactly."

Riley let out a husky giggle and moved on to washing El's back. She worked her way down until she was crouched at El's feet looking up lasciviously. "Wanna get something pierced, while we're at it? Maybe get some ink? Your ID says you're twenty-one. You could even get a bottle of gin if you wanted."

"I could, couldn't I?"

"Fuck *could*. *Should*, is more like it."

El poked her nose indulgently. "That stuff all costs money."

"It's on your mother. I made about two grand before I stopped taking money out of your account."

With a gasp, El took hold of Riley's wandering hands. "You are clever."

"Except when you go all poetic. Then I'm an idiot. It's intimidating as fuck, but I love it."

While Riley dried off, El sat bundled on the toilet and watched her. The urge to record it all was there. She needed to quantify it, preserve this moment somehow, but until it was safe, she was on hiatus from her platform. She needed a new way to lock it all in ink.

"I want a tattoo. Can we get one together?"

Riley was wearing a towel like a skirt, her breasts and pigments bared. She looked up from her computer in surprise. "You mean, like . . . matching tattoos?"

"Yes. Would you do that with me?" El bit her lip, watching Riley's face for even the slightest hint of hesitation. "We can get something simple, I don't care. I think . . . maybe, you know . . . if you don't want anything specific—"

"Fuck yes! Let's do it!"

"Really?"

"I love that stuff, El! I designed all my own art, you know."

El's mouth dropped open. "You did?"

Riley's brows were dancing on her forehead. "Wow, I guess we found something you *didn't* know about me! I grew up in a tattoo parlor. I know my way around."

"I love you!"

Riley returned to her computer with a shy grin. On the screen was a blue dot reading from an address that seemed to be somewhere in California. "Is that just your default? Like do you just go, *Brain is on pause, I love Riley.*"

"Yes."

She flushed crimson from her hair to her first rib. "Okay. Just making sure."

"You're mine, aren't you? I'm allowed."

Riley turned, one lithe and embellished arm slung across the back of the chair. The dark eyes that peeped out at El were mischievous and adoring all at once. "Yeah. That seems right."

"So what design are we getting tattooed?"

Riley put her chin atop her arm and looked at the ceiling. "I think I have an idea."

27
Snowflakes

appy's Tattoos was extremely cozy—one long glass case with a few feet of space on either side and a single tattooing table in a curtained area. It boasted a large bay window with a raised platform, on which stood several painted mannequins in wigs and subculture gear. It wasn't the best neighborhood or even the cleanest-looking parlor, but the online reviews were stellar. El seemed ecstatic as she jumped out of her seat, hot pink mane bouncing. That was all Riley could hope for.

Since the first time they'd spoken beneath the tree, understanding that emptiness she saw in El's eyes had been Riley's ambition. Now as she was tugged indoors, she realized she had a new one.

Riley wanted to banish every sorrow, fill up every emptiness, and crush every enemy. She wanted to see El happy, for once and for all.

A thin woman who seemed in her sixties appeared. She had spiky white hair streaked with pale violet and arms that read like a catalogue of important life events in vintage punk rock culture. A few long strings of glass beads dangled from her neck and her bright pink lips gave them a huge smile.

"I'm Happy!" Riley wondered how many people replied with their own emotional state before realizing she was telling them her actual name. "You must be the duo from the phone?"

"That's us." Laying the drawing out on the counter, Riley finally unfolded it. She'd kept it hidden from El all morning, though the girl begged and pleaded to be in on the surprise. El let out a gasp and clapped a hand over her mouth, a mannerism her mother had likely instilled in her.

"Oh, wow!" The artist spun the page of hotel stationary around and dragged a finger over the pen strokes. Hidden within the pale fractals were the deeper meanings. "This is like those pendants they had in Victorian times. For the queen, yeah? Like . . . the frost fair, right?"

Riley nodded, her face burning hot as El continued to squeeze her hand. "Yeah, so the initials superimpose and make the arms of the snowflake."

Lifting a pair of magnification glasses, Happy scrutinized the angular script. "Hmm . . . A rounded E and G and a more angular R and V. I love the shading work here. You do this with a plain old Bic?"

She managed a little nod, though she felt strangely self-conscious.

"I dig it! I can definitely turn out a precise graphic from this! You mind if I play with the font a little?"

"Not at all!"

El's smile was constant. As the artist excused herself to her computer equipment, she threw her arms around Riley's neck and raked her fingers over Riley's scalp. "It's perfect. Thank you."

Riley's mind was a fuzzy mess. As thoughts manifested, they quickly diffused out into her simmering blood. The only tangible things were the smell of the new dye in El's hair, the tingle that moved over her skin when El touched her, the constant throbbing in her ears. Words came out jumbled. Details vanished into the ether. She just wanted to bury her face in El's neck and coo.

"This isn't fair," she whispered.

El's hands tucked into her back pockets and tugged her hips closer. "What isn't?"

"I feel like I'm on drugs, but you're perfectly fine. Like . . ." She lost her train of thought and had to search for it briefly along the curve of El's collarbone. "I'm supposed to be making all the moves, planning things, but this is so . . . strange . . . and you've had two years . . . two fucking years to cope. I'm behind."

El was chuckling quietly, strands of electric rose framing her cheekbones. She nipped at Riley's nose and pressed their foreheads together. "Why do you have to make all the moves?"

She let out a contented sigh. "I'm older. I've had girlfriends. Also, I really want to impress you . . . because you know . . . I am so dumb right now, and somehow you're so rational. It's unnerving."

"You know what you are?"

"Hmm?"

El's mouth found hers, tongue moving with such command it pulled Riley forward off her feet and would have sent her staggering if not for the counter. Left gasping for air, she stared at El's mischievous face in awe.

"You're my champion: a big scary wolf who secretly likes belly scratches."

"Belly scratches is code for . . . sexy stuff, right?"

"In this case, yes."

"Oh, okay."

El laughed at her goofy grin. "You're the same color as your hair."

"Can't help it." She fluffed her shaggy head in a mea culpa. "When you came to Sam's that first time, I thought you were there to make fun of me. You looked like someone had dared you to come in and talk to me, and you were chickening out, but it was this, yeah?"

El bowed her head and closed her eyes. "Yes, that's exactly what I felt."

"But like . . . when was the first time you saw me? I don't remember when we crossed paths. I was a little bit . . . you know, defensive."

"It was your first day." El hesitated, seemingly constructing yet another poem. Riley was beginning to read her, learn the cadence of her ideas as they moved through her body. El's rhythm was soothing. It subdued every writhing anxiety, just to stand there and watch her think.

"I washed up on the front steps, trying to find the energy to face another day. Mama had just thrown me out of the car and threatened to starve me for a week if I didn't raise my Geometry score. I was so ashamed. If you can believe it, I thought I deserved it. I felt like she was doing her best and I was just this tragically awful daughter. I felt guilty and helpless because I didn't know how to be the thing she wanted me to be. There had to be something wrong with me."

Riley opened her mouth to curse.

"I know. But it's what I felt then. I was sure I had to be an evil person to hate my own mother when she was trying to teach me. I never knew anything else. I didn't know I needed to question my life. At the same time, I was still so sure it was unfair, but how does a person make those two things coexist? It's impossible and it's exhausting and eventually something has to give, or you die. I was just so tired, then I heard this loud sound and I turned around and there you were, like you'd just appeared with a clap of thunder. You took off your helmet and there was this gorgeous face . . ." El looked up and Riley's breath caught in her throat at the perfect mingling of wistful admiration. "You had an expression that said *If anyone says one goddamn thing to me about anything, I am going to bite off their nose, and they'll thank me for clearing their sinuses*! That was when your hair was longer, and it had the streaks in it. It glowed royal purple in the sunlight, and you just seemed to sparkle."

"All the studs," Riley muttered.

The feeble joke won her a forbearing shake of the head. "You were a queen. You glanced at me as you walked by, like you were daring me to pick a fight."

With a sudden jolt, Riley's memory rose from the depths and kicked up moments buried beneath two years of dust. There was the girl in her denim skirt and pink blouse, her dark hair in a single braid and her pale blue eyes wide in astonishment. She'd been so pretty, so primly assembled, so dyed-in-the-wool Southern Belle that Riley was sure she must be one of the mean girls.

"Oh my god, I remember!"

"You looked so confident and so . . . *badass*, and everything I wasn't. I couldn't help but be curious, and well . . . smitten. I spent my entire day trying to figure out your name without directly asking anyone. That's why I called you R at first, because no one could remember your name except that it started with an R or something."

Riley stared into space in shock. "That fast."

One bare and shapely shoulder hitched up. "I was lost . . . and waiting, but I didn't know what I was waiting for. It was you. Everyone I knew lived like I did. You had the secret thing I needed to see."

Riley shook her head, suddenly anxious again. This was the issue that had made sleeping so difficult for so many days. If this was some kind of worship, no matter how good it felt to be adored, she didn't want it. She had a temper, and a temper like hers could do terrible things with that kind of power. Riley did not want to be on a pedestal. She wanted to look El in the eye.

As she began to raise her objection, however, El silenced her with a soft peck that tickled and teased and tempted all at once.

"It's not like that, Riley. You have no idea how worthless I have always felt, and you flipped everything around so I could see clearly."

"El—"

"Listen to me. I'd never kiss you if I thought it was a bargain. There's no debt here. It's not like that at all."

"Then what is it?"

"I know I have value, or my mother wouldn't have worked so fucking hard to destroy me. I am strong. I want you, not because you can help me, but because we are the same. I *want* to be me, but the me that's with you, not the me that's without you."

Riley could no longer keep time by anything but El's shallow breath and the tiny kisses she gave. All the concerns of the previous week were warded off, threats held at bay because nothing could ever be so audacious as to ruin this perfection.

"I like who I am with you too."

Wrapping her up again, El nuzzled her. "Must mean you love me."

"You couldn't guess that, already?" she breathed in El's ear.

"I did."

Riley's mouth dried up. All that time she'd been counting the minutes until she could run, all those days she'd been gritting her teeth or clenching her fists, all those days she'd thrown punches and insults, all those days . . . someone had been back to back with her against the world. Someone had turned her into a poem, a song, and she'd been too busy to hear it. She'd missed the opportunity of El, because she was afraid. She was supposed to be clever, but if she couldn't even learn a lesson right in front of her, what was she doing going out into the world alone?

"I'm so grateful you're here, Riley."

"Come on," she rasped. "I'm the one who's grateful."

El's confusion was adorable. Riley couldn't help but praise her for it with a peck to the cheek. Looking into such a forgiving mirror as those two eyes, she knew she was going to have to start asking a hell of a lot more from herself.

"I don't think about the future. I don't try to imagine."

"Why?"

"Because things end." Her voice caught. Tears slipped along the bridge of her nose. El caught them and wiped them away. "I just . . . I never thought about who I could be, I guess, but I could be . . . I could be someone good for you. I think."

"You already have been."

Riley blinked furiously and couldn't stop the grin. "Makes it easier . . . knowing where you've already been."

"True."

"Okay!" Happy returned from the back. In her hand she had an immaculate copy of the sketch, lines cleaned with computer accuracy. The snowflake was crisp, and the letters wove and reflected an external light source. The artist stepped back into the conversation smoothly, her warm demeanor so comforting, Riley forgot her mascara was probably dribbling down her face.

"It's so pretty!" El murmured. "Where should we get them?"

"I was just about to ask you!"

El leaned over the drawing. "I want to be able to see it. Can I get it on my arm?"

Riley shrugged off her coat and brought out her right elbow. In the crook of it was her first tattoo, a bold compass rose. "Like this?"

"Yes! What about on the other arm?"

"Works for me."

Happy tapped the image and nodded. "It will look good, because they're similar shapes. So left arm on both?"

El bounced in place. When Happy handed them the paperwork, she filled hers out with a kind of gleeful flourish, wiggling her backside to the rock music blasting over the speakers. This was an important step for El, a physical mark that couldn't be undone, a scar the very shape and color of her spirit.

All Riley's ink was special to her—marks of where she'd gone and who she'd always been. But this was different. This was a declaration of who she would be and where she planned to go.

This was a promise.

On the tattooing table, El's glee faltered a bit. She looked pale against the bed of her vibrant hair. As Happy prepped the needle, wrapped it in plastic and dipped it in the dark paint, El's hand shot out and clamped around Riley's wrist. "Does it hurt a lot?"

"Like being scratched a bunch. Not too bad. Way less than you think."

"Less than falling out of a moving car?"

Riley let out a dark chuckle. "Yeah. Way less than that."

El pressed her lips shut with a nod.

Happy flipped the switch and set to work in a singsong buzz. Though El's features were at first contorted in a grimace, she soon relaxed. Her fingers released Riley, and she sat up to watch the progress through hooded eyes.

The snowflake crystalized on El's arm in a smear of deep blue and purpled blood. Happy's lines were incredibly precise, and though her gaze was narrowed on her work, she smiled as if she were singing.

"Snowflakes are all unique, you know. A bunch of vapor that sort of condenses, like magic. Things just drawn together that cling and make this perfect mathematical shape, always symmetrical, always different." She picked up more ink, her glasses on the tip of her narrow nose. Glancing over them at Riley, she winked. "People talk a lot of shit about snowflakes, these days, but that's because they're dumber than a sack of bricks and don't know they're oppressing themselves."

El's adrenaline was fading. She shivered a bit as her eyes rolled to the black ceiling. "If I have to hear one more fucking word about safe spaces and trigger warnings being the death of independent thought, I swear . . ."

Happy let out a snort. "Cracks me up. God made you in His image, says you're unique and beloved, but not them, right? God says turn the other cheek, but that's for them to do when you hit them with a tiki torch, yeah? Not something that applies to you. God knows everything and can do anything and His creation is perfect . . . except when you disagree with it. An omnipotent deity who makes the Devil, but can't kill him? What kind of God is that? A pretty human one if you ask me."

"Looks a lot like my mother, actually," El said, lying back against the vinyl pillow. "Man made God in his own image. Not the other way around."

"Yeah, and used it as an excuse to be complete assholes."

Riley crossed her arms. "It's a dull life, if you're so bored you have to be all up in someone else's business. Go learn crochet or computer programming and shut the fuck up."

Happy's brows went up in agreement. There was a blank slash across her brow where a piercing had probably been in her rebellious days. "Snowflakes are made by the biting wind and the bitter cold and the lightning. Storms at deadly altitude sculpting flawless geometry that looks soft as a feather, but can level a city if you get enough of them together. Can't think why that's weak. Completely terrifying if you ask me."

El wore a soft smile and her lids fluttered, as if she were sleeping deeply. The shading work would take a little while. Casting her eye to the front of the shop, Riley tossed her jacket over her chair. "I'm gonna go get us some drinks, okay babe? You'll want one for after. You all right here?"

The girl nodded, though she looked as if she were already in a dream state. Unable to resist, Riley dipped over her forehead and left a kiss as a farewell.

"See you in a minute."

Outside in the bright sunlight, she dropped her shades and looked along the wide street. As they had ridden in, she'd spotted the thrift shop a few blocks away. Riley chewed her lip and sized the window display by eye. The leather jacket seemed a perfect fit, though El probably wouldn't be too psyched about the fringe. That's what scissors were for, though. Pressing her nose to the glass, she found the tag and knew it was too good to pass up.

The hanger was brought down. Inside and out the jacket was in great condition, all the zippers working. It was softer than she'd expected, a dark green lambskin, but the collar had the definite weathering of someone who'd worn a helmet. The money changed hands—another portion of her *per diem* that went to a worthy cause—thumbing her nose at El's mother.

Triumphant, Riley walked to the gas station and got two Slurpees, an indomitable grin in place. Nothing could fuck up this feeling. She was energized, strong, unbreakable.

Until the black SUV screeched around the corner, and a jarhead in a buzzcut shot her dead with a glare.

28
Bound

A car horn blared, deafening as it cut into Riley's skull. The driver of the vehicle revved the engine in threat, but she didn't move from the crosswalk. She stared at the front of the tattoo parlor, at the place where El had been when the men threw her into the SUV. She knew she had to take charge of her limbs, to mount her bike and race after them, but her temper—that demon in her soul from the get-go—had abandoned her.

El was gone again.

In only two days, El's companionship had taken root and burrowed so far down into Riley, that all the gears of rage and ferocity had ground to a halt. Finding the girl had been the all-consuming goal. Speaking her heart even in the most jumbled words, had been her one desire. Suddenly, she was a machine without a navigator, and knowing they'd taken El from her inspired nothing but abject and disarming misery.

A chorus of horns continued to demand she cross or cut bait. The one-way street had a line of vehicles backed up all the way to the freeway exit. Two windows had rolled down and people were shouting at her.

"Goddamn it, get out of the way! Are you crazy? What's wrong with you?"

A man rushed toward her, looking so overcome with anger that he wanted to strangle her. He snapped his fingers repeatedly, as if he thought she was hypnotized and only he could wake her. "Hey! Hey! You stupid—"

"Did you call 911?" Riley looked at him. He stopped dead in his tracks at her expression.

"Oh, I'm gonna call the cops if you don't fucking move!"

It wasn't enough. Riley needed more. She needed a spark, a catalyst. She needed to turn this emotional engine over and get it moving again.

"A girl was just thrown into a car, or were you so busy bitching about five minutes of your day that you didn't notice?" She pointed to the shop and the tire marks on the asphalt. Happy was nowhere to be found. Riley wondered if they'd hurt the woman and suspected it must be so. "She was screaming for help and you did nothing!"

"Get. Out. Of. The. Road. Bitch!"

Riley closed her eyes as the forge in her chest began to warm. She could hear her own robotic voice from far away, smooth as steel and foreboding as fuck.

"What did you call me?"

He took a step toward her. She began to flex her fist until she realized she was still holding the Slurpee. Her heart sent a fearsome thud of motivating pain through her. In one smooth arc, she launched the drink full force at the polished windshield of his shiny car.

He let out a wail. "What the hell?!"

"Thanks for that."

Riley cracked her neck and looked both ways. Jogging swiftly through traffic, she skidded into the parlor. A loud banging came from the rear of the shop. Riley flung aside the curtain and found that her chair had been shoved beneath a doorknob on a utility cupboard.

Happy was unscathed, but clearly shaken. Despite the fact that she'd been imprisoned in her own closet and had one of her clients literally kidnapped from her chair, she patted Riley down with heavily ringed hands.

"Are you okay? Oh my god. Did they hurt you?"

"I'm fine." Riley took hold of her hands. "What happened?"

"I was just finishing up and these fucking goons bust in. They just grabbed your girlfriend and dragged her out! Oh my god, I need to call the cops!"

"No!" She shook her head darkly. "Don't bother. I know who they are and where they're going."

Certain that Happy was all right, Riley sat the woman on her own table and ran back to the design computer. With a jiggle of the mouse, she was online, fingers flying at top speed to log into accounts and enter passwords. The blue dot pinged as the map manifested from the satellite feeds. The SUV was on the move to Interstate 80, headed east.

Were they going to drive El back across country?

And how had they been discovered? El had ditched the iPhone...

Unless they weren't tracking El.

"Oh fuck you, you assholes," Riley swore, because she knew she had to be to blame. They'd acted so surprised to see her at the diner, but if they'd known about her from the beginning, if Mama had betrayed her despite the admonitions to the contrary, then they would know what she was driving. Her bike had been *right* there for them to see. They must have done the same thing to her that she'd done to them.

"Oh Mama . . . am I gonna fuck you up and enjoy every second of it."

A siren tore at the air suddenly, and flashing lights flickered on the monitor. Someone had apparently called the cops, though the only people she'd seen on the street were the cars she'd barricaded, and no one would come that quickly to defend a man's car from slushed ice. A shop owner could have called about El, but in this neighborhood, if a guy right across the street decided to ignore it, then it was likely everyone else would too. So who had called the police?

Riley's flesh ran hot and then deathly cold, and every cell seemed to sink into the ground. She knew the answer all too well.

The artist saw the screen over Riley's shoulder as she shut down the programs. With a few shaky steps, Happy moved toward the front of the shop. "What do you want me to tell them?"

Riley blinked in astonishment. "What?"

"I've been around the block, *chica*. I don't know what the fuck is going on, but I'm guessing you don't want the popo involved." The penciled brows twisted with quirky wryness. "Just tell me *they're* the dickbags."

Riley looked out the window. The black and whites had come to rest at angles and the sirens choked off like a bird drowning. The mannequins looked so patriotic, flipping off the world in alternating red and blue while the uniforms unpacked like clowns.

"It's a long fucking story."

"Give me the Cliff's Notes."

Riley's jaw dangled, but she was beginning to feel a kinship with this woman. It was like seeing herself in forty years. "It's some Shakespearean shit, but yeah. They're the dickbags."

Happy let out a long-suffering sigh. "You want me to mention your friend getting black-bagged or not?"

"Only tell them if they ask."

"But, why *wouldn't* they . . ." Happy looked back and forth between the door and Riley. The cops had their weapons drawn and were scrambling behind their open car doors for cover. "How the fuck did the cops get here so quickly?"

"*They* called. As payback to jam me up so I can't chase them."

Riley reached for her coat and unzipped the pocket. The ATM card and knife were side by side. In one swift move, she opened the utility closet and dropped them into an open box of ink bottles. When she turned around, Happy's eyes were rolling.

"Keep the knife safe, but shred the card. Thanks for being cool."

The artist shook her head, just as the megaphone peeled their eardrums with the equivalent of audible acid. "This is the Richmond Police Department. Please exit the building with hands up!"

"Jesus fucking Christ. My neighbors already hate me," Happy growled. "Where were they last year when someone threw a rock through my door, huh?"

At the entrance, Riley tapped her on the shoulder and tucked a set of keys into Happy's back pocket. "They're gonna arrest me. I don't want them to search or impound my bike. Say it's yours. I'll come back for it."

"Sick ride like that will look good in my window," Happy muttered permissively.

On the sidewalk, they were ordered to turn around and drop to their knees. As soon as they were in position, Happy began to loudly declare her rights as the owner of the property. Propped up against a cop car, Riley overheard them explain to her that they had been answering an anonymous call of an armed robbery in progress. As Riley's pockets were searched for her wallet, and her identification was run for warrants, Happy was allowed to sit in a car without cuffs.

"There's no robbery! She's a paying customer! You're disrupting my business!"

Two officers were sitting in the front seat of the car next to her. They appeared to be looking at their computer monitor. She knew what they were seeing. No doubt, when she'd stopped calling in, Mama had reported her to the police back home and used her clout to get a warrant issued for Riley's arrest. The mercenaries may even have known this had been done when they'd repaid Riley for her stunt at the café. But now that the police had her ID, it was finished.

"Fuck," she whispered, putting her forehead to the roof of the car. Eighteen for a week and already arrested for theft. So much for proving everybody wrong.

Riley knew that each breath was one more moment El was in their hands, being dragged back into that hell she'd escaped. She could only hope that those four were at least honorable in that respect, though given their track record, she doubted it. In their custody, El might be safe from the outside world, but what about them? What would they do to her?

After an eternity, the officers returned to her and informed her she was under arrest. She was searched and asked about her property, making no mention of the bike. Cuffed and locked in a patrol car, Riley caught one last look at Happy as she was driven away. The woman's arms were outstretched in disbelief and concern. They'd only just met, but something told Riley that her bike would be safe in Happy's care.

All the way to the jail, Riley tried to recall every detail her father had given her about what it was like to be arrested. It was extremely unlikely that Mama Glasse could get a prosecutor or judge to sign off on a warrant that didn't contain bail for such a small offense as theft of an ATM card. Truth was, even if she'd stolen ten grand in diamonds, they probably still wouldn't set the bail any higher than five hundred dollars. If that proved true, she could post the bond and be out by the following day.

Riley just had to be patient.

She said nothing as they photographed her and put her hands over the fingerprinting scanner. When the officer filled out the paperwork, she gave one-word replies. The holding area had a phone in it. Riley called her father and dropped the bad news.

"I'm going to kill her," he rumbled.

She lowered her voice. "Dude . . . Dad . . . can you not say shit like that right now!"

"I'm sorry Rye, I just get—"

"You're fucking up my motivational fantasies, okay? *I'm* the one who gets to kill her? *Claro*?"

He chuckled. "*Claro*. Do you want me to call a lawyer?"

"Naw. This is a cake walk. Bail can't be high, right?"

His noise of doubt was like an engine idling. "Knowing her, I'd say she'd find a way to keep you there while she does whatever she is going to do to El."

The chilly air and loud sounds broke through her defenses. Riley shivered and folded up on herself. "Yeah, but Dad, I didn't take anything from her. It's all lies."

"The arresting officers don't care. They'll hand you the bail the warrant says you're granted. And if she managed to convince a judge that you're violent, a flight risk, or that you committed felony level theft, you're fucked."

Riley buried her face in her hand. "What do I do?"

"I'll call my lawyer."

She didn't want him going through this again, digging up all those bad memories. She didn't want him drawing any of Mama's attention to himself. "No! I swear . . . I think . . . I can handle this. Don't worry about me. Just call the tattoo parlor and talk to Happy about Aella. She seemed cool, but make sure she knows someone is coming for the bike."

"Rye—"

"I'm fine! I'll call you when I'm out."

"Rye, goddamn it! You don't always have to be hard. Do you understand?"

She squeezed her eyes shut. She could see the terror in El's face all over again, see that image of her on the ground of that broken-down shack in the woods. El was counting on her. Riley was the only one who could do anything. She didn't have time to cry.

He sighed when her silence grew too long. "Is there anyone in holding with you?"

"No."

"When you hang up, I want you to go into a corner and let out what you feel. The cops see it all the time. They won't care. It won't change your situation for the worse, okay? Do you hear me?"

"Dad—"

"Do it!" he commanded.

He was seldom stern, but when he was, she could hear the prisoner, the gang member, the survivor. If she didn't obey, the consequences wouldn't come from him. They'd come from the universe, because he was sharing a hard-won truth with her.

"Okay."

"Call me when you're out."

"I love you."

"I'm proud of you."

Her laugh came out oddly emotional. She dragged her hand over her face and stared at slippers they'd given her in place of her massive boots. "Yeah? For being a chip off the old block or for getting arrested?"

"For standing your ground. You're strong enough. You can handle this. I'm not worried. But you gotta feel it, Rye. Get the emotions outta the way, so the mind can work in peace."

The shivering intensified. Riley could barely grip the receiver. Finally, the goodbyes came, and she could hang up and fall to pieces. With her back to a corner, knees to her chin, she sobbed. Each shudder brought her closer to the ground.

How could she have been so stupid? She'd been so caught up in El that she had failed the girl. It was more than that, though. So much more. In two weeks, she'd skipped out on graduation, her job, traveled nonstop, nearly killed a man, found love and lost it, all to end up in a jail cell with her newfound self-worth crushed under the stiletto heel of an entitled racist bigot. Things most people saw as a lifetime of events, she'd crammed into one week, and given herself absolutely no time to *feel* any of it. All at once, it tumbled out, and she didn't try to stop it.

The sounds of her weeping echoed off the cinderblock and down the corridor. Before long, a female deputy turned up. She leaned against the wall, imperious despite her frumpy uniform, and cleared her throat meaningfully.

"You okay? The phone is there for you to use."

"I used it."

The officer extended a few brown paper towels through the bars. Riley scrambled to her feet and took them.

"First time in here?"

"Yeah."

The woman dropped her chin and eyed Riley. "*Last* time in here?"

Blowing her nose, Riley shook her head. "Fight the power."

"Joking only gets you so far, kid."

Riley fixed her with a glare. "Who's joking? I'm only in here because a privileged racist with a Senator for a husband lied to the sheriff."

The officer raised her brow. "Well, at least you got the innocent act down."

"I can prove it dead-to-rights in about five minutes flat, but so what, right? I'm a hoodlum, right? Who the fuck cares? Just give me my bail so I can go to court. Then they have to listen to me."

The deputy rolled a mint around her mouth as she seemed to search Riley's aura. She mimicked, dragging the tongue ring back and forth across her teeth, hanging from the bars like a caged animal. The woman's demeanor remained relaxed and confident. She had the look of a mother about her, with an unnerving gaze. Given her age, she had probably been at this job for a while.

"Tell me the story," she said finally.

"Don't you have better shit to do?"

The deputy tilted her head sardonically. "It's a slow day."

"Just let me post and get the fuck out of here."

"I came in to do just that. You got a spare three hundred bucks lying around?"

"Yeah, actually."

"It stolen too?"

Riley made a face and wrapped her arms through the bars. "Naw, it's the salary I was paid by the bitch who put me in here, after I signed a fucking contract not to legally disclose. So let me post."

The deputy was frowning and finally, she moved away from the wall. Unbuttoning a pouch on her belt, she withdrew a tiny notepad. "Spit it out."

"You miss the bit about the NDA?"

"If this woman filed a false police report to put you in here, then she's committed a crime. NDAs can't legally conceal criminality. So . . . spit it out."

Stunned, Riley gripped the bars as if dangling above the gaping maw of hell. It wasn't until her hands went numb that she thought to reply.

"Why do you care?"

The deputy shrugged nonchalantly. "Like I said, it's a slow day and I was young once. Back when dinosaurs roamed."

29
Slumber

"What the *hell*?"

Happy's voice was all wrong. El sat up in alarm and swung her legs off the table, the plastic dressing on her tattoo crinkling. Heavy boots trampled the tile. A huge shadow loomed over the curtain and a massive arm jerked it aside. Looking up, she saw a face she recognized.

In one shallow breath, her soul momentarily evacuated her body, realized it was still tethered, and then slammed home painfully.

"Well, here we are!" The man had a mean look in his eye. "Wow, you just went full-on freak, didn't you? Your mama's gonna be pissed."

El took a deep breath and tilted her chin. Mere days ago, she'd been afraid, but that was because she hadn't seen anything of the world. It seemed ominously large and full of threats. Now, she'd met some of those threats and survived them. As she glared at this man sent to force her into submission, she realized that she'd survived every terrible thing that had ever happened to her. Nothing she'd ever experienced had defeated El.

Mama would never have power over her again.

"I don't give a fuck what she thinks."

He put his hand on his hip. Beneath his windbreaker was a bulky shape she was sure was a gun. Behind him, Happy was grappling with the man she'd seen try to board the train. A third stood at the window seemingly keeping watch while the fourth was talking on the phone in a hushed tone. All of them were smiling like jackals.

Happy struggled. The man holding her swung back an arm and slapped the woman so hard that she stumbled, then hurled her against a wall. Happy let out a grunt as she slid to the floor, holding her face in her hand. El leaped to help her, but the man took hold of her hair and tugged. As she thrashed and kicked, he wound her hair up tight around his fist and twisted a well-muscled forearm around her waist.

"Leave her alone! She doesn't have anything to do with this!"

No one paid her shout any mind. Happy's guard picked her up and dragged her kicking and thrashing to the closet. A chair was propped against the doorknob and held despite the woman's banging.

The man on the phone hung up. "Let's go."

Before she could get another word out, El was picked up and thrown over his shoulder, the wind completely knocked out of her. Gasping and writhing, she was carried straight out the front door in broad daylight. The trunk of the SUV was open, and the three back seats were folded flat. A length of chain was coiled on the ground. Spotting it and the handcuffs beside it, El let out a shriek and brought her knee down into the man's chest. With an oof, his arms went slack. El landed hard on the concrete, for an instant knocked senseless. It was all the time needed for the man to recover. Though she screamed and bucked, he dragged her back by her ankles and lifted her over his head.

El scanned the street for help, just in time to spot Riley fighting traffic across the street. The girl came to a dead stop, breathing as if she'd torn down the street at top speed. Their eyes met for one charged breath, long enough for El to shake her head.

Riley couldn't win this fight.

El hit the backs of the raised seats and crumpled onto the floor of the vehicle. A handcuff was clasped around her ankle and through a link in the chain. Instinctively, she reached for the manacle, only to feel a sharp pain in her neck. Instantly, her equilibrium went cockeyed, and before she could fully register that she'd just been injected with something, the world vanished.

When she next awakened, her head ached in a constant pulsing rhythm. The passing lights of other cars stabbed through her skull and made her nauseous. When her whimper was heard, the oldest of the four men leaned over the back seat and held a water bottle to her lips. Her mouth felt stuffed with cotton no matter how much she slurped.

"She awake?"

"Yeah. That shit really knocked her for a loop."

"You gave her enough to take one of us out," another said with a laugh. "Lucky she didn't die."

"Come on, man, they'd give her more than that for a surgery."

El worked at clearing her throat, which felt caked with dust. When she lifted her head from the carpet, her face stuck. When she rubbed it, there was a deep, pockmarked impression on the skin of her cheek as if she'd been lying in one position for hours.

"Why . . . why are you doing this?" she whispered. "I don't understand."

The older man stared at her for a long moment, his face slowly wrinkling up on itself as if he too was bothered by the situation. His apparent misgivings confused her for only a moment, and then suddenly it all made sense. These men weren't being paid to break the law. They were digging their way out of debt.

The older man turned away, his voice a monotone. "Worry about yourself."

"If you think this is going to change anything, you're wrong." El dragged her leaden body upright and rubbed at the mark around her ankle. "Because she's going to hold *this* over your heads for the rest of your lives. Every time she wants something, it will be *Remember that time I paid you to abduct a child?* and she'll get it, because you all have lives she can ruin."

"Shut up," grunted the driver.

"Okay, as long as you're into self-delusion."

There was no way any of them were going to let her go. Perhaps it was revenge, a way of making them suffer a modicum of the anxiety she had endured for over a week, that urged her to keep talking. El had no idea what they might do, what Mama had told them to do, but whatever that was, she was outnumbered anyway. She might as well score a few points.

She'd been afraid all her life. It had never done her any good. The only times anything had changed was when she stopped letting herself be paralyzed by that fear.

"I lived in a mansion, I had designer clothes, I am good at school. If I ran away, then maybe you should think about why. My mother is a monster and some day, you're all going to really kick yourselves—"

The driver seemed to be their leader. When he shouted for her to be quiet, the older man flinched slightly and shifted in his chair so that she could no longer look to him for signs of what the others might be thinking.

"I have to go to the bathroom."

With a sudden jerk of the wheel and screech of tires, the SUV veered into the shoulder and lurched to a halt. Orange flashers blinked into the night. The driver slammed his door and lifted the rear gate, dragging her toward him by the chain. The highway around them was abandoned. Desert terrain stretched out in all directions, featureless and desolate, dotted with sagebrush. In the distance, a range of peaks jutted from the flat earth, standing out in the full moonlight.

How long had she been unconscious?

The locks were opened, but her captor didn't appear to be at all concerned about letting her go. In fact, he seemed to take pleasure in shoving her toward the ditch beside the road, even going so far as to laugh when she stumbled into the dirt.

"Go on," he coaxed, leering at her malevolently.

So it was going to be humiliation? That was how they thought they were going to keep her obedient. Tears burned in her eyes for an instant, until the chill wind caught her hair and caused a bracing chain reaction in her body.

As she undid her jeans and squatted down, she grinned at him. Mama really must have fed him a line or two. She must have left out the time she'd had a fit in the crowded pediatrician's office, charging him with encouraging El to have sex by prescribing her birth control for cramps. Or the time Mama had dragged her through a church potluck covered in vomit, accusing her of purposefully making herself sick so that she could go home. Or the time at the park when she was five and split her face open on a metal slide, and Mama had told her she could just sit there and bleed, because good girls didn't roughhouse like boys. Perhaps she'd neglected to talk about how there was no crying in the Glasse house. If one tear was shed . . . the punishments were horrifying.

Mama had been humiliating her for her entire life—blaming her for things outside her control, turning bodily functions into shameful events, transforming all her failures into sympathy credits for being such a long-suffering mother. There wasn't one thing these men could do that was any worse than what Mama had done. In fact, they were just one more way Mama was trying to hurt her, an extension of that woman's reach.

She stood up and fastened her pants with a shake of her head. "She must really have you dead to rights, to make you stand there watching a teenager pee. Did she convince you to watch me take a shit too? Or is that just the kind of thing you enjoy?"

His face contorted. "I have no qualms about gagging you."

"Guess you'll have to then, because no one is ever going to tell me to shut up again." She crossed her arms and when he took a step toward her, she stepped back. "I'm not my mother. Whatever she's done to you, she's done just as bad to me, I promise you. You're not going to hurt her by hurting me, because she doesn't care. I'm not her daughter. I'm her victim, who legally has to sit there and take it until I can get the fuck out of that house."

He gritted his teeth and took another step. She backed up again.

"I'm not my mother. I hate her just as much as you do. In fact, probably *more* than you do, because she was *supposed* to care for me."

"Get back in the car. She's told us to use whatever force we want."

"So that makes it okay?" She turned her back to him. If he wanted her to get back in the car, he was going to have to put her there. Every time.

He obliged, storming up behind her with another syringe of slumber.

Her eyes opened on a plain gray ceiling, blurring in and out of focus. El tried to touch her numb face, only to find that her wrists were restrained. Vision churning from side to side, stomach unsettled, she looked down to her toes. Her arms and legs were all shackled to a hospital bed. There were, however, no machines, no IV. It was just an empty room, with padded, soundproofed walls and a door with a tiny window.

A cold sweat stood out on her skin as the truth set in. This was the last measure, the only option open to Mama. She couldn't have El arrested, because that would cast aspersions on the family. But if El was confined to a mental ward for *her own good,* then no one would ever judge Mama at fault. She was just a poor distraught mother, doing her best despite her daughter's illness. El was just a feather to be worn in Mama's couture cap. Her feelings, her personality, her desires all meant nothing, and now they'd been equated to a malfunctioning brain. It was a different game now, because her word was now worthless. no matter what she said about her mother, no one would believe her.

El turned her head and threw up.

It seemed forever before anyone checked on her. When they did, they said nothing. It was as if she didn't even merit an introduction. The orderlies just stripped her pillow case and smeared a few wet towels on the floor, then left her to the insulated paralysis of depression and a partially medicated mind.

At some point, El took up counting. When she'd tallied what she believed to be almost a half hour, her thoughts diving in and out of drowsiness, a man in a white coat appeared. He had a plastic smile and the bedside manner of a sugar-coated tongue depressor.

"How are we today?" he trumpeted as he took her pulse right over the top of the angry red scab of her tattoo. The skin itched terribly.

"Where am I?"

El had no idea how much time had truly passed, how many days it had been since she'd seen Riley in the middle of the street, face pale with panic. If that was to be her last memory of her champion, then perhaps she didn't really want to know.

"You're in a hospital."

The chemicals in her blood were an excellent inoculation against giving a shit. Suddenly, all traces of concern vanished, and she was left with the burning resentment. Laws that allowed such things—a system so broken and rigged against any child that didn't conform— *had* to be written by men like her father. Unfeeling regulations, based on numbers and forms, legalese and two-thousand-year-old words written by other misogynistic, straight, old men.

For that long, people like her had been silenced in ways much like this, while those same men talked about how much progress had been made, and their wives smiled demurely and nodded like animatronic embodiments of virtue. Then there were women like her Mama, programmed to preserve her appearance by any means necessary.

All of them living as if they'd never die, as if it would never actually happen. As if they wouldn't one day be looking at a ceiling just like this and facing all their mistakes alone. They called her crazy, but if that was *normal*, El would rather be a freak.

She erupted into bitter laughter.

The frown touched only the top of his forehead as the doctor made some notes on his clipboard. "You seem upset."

"Upset?" El jerked hard on the shackles, pleased to watch him flinch. He likely had a difficult job, if he had the moral flexibility to take any random, unconscious teenaged girl on the word of her mother. "You'd be upset too, if your abusive mother decided to have you installed in a straightjacket because you dared to disagree."

He cocked his head to one side, the vague smile back in full force. "Your mother is concerned. From what she tells me, you seem to be suffering some dysphoria, some anxiety, paranoia—"

"Yeah?"

All El's cautious, anonymous revelations on the internet had all been some kind of exercise. It was as if she was testing her identity in the world, running a focus group on the person she wanted to be. She'd been hiding from the absolutes, from decisiveness because those had consequences that could be painful. That final look on Riley's face was the worst suffering she could remember enduring, the most painful emotion she had ever felt.

There were no consequences anymore.

"From where I sit, you're depriving someone of their civil rights, but I suppose that just makes me *combative*, right?"

"All these sudden changes you've made—your hair, the tattoo, your clothing . . . that's not important?"

El relaxed against the pillow. "I'm sure it seems sudden to people like you, because girls aren't allowed to have emotions that build like compressed fire. We're not allowed to explode. We don't have the strong exterior to suppress all that, do we? And how could our lives be that miserable anyway, since we are handed everything we should want?"

"And the injuries?"

"What injuries?"

"You don't remember taking those medications and cutting yourself?"

"What are you talking about?"

His smile ticked as he helpfully lifted the thin blanket over her. Across her upper thigh was a thick gauze pad. Dread built in her as he carefully peeled the dressing to reveal a series of deep, parallel gashes that had been sutured. The flesh was bruised and scabbed, an injury at least two days old and sure to scar.

El collapsed back against the pillow and stared blankly at the ceiling.

She should be shocked, but she couldn't be anymore. She didn't have the energy.

"What about those, Elyrra?"

"Why don't you ask my mother? She's the sane one, right?"

"I'm prescribing you some medications. They'll make you sleepy. We don't want anything to happen to those stitches, right?"

He took a needle from his pocket and a bottle of clear fluid. As he stuck it into her thigh, El's thoughts battered against this impassible barricade and shattered.

If this was how her life was going to be, she was better off asleep.

30
Glass Houses

The glow of the computer monitor cast spiderlike shadows as it struck the filming equipment. Riley spun the chair in a slow circle as outside the closed door of the office, Mama marched through her polished home shouting at the staff. She was grateful that the walls of the studio were lined in acoustic tiles. Her veins throbbed with an eager meter that she controlled with breath.

For the last several days, Riley had been piecing together the trap, questioning every detail, prognosticating every possible outcome and reaction Mama might have. The script was written, the pieces aligned, the timing worked out. Everything that happened from this moment on was entirely in Mama's hands.

Which meant Riley didn't need to worry at all.

The light clicked on as the office chair was in mid-swing. Mama let out a gasp.

"Hello, Mama."

Though she was obviously surprised to find Riley sitting there, Mama lifted her nose in indignation. "*What* are you doin' here?"

That heavy-handed *H* earned a vengeful grin. "You mean, *what* am I not doin' in a cell?"

"I warned you, sugar." Mama stepped inside oozing contempt. Behind her, Lizabet hovered. She gave Riley a nod of solidarity before the door was slammed in her face. "You knew the consequences of crossing me."

"Oh, sure," Riley replied in a measured tone. "And now *you're* going to find out the consequences of crossing *me*."

Mama snorted and retrieved her phone from her pocket. "I am callin' the police."

Riley lifted a hand and poised a finger ominously over the keyboard. "I wouldn't do that if I were you."

Unconvinced, Mama shrugged off her hesitation with an aloof glance and dialed. "You can't just waltz into people's—"

"Bitch, save the waltzing for cotillions. Your housekeeper let me in."

"This is my private office!"

"Whoops! I'm sure she gives a shit, since her letter of resignation is literally sitting right here, and she's packing her bags as we speak. Maybe you should have locked the door." Riley moved her finger from above the trigger and propped her chin in her hand nonchalantly. "Oh *right*, if you did that, you wouldn't be able to follow El's blog, because how would she write it? Bad habit to pick up. No security, no passwords, all this information just . . . sitting here."

The woman's umbrage dimmed, and beneath the paralyzed lines of her face, concern was growing. "*What* are you talkin' about? There isn't one thing on there worth anythin'."

"You sure about that?"

Mama dropped her arm and went deathly still. Her skin was blotchy, her eyes enormous. Her breath came so shallowly that it wasn't even discernible.

Riley reclined comfortably in the black leather chair and put her feet up on the desk. "From the beginning, I've had a difficult time figuring out what the deal was. I mean . . . how is it possible that a woman could so hate her own daughters? How could she be so vicious? There's something deeper going on. There's some serious psychological issues at play here. People like that don't have just one flaw. They have so many skeletons they have to rent storage sheds to keep them in. Like the one you have over in Charlotte that—"

"You get the *hell* outta my house!"

"No." Riley steepled her fingers. She couldn't help a tiny chuckle at the awareness slowly taking the hateful shine off Mama's gaze. "I'm comfortable on your throne. Besides . . . you really don't want me leaving with all the terrible things I could do. El and I have that in common."

Mama looked around the room as if seeing it for the first time. As she caught sight of her own cameras, equipped with motion sensors and pointed at a number of useful angles, she seemed to relax. "Are you threatening me?"

"I turned them off."

Sweeping up to the tripod, Mama swung the lens around with a vindictively contorted smirk and pointed it directly at Riley. "It has a manual switch. Now *why* on earth are you going through my private computer?"

Riley cracked her neck. "Because I thought all your account passwords needed updating. Oh, and I removed the batteries from your cameras. They needed replacing too."

Mama furiously smashed the button. When nothing happened, she shoved the tripod over and stood there fuming.

"I even made a little podcast and video of my own, just for your family-values groupies. They are scheduled to go live tomorrow. In exactly fifteen hours, to be precise."

As if her brain had suddenly shorted out, Mama's expression vanished. With a sickeningly ratcheted movement, the woman gathered herself up to her full height. She looked down her nose at Riley with two inhuman cobalt slits.

"*Excuse* me?"

"*Esto es lo que mi familia mexicana llama un*"—Riley framed comedic air quotes—"stand-off."

Mama's lip began to curl back on her perfectly aligned porcelain veneers. "You fucking little bitch."

"Stole my line, lady."

"You *think* . . . you can sneak into my *home* and threaten *me*?" Her pitch rose with each word, goading every part of Riley that had ever wanted to haul off and punch this woman in the face. The temper remained quiet, however, soothed into slumber by the simple perfection of this plan and the rewards that awaited the risk. "This is my *house*!"

The shriek was dampened nicely by corrugated foam tiles. As the silence closed back in, Riley yawned. "If you don't calm down, you'll regret it."

"Don't you tell me to *calm down*! I will *end* you! You think you're safe from me, you disgusting whore?" She stepped forward, shivering with rage, flecks of spit spattering as she swore. "I know *every* fucking judge in this jurisdiction and some very dangerous people. I promise you, your father's parole is over! *Over*!"

Riley smiled. "I told you before . . . I'm not your daughter. You can't bully me. And also, unlike your daughter, I have family who care about me and have my back. People to witness what you've done and say enough is enough. Isn't that right, Dad?"

His voice was mighty, even though it came from the tiny speaker of her phone. "I've always got your back, Rye. And I don't know who this woman thinks she knows, but I can promise you . . . I know worse."

The surprise sent Mama back a full stride. From head to toe, she began to shake. To some, it might look like fury, or perhaps terror, but Riley had an old soul and she'd seen a few things.

As Mama staggered back toward the tiny kitchenette and the bottle of bourbon in her cupboard, Riley heaved a great sigh. "What you've done to your kids, you did because you hate your life. You hate it and you don't know why you do. You're supposed to love it. That's what they told you. But no, you hate it and you resent them."

Mama tossed back the drink and sloshed another into the tumbler. "Fuck you. You don't know anything about my life."

"I know it doesn't look anything like the life you pretend to have." She waved a gloved hand over the production suite. "On the internet you're a model citizen, a perfect mother, a devout sister of the faith. In real life, you're a drunk, abusive hypocrite."

Another drink vanished. "Look at you? A worthless skank with a murderer for a daddy? Living out of a fucking trailer?"

Riley glanced at the phone, but her father said nothing. "The difference is, I've never claimed to be anything I'm not. So you get it, right? While you're busy wasting all this energy trying to keep your secrets and lies straight . . ." Riley put down her feet and stood up. "I don't have a straight bone in my body, and I have energy to burn. And boy . . . have you lit a fucking match."

Mama was still shaking. Her third tumbler of liquor was clutched in a white hand, long French nails curved around the crystal-like talons. Her features were hard, and her jaw flexed as if she was grinding her teeth.

Riley crossed her arms. "You hired me to find your daughter, and I have. I know you've put her in that hospital on a mental health hold. I know you think you can have her committed and medicated until she actually does have a breakdown. And even if they release her, nothing she says will ever matter, because she's a nutcase. It's in her record, right?"

"You're . . . *sick*," Mama spat. "I'm entitled to protect my daughter from all spiritual evils!"

"What you did wasn't protection. It was abuse."

"Says a *liberal* society!"

"It's liberal because it has to be, so that we can all coexist, no matter what our backgrounds, duh." She smiled wickedly. "Unless of course you're about to tell me you don't think *those sorts* ought to be allowed to exist . . ."

"Maybe they shouldn't!"

With one hand, Riley tapped the enter key. The printer revved up with a high-pitched whine and began churning out paperwork. "The last time we were in this room, you made me sign a bullshit contract. You thought I didn't know what it was. You thought I'd be scared. You were wrong."

While Mama hurled curses at her, Riley gathered up the printouts and plucked a pen from the cup. She laid them out neatly on the desk with a smile.

"—That contract is legally bindin'! If you tell anyone *anythin'* about this—"

"No, it isn't. You voided it the moment you opened your stupid mouth, and when your husband finds out what's happened, he'll tell you the same thing."

The woman's jaw hung open for a moment of self-doubt, and when it finally snapped shut, Riley saw what she'd been waiting for: fear. With a grin, she let the other shoe drop.

"From the moment I came into the office the first time, I've recorded our conversations. Now, you may be looking back thinking *I haven't said anything wrong*, but that's not entirely true. It may not be wrong to you, but to the rest of the world looking in? Way wrong.

I've recorded you hiring a person to commit what you believed to be illegal acts to retrieve your daughter. I have you admitting to hiring a boy you knew to be a bigot to perpetrate a sexual assault against a minor. I've got you advocating hate crimes. I've got you for delinquency, by refusing to press charges against a man who attacked a minor. Blaming the victim. Recruiting four men to illegally abduct your daughter across state lines, which is a felony. I even have you threatening to lie to police. And you know what? They'll take me seriously. Do you know why?"

It looked as if Mama was about to be sick. Her vanilla skin had turned green. Her bottom lip was trembling.

"Because you actually went and fucking did it." Riley stepped out from behind the desk and slid the contract further over its surface. "I got arrested in California, you know?"

"They'll never believe you," Mama whispered. "You thief."

Riley could only laugh. "Man, with your stubbornness and drive, you could have actually done something worthwhile instead of turning into Lady Macbeth with a side of Elizabeth Bathory. But come on, I'm telling you why you don't want to fuck with me. You might want to listen this time, since apparently, you didn't actually read all the helpful essays your daughter wrote on the subject."

Riley leaned back against the desk, enjoying every creak and drag of her leather riding gear as it perforated the ballooning tension. Mama seemed to be struggling with an unseen force. Every time she thought to lunge forward, something held her back, and every time her mouth opened to unleash another invective, her lips parted uselessly. Power was trading hands.

The magic was shifting to a new mistress.

"Funny thing happened on the way to the correctional facility. I met this great classifications deputy, named Wanda. She's been in her job for almost twenty-five years, you know, and she really takes the arrests of young people seriously. Like a mission. And she really fucking despises racists, which . . . I gotta say, really greased the wheels when I said your name. Wowza."

Mama brought the glass to her lips and sucked down the few amber sips that sloshed into her face. "I don't give a damn about—"

"She listened to my story, even though, like . . . no one would believe a *skank* like me. Even went and got my phone out of lockup, and then she called some detective friends of hers and they phoned the issuing jurisdiction. Asked to speak to the DA who'd requested the warrant for my arrest. Apparently, he found the recordings really informative."

Riley sniffed. The sickly sweet alcohol wafting on the air-conditioned breeze mingled with Mama's perfume in a disgusting cloud. The woman was completely silent, staring vaguely into space as if watching her future corrode.

The perfect time to finish it.

"I didn't even have to post bail," Riley murmured. "The DA just dropped the whole thing. Probably didn't want it to get out that he'd had any dealings with you. I mean why risk his career over a tiny case like mine? You thought you could intimidate me with that, but see, that was stupid, because I grew up on the wrong side of the tracks. Nothing intimidates me."

Mama scowled at her. The witch apparently understood finally that she couldn't play the old games, because none of them would work. It was like watching a snake shed, as the face pinched up on itself. Suddenly, Mama was looking her in the eye, not as someone she could control, but as someone practicing the same craft.

"Clever."

"That's what they call me. I love your daughter. She's an incredible person in spite of all you've done, and I'm going to take good care of her, no matter what you say. I know . . . I *know* it fucking kills you that she might be happy, but I don't care. You're not going to stop me."

Riley tapped the stack of paper. "This is the paperwork you need to release her from that place. You're going to sign it. Then you're going to agree not to bother her for the next five and a half months. She's going to move out a bit early and you're not going to do one thing about it. If anything, and I mean *anything*, happens to disrupt that, we'll just see what happens, huh?"

Mama let out a laugh that would have sent a super villain for their vocal coach. "You think that a few recordings of me doing my Christian duty are gonna matter with the kind of people I know? Those idiots would burn a cross on your yard as soon as look at you, sugar. They don't give a dried-up turd about anything I've done. And there's enough good-ole-boy cops and jurists in this county to shove everything under the rug in a heartbeat."

Riley let her have her mirth with a stoic face. When she didn't evince any sign of backing down, Mama's baleful smile dimmed.

"I thought you'd say that. That's kind of why I just recorded you saying it." Riley turned off the recording app and tilted her head. "Man! You just don't *learn*! You should know that I mention El's blog in the videos, which of course means they'll get to read all her details about your child abuse. I reprogrammed all your email accounts, printed off all your bank statements, downloaded the entire file off your keystroke tracker, and data-mined your text messages from the cloud. I read some of your husband's conversations with his staffers, a few of your insider trading tips, and even a really great bunch of convos with some blocked numbers I'm pretty sure are the four guys who dragged El back. Four guys whose names I know, because I also downloaded all your recent NDA files. I dug up your entire life, and it's all on the internet timed to fall like an axe from God's hand."

Mama was silent. Riley looked her up and down. "You remember *that* guy, right? God? The one who said he had a day for all the proud and lofty, on which they would be humbled? Guess what, bitch . . . the day is on your fucking Google calendar, because I hacked that too."

Mama had drawn up on herself as if about to pounce, the tumbler twisted up in her arms. She stared savagely at the paperwork on the desk as if assailed by the scent of burning flesh.

Riley took her cue, retrieving her phone and the several external drives she'd used. "Sign the paperwork. Deliver it to me at the facility tomorrow by ten. If you don't do this, I will expose you for the fraud you are."

"I'll have you arrested for theft," Mama hissed.

"Yeah? So what? I've already been down that road and if you think I wouldn't happily do two years in county for your daughter, you're fucking stupid. And by then, the damage will be done and I get a day in court to do even more. *You* on the other hand . . . you've never been called on your bullshit. You have no idea how bad it can get. You wanna find out? Test me."

At the office door, she stopped and tried one last time. Not because Mama deserved it, or would ever change, but because Riley had made a decision about the kind of person she would be from that moment forward.

It wasn't enough to end shit once. She had to end it forever.

"What's stupid is, none of this would have happened if you hadn't been so caught up in crushing your daughter's identity. You just had to leave the computer as bait. Your psyche just fucking *relied* on that like an addiction—what you got out of controlling her meant more to you than good common sense. Because of that . . . you lost. That's some Greek Tragedy level shit, right there."

A whistling sound was her only warning. Riley ducked just as the crystal tumbler exploded on the wall near her head. The force sent shards in every direction and practically converted the bourbon into a mist, but Riley's armor was impervious.

"Meet me outside the facility at ten. And if you ever come near us again, I will turn every single detail of what I have over to the press. You and your husband will lose everything you ever cared about."

31
Broken Spell

As she sat in the circle, El saw more similarities than differences. A few of the others had nervous ticks, scabs where they'd clawed themselves. One had obvious bindings around her wrists. Every woman stared at their shoes or rolled their heads to the side, refusing to acknowledge any of it. Almost every single one had a story of abuse and neglect, remnants of the girls they used to be. And yet, they were still girls. The law kept them here, the orderlies spoke to them like infants, and stimulation and mental exercise were strictly controlled.

For their own good—El heard repeated at least five times a day, but where was the dignity? What was *good for them* should grant them at least that.

"Elyrra, you haven't shared yet."

She took a deep breath. "I don't have anything to say to you."

"What's a'matter? We ain't good enough?" one young lady snarled.

El had grown accustomed to her outbursts. She sighed and shook her head. "Has nothing to do with these ladies. It's you I don't like."

The therapist didn't bat an eye. "Talk about that, then."

"No point, because to you it's a symptom of something. Really, I just don't like you, because you're keeping me here against my will."

"It's for—"

"No. It isn't. These cuts? I didn't do them. My mother did. And the medications you say I took? They did it to me."

The therapist tilted her head. "Who are *they*?"

"The four men who kidnapped me from the tattoo parlor where I got this. Go ahead, call the owner. She was there. But no, you won't, because I'm just a girl who has lost her mind. Never listened to me before I supposedly lost my mind, but so what."

"You sound as if you feel very helpless."

El couldn't help her laugh. It erupted and echoed over the walls, agitating a few of the others. "No. I don't feel helpless, that's why I'm here. I know how to deal with my mother, and she knows it too. Every time she does something to me, she is teaching me just how strong I need to be and just what I need to do. No matter how many times she tries to hurt me, I am going to leave and keep going. Until she stops or dies. That's terrifying to her. So, here I am."

A few faces lifted, one wearing the ghost of a smile. In them, El saw reflections of the girl she had been, the one before Riley. The one before she had focused her thoughts on deciphering Riley's confidence, her strength, her clever mind. The girl before that revelation that life could be different. Now these women were looking at her the same way, like they'd never seen anything like her before. Especially not in the mirror.

That was the real tragedy.

"Tell us about—"

"I'm finished sharing, thank you."

"Elyrra, you know that therapy is participation. We're not here to tell you what's wrong with you. We're here to give you support for anything you might be feeling."

"I don't trust *any* support that comes from the hand of my abuser."

The woman pushed her glasses up her nose. "Your mother?"

"Did you hear me say that she cut me? While I was asleep?"

"Why would she do that?"

The tiny skeptical smile was so subtle the doctor likely didn't even know she'd done it, but it was enough to put El's teeth on edge. She'd grown tired of the subdued religious rhetoric, the refusal to embrace her name, the way some of the girls were treated when they discussed their gender. El hated it, and even if these doctors were actually wonderful people whom she was seeing the worst possible light, the fact that they wouldn't listen to her was enough to assure her that she was thinking clearly.

"Probably so that she'd have a legal reason to index me into this fucking place."

"That's a serious allegation."

"You know what I'm just realizing is hilarious?"

The doctor looked around the circle. Every girl was watching, something El was about to use against her.

"Everyone always tells the victim it's serious. We were the first people to know that! You get that, right? We were the ones who suffered, who bled, who built up the courage to speak about what was being done to us, and instead of turning to the abusers and saying this is serious, you look at us. You look at the victim and ask them if they know what ruin they're about to bring to someone who hurt them. Do you think that's right?"

Agreement was passing through the circle in a wave. The therapist glanced at the clock. She was about to use time as an escape. Well, then El would make it brief.

"Every person in this room is a woman and is in search of mental health, two of the most victimized groups. Some of them are people of color, some are disabled. More layers of victimization. Every single one of us ends up here, in a sharing circle where we're told it's *serious*. Yeah, it's *serious*. So *serious* you don't take any of it seriously. And you expect us to trust you? To get better?"

A few of the patients had begun to rock. The ones who had difficulty with social settings began responding to the tension with ticks and laughter. The woman who'd first criticized her let out a guffaw and flapped her hands.

"Thank you! I hate that! I hate that word."

"Yes . . . well, you've made an excellent point Ely—"

"My name is El, and if I have to tell you again, you won't like the name I start calling *you*."

She fixed the woman with a stern glare as a giggle went through the gathering.

More than once, the doctor had let group therapy run over to address the trailing revelations of the circle. Today, however, she dismissed it immediately, and gathering her things, left the patients to the orderlies. El was escorted to her room to await her afternoon lunch tray and the cup of pills.

The first two days, she'd swallowed them. On the third, she learned to vomit. They were perhaps necessary for those with serious troubles and difficulty with self-restraint, but as El sat on her bed, she knew it wasn't restraint that was her dilemma. It was the opposite. She needed to stand up for herself.

Even as she calmed herself down from the encounter, she found her palms sweaty and her heart racing. She'd gotten better at framing words, at spitting out precisely what she meant to say, though the emotions were turbulent. If she had a little longer, she might be able to get someone to listen to her. She just had to remain calm and patient, and hold tight to the rational.

Nothing was more grounding than the memory of Riley's touch, her smile, the subtle diffidence in her affection. Nothing was as joyful as Riley revealing she knew how to make napalm. Nothing was more rational than Riley's story of her journey cross-country and all the lengths she'd gone to just to track El down.

Somewhere out there, Riley was still stomping through the dirt, doing whatever it took. El had to trust that, and even if she never saw that beautiful face again, even if Riley never came for her, it didn't matter, because Riley *existed*, and that was enough to teach El all she needed to know about the world.

The door opened. El stood up beside the table, but the orderly didn't have a tray. Instead, he waved her out into the hall.

"Someone is here to see you."

"I thought visiting time was in the afternoon."

The man said nothing. El stepped out into the hallway, surprised that he didn't follow closely on her heels. Near the nurses' station, a uniformed staff member with a terse demeanor drew her into an office. Several of the doctors were standing around the walls, all of them talking at once. Her appearance silenced the debate. A person seated in the chair turned around, but El recognized her before their eyes even met.

Her fists clenched. It was the first time in days she'd looked her mother in the eye, and while she would have expected a return to meekness, all she felt was contempt.

"I have nothing to say to this woman." Mama's mouth fell open, but El cut her off. "I don't ever want to see her again. If she comes, I won't visit with her."

She turned on her heel, but the orderly blocked the door.

"Elyrra, your mother has signed the paperwork to take you home."

El scowled at her feet. It probably didn't feel as good for Mama not to be the torturer. It was probably the only thing she didn't want to pay someone to do.

The doctor cleared his throat. "We've told her we don't think it's in your best interests. If you did hurt yourself, then your health is in jeopardy. If you didn't hurt yourself, then . . ."

Mama let out a huff. She seemed impatient, and her usually perfect makeup and flawless condescension were very different. She looked as if she hadn't slept in days. Something about her wandering, glassy gaze told El that it wasn't motherly concern that brought her here. She was nervous and, remarkably, sober.

Mama fidgeted in her seat as if looking for the right words. "I've told them that I've arranged an alternative treatment for you but—"

"I'm not going anywhere with you."

Teeth clenched, Mama managed a pained smile. It was clear she didn't like being the one in the room with the least control of the situation, and for a moment, El took pleasure in watching her squirm.

"You wouldn't be with me. Riley is going to take you to treatment."

El sucked down air. For a moment, she could swear she'd misheard. "What?"

Mama gave a little shake of her shoulder. "Riley is waiting downstairs."

"Prove it."

Waving toward the window, Mama fell oddly silent. She was the shadow of her former self, and didn't even criticize when El ran to the opening and looked out. Parked in the lot was the old bike, with Riley's helmet chained in place.

"Elyrra?"

El turned back to the expectant doctors, putting a damper on her elation with pointed stares. This was a line. She either had to take back the accusations she'd made of her mother in order to be released into her care, or she had to hold her ground and stay put. If she held to it, what would happen? If she pushed and pushed and went to court, she'd just end up in foster care, and that was assuming it was all accomplished by her eighteenth birthday. If she took back all the *serious allegations*, her mother would not only get away with it, she'd have medical records that called El a compulsive liar.

She turned on Mama, examining her sunken features carefully before she responded. "You *want* me to go with her?"

"That's the arrangement, yes." Mama nodded curtly, her eyes on her nails. "It's all been worked out."

El's mouth twitched. She'd never seen her mother defeated, but this must be what it looked like. The price to be paid for such triumph was the lie. People always said the truth brought freedom. They didn't know Mama.

For now, El could be a liar.

"I believe . . . uh . . . I think that cutting incident may have been a misunderstandin.'" Mama interrupted, just as she opened her mouth. "That's *why* I'm here."

The group therapist was frowning, El's story fresh in her mind from the circle. "How can self-harm be a misunderstanding?"

"My attorney has the matter. I don't believe El did it to herself, as I've said." Mama gave the woman a snide look. "She was drugged and assaulted, and we will handle it. Now, may I please remove my daughter?"

El was dismissed from the room. Down the hall, she found another window and searched eagerly for other signs of Riley. What had she done? What had she said to beat Mama? It had to be so clever! It had to be magical. Riley was too spellbinding for it not to be.

Hyper-vigilant to her mother's moods, she heard the elevated tones of what had always been called a *discussion*. For the first time in her life, she was glad that Mama always got her way.

Well . . . almost always.

The door opened. Mama swept by her and hooked her arm. On their way through the various checkpoints, Mama said nothing to her, instead choosing to focus on the dial of her watch. El was nearly shoved down the steps, and when she put her foot down and wrenched her arm free, her mother looked as if she would just as soon scalp El as save her.

"Elyrra, I don't have time—"

"Hey there, Snow."

El looked up. There, haloed in sunlight from the open door, stood a victorious Riley. The emotions hit her like a blow to the stomach, robbing her of the words she needed to say. El was left blinking back tears and trembling.

Riley kicked away from the doorway and took her hand. "Sick duds. You going for *Silent Hill* Chic?"

She flung her arms around Riley's neck, burying her thoughts in the scent and the feel of her skin. "I don't know what that is."

"It's cool." In her ear, Riley let out a soft breath. "I missed you."

"Not as much as I missed you."

"I don't know. I was pretty jacked. I've been pounding energy drinks and chewing my nails. I was so worried."

"Oh, puh-lease," Mama snorted. "Can you *not* hump my daughter like a horny—"

Riley lifted her head off El's shoulder to comment, but El snapped before she could. "Don't talk to her like that. Ever. Do you understand me, Mama?"

Before El's eyes, Riley's fierce mask slipped. She nestled her forehead back in place and let El be strong on her behalf.

"Don't talk like that to—"

"Take a walk, Mama, or I swear you'll regret it."

Surprisingly, with a huff, Mama obliged, wandering off in a meandering trail of unfinished invectives and stuttered nonsense.

Giggling, El leaned back and took in the view. There she was, Riley Vanator, in all her smug glory, with some added ornamentation. Sticking out her left arm, Riley presented the replica of the snowflake tattoo.

"Happy was so *unhappy* she did it for half price."

El's face was sore from the strength of her smile and warm with contentment. "Where's Aella? What happened after . . . I don't even know what day it is!"

Riley kissed her suddenly and possessively. Surrendering to the communion of it, El forgot where she was. She forgot about her mother. She forgot she'd just been locked behind bulletproof glass windows. Parting, El felt as if the last several weeks had all been some kind of hallucination. She would scarcely have believed it if not for the signs on her body.

"I actually have no idea what day it is either. I've been a bit preoccupied."

El laughed. Her mother had gone to her car and was sitting in the front seat, banging her hands on the steering wheel and waiting impatiently. With a knowing shake of her head, she nudged Riley.

"What did you have to promise her?"

"That I wouldn't destroy her. I'm giving back the keys to the kingdom."

"What?"

"I'll explain later." Riley looked her over. "Are you okay?"

"I'm hurt, but since when is that news?"

Pulling her close, Riley drew her into a kind of meditation. Foreheads touching, fingers laced and clenched, they stood there breathing.

"Go say what you need to say," Riley whispered. "You never have to see her again. She's never going to hurt you again, okay? So say what you need to."

"I love you." El smiled. "That's all I need to say."

Riley broke the prayer to look her in the eye. The stare was so deep and intense, El found she could scarcely think as her soul was turned over carefully and then installed back in her body.

"Are you forgiving her?"

El looked across the grounds at her mother's car. "No. She doesn't deserve anything from me, least of all the permission to blame me for what she did to herself. She gets apathy. That's it."

"You're not angry?" Riley's mouth hung open in obvious astonishment.

"I am, but I'm not going to play her game anymore. The spell is broken. I'm finished. She means nothing to me. Nothing. And as soon as we leave, she'll know that."

Riley draped an arm around her shoulders with a smile. "Well, shit, let's blow this horror fest. Where to first?"

El put on the helmet and leather coat, laughing. "First, I want to change clothes, then . . . how about ice cream?"

"You read my mind."

Riley swung her leg over and started the bike. The sound still sent a thrill through El. As she settled carefully into her place at Riley's back, she caught sight of her mother's stricken face.

And dropped the visor.

Epilogue

El opened the box and couldn't suppress the shudder of accomplishment that went through her. It was like a dream, seeing all the copies nestled there in their wrapping, her name in print, the story of her life out in the world. First volley of what was sure to be a war, the cover was deceptively demure. She autographed a copy and tucked it into an envelope.

Stowing the books in her top rack, she donned her helmet and started up the new bike. It ran beautifully, cutting an aerodynamic green groove through traffic. She rode like she was flying, her heart tumbling in the breeze, her mind singing.

Back at their apartment, Riley was perched on a kitchen chair, a myriad of legal tomes and FBI manuals fortifying her in a disassembled discussion of search and seizure. El would have been bleary-eyed within the first paragraphs, but Riley was chewing jargon with a side of gummy bears and using highlighters in some kind of pop-art cryptography. She was a knight who belonged on that wall, fighting that fight, and El loved her even more for it.

Riley blew a kiss. "You have a good day?"

"Yup!" El set her helmet down and unzipped her boots. Within moments, she was in Riley's lap, tangled in a love knot. The test prep was forgotten as they took a few moments for each other.

"How was the bike?"

"Amazing. I love the tune-up. Purrs now."

Riley nodded "She's a hellcat. If she don't purr, we got problems."

El couldn't keep it secret anymore. The pressure within was too great. "My advance copies came."

Riley's grin was the mischievous challenge of old. "You do it? The thing?"

"Of course! Wrote a sweet little note and everything."

The laugh evolved into a howl and a high five. "I saw another television commercial today. Almost fired a shot into the TV. Would've gotten me into trouble with the Academy, but might have been worth it."

El curled up in Riley's arms and closed her eyes. Since her father had announced his candidacy for president, El had stopped watching television. Her agent agreed it was best, and every day would email with campaign updates and platform promises. He was running on values yet again, misleading the world that his family was perfect and godly. According to the charming picture Mama had concocted, El was simply busy with college and not terribly political. She'd even hinted in her podcast that El had cognitive difficulties, spinning El's silence and low profile into another unearned credential, another point of sympathy for her cult following of nationalists.

Riley caressed her spine and gently rocked her, somehow knowing it wasn't all jubilation. "Hey . . . Look at me."

Dutifully, she lifted her face. Ever the champion, Riley fixed her with a calm and centering stare. "They did this to themselves."

"I know."

Curating the blog into book form—at last telling the world what she'd been through, who her parents truly were, and what they stood for—wasn't about punishment, though it likely would damage them. Even though she had long ago resigned herself to the fact that her mother was a stranger to her, some part of her still hoped the woman would learn a lesson. It was that optimism that separated her from people like her parents. Mama Glasse could only care about herself.

"What did you put in the note?" Riley whispered.

"Thanks for all your help with content development. Good luck with the election. Sincerely, El Vanator."

Riley's chuckle lifted the hairs on the back of her neck and simultaneously soothed and invigorated her. She tipped forward and brought their mouths together. Riley's tongue was sweet and seductive. El missed the metal stud through it, retired to the moments when they weren't adulting. Riley's hair had gone dark, though she sometimes still streaked it with paint. Most days, her tattoos were covered in business casual, but she was still ferocious and fashionably antifa.

"You are one hell of a chick, El."

El nuzzled her, displacing a pen from behind her ear. "I'm a snowflake. Don't fuck with me or I'll bury your village."

Dear Reader,

Thank you for reading Kristina Meister's *Love Under Glasse*!

We know your time is precious and you have many, many entertainment options, so it means a lot that you've chosen to spend your time reading. We really hope you enjoyed it.

We'd be honored if you'd consider posting a review—good or bad—on sites like **Amazon, Barnes & Noble, Kobo, Goodreads, Twitter, Facebook**, **Tumblr,** and your blog or website. We'd also be honored if you told your friends and family about this book. Word of mouth is a book's lifeblood!

For more information on upcoming releases, author interviews, blog tours, contests, giveaways, and more, please sign up for our weekly, spam-free newsletter and visit us around the web:

　　Newsletter: riptidepublishing.com/newsletter

Thank you so much for Reading the Rainbow!

Tritonya.com

TRITON
BOOKS

AN IMPRINT OF RIPTIDE PUBLISHING.

Acknowledgments

A huge thank you to my agent, Laurie McLean; my chief beta reader, Jill Ford; my editor, May; and my many San Francisco Writers' Conference cohorts who offered tremendous support and feedback.

Also by Kristina Meister

Cinderella Boy

About the Author

Kristina Meister is an author of fiction that blurs genre. There's usually some myth, some mayhem, and some monsters. Kristina's fond of creative swearing and has an obsession with folklore and pop culture, adding humor and complexity to her work. Her story *Cinderella Boy* was the first book selected for RuPaul's Love Yourself Library.

She and her mad-scientist husband live in California with their poodles Khan and Lana, and their daughter Kira Stormageddon, where they hoard Nerf toys, books, and swords—in case of zombie apocalypse.

Follow her on Twitter @kristinameister and on Facebook at facebook.com/kristina.meister.